DREAD AND DELIGHT

DREAD AND DELIGHT

A Century of Children's Ghost Stories

Edited by

Philippa Pearce

Oxford   New York

OXFORD UNIVERSITY PRESS

1995

Oxford University Press, Walton Street, Oxford OX2 6DP

Oxford New York

Athens Auckland Bangkok Bombay
Calcutta Cape Town Dar es Salaam Delhi
Florence Hong Kong Istanbul Karachi
Kuala Lumpur Madras Madrid Melbourne
Mexico City Nairobi Paris Singapore
Taipei Tokyo Toronto
and associated companies in
Berlin Ibadan

Oxford is a trade mark of Oxford University Press

British Library Cataloguing in Publication Data

Data available

Library of Congress Cataloging in Publication Data

Dread and delight: a century of children's ghost stories /
edited by Philippa Pearce.
p. cm.
Includes bibliographical references.
Summary: Forty ghost stories from English-speaking countries,
written in the twentieth century by such well-known authors as A.C.
Benson, Eleanor Farjeon, Joan Aiken and Leon Garfield.
1. Ghost stories. 2. Children's stories.
[1. Ghosts—Fiction. 2. Short stories.]
I. Pearce, Philippa.
PZ5.D7475 1995 [Fic]—dc20 95–4123

ISBN 0–19–212605–9

1 3 5 7 9 10 8 6 4 2

Typeset by Pure Tech Corporation, Pondicherry, India
Printed in Great Britain
on acid-free paper by
Bookcraft (Bath) Ltd
Midsomer Norton, Avon

ACKNOWLEDGEMENTS

IN making this anthology, I have been helped by advice and suggestions, loans of books, and gifts of time from many generous people. I am grateful to them all, and particularly thank the following: Jonathan Appleton, Editor of the Australian *Rippa Reading*; Laura Cecil; Margaret N. Coughlan of the Library of Congress; Richard Dalby, Rosemary Pardoe, and Barbara Roden, all of the Ghost Story Society; and the staff of the Cambridge University Library and the Library of Homerton College, Cambridge.

CONTENTS

Contents

INTRODUCTION

HERE is a collection of children's ghost stories which I have tried to make into a history, or at least a chronology, of the genre. As histories go, this one turns out to be surprisingly short. Surprisingly, considering the well-known fascination of the supernatural for so many people of all ages and in all ages.

As late as 1952—and by then children's literature in Britain had been flourishing for some two hundred years—Lord David Cecil could suppose that Christopher Woodforde's collection of stories, *A Pad in the Straw*, was the first of its kind. In his Prefatory Note he wrote:

> Dr Woodforde is breaking new ground. Stories for the young, except fairy tales and fantasies, belong to the same categories as stories for grown up people; only they are, as it were, transposed into a treble key. We have seen this process applied to thrillers, historical romances, detective stories, and stories of domestic life. Dr Woodforde is the first writer I know of to have applied it to the ghost story.

David Cecil perceived the beginning of a trickle that, before the end of the twentieth century, would become a flood of ghost stories for children. But what about the antediluvian period? Were there really no ghost stories at all for children before the middle of the twentieth century?

In the folk-tales and legends of oral tradition ghosts abounded; but such tales, of course, were originally not more for children than for adults. By the nineteenth century, with the emergence of a new reading public, the oral tradition was narrowing. Yet the telling of traditional tales, particularly ghost stories, was still popular, especially at Hallowe'en and Christmas. In *The Pickwick Papers* the whole family at Dingley Dell, including guests and servants, would assemble in the great kitchen: 'Here we wait, until the clock strikes twelve, to usher Christmas in, and beguile the time with forfeits and old stories' (ch. 28).

Dickens is the great literary exploiter of Christmas and its story traditions. His first Christmas book, *A Christmas Carol* (1843), is a ghost story; and the Christmas numbers of his *Household Words* and *All the Year Round* often feature the supernatural. But these ghost stories are for family reading—an inclusive, undifferentiated readership. Nothing particularly for children.

Yet, buried among the papers of *The Uncommercial Traveller* (1861) is 'Nurse's Stories', including something uncommonly like an original ghost story for children—a story *told* first of all, only later written down. The tale is of a shipwright called Chips who has sold his soul to the Devil for a quantity of ship's chandlery together with—the unwanted part of the bargain—a truly diabolical rat:

Chips resolved to kill the rat, and, being at work in the Yard one day with a great kettle of hot pitch on one side of him and the iron pot with the rat in it on the other, he turned the scalding pitch into the pot and filled it full. Then, he kept his eye upon it till it cooled and hardened, and then he let it stand for twenty days, and then he heated the pitch again and turned it back into the kettle, and then he sank the pot in water for twenty days more, and then he got the smelters to put it in the furnace for twenty days more, and then they gave it him out, red-hot, and looking like red-hot glass instead of iron—yet there was the rat in it, just the same as ever! And the moment it caught his eye, it said with a jeer:

> 'A Lemon has pips
> And a Yard has ships
> And *I*'ll have Chips !'

This and other stories, some ghostly, some not, all terrifying, were told to the infant Dickens by his Nurse. According to Dickens, she tormented him by insisting on telling him stories he hated. But how accurately is Dickens remembering those childhood feelings? In most people's experience, a child of, say, 5 cannot be made to pay attention to a story he doesn't really want to hear. It seems more likely that the infant Dickens succumbed to the peculiar charm of the ghost story—the blending of dread and delight.

The Victorian period is rich in writers and tellers of ghost stories for adults; and if, on the whole, adults did not provide ghost stories for children, certainly children told them to each other. One example among many is A. C. Benson recalling his schoolboy adoration for an older boy at Eton: 'I never spoke to him till the blissful day when I had gone to Henley, and, tired of heat and noise, made my way to the station to return. He got into the same carriage and told me ghost stories . . .'[1]

The adults who were interested in ghostly fiction had sometimes a markedly childlike sense of the pleasure there can be in fear—in safe fear. This was something that Lord Halifax (1839–1934) could afford (in every sense of the word) to indulge in. E. F. Benson (the brother of A. C. Benson and a noted ghost-story writer, although not for children) was a friend and knew well one of the family houses:

---

[1] Quoted in David Newsome, *On the Edge of Paradise* (Murray, 1980), 30.

Garrowby, on the hills beyond the plain of York. What I best remember of a day's excursion there is being shut into some big dark chest or cupboard at one end of the house and being told to open a door or push a panel on the side of it and walk along a passage that would be disclosed. The passage turned sharply, and immediately round the corner was an awesome figure against the wall with a mask for a face. After recovering from this shock, one had to continue the solitary pilgrimage; it was dark and as one shuffled along in the gloom there were strange tappings and chucklings from which it was easy to imagine the most sinister causes. This passage was Halifax's gleeful contrivance for producing a pleasing terror in those who, like himself, appreciated the childish luxury of being frightened and uneasy. . . . He loved the ghost stories of fiction, whose only object is to terrify. I wrote several, as desired, for his especial discomfort, and read them aloud to him. He was getting rather deaf, and sat close, with his hand up to his ear; and, if the story was fulfilling its aim, he got more and more uncomfortable and entranced. 'It's too frightful,' he said, 'Go on, go on. I can't bear it.' The passage at Garrowby was his own original ghost story in bricks and mortar.[2]

Comparably, M. R. James, as a Fellow of King's College, Cambridge, played ghost-games in the Fellows' Garden with friends from his own and other colleges. The Garden lay remote from the main College buildings, and it was densely grown just inside its boundary with ferns, shrubs, and overarching and large trees behind whose boles a man—or a spectre—might conceal himself. Through these a path wound its gloomy way. One player had to attempt the circuit at a steady walk, not faltering or breaking into a run, not crying out or exclaiming in any way. Meanwhile, others, hidden along the sides of the path, 'either made eerie noises as the victim passed, or gently clutched at his clothes, and so on. . . . Monty was particularly good at making ghostly noises.'[3]

Any account of the development of ghost fiction must pause respectfully at the name of M. R. James. He is pre-eminent. He wrote only one book for children, *The Five Jars* (1922): this has what might be called a ghost element, but the story is too long for the present collection. If it were not for James's own admissions, the casual reader of his collected ghost stories might never identify the two that were originally for children: 'A School Story', which was 'made up for the benefit of the King's College Choir School',[4] published first in *More Ghost Stories of an Antiquary* in 1911, but read aloud probably some years earlier; and

[2] E. F. Benson, *Final Edition* (Longman, 1940), 84–5.
[3] Professor Charles Fletcher, quoted in Michael Cox, *M. R. James: An Informal Portrait* (Oxford University Press, 1983), 98.
[4] See Preface to M. R. James, *The Complete Ghost Stories* (Arnold, 1931).

'Wailing Well' 'written for the Eton College troop of Boy Scouts and read at their camp-fire at Worbarrow Down in August 1927.'[5]

The usual method of M. R. James with his Christmas ghost stories for adults was to write down his narrative, sometimes writing up to the last minute, even as the audience of friends was assembling in his College rooms. He 'emerged from the bedroom, manuscript in hand at last, and blew out all the candles but one, by which he seated himself. He then began to read, with more confidence than anyone else could have mustered, his well-nigh illegible script in the dim light.'[6] His first presentation of 'A School Story'—with which this collection starts—was at Christmas, and the entertainment must have been very similar, only for boys instead of for grown men.

At once interesting points are raised. How is it that a story primarily for children can appear, without self-identification, in a collection for adults? For publication, there is reason to suppose that the story has in part been rewritten upwards in age—surely an unusual occurrence. But how aware was James—as a writer for children should be—of his responsibilities? Already, in writing for adults, he speaks of the sin of 'stepping over the line of legitimate horridness'. He observes certain restraints: 'It is very easy to be nauseating. I, *moi qui vous parle*, could undertake to make a reader physically sick, if I chose to think and write in terms of the Grand Guignol.'[7] What he considered unacceptable for children is very clearly demonstrated by the appalling Mr Karswell in 'Casting the Runes'. Mr Karswell invites the children of the village to a party ending in a magic lantern show. The local parson, Mr Farrer, attended the occasion:

[Mr Karswell] began with some comparatively mild things. Red Riding Hood was one, and even then, Mr Farrer said, the wolf was so dreadful that several of the smaller children had to be taken out. . . . Well, the show went on, and the stories kept on becoming a little more terrifying each time, and the children were mesmerized into complete silence. At last he produced a series which represented a little boy passing through his own park—Lufford, I mean—in the evening. And the poor boy was followed, and at last pursued and overtaken, and either torn in pieces or somehow made away with by a horrible hopping creature in white, which you saw first dodging about among the trees, and gradually it appeared more and more plainly. Mr Farrer said it gave him one of the worst nightmares he ever remembered, and what it must have meant to the children doesn't bear thinking of.

[5] M. R. James, *The Complete Ghost Stories*.
[6] Unpublished reminiscences of Oliffe Richmond, quoted in Cox, *M. R. James*, 134.
[7] M. R. James, 'Some Remarks on Ghost Stories' in the *Bookman* (Dec. 1929), 171.

Disapproval of Mr Karswell's story-telling is self-evident; and later he comes to a very bad end, both ghostly and ghastly.

M. R. James was one of a tiny group of ghost-writing friends whose careers flitted to and fro between Eton and Cambridge. A. C. Benson, as a housemaster at Eton, every Sunday evening used to tell his own ghost stories, leisurely and ornate, dark yet bracingly moralistic, to the boys who congregated in his rooms to hear him. The stories were later published in two volumes. H. F. W. Tatham, also an Eton housemaster, told Sunday evening ghost stories that were sometimes almost Christian fables. They made one volume. As M. R. James said in self-mockery of his own story-telling: 'all very pedestrian and Anglican and Victorian.'

Another contemporary, William James Wintle, starting from very different beginnings (he was the son of a coachman and a domestic servant), ended by telling—and publishing—his stories not all that differently. He became an oblate in the Abbey on Caldey Island and told his ghost stories on Sunday evenings to the alumni (boys aged usually 13 to 16) in the Abbey's little school. His book, *Ghost Gleams: Tales of the Uncanny* (1921), is dedicated to eight named listeners. His story 'The Light in the Dormitory' must have seemed to them a close reflection of their way of life and where they lived.

Two later writers seem to class themselves with this group. J. S. Leatherbarrow, later a Canon of Worcester Cathedral, was inspired by his reading of M. R. James to tell his own ghost stories at Scout and Youth camps in the 1930s. These were published several decades later. Finally comes Christopher Woodforde himself, Chaplain of New College at Oxford, whose *A Pad in the Straw* was dedicated 'To the eight boys who first asked me to tell them a story.'

Apparently, then, there were writers of children's ghost stories before Christopher Woodforde, but only a very few. They form, with him, an oddly homogeneous group. They all wrote stories, but relied on audiences before readerships: in this way, they looked back to—of all people!—Dickens's Nurse, and so to the old oral tradition. Their output of stories was small—even the enormously prolific A. C. Benson produced only two volumes. The group was very male-dominated, and most noticeably was outside the mainstream of children's literature. For instance, none of these ghost collections (perhaps one should except *A Pad in the Straw*) was illustrated, whereas the great majority of books for children always had been.

In the mainstream, there were popular writers for children from whom one might have expected regularly to have had children's ghost stories. E. Nesbit (1858–1924) wrote macabre stories very successfully for adults; and her imagination had been M. R. Jamesian from childhood: 'One used to lie awake in the silence, listening, listening to the pad-pad of one's own heart, straining one's ears to make sure it was not the pad-pad of something else, something unspeakable creeping towards one out of the horrible dense dark.'[8] In childhood she had had nightmar- ish experiences—one being her belief that she had seen the ghost of her dead father, and another a sight-seeing visit to the gruesome 'Bordeaux mummies'. As a child, she prayed 'fervently, tearfully, that when I should be grown up I might never forget what I thought, felt, and suffered then.'[9] She remembered her childhood fears only too well: the few easily traceable Nesbit ghost stories for children are milk-and-water pieces, written entirely without her usual flair.

Perhaps, too, as someone who wrote for a living, E. Nesbit had a restricting awareness of what would be considered acceptable by adults— by the adults who, on the children's behalf, publish magazines and books, sell them, and buy them for homes, schools, or (nowadays) for libraries. Here, as always in the history of children's literature, is seen the confronta- tion of what adults think ought to be provided for children, and what children might actually enjoy. In any period, for varying reasons, it is unlikely that the two will exactly coincide.

Sadly and against all expectation, there is no Nesbit story in this collection.

Another prestigious writer for children was Walter de la Mare (1873– 1956). His ghost stories for adults—for instance, 'Seaton's Aunt'—are well known. In his prose fiction for children there are only ghost refer- ences. In 'The Scarecrow' old Mrs Lamb 'sat in her chair with her cup in her hand, and munching her toast . . . I asked her what the ghost her husband saw was like. "Well", she said, "it was like (*crunch, crunch*), it was like, he told me, seeing something with your eyes shut. It made him feel very cold; the bedroom went black; but he wasn't frightened." ' Later in the story, Mr Bolsover recalls how, as a boy, he had met a fairy: 'As I came stumping I suddenly went cold all over, and I firmly believe my cap had pushed itself up a little on the top of my head, owing to the hair underneath trying to stand on end.' De la Mare's fairies were not the gauzy-winged dainty little creatures fake-photographed in Conan Doyle's *The Coming of the Fairies* (1922), but creatures of stature, mystery, and power: in their effect, indeed, rather like ghosts. There had been some association in people's minds from ancient times. The historian,

---

[8] 'My Schooldays' in *Girl's Own Paper* (Oct. 1896–Sept. 1897), quoted in Doris Langley Moore, *E. Nesbit* (Benn, 1967).

[9] Ibid.

Keith Thomas, in a chapter entitled 'Ghosts and Fairies', writes: 'Elves and fairies were either devils or diabolical illusions, declared a number of late medieval writers. This hostility was strengthened by the Reformation, whose theologians took away the remaining possibility that *fairies might be the ghosts of the dead.*'[10]

In this collection I have included de la Mare's 'Miss Jemima' with a personal justification. In childhood I had loved the story, experiencing what seemed an authenticating dread and delight: at the heart of the story, I was aware of a Presence, seductive, accusatory, malevolent. Rereading yet again as an adult, I was startled to realize that a fairy (or faery) had been specified—even described. So, in actuality, there was no ghost at all—although there were many of the usual accompaniments: the church and its graveyard, the death that inspires guilt, the corruption of innocence, the temptation to evil. As an adult reader, I became aware of faint, distorted echoes of Henry James's *The Turn of the Screw* (1898), which Walter de la Mare much admired.

Eleanor Farjeon (1881–1965) has less of a reputation now than during her lifetime. The increasing sophistication of children, although often only superficial perhaps, has told against her work. She wrote her stories—often fantasies—with elegance and whimsicality and a certain sunniness (or moonshine). De la Mare's 'Miss Jemima' felt to me like a ghost story, and—strictly—isn't; Farjeon's 'Elsie Piddock Skips in her Sleep' feels not at all like a ghost story, but must be. For Elsie comes back to skip for her village when she is 109 years old. *Just* possible, of course; 'but that wasn't the end of Elsie Piddock, she has never stopped skipping . . . If you go to Caburn you may catch a glimpse of a tiny, bent figure, no bigger than a child, skipping all by itself in its sleep . . .' 'Elsie Piddock Skips in her Sleep' has been a favourite with story-tellers, and one can see why.

Compilers of ghost anthologies for adult readers have rummaged successfully through the magazines that began to proliferate by the end of the nineteenth century. At the beginning of 'A School Story', it is supposed that schoolboys inventing ghost stories got their ideas from, say, the *Strand Magazine*. At that time the *Strand* certainly had plenty of fiction by top writers, including ghost fiction. There was also a story corner for children, where several of E. Nesbit's novels, such as *The Amulet*, were serialized. But schoolboy readers would have had to steal any ghostly ideas from outside that story corner.

---

[10] Keith Thomas, *Religion and the Decline of Magic* (Weidenfeld, 1971), my emphasis.

Children's own magazines and annuals and other miscellanies are not much more help—even Lady Cynthia Asquith's enterprising compilations, such as *The Treasure Cave* in 1928. *Little Folks* (1871–1933) indulged in fantasy but not in ghosts. *Joy Street* (1923–1939) only occasionally included some mild ghost fiction—although it was the first publisher of 'Miss Jemima'. *The Boy's Own Paper* (1879–1967), an outstandingly successful publication, concentrated on stories of action and adventure, school stories, historical fiction, sport, and manly hobbies. No ghost fiction.

In the USA the periodical *Saint Nicholas* (1873–1939) was immensely popular with children; still it observed a censorship of silence on the supernatural. One early story throws incidental light on all this: a story of settlers and Indians, called 'My Grandmother's Grandmother's Christmas Candle' by Hezekiah Butterworth (1839–1905).[11] One of the characters, Silas Sloan, is asked to tell a story to the company assembled before the great kitchen fire:

Si—as he was called—was relating an account of a so-called haunted house, where, according to his silly narrative, the ghost of an Indian used to appear at the foot of an old woman's bed; and some superstitious people declared that the old lady one night on awaking and finding this ghostly Indian present, put out her foot to push him away, and pushed her foot directly *through him*. What a brave old lady she must have been, and how uncomfortable it must have been for the ghost!

The sarcastic reporting of the story ends with a reflection of some severity: 'People who relate so-called ghost stories are often cowardly, and it is usually a cowardly nature that seeks to frighten children.'

There was a continuing unwillingness of adults to admit that most children wanted—perhaps *needed*—the experience of safe fear and of a certain kind of awe. Writers for children censored themselves. In the 1940s, in Britain, appeared a timid, good-natured little American ghost called Georgie. He was pictured very like a toddler swathed in his mother's white tablecloth, a charming apparition on a neighbour's doorstep some Hallowe'en. He was the creation of Robert Bright (1902–1988), writer and illustrator for children:

Bright recalls that the idea for Georgie stemmed from his own children badgering him to make up for them a ghost story. While they probably wanted a tale of dread and awe, it was to Bright's ultimate advantage as a publishable writer

[11] Hezekiah Butterworth, 'My Grandmother's Grandmother's Christmas Candle' in *St Nicholas*, 13 (1886).

for the young that he decided against doing a genuine ghost story. Instead he chose a tongue-in-the-cheek treatment of the supernatural.[12]

The result was 'Georgie', popular with readers (or listeners) probably aged about 4 to 7.

With 'Georgie', only the first of a 'Georgie' series, we have reached a period when writers were making efforts, professionally directed, to write ghost stories that would lean on the old traditions and yet be for a carefully assessed readership of children.

At this point in the history of the children's ghost story, it is convenient to pause for breath, before going forward into the bewildering proliferations of the second half of the twentieth century. Here the search is easy; the difficulty lies in choosing among so many.

The rules which I have been observing remain the same. Every story must be complete in itself. It must be written in English (no translations), although not necessarily coming from within the UK.[13] The story must be an original fiction—although some of these stories are clearly *inspired* by traditional tales. And—most importantly—the fictions must originally have been intended for children; and they must truly be ghost stories. (No science fiction, for instance; and certainly no hoaxes.)

At once two large questions are begged: what age am I supposing these child-readers to be; and what exactly is a children's ghost story?

Over the long period of childhood, of course, children are of different ages, and of different reading ages roughly to correspond. They may also seem to be of more than one reading age at the same time: it has become accepted that, on occasion, children may choose to read well below and also even above their usual reading age. The texts have, of course, to be of sufficient interest, or, at least, of sufficiently comforting familiarity.

Meanwhile, what adults think that children can or should read seems always to be changing. Ghost stories written for adults in the first half of the twentieth century have been picked over by anthologizers and selectively re-published for children in the second half of the century. Alfred Hitchcock's very popular anthologies are examples. And his collections are intended for an entirely new category of child-readers who are hardly still children: teenagers, or (a later term) Young Adults.

[12] Patrick Groff in *Twentieth Century Children's Writers*, ed. D. L. Kirkpatrick (Macmillan, 1978).

[13] In 1984 J. A. Cuddon, in his Introduction to *The Penguin Book of Ghost Stories* estimated that more than nine-tenths of all ghost stories were written in English, anyway.

Among such complications one has to pick a wary way. On the whole and very roughly, most children's ghost stories seem to be for readers over the age of, say, 10. But I have decided, anyway, to ignore rigid categorization by age. I include here not only 'Georgie' but also Dorothy Edwards's 'The Old White Ghost and the Old Grey Granddad' for variety and to demonstrate more widely the development of the genre.

And what exactly is a children's ghost story? As David Cecil pointed out, it is really the adult ghost story 'transposed into a treble key'. It does not necessarily confine itself to ghosts, as revenants. Ghostly, or super-natural, is a better description of some of the stories here. Ruskin Bond, for instance, contributes the story of an Indian poltergeist; Arthur Machen writes of a *doppelgänger*. The transposition from adult to juvenile does make changes, however. In ghost stories for children—especially for younger children—there is a prevalence of the wistful, the whimsical, the downright comic. The authors, anxious for their young readers, clearly try to keep in balance the frightening and the reassuring.

I, too, have tried to keep a balance. What I have particularly excluded are ghost stories so anti-ghostly in their effect that they condemn themselves on the grounds of dishonesty of the imagination. I have also excluded horror stories for children. 'If there is a theme that ought to be kept out of the ghost story, it is that of the charnel house,' said M. R. James, adding, perhaps obsessively: 'That and sex.'[14] Between the First and Second World Wars a series called *Not at Night* was published for adults, and I have heard of at least one schoolmaster who used it as bedtime reading for his boys. The editor of a *Not at Night* anthology of 'the best stories' wrote that 'from the first I set myself against "literature".... No amount of style could persuade me to select a story that lacked genuine, unadulterated horror.'[15]

The great increase in ghost fiction for children in the second half of the twentieth century included—very fortunately for my purposes—a large number of *short* stories. Enthusiasts, such as Aidan Chambers, began commissioning original ghost stories for anthologies for children. A writer with the inclination and the ability might contribute to several different anthologies over the years, then retrieve his or her stories, add a few new ones, and publish a collection under one authorship. The genre flourished.

Nevertheless, choosing for this anthology has sometimes been frustrating. Some writers with ghost stories here have even better ones which—

---

[14] M. R. James, 'Ghosts—Treat them Gently' in the *Evening News*, 17 Apr. 1931.

[15] Christine Campbell Thomson (ed.), *Not at Night* (Selwyn & Blount, 1936).

alas!—are far too long to qualify. Leon Garfield's *The Ghost Downstairs* (1972) and Penelope Lively's *The Ghost of Thomas Kempe* (1973) are examples. Joan Aiken's work presents a different problem: she has written so many good short ghost stories for children that choosing was particularly hard. And Ruth Brown's *One Stormy Night* (1992), a story of great charm, could not be included since it is told entirely in pictures; no words at all.

Until almost last I have left the question of the real suitability of ghost stories for children. Certainly they can entertain, and that is no small virtue. The fear they induce should be pleasurable—the delight is in the dread, and the fear should be imagination-widening. Fear becomes awe and wonder: the Present relates itself to the Past, the Known to the Unknown—to the Unknowable.

The last story in this collection, John Gordon's 'The Burning Baby', highlights the issue of suitability and appears to contrast sharply with the first story, 'A School Story' by M. R. James. (I have cheated a little on the chronology to secure the comparison.) The teenage seduction, unwanted pregnancy, and resultant murder in Gordon's plot would have been abhorrent to M. R. James. Yet the stories share an ancient morality. One of the offices of a revenant was the pitiless haunting of the guilty, when the ordinary machinery of detection and punishment was for some reason ineffective. In 'A School Story' there is a strong implication of revenge, itself 'a kind of wild justice'. And in 'The Burning Baby' the seducer–murderer is executed by the ghost of his own unborn child. Note that in both stories a schoolchild is the witness and reporter of events.

The first and last of the stories chosen are separated by almost a hundred years, making the whole collection fit neatly—perhaps suspiciously neatly—inside the century. I have tried to find a children's ghost story published before 1900; it has proved impossible, even with the help of others much more knowledgeable than myself. No doubt one such story will turn up after the publication of this volume, to falsify its title. I even hope so.

Finally, what about any reality that lies behind ghost stories for children? To begin with, these stories are all fictions. Children reading them may shiver and shake (or sigh, or laugh): they are not asked to *believe*, except temporarily. Talking to adults about ghost fiction, I have found curious correlations. On the whole, those who absolutely believe in the supernatural, or absolutely disbelieve, are not much interested in the fictions. One can see why. It is the doubtful, the half or even quarter believers who like ghost stories. Doctor Johnson himself said of the

supernatural: 'All argument is against it; but all belief is for it.' Nowadays, in an age of scientific and technological sophistication, one would
expect the balance to be tipped against belief; yet ghost fiction—especially for children—thrives.

Walter de la Mare was surely at least a half-believer. He wrote sym-
pathetically of the *Proceedings* of the Society for Psychical Research, but
went on to ask: 'How do even the best of these records compare in mere
reading value alone, quite apart from significance, persuasiveness, depth
and memorability, with the best of their kind in fiction?'[16]

He added, very pertinently: 'All depends, of course, not only on what
is told, but on who tells it, and whom it is told to.'

PHILIPPA PEARCE

Great Shelford
August 1994

---

[16] Introduction to *The Ghost Book*, ed. Colin de la Mare (Faber, 1931).

M. R. JAMES

A School Story

Two men in a smoking-room were talking of their private-school days. 'At *our* school,' said A., 'we had a ghost's footmark on the staircase. What was it like? Oh, very unconvincing. Just the shape of a shoe, with a square toe, if I remember right. The staircase was a stone one. I never heard any story about the thing. That seems odd, when you come to think of it. Why didn't somebody invent one, I wonder?'

'You never can tell with little boys. They have a mythology of their own. There's a subject for you, by the way—"The Folklore of Private Schools".'

'Yes; the crop is rather scanty, though. I imagine, if you were to investigate the cycle of ghost stories, for instance, which the boys at private schools tell each other, they would all turn out to be highly-compressed versions of stories out of books.'

'Nowadays the *Strand* and *Pearson's*, and so on, would be extensively drawn upon.'

'No doubt: they weren't born or thought of in *my* time. Let's see. I wonder if I can remember the staple ones that I was told. First, there was the house with a room in which a series of people insisted on passing a night; and each of them in the morning was found kneeling in a corner, and had just time to say, "I've seen it," and died.'

'Wasn't that the house in Berkeley Square?'

'I dare say it was. Then there was the man who heard a noise in the passage at night, opened his door, and saw someone crawling towards him on all fours with his eye hanging out on his cheek. There was besides, let me think—Yes! the room where a man was found dead in bed with a horseshoe mark on his forehead, and the floor under the bed was covered with marks of horseshoes also; I don't know why. Also there was the lady who, on locking her bedroom door in a strange house, heard a thin voice among the bed-curtains say, "Now we're shut in for the night." None of those had any explanation or sequel. I wonder if they go on still, those stories.'

'Oh, likely enough—with additions from the magazines, as I said. You never heard, did you, of a real ghost at a private school? I thought not; nobody has that ever I came across.'

'From the way in which you said that, I gather that *you* have.'

'I really don't know; but this is what was in my mind. It happened at my private school thirty odd years ago, and I haven't any explanation of it.

'The school I mean was near London. It was established in a large and fairly old house—a great white building with very fine grounds about it; there were large cedars in the garden, as there are in so many of the older gardens in the Thames valley, and ancient elms in the three or four fields which we used for our games. I think probably it was quite an attractive place, but boys seldom allow that their schools possess any tolerable features.

'I came to the school in a September, soon after the year 1870; and among the boys who arrived on the same day was one whom I took to: a Highland boy, whom I will call McLeod. I needn't spend time in describing him: the main thing is that I got to know him very well. He was not an exceptional boy in any way—not particularly good at books or games—but he suited me.

'The school was a large one: there must have been from 120 to 130 boys there as a rule, and so a considerable staff of masters was required, and there were rather frequent changes among them.

'One term—perhaps it was my third or fourth—a new master made his appearance. His name was Sampson. He was a tallish, stoutish, pale, black-bearded man. I think we liked him: he had travelled a good deal, and had stories which amused us on our school walks, so that there was some competition among us to get within earshot of him. I remember too—dear me, I have hardly thought of it since then!—that he had a charm on his watch-chain that attracted my attention one day, and he let me examine it. It was, I now suppose, a gold Byzantine coin; there was an effigy of some absurd emperor on one side; the other side had been worn practically smooth, and he had had cut on it—rather barbarously—his own initials, G. W. S., and a date, 24 July, 1865. Yes, I can see it now: he told me he had picked it up in Constantinople: it was about the size of a florin, perhaps rather smaller.

'Well, the first odd thing that happened was this. Sampson was doing Latin grammar with us. One of his favourite methods—perhaps it is rather a good one—was to make us construct sentences out of our own heads to illustrate the rules he was trying to make us learn. Of course that is a thing which gives a silly boy a chance of being impertinent:

there are lots of school stories in which that happens—or anyhow there might be. But Sampson was too good a disciplinarian for us to think of trying that on with him. Now, on this occasion he was telling us how to express *remembering* in Latin: and he ordered us each to make a sentence bringing in the verb *memini*, "I remember." Well, most of us made up some ordinary sentence such as "I remember my father," or "He remembers his book," or something equally uninteresting: and I dare say a good many put down *memino librum meum*, and so forth: but the boy I mentioned—McLeod—was evidently thinking of something more elaborate than that. The rest of us wanted to have our sentences passed, and get on to something else, so some kicked him under the desk, and I, who was next to him, poked him and whispered to him to look sharp. But he didn't seem to attend. I looked at his paper and saw he had put down nothing at all. So I jogged him again harder than before and upbraided him sharply for keeping us all waiting. That did have some effect. He started and seemed to wake up, and then very quickly he scribbled about a couple of lines on his paper, and showed it up with the rest. As it was the last, or nearly the last, to come in, and as Sampson had a good deal to say to the boys who had written *meminiscimus patri meo* and the rest of it, it turned out that the clock struck twelve before he had got to McLeod, and McLeod had to wait afterwards to have his sentence corrected. There was nothing much going on outside when I got out, so I waited for him to come. He came very slowly when he did arrive, and I guessed there had been some sort of trouble. "Well," I said, "what did you get?" "Oh, I don't know," said McLeod, "nothing much: but I think Sampson's rather sick with me." "Why, did you show him up some rot?" "No fear," he said. "It was all right as far as I could see: it was like this: *Memento*—that's right enough for remember, and it takes a genitive,—*memento putei inter quatuor taxos.*" "What silly rot!" I said. "What made you shove that down? What does it mean?" "That's the funny part," said McLeod. "I'm not quite sure what it does mean. All I know is, it just came into my head and I corked it down. I know what I *think* it means, because just before I wrote it down I had a sort of picture of it in my head: I believe it means 'Remember the well among the four'— what are those dark sort of trees that have red berries on them?" "Mountain ashes, I s'pose you mean." "I never heard of them," said McLeod; "no, *I'll* tell you—yews." "Well, and what did Sampson say?" "Why, he was jolly odd about it. When he read it he got up and went to the mantelpiece and stopped quite a long time without saying anything, with his back to me. And then he said, without turning round, and rather quiet, 'What do you suppose that means?' I told him what I thought; only I couldn't remember the name of the silly tree: and then he wanted to know why I put it down, and I had to say something or other. And after that he left off talking about it, and asked me how long I'd been here, and where my people lived, and things like that: and then I came away: but he wasn't looking a bit well."

'I don't remember any more that was said by either of us about this. Next day McLeod took to his bed with a chill or something of the kind, and it was a week or more before he was in school again. And as much as a month went by without anything happening that was noticeable. Whether or not Mr Sampson was really startled, as McLeod had thought, he didn't show it. I am pretty sure, of course, now, that there was something very curious in his past history, but I'm not going to pretend that we boys were sharp enough to guess any such thing.

'There was one other incident of the same kind as the last which I told you. Several times since that day we had had to make up examples in school to illustrate different rules, but there had never been any row except when we did them wrong. At last there came a day when we were going through those dismal things which people call Conditional Sentences, and we were told to make a conditional sentence, expressing a future consequence. We did it, right or wrong, and showed up our bits of paper, and Sampson began looking through them. All at once he got up, made some odd sort of noise in his throat, and rushed out by a door that was just by his desk. We sat there for a minute or two, and then—I suppose it was incorrect—but we went up, I and one or two others, to look at the papers on his desk. Of course I thought someone must have put down some nonsense or other, and Sampson had gone off to report him. All the same, I noticed that he hadn't taken any of the papers with him when he ran out. Well, the top paper on the desk was written in red ink—which no one used—and it wasn't in anyone's hand who was in the class. They all looked at it—McLeod and all—and took their dying oaths that it wasn't theirs. Then I thought of counting the bits of paper. And of this I made quite certain: that there were seventeen bits of paper on the desk, and sixteen boys in the form. Well, I bagged the extra paper, and kept it, and I believe I have it now. And now you will want to know what was written on it. It was simple enough, and harmless enough, I should have said.

'"Si tu non veneris ad me, ego veniam ad te,"

which means, I suppose, "If you don't come to me, I'll come to you." '

'Could you show me the paper?' interrupted the listener.

'Yes, I could: but there's another odd thing about it. That same afternoon I took it out of my locker—I know for certain it was the same bit, for I made a finger-mark on it—and no single trace of writing of any kind was there on it. I kept it, as I said, and since that time I have tried various experiments to see whether sympathetic ink had been used, but absolutely without result.

'So much for that. After about half an hour Sampson looked in again: said he had felt very unwell, and told us we might go. He came rather gingerly to his desk and gave just one look at the uppermost paper: and I suppose he thought he must have been dreaming: anyhow, he asked no questions.

'That day was a half-holiday, and next day Sampson was in school again, much as usual. That night the third and last incident in my story happened.

'We—McLeod and I—slept in a dormitory at right angles to the main building. Sampson slept in the main building on the first floor. There was a very bright full moon. At an hour which I can't tell exactly, but some time between one and two, I was woken up by somebody shaking me. It was McLeod; and a nice state of mind he seemed to be in. "Come," he said,—"come! there's a burglar getting in through Sampson's window." As soon as I could speak, I said, "Well, why not call out and wake everybody up?" "No, no," he said, "I'm not sure who it is: don't make a row: come and look." Naturally I came and looked, and naturally there was no one there. I was cross enough, and should have called McLeod plenty of names: only—I couldn't tell why—it seemed to me that there *was* something wrong—something that made me very glad I wasn't alone to face it. We were still at the window looking out, and as soon as I could, I asked him what he had heard or seen. "I didn't *hear* anything at all," he said, "but about five minutes before I woke you, I found myself looking out of this window here, and there was a man sitting or kneeling on Sampson's window-sill, and looking in, and I thought he was beckoning." "What sort of man?" McLeod wriggled. "I don't know," he said, "but I can tell you one thing—he was beastly thin: and he looked as if he was wet all over: and," he said, looking round and whispering as if he hardly liked to hear himself, "I'm not at all sure that he was alive."

'We went on talking in whispers some time longer, and eventually crept back to bed. No one else in the room woke or stirred the whole time. I believe we did sleep a bit afterwards, but we were very cheap next day.

'And next day Mr Sampson was gone: not to be found: and I believe no trace of him has ever come to light since. In thinking it over, one of the oddest things about it all has seemed to me to be the fact that neither

McLeod nor I ever mentioned what we had seen to any third person whatever. Of course no questions were asked on the subject, and if they had been, I am inclined to believe that we could not have made any answer: we seemed unable to speak about it.

'That is my story,' said the narrator. 'The only approach to a ghost story connected with a school that I know, but still, I think, an approach to such a thing.'

The sequel to this may perhaps be reckoned highly conventional; but a sequel there is, and so it must be produced. There had been more than one listener to the story, and, in the latter part of that same year, or of the next, one such listener was staying at a country house in Ireland.

One evening his host was turning over a drawer full of odds and ends in the smoking-room. Suddenly he put his hand upon a little box. 'Now,' he said, 'you know about old things; tell me what that is.' My friend opened the little box, and found in it a thin gold chain with an object attached to it. He glanced at the object and then took off his spectacles to examine it more narrowly. 'What's the history of this?' he asked. 'Odd enough,' was the answer. 'You know the yew thicket in the shrubbery: well, a year or two back we were cleaning out the old well that used to be in the clearing there, and what do you suppose we found?'

'Is it possible that you found a body?' said the visitor, with an odd feeling of nervousness.

'We did that: but what's more, in every sense of the word, we found two.'

'Good Heavens! Two? Was there anything to show how they got there? Was this thing found with them?'

'It was. Amongst the rags of the clothes that were on one of the bodies. A bad business, whatever the story of it may have been. One body had the arms tight round the other. They must have been there thirty years or more—long enough before we came to this place. You may judge we filled the well up fast enough. Do you make anything of what's cut on that gold coin you have there?'

'I think I can,' said my friend, holding it to the light (but he read it without much difficulty); 'it seems to be G.W.S., 24 July, 1865.'

A. C. BENSON

Out of the Sea

IT was about ten of the clock on a November morning in the little village of Blea-on-the-Sands. The hamlet was made up of some thirty houses, which clustered together on a low rising ground. The place was very poor, but some old merchant of bygone days had built in a pious mood a large church, which was now too great for the needs of the place; the nave had been unroofed in a heavy gale, and there was no money to repair it, so that it had fallen to decay, and the tower was joined to the choir by roofless walls. This was a sore trial to the old priest, Father Thomas, who had grown grey there; but he had no art in gathering money, which he asked for in a shamefaced way; and the vicarage was a poor one, hardly enough for the old man's needs. So the church lay desolate.

The village stood on what must once have been an island; the little river Reddy, which runs down to the sea, there forking into two channels on the landward side; towards the sea the ground was bare, full of sand-hills covered with a short grass. Towards the land was a small wood of gnarled trees, the boughs of which were all brushed smooth by the gales; looking landward there was the green flat, in which the river ran, rising into low hills; hardly a house was visible save one or two lonely farms; two or three church towers rose above the hills at a long distance away. Indeed Blea was much cut off from the world; there was a bridge over the stream on the west side, but over the other channel was no bridge, so that to fare eastward it was requisite to go in a boat. To seaward there were wide sands, when the tide was out; when it was in, it came up nearly to the end of the village street. The people were mostly fishermen, but there were a few farmers and labourers; the boats of the fishermen lay to the east side of the village, near the river channel which gave some draught of water; and the channel was marked out by big black stakes and posts that straggled out over the sands, like awkward leaning figures, to the sea's brim.

Father Thomas lived in a small and ancient brick house near the church, with a little garden of herbs attached. He was a kindly man, much worn by age and weather, with a wise heart, and he loved the quiet life with his small flock. This morning he had come out of his house to look abroad, before he settled down to the making of his sermon. He looked out to sea, and saw with a shadow of sadness the black outline of a wreck that had come ashore a week before, and over which the white waves were now breaking. The wind blew steadily from the north-east, and had a bitter poisonous chill in it, which it doubtless drew from the fields of the upper ice. The day was dark and overhung, not with cloud, but with a kind of dreary vapour that shut out the sun. Father Thomas shuddered at the wind, and drew his patched cloak round him. As he did so, he saw three figures come up to the vicarage gate. It was not a common thing for him to have visitors in the morning, and he saw with surprise that they were old Master John Grimston, the richest man in the place, half farmer and half fisherman, a dark surly old man; his wife, Bridget, a timid and frightened woman, who found life with her harsh husband a difficult business, in spite of their wealth, which, for a place like Blea, was great; and their son Henry, a silly shambling man of forty, who was his father's butt. The three walked silently and heavily, as though they came on a sad errand.

Father Thomas went briskly down to meet them, and greeted them with his accustomed cheerfulness. 'And what may I do for you?' he said. Old Master Grimston made a sort of gesture with his head as though his wife should speak; and she said in a low and somewhat husky voice, with a rapid utterance, 'We have a matter, Father, we would ask you about—are you at leisure?' Father Thomas said, 'Ay, I am ashamed to be not more busy! Let us go within the house.' They did so; and even in the little distance to the door, the Father thought that his visitors behaved themselves very strangely. They peered round from left to right, and once or twice Master Grimston looked sharply behind them, as though they were followed. They said nothing but 'Ay' and 'No' to the Father's talk, and bore themselves like people with a sore fear on their backs. Father Thomas made up his mind that it was some question of money, for nothing else was wont to move Master Grimston's mind. So he had them into his parlour and gave them seats, and then there was a silence, while the two men continued to look furtively about them, and the goodwife sate with her eyes upon the priest's face. Father Thomas knew not what to make of this, till Master Grimston said harshly, 'Come, wife, tell the tale and make an end; we must not take up the Father's time.'

'I hardly know how to say it, Father,' said Bridget, 'but a strange and evil thing has befallen us; there is something come to our house, and we know not what it is—but it brings a fear with it.' A sudden paleness came over her face, and she stopped, and the three exchanged a glance in which terror was visibly written. Master Grimston looked over his shoulder swiftly, and made as though to speak, yet only swallowed in his throat; but Henry said suddenly, in a loud and woeful voice: 'It is an evil beast out of the sea.' And then there followed a dreadful silence, while Father Thomas felt a sudden fear leap up in his heart, at the contagion of the fear that he saw written on the faces round him. But he said with all the cheerfulness he could muster, 'Come, friends, let us not begin to talk of sea-beasts; we must have the whole tale. Mistress Grimston, I must hear the story—be content—nothing can touch us here.' The three seemed to draw a faint content from his words, and Bridget began:—

'It was the day of the wreck, Father. John was up betimes, before the dawn; he walked out early to the sands, and Henry with him—and they were the first to see the wreck—was not that it?' At these words the father and son seemed to exchange a very swift and secret look, and both grew pale. 'John told me there was a wreck ashore, and they went presently and roused the rest of the village; and all that day they were out, saving what could be saved. Two sailors were found, both dead and pitifully battered by the sea, and they were buried, as you know, Father, in the churchyard next day; John came back about dusk and Henry with him, and we sate down to our supper. John was telling me about the wreck, as we sate beside the fire, when Henry, who was sitting apart, rose up and cried out suddenly, "What is that?" '

She paused for a moment, and Henry, who sate with face blanched, staring at his mother, said, 'Ay, did I—it ran past me suddenly.' 'Yes, but what was it?' said Father Thomas trying to smile; 'a dog or cat, me-thinks.' 'It was a beast,' said Henry slowly, in a trembling voice—'a beast about the bigness of a goat. I never saw the like—yet I did not see it clear; I but felt the air blow, and caught a whiff of it—it was salt like the sea, but with a kind of dead smell behind.' 'Was that all you saw?' said Father Thomas; 'belike you were tired and faint, and the air swam round you suddenly—I have known the like myself when weary.' 'Nay, nay,' said Henry, 'this was not like that—it was a beast, sure enough.' 'Ay, and we have seen it since,' said Bridget. 'At least I have not seen it clearly yet, but I have smelt its odour, and it turns me sick—but John and Henry have seen it often—sometimes it lies and seems to sleep, but it watches us; and again it is merry, and will leap in a corner—and John saw it skip upon the sands near the wreck—did you not, John?' At these words the two men again exchanged a glance, and then old Master

Grimston, with a dreadful look in his face, in which great anger seemed to strive with fear, said, 'Nay, silly woman, it was not near the wreck, it was out to the east.' 'It matters little,' said Father Thomas, who saw well enough this was no light matter. 'I never heard the like of it. I will myself come down to your house with a holy book, and see if the thing will meet me. I know not what this is,' he went on, 'whether it is a vain terror that hath hold of you; but there be spirits of evil in the world, though much fettered by Christ and His Saints—we read of such in Holy Writ—and the sea, too, doubtless hath its monsters; and it may be that one hath wandered out of the waves, like a dog that hath strayed from his home. I dare not say, till I have met it face to face. But God gives no power to such things to hurt those who have a fair conscience.'—And here he made a stop, and looked at the three; Bridget sate regarding him with a hope in her face; but the other two sate peering upon the ground; and the priest divined in some secret way that all was not well with them. 'But I will come at once,' he said, rising, 'and I will see if I can cast out or bind the thing, whatever it be—for I am in this place as a soldier of the Lord, to fight with works of darkness.' He took a clasped book from a table, and lifted up his hat, saying, 'Let us set forth.' Then he said as they left the room, 'Hath it appeared to-day?' 'Yes, indeed,' said Henry, 'and it was ill content. It followed us as though it were angered.' 'Come,' said Father Thomas, turning upon him, 'you speak thus of a thing, as you might speak of a dog—what is it like?' 'Nay,' said Henry, 'I know not; I can never see it clearly; it is like a speck in the eye—it is never there when you look upon it—it glides away very secretly; it is most like a goat, I think. It seems to be horned, and hairy; but I have seen its eyes, and they were yellow, like a flame.'

As he said these words Master Grimston went in haste to the door, and pulled it open as though to breathe the air. The others followed him and went out; but Master Grimston drew the priest aside, and said like a man in a mortal fear, 'Look you, Father, all this is true—the thing is a devil—and why it abides with us I know not; but I cannot live so; and unless it be cast out it will slay me—but if money be of avail, I have it in abundance.' 'Nay,' said Father Thomas, 'let there be no talk of money— perchance if I can aid you, you may give of your gratitude to God.' 'Ay, ay,' said the old man hurriedly, 'that was what I meant—there is money in abundance for God, if He will but set me free.'

So they walked very sadly together through the street. There were few folk about; the men and the children were all abroad—a woman or two came to the house doors, and wondered a little to see them pass so solemnly, as though they followed a body to the grave.

Master Grimston's house was the largest in the place. It had a walled garden before it, with a strong door set in the wall. The house stood back from the road, a dark front of brick with gables; behind it the garden sloped nearly to the sands, with wooden barns and warehouses. Master Grimston unlocked the door, and then it seemed that his terrors came over him, for he would have the priest enter first. Father Thomas, with a certain apprehension of which he was ashamed, walked quickly in, and looked about him. The herbage of the garden had mostly died down in the winter, and a tangle of sodden stalks lay over the beds. A flagged path edged with box led up to the house, which seemed to stare at them out of its dark windows with a sort of steady gaze. Master Grimston fastened the door behind them, and they went all together, keeping close one to another, up to the house, the door of which opened upon a big parlour or kitchen, sparely furnished, but very clean and comfortable. Some vessels of metal glittered on a rack. There were chairs, ranged round the open fireplace. There was no sound except that the wind buffeted in the chimney. It looked a quiet and homely place, and Father Thomas grew ashamed of his fears. 'Now,' said he in his firm voice, 'though I am your guest here, I will appoint what shall be done. We will sit here together, and talk as cheerfully as we may, till we have dined. Then, if nothing appears to us,'—and he crossed himself—'I will go round the house, into every room, and see if we can track the thing to its lair: then I will abide with you till evensong; and then I will soon return, and lie here to-night. Even if the thing be wary, and dares not to meet the power of the Church in the day-time, perhaps it will venture out at night; and I will even try a fall with it. So come, good people, and be comforted.'

So they sate together; and Father Thomas talked of many things, and told some old legends of saints; and they dined, though without much cheer; and still nothing appeared. Then, after dinner, Father Thomas would view the house. So he took his book up, and they went from room to room. On the ground floor there were several chambers not used, which they entered in turn, but saw nothing; on the upper floor was a large room where Master Grimston and his wife slept; and a further room for Henry, and a guest-chamber in which the priest was to sleep if need was; and a room where a servant-maid slept. And now the day began to darken and to turn to evening, and Father Thomas felt a shadow grow in his mind. There came into his head a verse of Scripture about a spirit which found a house 'empty, swept and garnished,' and called his fellows to enter in.

At the end of the passage was a locked door; and Father Thomas said: 'This is the last room—let us enter.' 'Nay, there is no need to do that,'

said Master Grimston in a kind of haste; 'it leads nowhither—it is but a
room of stores.' 'It were a pity to leave it unvisited,' said the Father—
and as he said the word, there came a kind of stirring from within. 'A rat,
doubtless,' said the Father, striving with a sudden sense of fear; but the
pale faces round him told another tale. 'Come, Master Grimston, let us
be done with this,' said Father Thomas decisively; 'the hour of vespers
draws nigh.' So Master Grimston slowly drew out a key and unlocked
the door, and Father Thomas marched in. It was a simple place enough.
There were shelves on which various household matters lay, boxes and
jars, with twine and cordage. On the ground stood chests. There were
some clothes hanging on pegs, and in a corner was a heap of garments,
piled up. On one of the chests stood a box of rough deal, and from the
corner of it dripped water, which lay in a little pool on the floor. Master
Grimston went hurriedly to the box and pushed it further to the wall. As
he did so, a kind of sound came from Henry's lips. Father Thomas
turned and looked at him; he stood pale and strengthless, his eyes fixed
on the corner—at the same moment something dark and shapeless
seemed to slip past the group, and there came to the nostrils of Father
Thomas a strange sharp smell, as of the sea, only that there was a taint
within it, like the smell of corruption.

They all turned and looked at Father Thomas together, as though
seeking a comfort from his presence. He, hardly knowing what he did,
and in the grasp of a terrible fear, fumbled with his book; and opening
it, read the first words that his eye fell upon, which was the place where
the Blessed Lord, beset with enemies, said that if He did but pray to His
Father, He should send Him forthwith legions of angels to encompass
Him. And the verse seemed to the priest so like a message sent instantly
from heaven that he was not a little comforted.

But the thing, whatever the reason was, appeared to them no more at
that time. Yet the thought of it lay very heavy on Father Thomas's heart.
In truth he had not in the bottom of his mind believed that he would see
it, but had trusted in his honest life and his sacred calling to protect him.
He could hardly speak for some minutes—moreover the horror of the
thing was very great—and seeing him so grave, their terrors were
increased, though there was a kind of miserable joy in their minds that
some one, and he a man of high repute, should suffer with them.

Then Father Thomas, after a pause—they were now in the parlour—
said, speaking very slowly, that they were in a sore affliction of Satan,
and that they must withstand him with a good courage—'and look you,'
he added, turning with a great sternness to the three, 'if there be any
mortal sin upon your hearts, see that you confess it and be shriven

speedily—for while such a thing lies upon the heart, so long hath Satan power to hurt—otherwise have no fear at all.'

Then Father Thomas slipped out to the garden, and hearing the bell pulled for vespers, he went to the church, and the three would go with him, because they would not be left alone. So they went together; by this time the street was fuller, and the servant-maid had told tales, so that there was much talk in the place about what was going forward. None spoke with them as they went, but at every corner you might see one check another in talk, and a silence fall upon a group, so that they knew that their terrors were on every tongue. There was but a handful of worshippers in the church, which was dark, save for the light on Father Thomas's book. He read the holy service swiftly and courageously, but his face was very pale and grave in the light of the candle. When the vespers were over, and he had put off his robe, he said that he would go back to his house, and gather what he needed for the night, and that they should wait for him at the churchyard gate. So he strode off to his vicarage. But as he shut to the door, he saw a dark figure come running up the garden; he waited with a fear in his mind, but in a moment he saw that it was Henry, who came up breathless, and said that he must speak with the Father alone. Father Thomas knew that somewhat dark was to be told him. So he led Henry into the parlour and seated himself, and said, 'Now, my son, speak boldly.' So there was an instant's silence, and Henry slipped on to his knees.

Then in a moment Henry with a sob began to tell his tale. He said that on the day of the wreck his father had roused him very early in the dawn, and had told him to put on his clothes and come silently, for he thought there was a wreck ashore. His father carried a spade in his hand, he knew not then why. They went down to the tide, which was moving out very fast, and left but an inch or two of water on the sands. There was but a little light, but, when they had walked a little, they saw the black hull of a ship before them, on the edge of the deeper water, the waves driving over it; and then all at once they came upon the body of a man lying on his face on the sand. There was no sign of life in him, but he clasped a bag in his hand that was heavy, and the pocket of his coat was full to bulging; and there lay, moreover, some glittering things about him that seemed to be coins. They lifted the body up, and his father stripped the coat off from the man, and then bade Henry dig a hole in the sand, which he presently did, though the sand and water oozed fast into it. Then his father, who had been stooping down, gathering somewhat up from the sand, raised the body up, and laid it in the hole, and bade Henry cover it with the sand. And so he did till it was nearly hidden. Then came a horrible thing; the sand in the hole began to move and stir, and presently a hand was put out with clutching fingers; and Henry had dropped the spade, and said, 'There is life in him,' but his father seized the spade, and shovelled the sand into the hole with a kind of silent fury, and trampled it over and smoothed it down—and then he gathered up the coat and the bag, and handed Henry the spade. By this time the town was astir, and they saw, very faintly, a man run along the shore eastward; so, making a long circuit to the west, they returned; his father had put the spade away and taken the coat upstairs; and then he went out with Henry, and told all he could find that there was a wreck ashore.

The priest heard the story with a fierce shame and anger, and turning to Henry he said, 'But why did you not resist your father, and save the poor sailor?' 'I dared not,' said Henry shuddering, 'though I would have done so if I could; but my father has a power over me, and I am used to obey him.' Then said the priest, 'This is a dark matter. But you have told the story bravely, and now will I shrive you, my son.' So he gave him shrift. Then he said to Henry, 'And have you seen aught that would connect the beast that visits you with this thing?' 'Ay, that I have,' said Henry, 'for I watched it with my father skip and leap in the water over the place where the man lies buried.' Then the priest said, 'Your father must tell me the tale too, and he must make submission to the law.' 'He will not,' said Henry. 'Then will I compel him,' said the priest. 'Not out of my mouth,' said Henry, 'or he will slay me too.' And then the priest said that he was in a strait place, for he could not use the words of confession of one man to convict another of his sin. So he gathered his things in haste, and walked back to the church; but Henry went another way, saying 'I made excuse to come away, and said I went elsewhere; but I fear my father much—he sees very deep; and I would not have him suspect me of having made confession.'

Then the Father met the other two at the church gate; and they went down to the house in silence, the Father pondering heavily; and at the door Henry joined them, and it seemed to the Father that old Master Grimston regarded him not. So they entered the house in silence, and ate in silence, listening earnestly for any sound. And the Father looked oft on Master Grimston, who ate and drank and said nothing, never raising his eyes. But once the Father saw him laugh secretly to himself, so that the blood came cold in the Father's veins, and he could hardly contain himself from accusing him. Then the Father had them to prayers, and prayed earnestly against the evil, and that they should open their hearts to God, if He would show them why this misery came upon them.

Then they went to bed; and Henry asked that he might lie in the priest's room, which he willingly granted. And so the house was dark, and they made as though they would sleep; but the Father could not sleep, and he heard Henry weeping silently to himself like a little child.

But at last the Father slept—how long he knew not—and suddenly brake out of his sleep with a horror of darkness all about him, and knew that there was some evil thing abroad. So he looked upon the room. He heard Henry mutter heavily in his sleep as though there was a dark terror upon him; and then, in the light of the dying embers, the Father saw a thing rise upon the hearth, as though it had slept there, and woke to stretch itself. And then in the half-light it seemed softly to gambol and play; but whereas when an innocent beast does this in the simple joy of its heart, and seems a fond and pretty sight, the Father thought he had never seen so ugly a sight as the beast gambolling all by itself, as if it could not contain its own dreadful joy; it looked viler and more wicked every moment; then, too, there spread in the room the sharp scent of the sea, with the foul smell underneath it, that gave the Father a deadly sickness; he tried to pray, but no words would come, and he felt indeed that the evil was too strong for him. Presently the beast desisted from its play, and looking wickedly about it, came near to the Father's bed, and seemed to put up its hairy forelegs upon it; he could see its narrow and obscene eyes, which burned with a dull yellow light, and were fixed upon him. And now the Father thought that his end was near, for he could stir neither hand nor foot, and the sweat rained down his brow; but he made a mighty effort, and in a voice which shocked himself, so dry and husky and withal of so loud and screaming a tone it was, he said three holy words. The beast gave a great quiver of rage, but it dropped down on the floor, and in a moment was gone. Then Henry woke, and raising himself on his arm, said somewhat; but there broke out in the house a great outcry and the stamping of feet, which seemed very fearful in the silence of the night. The priest leapt out of his bed all dizzy, and made a light, and ran to the door, and went out, crying whatever words came to his head. The door of Master Grimston's room was open, and a strange and strangling sound came forth; the Father made his way in, and found Master Grimston lying upon the floor, his wife bending over him; he lay still, breathing pitifully, and every now and then a shudder ran through him. In the room there seemed a strange and shadowy tumult going forward; but the Father saw that no time could be lost, and kneeling down beside Master Grimston, he prayed with all his might.

Presently Master Grimston ceased to struggle and lay still, like a man who had come out of a sore conflict. Then he opened his eyes, and the Father stopped his prayers, and looking very hard at him he said, 'My son, the time is very short—give God the glory.' Then Master Grimston, rolling his haggard eyes upon the group, twice strove to speak and could not; but the third time the Father, bending down his head, heard him say in a thin voice, that seemed to float from a long way off, 'I slew him . . . my sin.' Then the Father swiftly gave him shrift, and as he said the last word, Master Grimston's head fell over on the side, and the Father said, 'He is gone.' And Bridget broke out into a terrible cry, and fell upon Henry's neck, who had entered unseen.

Then the Father bade him lead her away, and put the poor body on the bed; as he did so he noticed that the face of the dead man was strangely bruised and battered, as though it had been stamped upon by the hoofs of some beast. Then Father Thomas knelt, and prayed until the light came filtering in through the shutters; and the cocks crowed in the village, and presently it was day. But that night the Father learnt strange secrets, and something of the dark purposes of God was revealed to him.

In the morning there came one to find the priest, and told him that another body had been thrown up on the shore, which was strangely smeared with sand, as though it had been rolled over and over in it; and the Father took order for its burial.

Then the priest had long talk with Bridget and Henry. He found them sitting together, and she held her son's hand and smoothed his hair, as though he had been a little child; and Henry sobbed and wept, but Bridget was very calm. 'He hath told me all,' she said, 'and we have decided that he shall do whatever you bid him; must he be given to justice?' and she looked at the priest very pitifully. 'Nay, nay,' said the priest. 'I hold not Henry to account for the death of the man; it was his father's sin, who hath made heavy atonement—the secret shall be buried in our hearts.'

Then Bridget told him how she had waked suddenly out of her sleep, and heard her husband cry out; and that then followed a dreadful kind of struggling, with the scent of the sea over all; and then he had all at once fallen to the ground and she had gone to him—and that then the priest had come.

Then Father Thomas said with tears that God had shown them deep things and visited them very strangely; and they would henceforth live humbly in His sight, showing mercy.

Then lastly he went with Henry to the store-room; and there, in the box that had dripped with water, lay the coat of the dead man, full of money, and the bag of money too; and Henry would have cast it back into the sea, but the priest said that this might not be, but that it should be bestowed plentifully upon shipwrecked mariners unless the heirs should be found. But the ship appeared to be a foreign ship, and no search ever revealed whence the money had come, save that it seemed to have been violently come by.

Master Grimston was found to have left much wealth. But Bridget would sell the house and the land, and it mostly went to rebuild the church to God's glory. Then Bridget and Henry removed to the vicarage and served Father Thomas faithfully, and they guarded their secret. And beside the nave is a little high turret built, where burns a lamp in a lantern at the top, to give light to those at sea.

Now the beast troubled those of whom I write no more; but it is easier to raise up evil than to lay it; and there are those that say that to this day a man or a woman with an evil thought in their hearts may see on a certain evening in November, at the ebb of the tide, a goatlike thing wade in the water, snuffing at the sand, as though it sought but found not. But of this I know nothing.

H. F. W. Tatham

Manfred's Three Wishes

MANFRED gnawed his fingers with rage and jealousy, and thought bitterly of schemes of vengeance; but none seemed safe to him, as he turned them over in his heart. His enemy was rich and popular, and even if he succeeded in bringing about his death, he could not see how he could himself escape detection and punishment. Even if he did escape, he would perhaps have to face exile and poverty; while there was the third chance, too terrible almost to think of, of failing in his attempt and meeting with punishment himself, a laughing-stock to his enemies.

So he sat and gnawed his fingers, and no light came to him—at least, for a while. Then suddenly he started up, and, flinging back the hair from his forehead with a characteristic gesture, 'I will do it,' he said.

Some hours had passed, and the shades of evening were beginning to fall, when, wrapped in a long hooded cloak, Manfred set forth from the city towards the great dark wood which fringed the slope of the neighbouring hills. He walked swiftly, like one bent on some errand of importance, that required haste; and such indeed his errand was, for he was on his way to consult the great wizard of the forest, of whom men spoke with awe and bated breath, as of the Evil One himself. The wizard dwelt in a dark and lonely house in the thickest part of the wood, and few dared to pass near it even in the daytime. As Manfred made his way along the forest path, a hundred sounds and sights of ill-omen encountered him and seemed to forbid his passage. Now the hoot of an owl, now the howl of a wolf, awoke the melancholy echoes of the wood; at another time the branches of the trees, rubbed together by the night wind, sent forth a dreary wailing sound, like the crying of a lost spirit; or some creature of the night, wild-cat, or stoat, or serpent, slipped across the path in front, and vanished rustling amid the bushes that fenced it in on either side. But Manfred pressed on, and in the heat of his desire for vengeance felt in his heart no chill of premonitory fear.

By and by he came to a clearing in the heart of the wood, and saw the dark bulk of the wizard's house rise before him. As he approached, a light suddenly shone out in an upper room, and the great door of the house swung open of its own accord, showing a dark entry beyond, presently illumined by a lamp held at the head of the stairs by some one scarcely seen, who, addressing him by name, bade him enter. Manfred started at finding himself thus known, but obeyed the command and passed into the house and up the stairs, and thence into the room which the figure with the lamp had already entered.

Manfred had anticipated the ordinary terrors associated with a necromancer's abode, the skulls and bones, the familiar in shape of cat or toad, the crocodile hung from the roof; but there were none of these here. The room was circular, and perfectly black, both walls and floor and ceiling; the lamp dimly illumined it, and showed that besides two chairs it contained but one object—a brazier in which coals burned redly.

The magician crouched behind the brazier, and regarded Manfred with open, unwinking eyes. His face was smooth and yellow, like parchment, and even his lips appeared of the same colour. There was no hair on his face or on any part of his head.

Manfred looked at him, and for the first time fear came into his heart. But he mastered it by an effort, and was about to speak when the wizard anticipated him. 'I know your will,' he said; and his voice seemed to come from very far away. Manfred bowed his head, and the wizard went on. 'You seek vengeance, wealth, and power,' he said; 'and these you shall have; shall he not?' he continued, suddenly inclining his head to the right, as if listening; and Manfred thought he heard a voice whisper, 'He shall have these,' and a low crooning laugh followed.

The wizard rose to his feet, and drew from his breast three packets. 'This is for vengeance,' he said, and he cast from the first a red powder on the coals in the brazier. A crimson flame burst forth, and rose high in the air, licking the ceiling of the room. 'Your vengeance shall be complete,' said the wizard; and with that the flame died down again and only the coals glowed as before.

A second time the wizard drew a packet from his breast. This time the powder was yellow, and when he cast it on the red coals a flame of a deep golden hue started up from them. As before, it licked the ceiling of the chamber, and then sank again, as the wizard said, 'You will attain your desire, and become rich.'

The third packet that was drawn forth contained powder of a purple hue. It was flung into the brazier, and a flame of rich royal purple started up from the coals. But at that moment a wind swept through the room, and the flame, instead of rising to the roof, was whirled downwards and sideways, and presently died out. And the wizard sat silent.

Manfred stared at the glowing coals and the yellow face. But he dared ask no more, and presently, passing down the stairs and out of the house, went forth again into the darkness of the wood. As he crossed the threshold he fancied he heard the wizard—or was it some one else?— laugh in the room above. But he flung back his hair from his forehead and passed out.

Down through the wood he went, and over the open plain that lay between it and the town. When he was about half-way across this, he caught a glimpse of a man on his left walking slowly in the same direction. Something seemed familiar in the man's gait and figure, though the light was dim, and Manfred, slipping behind a great stone, gazed eagerly at him. At that moment the moon shone through a cloud, and Manfred recognised the features of his enemy. The chance of vengeance had come, and that soon.

Coming forth from behind the stone, Manfred, with his drawn knife in his hand, swiftly and silently crept after the man. In a few seconds he was close behind him, and raising the knife, stabbed him with all his force between the shoulders.

The hot blood spirted out over his hand, and the man, with a horrid gurgling groan, sank to the ground and lay on his face, clutching at the earth with his finger-nails. Manfred stood and watched him. Presently he lay still, and Manfred, turning him over, saw that he was dead.

It was plainly needful at once to conceal the body. In all that flat plain there was no stream or chasm or bush into which it could be cast. But Manfred, looking round, saw that some one had been digging close by and had left his spade behind. Recognising this as part of the luck promised him by the wizard, he hastily dragged the body behind the great stone, and digging a deep grave, flung it in and piled the earth over it. Then, turning his back on the city, he hurried towards the frontier, safe for a while from all detection or pursuit, and trusting in his lucky star to win riches in another land.

Years passed by. Manfred, under another name, had prospered and grown wealthy, and now, led by instinct, he was returning to his native land. He had crossed the frontier in the early morning, and had reached a low hill from which the flat plain that he remembered so well stretched right up to the city walls. But when he looked out from the hill-top he hardly recognised the place. A great suburb of the city extended over the plain to within a mile or two of where he stood, so that even the wizard's wood was now quite close to the outermost houses. This suburb was well built, with stately houses and temples, and large open spaces, green with grass and trees. But Manfred did not gaze long. He quickly started to ride down the hill. Half-way down it his horse started and shied violently at some movement in the bushes that bordered the road. Manfred tried to steady it, but the animal plunged in uncontrollable terror, and finally slipped and fell heavily, throwing its rider to the ground. Manfred started up at once and, finding himself uninjured, seized his horse's bridle, and pulled it to its feet; but when erect it stood shaking all over, and Manfred soon noticed that it had lamed itself, since it could only put the tip of the hoof of one of its forelegs to the ground. It was plainly impossible to ride it any farther.

Manfred stood doubting how he should proceed. At that moment something came out of the bushes at the side of the road—clearly the animal that had made the rustling noise that frightened Manfred's horse. Manfred soon saw that it was another horse; but he was startled at the strangeness of its appearance. Its colour was piebald, and it had but one eye; and its gaunt body and long neck and ill-shaped head gave it an uncanny look. But it was plainly in sound condition, and it came and stood quietly beside Manfred, as if expecting him to mount it. The man did not hesitate. To transfer the saddle and bridle from his own horse to the other was the work of a moment, and he was soon again upon his way. It was not long before he came to the gate of the town. He had met one or two people before he reached it, and they had surprised him by either gazing at him in astonishment or running away at full speed so as to reach the gate before him. He put this down to the strange appearance of his horse; but this could not account for the fact that when the gate was flung open and he rode in, the doorkeeper bowed low before him with an air of deep reverence, and the streets were rapidly filling with a crowd that lined them on both sides, and soon broke into loud cheering as Manfred passed between their ranks. Utterly at a loss what to make of these proceedings, he rode on by a street that led him to a large open space in the new suburb. In the middle of this space stood a great altar, hewn out of a single stone—a stone that Manfred had seen before, though he did not recognise it now. The great space was filling with people, and a group came forward to meet Manfred, headed by an old man—plainly a priest—dressed in a long white robe and crowned with a wreath of leaves. When he came close to Manfred he kneeled on one knee, as did those who accompanied him, and hailed him as Lord and King.

Manfred reined up his horse and sat thunder-struck. Vengeance and wealth were his; now power had come suddenly. But he thought there must be some error, and he spoke roughly. 'I am no king,' he said. But the priest bowed lower still. 'You are our king,' he said, 'named so by the oracle.' And he went on to explain that their king had died suddenly a few days before, leaving no heir, and that the oracle had said a new king would come to them from the east, a stranger riding on a one-eyed piebald horse, and that this was why they hailed him as Lord and King.

Manfred sat for a while; then, dismounting, he advanced towards the great altar, and laying his hand upon it, faced the assembled people. The sun shone full upon him for a moment, as he flung back his hair from his forehead with a gesture characteristic but long forgotten. And at that a woman's voice was raised shrilly somewhere in the crowd.

The people looked round in surprise, as an old woman pushed her way to the front, and, raising her hand, cried out, 'That is no stranger, and shall be no king; it is Manfred the murderer.' And a cloud crept over the sun and a low rolling of thunder filled the air, and some thought the earth trembled under their feet.

Manfred faced the woman. Indignant cries began to rise around her, and some sought to pull her back. But Manfred bade them let her go. 'Woman,' he said, 'I know not of what you speak; I am not Manfred, nor a murderer.' Once more the thunder rolled, and the woman, nothing daunted, looked Manfred in the face. Her grey hair fell loose upon her shoulders, and her eyes shone wildly as she made answer, 'You are Manfred, who slew my son twenty years ago this day, and hid his body and fled. Will you lay your hand on the altar and swear that you are not he?'

Manfred was very pale, but his voice was firm as he answered, 'I will swear,' and he laid his hand upon the altar. 'I swear that I am not Manfred,' said he, 'and am innocent of the blood of this man.' There came a flash of blinding light, against which Manfred and the great altar-stone stood out as black as night; and with the light the thunder crashed overhead. A cry of alarm rose from the throng; and then the earth heaved, and the great altar reeled, and those who stood near saw an arm thrust forth from the ground close to where Manfred stood. The arm was that of a skeleton—knotted, and black, and crusted with mould; and when Manfred saw it he fell upon the ground with a dreadful cry, and the open hand came down upon his throat. When they raised him up he was dead, and his face was black and his eyes stood out like those of a strangled man.

WILLIAM J. WINTLE

The Light in the Dormitory

THE Abbey of St Placidus stood in a valley between the mountains, and was hidden from the few travellers who passed through that lonely region by a thick belt of trees. It was several miles from the nearest town; and the road through the valley led to no place of any importance. It was therefore rarely used except by the dependents of the Abbey and a few other peasants.

Thus disturbance from the outside world was quite unknown; and the peace of the community was rarely broken by any disquiet from within. The monks spent their days in the silence of prayer and recollection; and the daily round of Offices in the Church and work about the house, gardens and farm, fully occupied their time and thoughts.

Speaking generally, the monks ran elderly. Most of them were well over forty—a few were over eighty—and the Abbot was nearer sixty than fifty. He very properly maintained that no man had cut his wisdom teeth till he had passed fifty. But at the same time the community felt the need of some younger members. The old ones could not expect to live for ever in this world; there was plenty of work that called for strong, young hands; and the noviciate cried aloud for occupants.

So the Abbot took counsel with his brethren, and they agreed with him that something must be done to meet the situation. And the only thing that seemed at all possible was to try the experiment of an alumnate or school for boys who seemed likely to develop a vocation for community life later on. And that is how it came about that the old dormitory over the west cloister was now occupied by a dozen youths of rather lively disposition.

It was a decided change for the old dormitory, for it had been disused for twenty years past. No one appeared to quite know why; but there seemed to be a combination of reasons. For one thing, it was the part of the house farthest removed from the rest of the rooms, and so was a trifle inconvenient for those who lived in it. Then the stairs leading up to it were narrow and steep, and so were trying to elderly legs; the dormitory itself was cold in winter, and so did not agree with people subject to asthma and bronchitis; and the place was said to be bad to sleep in.

What this last objection meant was not very clear; but those who were old enough to have slept there when it was last used said that it was noisy. This was odd in a place where silence reigned both in the house and outside it; but the suggestion was that the wind somehow caught that part of the buildings and howled through chimneys and chinks. Queer noises were heard, which were put down to birds under the eaves or rats under the floor—anyway the place was noisy and unsuitable for light sleepers.

It was known as the old dormitory because it—with the west cloister beneath it—formed the sole surviving part of the ancient monastery which was pulled down when the present Abbey was built. It dated from the beginning of the thirteenth century, but had been considerably altered inside. Originally it had been one long, open dormitory, in which some twenty beds could have been arranged along the walls; but it was now divided into what were called cells, though they were merely cubicles open to the gangways down the centre.

Thus, while the occupants of the cubicles had a certain amount of privacy, they could see anyone who passed down the dormitory; and as the partitions between the cubicles were only some eight feet high, a good portion of the old oak roof was visible from all of them.

The boys were a very varied set, who got on well together as a rule; but we are only now concerned with one of them. This was Brother Bernard, who on account of being the eldest and steadiest had been made prefect of the alumnate. This meant that he had general charge of the others, under the monk who was their immediate superior, and was held responsible for their good behaviour. He was a youth of seventeen; and he had his hands full!

His cubicle was that next to the stairs, and was so arranged that it commanded a rather larger view of the dormitory than the others. It was his duty to see that everyone was in his cell immediately after Compline, and that all lights were out half an hour later. There was no gas or electric light in this ancient building: the dormitory was rather ineffectually lighted by some hanging oil lamps.

It was Brother Bernard's business to put these out, and to see that everybody was in bed by that time. Then he returned to his cubicle; and it was usually about a quarter of a minute later when steady breathing told the shadows that he was fast asleep. And the steady breathing did not as a rule cease until the bell rang to wake the community in the morning.

But one night he woke up with a start, and was just in time to hear the Abbey clock strike midnight. He turned over and tried to go to sleep again, but without result. He had that queer feeling that somebody was about. But all was perfectly still and silent.

Then for the first time he noticed the light in the dormitory which was destined to have such a strange sequel. He was looking drowsily at nothing—for there was nothing to look at—when he saw it. It was just a patch of light shining on the roof about half-way down the room.

He at once thought that one of the alumni had got a bit of candle from the sacristy, and was enjoying a surreptitious spell of reading. This was forbidden; and it was his business to stop it. So he slipped out of bed, and went quietly down the passage between the cubicles. But everybody seemed to be fast asleep; there was no light in any of the cubicles; and there was no odour of a blown-out candle. When he looked up at the roof again, the light was gone.

This was distinctly curious; but Brother Bernard was too young to trouble his head about such a trifle. It was not until the thing happened again about a week later that he began to think it over. Much reading of detective stories, written by people who have never been detectives nor talked with detectives, had given that youth the idea that he was a born investigator; and he set to work with a relish to find out the mystery of the light in the dormitory.

Could it come from any of the cubicles? To this question he was able to give a pretty decided negative. He knew that nobody had a dark lantern or anything of that sort; and on both occasions he had made sure that no bit of candle was being burnt. Besides, when he came to think of it, the patch of light was too small and too sharply defined to be caused in that way. A candle would have lit up a considerable part of the roof and not a small patch of it.

Could the light have come from outside? Again he was obliged to answer 'No'. The old dormitory was lighted in the day by some narrow lancet windows. Had the light shone through one of these, it would have been a long strip of light and not a small patch. Besides, the windows overlooked the cloister garth, into which no one could enter at night; so that the notion of a strong bull's-eye lantern operated from the garth was quite out of the question.

But soon the mysterious light became still more mysterious. The next time that Brother Bernard woke up in the night and saw it there was a change. Before, it was a vague patch; but now it was more distinct and was in the shape of a cross. He rubbed his eyes and wondered if he was dreaming. Then he looked again, and it was clearly a cross. A moment later it disappeared. But it disappeared in a rather unusual way. It did not vanish either suddenly or gradually; but it went out from one side. First one arm of the cross vanished, then the upright, and then the other arm. Imagine that the cross had been pushed sideways behind a dark screen, and you will have a fair idea of what happened.

It must have been just about the same time, if not on the same night, that one of the monks had a queer dream which he related next day at recreation. Of course Brother Bernard knew nothing about this and only heard of it by chance some time later. The monk in question, who was a very level-headed man, had his cell overlooking the cloister garth, but on the side opposite to the old dormitory. He had heard nothing about the strange light that had been seen.

He dreamt that he was standing in the cloister when he saw a monk in front of him whom he failed to recognise by the back view. The monk was walking slowly away from him. It was apparently not one of the community; and he knew that no visitor had arrived. So he hastened to pass him, that he might see who it was. But the other also hastened, and turned the corner; where he seemed to vanish, for he was not to be seen a moment later.

The monk in his dream then thought that he turned back, and again saw the stranger before him. This time he stood still to watch, and saw him take some object out of the folds of his habit. Whatever this object may have been, it seemed to give out a faint light which shone on the roof of the cloister. Then the stranger walked to a certain spot in the old west cloister and appeared to step into the wall and vanish! At this point the monk woke up, and at that moment the Abbey clock struck midnight.

Brother Bernard continued to have disturbed nights, waking up without any apparent cause, but saw nothing more for two or three weeks. Then a night came when he was aroused at about twelve o'clock, and again saw the light on the roof. This time it was brighter than before— so much so that it drew him out of bed in spite of previous failures to discover the cause. He stepped out into the central passage, and there before him he saw what he took to be one of the monks.

This greatly puzzled him, for no one had any business there at night, except the infirmarian in case of sickness. But there was no one unwell in the alumnate over night; and, if anyone had been taken ill, the prefect must first have been called to fetch the infirmarian. It was very strange. It might possibly be the Abbot or Prior who had taken it into his head to go round and see that all was right. In any case, it was Brother Bernard's duty to ascertain who it was; so he stood and watched the figure, expecting that when it turned back he would see. But the mysterious monk did not turn back. He walked to the farther end of the dormitory, which ended in a blank wall without a door.

But as he walked, Brother Bernard noticed that the light on the roof went with him. It was just as if he was carrying a lamp turned upwards, except that the patch of light was as before in the shape of a cross. Yes; without a doubt the light was moving along. It continued to move until it came to the wall, and then it disappeared in the same curious way as before, just as if it had been pushed sideways behind a screen. Or it might be said to have vanished sideways into the end wall.

Brother Bernard was watching the light, and so he did not see what became of the monk. But when the light vanished, he looked for him— and saw nothing! In fact it was too dark to see anything. There was no moon; and the dormitory was in total darkness. Then it struck him as very strange that he should have been able to see the monk at all in the dark. He could only suppose that the light on the roof enabled him to see.

Up till now, he had said nothing to anyone about the light in the dormitory, as he had no special wish to be laughed at for foolish fancies. But now he thought it right to mention the matter to the Prior. To his surprise, he was taken at once to the Abbot, and was asked to repeat the story in full detail. A good many questions were asked; and he was told not to say anything to the other alumni but to report any further happenings at once.

He was considerably astonished to find his story taken so seriously; and he would have been still more surprised if he had learnt the reason. Things had been happening at the Abbey. In the first place, an old manuscript had been found among the documents stored in the library, which seemed to be part of a diary kept by one of the monks over a century ago. Amongst other things of interest, it contained an account of some curious happenings in the Abbey at that time. Several of the community had seen what they supposed to be a spectre monk, walking in the cloister at night. On several occasions he had been seen to vanish into the wall of the west cloister; and he seemed to carry something in the folds of his habit that gave out a faint light.

Another, and still older, document had come to light in the same place. This was very difficult to read, and seemed to have been purposely written in such style as to conceal some secret from any casual reader. But, so far as could be made out, it was intended to record the hiding of something of value on the Abbey premises, and to give a clue to the hiding place. The clue was apparently lost now, for the manuscript was torn badly and the latter part could not be read.

But something else had happened besides the finding of these two papers. Curious rustling sounds had been heard late at night in the old west cloister by a monk who had been sitting up late to finish some important work; and on going to see what it was he had caught a glimpse of what seemed to be a figure in black that melted into the wall.

He went to the spot where the figure had disappeared; and he thought that a faint patch of light shone on the roof just overhead; but it was very faint, and had gone before he could be quite certain that it was there.

The next time that Brother Bernard woke up in the night, he saw the dark figure more distinctly, and he also saw plainly that it was carrying something partly concealed in the folds of its habit. The light appeared to come from this. He plucked up his courage and ran lightly and silently down the central passage to the intruder. But, quick as he was, the visitor was quicker still and had vanished before he overtook him. But Brother Bernard was in time to detect a curious perfume that seemed to linger on the air for a moment. It was like the pleasant scent that comes from an old chest in which spices and perfumes have been stored long ago.

Now we have said that the youth had detective ideas; and he decided to lay a trap for the visitor. The next night, when all were in bed and he went round to put out the lamps, he fastened a piece of black cotton across the passage about a foot from the floor, in such fashion that anyone passing that way would inevitably break it.

Nothing happened that night nor the next; but on the third he again woke up and saw the mysterious monk standing half-way down the passage. This time he was turned partly towards Brother Bernard, who could now see that he was holding what appeared to be a golden cross which gave out a pale light that seemed to be reflected on the open roof of the dormitory. He seemed to hesitate for a few moments, then walked slowly down the passage way, appeared to push the cross into the wall and then to melt away. The figure walked right past the place where the black cotton was fixed; but, when Brother Bernard went to examine it, he found that it had not been broken. It was pretty clear from this that the intruder was not of solid flesh and blood. What then could he be made of?

When the Abbot heard this story, he decided that a watch should be kept by two seniors; and for over a week these two monks—much to their disgust—sat up in the old dormitory till after midnight. But nothing at all happened, and they said a good many things about the folly of paying attention to idle tales. But it was a little odd that both of these monks dreamed the next night that a monk stood by their beds and said something about a hiding place. But in the morning neither of them could remember what it was the visitor had said.

The suggestion was now made by somebody that the whole affair was a delusion of the evil one; and Brother Bernard was told to try to sprinkle the apparition with holy water the next time it was seen. So he provided himself with a sprinkler and waited for an opportunity.

It came about a week later, and the result was not at all what he expected. The mysterious visitor was standing opposite his cubicle when he woke up with a start. As soon as he saw this, he slipped out of bed and took up the sprinkler. But something caught him by the wrist and held his hand back. Meanwhile the apparition was moving slowly down the central passage. Three times Brother Bernard tried to use the sprinkler, but each time the same thing happened. The last time, his wrist was held so tightly and jerked back so sharply as to cause actual pain. But who did it? Certainly not the apparition; for that was going down the dormitory at the time.

So the experiment was tried again in a different way. A small stoup of holy water was hung on the end wall at the exact spot where the monk had so many times been seen to disappear. The result was curious, according to Brother Bernard's account the next morning. He woke up as usual and saw the monk going down the dormitory. When he came to the usual spot he did not vanish but stood still as if hesitating what to do. The watcher saw his chance and ran towards him. But again he was disappointed, for something caught him by the heel and he fell with a crash. When he scrambled to his feet, the apparition was gone.

This was distinctly vexing, for he could not tell how the mysterious monk got over the difficulty of having to pass through a stoup of holy water. But a few nights later he found out, for he saw him again. This time he did not attempt to interfere but simply watched. When the monk reached the end of the dormitory, he seemed to hesitate for a moment; then he appeared to push the cross he was carrying into the wall a little below the holy water stoup; after which he simply vanished. How he went, the watcher could not describe: he just was not there, and that was all that could be said.

Things now took a rather unpleasant turn for Brother Bernard. The whole story rested on his word; and every attempt to test the truth of it had failed. Several of the monks who had heard the history began to suggest that the whole business was imagination at first and romancing later. He was cross-questioned pretty sharply by the Prior more than once; and the Abbot took occasion to say a few words on the sin of lying.

So it was very fortunate for him that one or two small incidents happened at this time to confirm his story.

One of the boys was a little unwell, and the local doctor came to see
him. He was accompanied by a little terrier which came up to the
dormitory with him. Needless to say, the doctor was not in the habit of
taking a dog with him to see his patients; but in this case he had called
in the course of a country walk and had asked permission to bring the
dog in, as he did not want it to go chasing rabbits in his absence.

While the doctor was examining his patient, the terrier ran about the
dormitory. Presently it went to the wall at the end. It stopped suddenly,
hesitated for a moment, and then went slowly and suspiciously to the
very spot where the nocturnal visitor was in the habit of disappearing. It
went to sniff at the wall; darted suddenly back as if it had touched
something very hot; and then dashed howling out of the place.

The other incident was the merest trifle in itself, but was significant in
view of what had happened. A new boy joined the alumnate. He had
heard nothing about anything occurring in the dormitory; and it
chanced that he was placed in the bed nearest to the end wall. But in the
morning he asked to be moved, and could give no better reason than
that he felt afraid and that he thought he heard whisperings in the wall.
He was told not to be silly: but he was moved all the same.

And now things developed rapidly. Brother Bernard woke up a few
nights later to find the mysterious monk standing by his side and
bending over him. He at once moved away, but kept looking back as if
expecting to be followed. The boy got up and went with him; and, when
he thought it over afterwards, he was surprised that he did not feel in the
least afraid. The monk walked slowly down the dormitory. This time he
did not appear to be carrying anything; and the usual light on the open
roof was not there. But the moonlight was streaming through the
windows, and everything could be seen.

They reached the end wall; and then the monk stopped and pointed
to a spot below the holy water stoup. To his surprise, Brother Bernard
then saw distinctly a cross of light shining on the place. He turned to his
companion, meaning to ask him what it meant—but he was alone. The
monk had vanished completely.

He was not much taken aback by this. He was getting used to queer
things happening. So he just went quietly back to his cell again; and, as
he went up to the dormitory, he heard an alumnus talking in his sleep.
And the boy was saying, 'Open the wall, Father!'

Next day all this was duly reported to the Prior; and the Abbot
decided to make a search. A mason was sent for, and the end wall of the

old dormitory was opened at the place that Brother Bernard had indicated. It quickly became evident that the wall had previously been tampered with. Beneath the stone facing, the wall had been cut away and then loosely filled in with broken stone and mortar. This was cleared away, and then a box came to light. It contained a cross of gold, containing a relic for which the Abbey had been famed in the olden days, before the dissolution.

Brother Bernard had the honour of carrying it in the procession when it was solemnly conveyed back to the church and placed once more in its old position above the high altar. And since that day, the light in the old dormitory has been seen no more.

WALTER DE LA MARE

Miss Jemima

IT was a hot, still evening; the trees stood motionless; and not a bird was singing under the sky when the little old lady and the child appeared together over the crest of the hill. They paused side by side on the long, green, mounded ridge, behind which the sun was now descending. And spread out flat beneath them were the fields and farms and the wandering stream of the wide countryside. It was quite flat, and a faint thin mist was over it all, stretching out as if to the rim of the world. The little old lady and the child presently ventured a few further paces down the hillside, then again came to a standstill, and gazed once more, from under the umbrella that shaded them against the hot sun, on the scene spread out beneath them.

'Is *that* the house, Grannie,' said the child, 'that one near the meadow with the horses in it, and the trees? And is that *queer* little grey building right in the middle of that green square field the church?'

The old lady pressed her lips together, and continued to gaze through her thick glasses at the great solitary country scene. Then she drew her umbrella down with a click, placed it on the turf beside her, and sat down on it.

'I don't suppose the grass *is* damp, my dear, after this long hot day; but you never know,' she said.

'It's perfectly dry, Grannie dear, and *very* beautiful,' said the child, as if she could hardly spare the breath for the words. Then she too sat down. She had rather long fair hair, and a straight small nose under her round hat with its wreath of buttercups. Her name was Susan.

'And *is* that the house, Grannie?' she whispered once more. 'And *is* that the church where you did really and truly see it?'

The old lady never turned her eyes, but continued to overlook the scene as if she had not heard the small voice questioning; as if she were alone with her thoughts. And at that moment, one after another, a troop of gentle-stepping, half-wild horses appeared on a path round the bluff of the hill. Shyly eyeing the two strange human figures there in their haunts, one and another of them lifted a narrow lovely head to snort;

and a slim young bay, his mane like rough silk in the light, paused to whinny. Then one by one they trotted along the path, and presently were gone. Susan watched them out of sight, then sighed.

'This is a lovely place to be in, Grannie,' she said, and sighed again. 'I wish I had been here too when I was little. Please do tell me again about the—*you* know.'

Her voice trailed off faintly in the still golden air up there on the hill, as if she were now a little timid of repeating the question. She drew in closer beside her grannie, and pushing her small fingers between those of the bent-up, black-gloved hand in the old lady's lap, she stooped forward after another little pause, looked up into the still grey face with its spectacles, and said very softly, '*How* many years ago did you say?'

There was a mild far-away expression in the slate-grey eyes into which Susan was looking, as if memory were retracing one by one the years that had gone. Never had Susan sat like this, upon a green hill, above so immense a world, or in so hushed an evening quiet. Her busy eyes turned once more to look first in the direction in which the trotting comely horses had vanished, then down again to the farmhouse with its barns and byres and orchard. They then rested once more on the grey stone church—which from this height looked almost as small as a dolls' church—in the midst of its green field.

'*How* many years ago, Grannie?' repeated Susan.

'More than I scarcely dare think of,' said the old woman at last, gently pressing her fingers. 'Seventy-five, my dear.'

'Seventy-five!' breathed Susan. 'But that's not so very many, Grannie dear,' she added quickly, pushing her head against her grannie's black-caped shoulder. 'And now, before it is too late, please will you tell me the story. You see, Grannie, soon we shall have to be going back to the cab, or the man will suppose we are not coming back at all. *Please.*'

'But you know most of it already.'

'Only in pieces, Grannie; and besides, to think that here we are—here, in the very place!'

'Well,' began the old voice at last, 'I will tell it you all again, if you persist, my dear; but it's a little *more* than seventy-five years ago, for—though you would not believe it of such an old person—I was born in May. My mother, your great-grandmother, was young then, and in very delicate health after my father's death. Her doctor had said she must go on a long sea voyage. And since she was not able to take me with her, I was sent to that little farmhouse down there—Green's Farm, as it was called—to spend the months of her absence with my Uncle James and his housekeeper, who was called Miss Jemima.'

'Miss Jemima!' cried the little girl, stooping over suddenly with a burst of laughter. 'It *is* a queer name, you know, Grannie.'

'It is,' said the old lady. 'And it belonged to one to whom it was my duty to show affection, but who never much cared for the little girl she had in her charge. And when people don't care for you, it is sometimes a little difficult, Susan, to care for them. At least *I* found it so. I don't mean that Miss Jemima was unkind to me, only that when she was kind, she seemed to be kind on purpose. And when I had a slice of plum cake, her face always seemed to tell me it was *plum* cake, and that I deserved only plain. My Uncle James knew that his housekeeper did not think me a pleasant little girl. I was a shrimp in size, with straight black hair which she made me tie in a pigtail with a piece of velvet ribbon. I had little dark eyes and very skimpy legs. And though he himself was very fond of me, he showed his affection only when we were alone together, and not when she was present. He was ill, too, then, though I did not know *how* ill. And he lay all day in a long chair with a check rug over his legs, and Miss Jemima had charge not only of me, but of the farm.'

'*All* the milking, and the ploughing, and the chickens, and the pigs, Grannie?' asked Susan.

The old lady shut her eyes an instant, pressed her lips together and said, 'All.'

'The consequence was,' she went on, 'I was rather a solitary child. Whenever I could, I used to hide myself away in some corner of the house—and a beautiful house it is. It's a pity, my dear, I am so old and you so young and this hill so steep. Otherwise we could go down and—well, never mind. That row of small lattice windows which you can see belong to a narrow corridor; and the rooms out of it, rambling one into the other, were walled in just as the builders fancied, when they made the house three hundred years or more ago. And that was in the reign of Edward VI.'

'Like the Bluecoat boys,' said Susan, 'though I can't say I like the yellow stockings, Grannie, not that *mustard* yellow, you know.'

'Like the Bluecoat boys,' repeated her grandmother. 'Well, the house was simply a nest of hiding-places; and I was small—smaller even than you. I would sit with my book; or watch out of a window, *lean* out too sometimes—as if to see my mother in India. And whenever the weather was fine, and sometimes when it was not, I would creep out of the house and run away down that shaggy lane to the little wood you see there. There is a brook in it (though you can't see that) which brawls with a hundred tongues. And sometimes I would climb up this very hill. And sometimes I would creep across the field to that little church.

'It was there I most easily forgot myself and my small scrapes and troubles—with the leaves and the birds, and the blue sky and the clouds overhead, or watching a snail, or picking kingcups and cowslips, or staring into the stream at the fish. You see I was rather a doleful little creature: first because I was alone; next because my Uncle James was ill and so could not be happy; and last because I was made to feel more homesick than ever, by the cold glances and cold tongue of Miss Jemima.'

'Miss Jemima!' echoed Susan, burying her face in her amusement an instant in her hands.

'Miss Jemima,' repeated the old voice solemnly. 'But I was not only dismal and doleful. Far worse: I made little attempt to be anything else, and began to be fretful too. There was no company of my own age, for, as you see, the village is a mile or two off—over there where the sun is lighting the trees up. And I was not allowed to play with the village children. The only company I had was a fat little boy of two, belonging to one of the farm-hands. And he was so backward a baby, that even at that age he could scarcely say as many words.'

'I began to talk at one,' said Susan.

'Yes, my dear,' said her grannie, 'and you are likely, it seems, to go on talking the clock round.'

'Grannie, dear,' said Susan, 'I simply *love* this story—until—*you* know.'

'Now of all the places where I was supposed not to go to,' continued the old lady, 'that churchyard was the very one. My aunt, as I say, thought me a fantastic silly-notioned little girl, and she didn't approve of picking flowers that grow among tombstones. Indeed, I am not now quite sure myself if such flowers belong to the living at all. Still, once or twice in the summer the old sexton—Mr Fletcher he was called, and a very grumpy old man he was—used to come with his scythe and mow the lush grasses down. And you could scarcely breathe for the sweet smell of them. It seemed a waste to see them lying in swaths, butterflies hovering above them, fading in the sun. There never were such butter-cups and dandelion-clocks and meadow-sweet as grew beneath those old grey walls. I was happy there; and coming and going, I would say a prayer for my mother. But you will please understand, Susan, that I was being disobedient; that I had no business to be there at all—when I first came to know there was somebody else in the churchyard.'

'Ah! somebody else,' sighed Susan, sitting straight up, her eyes far away.

'It was one evening, rather like this one, but with a mackerel sky. The day before I had been stood in the corner for wearing an orange ribbon in my hair; and then sent to bed for talking to the grandfather's clock. I did it on purpose. And now—*this* evening, I was being scolded because I would not eat blackberry jam with my bread for tea. I was told it was because I had been spoilt, and was a little town child who did not know that God had made the wild fruits for human use, and who thought that the only things fit to eat grew in gardens.

'Really and truly I disliked the blackberry jam because of the pips, and I had a hollow tooth. But I told my aunt that my mother didn't like blackberry jam either, which made her still more angry.

' "Do you really think, James," she said to my uncle, "we should allow the child to grow up a dainty little minx like that? Now, see here, Miss, you will just stay there until you have eaten up the whole of that slice on your plate."

' "Well, then, Miss Jemima," I said pertly, "I shall stay here till I am eighty."

' "Hold your tongue," she bawled at me, with eyes blazing.

' "I can't bear the horrid——" I began again, and at that she gave me such a slap on my cheek that I overbalanced, and fell out of my chair. She lifted me up from the floor with a shake, set me in my chair again, and pushed it against the table till the edge was cutting into my legs. "And now," she said, "sit there till you are eighty!"

'A look I had never seen before came into my uncle's face; his hands were trembling. Without another word to me, Miss Jemima helped him rise from his chair, and I was left alone.

'Never before had I been beaten like that. And I was almost as much frightened as I was hurt. I listened to the tall clock ticking, "Wick-ed child, stub-born child," and my tears splashed slowly down on the ugly slice of bread-and-jam on my plate. Then all of a sudden I clenched and shook my ridiculous little fist at the door by which she had gone out, wriggled back my chair, jumped out of it, rushed out of the house, and never stopped to breathe or to look back, until I found myself sitting huddled up under the biggest tomb in the churchyard; crying there, if not my heart out, at least a good deal of my sour little temper.'

'Poor Grannie!' said Susan, squeezing her hand.

'There was not much "poor" about that,' was the reply. 'A pretty sight I must have looked, with my smeared face, green-stained frock and hair dangling. At last my silly sobbing ceased. The sky was flaming with the sunset. It was in June, and the air very mild and sweet. But instead of being penitent and realising what a bad and foolish child I was, I began to be coldly rebellious. I stared at the rosy clouds and vowed to myself I'd give Miss Jemima a fright. I'd rather die than go back to the house that night. And when the thought of my mother came into my mind, I shut it out, saying to myself that she could not have cared how much I loved her, to leave me like this. And yet only a fortnight before a long letter had come to me from India!

'Well, there I sat. A snail came out of his day's hiding-place; moths began to appear; the afternoon's butterflies all gone to rest. Far away I heard a hooting—and then a step. Cautiously peering up above my tombstone, I saw Maggie, one of the girls that helped on the farm. Her face was burning hot, and she was staring about her round the corner of the little church tower with her saucer blue eyes. She called to me, and at that my mouth opened and I made a shrill yelping squeal. She screeched too; her steel-tipped boot slipped on the flagstones; in an instant she was gone. And once more I was alone.'

'Ah, but you weren't *really* alone, Grannie,' whispered Susan, 'were you?'

'That was just what I was going to tell you, my dear. Immediately in front of my face stood some tall dandelion stalks, with their beautiful clocks, grey in the late evening light. And there were a few other gently nodding flowers. As I stared across them, on the other side of the flat gravestone a face appeared. I mean it didn't rise up. It simply came into the air. A very small face, more oval than round, its gold-coloured hair over its wild greenish eyes falling on either side its head in a curious zigzag way—like this, I mean.' The old lady took the hem of her skirt, and three or four times folded it together, then loosened it out.

'You mean, Grannie, as if it had been pleated,' said Susan.

'Yes,' said her grannie. 'I noticed that most particularly. And very lovely it looked in the reddish light. The face was not smiling, and did not appear to see me sitting there, no more than a lion does when he looks out of his cage at the people gathered round to see him fed. And yet I knew *she* knew that I was there. And though I did not think she minded my being there, I felt more frightened than I had ever been in my life. My mouth opened; I was clutching tight the grass on either side. And I saw nothing else as I stared into that tiny face.'

'That was the Fairy, Grannie,' said Susan, stooping forward again as if to make her words more impressive. The old lady glanced fixedly at the two blue eyes bent on her from under the brim of the round straw hat.

'At that moment, my dear, I did not know *what* it was. I was far too frightened to think. Time must have been passing, too, very quickly, for as I stared on, it was already beginning to be gloaming between us, and silent. Yes, much more silent even than this. Then, suddenly, behind me a low birdlike voice began to sing from out of the may-bushes, the notes falling like dewdrops in the air. I knew it was a nightingale. And at the very moment the thought came to me—That is a nightingale—the face on the other side of the rough grey stone vanished.

'For a few minutes I sat without moving—not daring to move. And then I ran, straight out of the churchyard by the way I had come, as fast as my legs could carry me. I hardly know what I thought, but as soon as I saw the lights in the upper windows of the farm, I ran even faster. Up under the ilexes, and round through the farmyard to the back door. It was unlatched. I slipped through, quiet as a mouse, into the kitchen, climbed into the chair, and at once devoured every scrap of that horrid bread-and-jam!

'And still, my dear, I don't believe I was really thinking, only dreadfully afraid, and yet with a kind of triumph in my heart that Miss Jemima should never know anything at all about the face in the churchyard. It was all but dark in the kitchen now, but I still sat on in my chair, even at last lifted the plate, and insolently licked up with my tongue every jammy crumb that was left.

'And then the door opened, and Miss Jemima stood there in the entry with a lighted brass candlestick in her hand. She looked at me, and I at her. "Ah, I see you have thought better of it," she said. "And high time too. You are to go straight to bed."

'If you can imagine, Susan, a cake made almost entirely of plums, and every plum a black thought of hatred, I was like that. But I said never a word. I got down from my chair, marched past her down the flagstone passage, and she followed after. When I came to my uncle's door, I lifted my hand towards the handle. "Straight on, Miss," said the voice behind me. "You have made him too ill and too unhappy to wish you good-night." Straight on I went, got into bed with all my clothes on, even my dew-wet shoes, and stared at the ceiling till I fell asleep.'

'You know, Grannie,' said Susan, 'it was very curious of you not even to undress at all. Why do you think you did that?'

'My dear,' said her grannie, 'at that moment I had such a hard, hot heart in me, that there was not any room for a why. But you see that little jutting attic window above the trees—it was in the room beyond that and on the other side of the house that I lay. And it's now seventy-five years ago. It may be there was even then a far-away notion in my mind of getting up in the middle of the night and running away. But whether or not, I was awakened by the sun streaming through my lattice window, for my bedroom lay full in the light of the morning.

'I could think of but one thing—my disgrace of the night before, and what I had seen in the churchyard. It was a dream, I thought to myself, shutting my eyes, yet knowing all the time that I did not believe what I was saying. Even when I was told at breakfast that my uncle was no better, I thought little of him, and gobbled down my porridge, with the one wish to be out of the house before I could be forbidden to go out. But the only sign of Miss Jemima was my dirty jam-stained plate of the night before, upon which she had put my hunch of breakfast bread. Yet although I was so anxious to get out, for some reason I chose very carefully what I should wear, and changed the piece of ribbon in my hat from blue to green. A rare minx I was.'

'You were, Grannie,' said Susan, clasping her knees. 'And then you went out to the churchyard again?'

'Yes. But all seemed as usual there; except only that a tiny bunch of coral-coloured berries lay on a flat leaf, on the very tombstone where I had hid. Now though I was a minx, my dear, I was also fairly sharp for my age, and after the first gulp of surprise, as I stood there among the nodding buttercups, the sun already having stolen over the grey roof and shining upon the hot tombstones, I noticed a beady dewdrop resting on the leaf, and the leaf of as fresh a green as lettuce in a salad. Looking at this dewdrop I realised at once that the leaf could not have been there very long. Indeed, in a few minutes the sun had drunk up that one round drop of water, for it was some little time before I ventured to touch the berries.

'Then I knew in my heart I was not alone there, and that that green dish had been put there on purpose, just before I had come. The berries were lovely to look at, too; of a coral colour edging into rose. And I don't think it was because I had long ago been warned not to taste strange fruit, but because I was uneasy in conscience already, that I did not nibble one then and there.

'It was very quiet in that green place, and on and on I watched, as still as a cat over a mouse's hole, though I myself really and truly was the mouse. And then, all of a sudden, flinging back my green dangling hat-ribbon, I remember, over my shoulder, I said half aloud, in an affected little voice, "Well, it's very kind of you, I am sure," stretched my hand across, plucked one of the berries, and put it into my mouth.

'Hardly had its juice tartened my tongue when a strange thing happened. It was as if a grasshopper was actually sitting in my hair, the noise of tiny laughter was so close. Besides this, a kind of heat began to creep into my cheek, and it seemed all the colours around me grew so bright that they dazzled my eyes. I closed them. I must have sat there for a while quite unconscious of time, for when I opened them again, the shadow had gone a pace or two back from the stone, and it was getting towards the middle of the morning.

'But there was still that dazzle in my eyes, and everything I looked at—the flowers and the birds, even the moss and lichen on the old stones, seemed as if they were showing me secrets about themselves that I had not known before. It seemed that I could share the very being of the butterfly that was hovering near; and could almost hear not only what the birds were singing, but what they were saying.'

'Just like the fairy-tales, Grannie.'

'Yes,' said the little old woman, 'but the difference is that I was not happy about it. The flush was still in my cheek, and I could hear my heart beating under my frock, and I was all of an excitement. But I knew in my inmost self that I ought not to feel like that at all; that I had crept into danger through my wicked temper; that those little unknown coral fruits on the tombstone had been put there for a trap. It was a bait, Susan; and I was the silly fish.'

'O Grannie, a "silly fish"!' said Susan. 'I can see you *might* feel wicked,' she added, with a sage little nod, 'but I don't *exacaly* see why.'

'That is just when it's most dangerous, my child,' said her grandmother, sharply closing her mouth very much indeed like a fish. 'But I must get on with my story, or we shall never be home.

'I sat on, keeping my eyes as far as I could fixed on the invisible place in the air where I had seen the face appear, but nothing came, and gradually the scene lost its radiance, and the birds were chirping as usual again, and the buttercups were the same as ever. No, not the same as ever, because, although it was a burning, sunny day, it seemed now that everything was darker and gloomier than usual on so bright a morning, and I skulked away home, feeling not only a little cold, but dejected and ashamed.

'As I went in through the gate between those two stone pillars you can just see by the round green tree down there, I looked up at the windows. And a dreadful pang seized me to see that their curtains were all drawn over the glass. And though I didn't know then what that meant, I knew it meant something sorrowful and tragic. Besides, they seemed like shut eyes, refusing to look at me. And when I went in, Miss Jemima told me that my uncle was dead. She told me, too, that he had asked to see me an hour or two before he died. "He said, 'Where is my little Susan?' And where you have been," added Miss Jemima, "is known only to your wicked wilful self." I stared at her, and seemed to shrink until she appeared to be twice as large as usual. I could not speak, because my tongue would not move. And then I rushed past her and up the stairs into a corner between two cupboards, where I used sometimes to hide, and I don't know what I did or thought there; I simply sat on and on, with my hands clenched in my lap, everything I looked at all blurred, and my lips trying to say a prayer that would not come.

'From that day on I became a more and more wretched and miserable little girl, and, as I think now, a wickeder one. It all came of three things. First, because I hated Miss Jemima, and that is just like leaving a steel knife in vinegar, it so frets and wastes the heart. Next, because of the thought of my poor uncle speaking of me so gently and kindly when he was at death's door; and my remorse that I could never now ask him to forgive me. And last, because I longed to see again that magical face in the churchyard, and yet knew that it was forbidden.'

'But, Grannie dear, you know,' said Susan, 'I never can see why you should have thought that then.'

'No,' replied the old lady. 'But the point was, you see, that I *did* think it, and I knew in my heart that it would lead to no good. Miss Jemima made me go next day into the room where my uncle lay in his coffin. But try as she might to persuade and compel me, she could not make me open my eyes and look at him. For that disobedience she sent me to my bedroom for the rest of the day.

'When all was still, I crept out across the corridor into another room, and looked out over the trees towards the little church. And I said to myself, as if I were speaking to someone who would hear, "I am coming to you soon, and nobody, *nobody* here shall ever see me again."

'Think of it; a little girl not yet nine, angry with the whole world, and hardly giving a thought to the mother who was longing to see her, and—though I didn't know it then—was very soon to be in England again.

'Well, then came the funeral. I was dressed—I can see myself now, as I stood looking into the looking-glass—in a black frock trimmed with crape, with a tucker of white frilling round the neck, and an edging of it at the sleeves; my peaked white face and coal-black eyes.

'It was, as you see, but a very little distance to my poor uncle's last resting-place, and in those days they used a little hand-cart on wheels, which the men pushed in front of us, with its flowers. And Miss Jemima and I followed after it across the field. I listened to the prayers as closely as I could. But at last my attention began to wander, and, kneeling there beside Miss Jemima in the church, my hands pressed close to my eyes, for an instant I glanced out and up between my fingers.

'The great eastern window, though you cannot see it from here, is of centuries-old stained glass, crimson, blue, green. But in one corner, just above the narrow ledge of masonry outside, it had been broken many, many years ago by the falling of a branch of a tree, and had been mended with clear *white* glass. And there, looking steadily in and straight across and down at me, was the face and form of the being I had seen beside the tombstone.

'I cannot tell you, Susan, how beautiful that face looked then. Those rich colours of the saints and martyrs surrounding that gold hair—living gold—and the face as pale and beautiful—far more beautiful than anything else I had ever seen in my life before. But even then I saw, too, that into the morning church a kind of shadowy darkness had come, and the stone faces on either side the window, with their set stare, looked actually to be alive. I gazed between my fingers, hearing not a single word of what the old clergyman was saying, wondering when anyone else would see what I saw, and knowing that the smiling lips were breathing across at me, "Come away, come away!"

'My bones were all cramped, and at last I managed to twist my head a little and peep up at Miss Jemima. The broad face beneath her veil had its eyes shut, and the lips were muttering. She had noticed nothing amiss. And when I looked again, the face at the window was vanished.

'It was a burning hot day—so hot that the flowers beside the grave were already withering before Miss Jemima took me home. We reached the stone porch together, and in its cold shadow she paused, staring down on me through her veil. "You will be staying on here for a while, because I don't know what else to do with you," she said to me. "But you will understand that this is my house now. I am telling your mother how bad a child you are making yourself, and perhaps she will ask me to send you away to a school where they know how to deal with stubborn and ungrateful beings like yourself. But she will be sorry, I think, to hear that it was your wickedness that brought that poor kind body to its grave over there. And now, Miss, as the best part of the day is over, you shall have your bread-and-butter and milk in your bedroom, and think over what I have said." '

'I think, Grannie,' cried Susan, bending herself nearly double, 'that that Miss Jemima was the most dreadful person I have ever heard of.'

'Well, my dear,' said her grandmother, 'I have lived a good many years, and believe it is wiser to try and explain to oneself people as well as things. Do you suppose she would have been as harsh to me if I hadn't hated her? And now she lies there too, and I never had her forgiveness either.'

Susan turned her head away and looked out over the countryside to the north, to where the roving horses had vanished, and where evening was already beginning gradually to settle itself towards night.

'And *did* you think over what Miss Jemima had said, Grannie?' she asked in a low voice.

'The first thing I did was to throw the bread-and-butter out of the window, and while I watched the birds wrangling over it and gobbling it up, I thought of nothing at all. It was cooler in the shade on that side of the house. My head ached after the sorrowful walk to the church and back. I came away from the window, took off my black frock, and sat there on the edge of my bed, I remember, in my petticoat, not knowing what to do next. And then, Susan, I made up my mind that I could not bear to be in Miss Jemima's house for a day longer than I need.

'I was just clever enough to realise that if I wanted to run away I must take care not to be brought back. I grew hot all over at the thought of such a shame, never thinking how weak and silly I was not to be able to endure patiently what could only be a few more days or weeks before another letter came from my mother. Then I tore a leaf from a book that was in my room—a Prayer-Book—and scrawled a few words to my mother, saying how miserable *and* wicked I had been, and how I longed to see her again. It's a curious thing, Susan, but I was pitying myself while I wrote those words, and thinking how grieved my mother would be when she read them, and how well Miss Jemima would deserve whatever my mother said to her. But I didn't utter a word in the letter about where I was going.'

'You didn't really *know* where you were going, Grannie,' whispered Susan, edging a little nearer. 'Did you? Not *then*, I mean?'

'No, but I had a faint notion whom I was going *to*; for somehow, from old fairy tales I had got to believe that human children could be taken away to quite a different world from this—a country of enchantment. And I remembered having read, too, about two children that had come back from there, and had forgotten their own English.'

'I know two poems about it,' said Susan. 'One about "True Thomas—Thomas the Rhymer," you know, Grannie, who stayed with the Queen of Fairyland for seven whole years, and another about . . . I do wonder—— But please, *please*, go on.'

'Well, I hid my little letter in a cranny in the wainscot, after sewing a piece of cotton to it so that I might pull it out again when I wanted it. The next morning, I got up early, and slipping on my clothes, tiptoed out of the house before breakfast, and made my way to the church. I thought deceitfully that Miss Jemima would be sure to find out that I was gone, and that if for a morning or two she discovered me quietly sitting in the churchyard she would not suppose at another time, perhaps, that I was not safely there again. Plots, Susan, are tangled things, and are likely to tangle the maker of them too.

'The old man who took care of the church, Mr Fletcher, to save himself the trouble of carrying the key of the door, used to hide it under a large stone beneath the belfry tower. I had watched him put it there. It was a fresh sparkling day, I remember, with one or two thin silver clouds high in the sky—angels, I used to call them—and I forgot for the moment in the brightness of it all my troubles, as I frisked along past the dewy hedges.

'My first thought was to make quite, quite sure about the Fairy Creature in the churchyard, my next to plan a way of escape. I gathered a bunch of daisies, and having come to the belfry door, I somehow managed to open it with the key which I dragged out from beneath its stone, and crept into the still, empty coolness. I had come to the conclusion, too, Susan, young though I was, that if the Fairy Creature or whatever she might be actually came into the church to me, it might be a proof there was no harm in her company, for I knew in my heart that I was in some mysterious danger.

'There are a few old oak pews in the little church, with heads carved upon them, and one or two have side seats that draw out from the wood into the aisle. On one of these I sat down, so that while I could be intent on my daisy-chain—just to show I had something to do there—I could see out of the corner of my eye the open door by which I had come in. And I hadn't very long to wait.

'In the midst of the faint singing of the wild birds, out of the light that lay beyond the stone church wall I spied her come stealing. My heart almost stopped beating, nor did I turn my head one inch, so that my eyes soon ached because they were almost asquint with watching. If you can imagine a figure—even now I cannot tell you how tall she was—that seems to be made of the light of rainbows, and yet with every feature in its flaxen-framed face as clearly marked as a cherub's cut in stone; and if you can imagine a voice coming to you, close into your ear, without your being able to say exactly where it is coming *from—that* was what I saw and heard beneath that grey roof down there on that distant morning, seventy-five years ago. The longer I watched her out of the corner of my eye, the more certain I became that she was using every device she knew to attract my attention, even that she was impatient at my stupidity, and yet that she could not or did not, dare to cross the threshold. And so I sat and watched her, fumbling on the while with my limpening daisy-stalks. Many strange minutes must have passed like this.

'At last, however, having fancied I heard a footfall, I was surprised out of myself, and suddenly twisted my head. She too had heard, and was standing stiller than a shadow on snow, gazing in at me. I suppose thoughts reveal themselves in the face more swiftly than one imagines. I was partly afraid, partly longing to approach closer. I wished her to realise that I longed for her company, but that danger was near, for I was well aware whose step it was I had heard. And, as I looked at her, there came a sharpness into her face, a cold inhuman look—not of fear, but almost like hatred—and she was gone. More intent than ever, I stooped over my daisies. And in the hush there was a faint sound as of an intensely distant whistle.

'Then a shadow fell across the porch, and there was Miss Jemima. It's a strange thing, Susan, but Miss Jemima also did not enter the church. She called to me from where she stood, in almost a honeyed voice: "Breakfast is ready, Susan." '

'I can imagine *exacaly* how she said that, Grannie,' said the little girl, 'because my name's Susan, too.'

'Yes, my dear,' said the old lady, squeezing her hand. 'It was passed on to you from me by your dear mother just because it was mine. And I hope you will always be the Susan I have *now*.' From near at hand upon the hill a skylark suddenly took its flight into the evening blue. The old lady listened a moment before going on with her story.

'Well,' she began again, 'I gathered up my apron and walked towards Miss Jemima down the aisle. Suddenly there came a slight rumbling noise, which I could not understand. Then instantly there followed a crash. And at Miss Jemima's very feet, in the sunlight, I saw lying a piece of stone about the size of a small plum pudding. Miss Jemima gave a faint scream. Her cheek, already pale, went white; and she stared from me to the stone and back again, as I approached her.

' "You were talking in there—in God's church—to someone," she whispered harshly, stooping towards me. "To whom?"

'I shook my head, and stood trembling and gazing at the stone.

' "Look into my face, you wicked child," she whispered. "Who were you talking to in there?"

'I looked up at last. "It's empty," I said.

' "There's a lying look in your eyes!" cried Miss Jemima. "And you are the child that goes into a sacred place to weave daisy-chains! Turn your face away from me. Do you hear me, Miss? Miserable little *Sorceress* that you are!"

'The word seemed to flame up in my mind as if it had been written in fire on smoke; and still I stared at the stone. I felt but did not see Miss Jemina steadily turn her head and look around her.

' "A few inches," she added in a low voice, "and you would have killed me."

' "Me!" I cried angrily. "What has it to do with *me*, Miss Jemima?"

' "Ah!" said she. "We shall know a little more about that when you have told me what company you find here where your poor uncle might hope to be at rest."

'It's a dreadful thing to confess, Susan, but up to that moment, though I had again and again cried by myself at memory of him, though tears were always in my heart for him, I hadn't thought of my uncle that morning.

' "And perhaps," added Miss Jemima, "bread and water and solitude for a day or two will help to persuade your tongue."

'I followed her without another word across the field, and in a few minutes was alone once more in my bedroom with a stale crust and a glass of water to keep me company.

'I should think if my angry tears had run into the water that morning, they would have actually made it taste salt. But I cried so that not even a mouse could have heard me. Every other thought was now out of my mind—for I dared not even talk to myself about the stone—but that of getting away from the house for ever. One thing I could not forget, however, and that was the word "sorceress." It terrified me far more than I can tell you. I knew in my young mind that Miss Jemima was treating me wickedly, however naughty I had been, and I knew too, in strange fear, that the stone might not have fallen by accident. I had seen the look on the Fairy's face and . . .' The old lady suddenly broke off her story at this point, and looked about her in alarm. 'My dear, we must go at once; the dew is beginning to fall, and the air is already colder.'

'Oh, Grannie,' said the child, 'how I wish we might stay—a little, *little* longer!'

'Well, my dear, so do I. For I am old, and I shall never see this place again. It brings many memories back. Who knows what might have happened if——'

'But, Grannie,' interrupted the child hastily, picking up the umbrella from the grass. 'Please tell me the rest of the story straight, straight, straight on as we go back.' It seemed to Susan, so still was her grandmother's face at that moment, and so absent her eyes—that she could not have heard her. The small aged eyes were once more looking carefully down on the scene below. For an instant they shut as if the old lady had thought so to remember it more completely. And then the two of them began slowly to climb the hill, and the story proceeded.

'No one disturbed me during the long morning,' continued the old voice, 'but in the afternoon the door was unlocked, and Miss Jemima opened it to show in the Reverend Mr Wilmot, who conducted the service in the church every other Sunday. I won't tell you all he said to me. He was a kind and gentle old man, but he didn't so much as think it possible there was any being or thing in the churchyard but its birds, its tombstones, and now and then a straying animal. He only smiled about all that, nor did he ask me Miss Jemima's question.

'He took my hand in his great bony one and begged me to be a good little girl. And I see his smiling face as he asked it. "Not only for your mother's sake," he said, "but *for goodness' sake.*"

' "I am sure, my dear," he went on, "Miss Jemima *means* to be kind, and all *we* have to do is to mean to be good."

'I gulped down the lump in my throat, and said, "But don't you think *sorceress* is a very wicked word?"

'He stood up, holding both my hands in his. "But my poor little lamb," he cried, "Miss Jemima is no more a sorceress than I am a Double Dutchman!" And with that he stooped, kissed the top of my head, and went out of the room.

'In a minute or two his footsteps returned. He opened the door an inch and peeped in. "Why, we are better already!" he smiled at me over his spectacles. Then he came in, carrying a plate with a slice of bread-and-jam upon it, and a mug of milk. "There," he said, "there's no sorcery in that, is there? And now you will be an obedient and gentle child, and think how happy Mamma will be to see you." '

'I think,' said Susan stoutly, 'that that Mr Wilmot is one of the kindest men I ever knew.'

Her grandmother looked down on her with a crooked smile on her face. 'He was so kind, Susan, that I never mentioned to him that the blackberry-jam on the bread was not a great favourite of mine! A moment after the sound of his steps had died away I heard the key once more in the lock. And what did I say to myself when he was gone? I looked forlornly at the plate, then out of the window, and I believe, Susan, that I did what they sometimes describe in the story-books—I wrung my hands a little, repeating to myself, "He doesn't understand. No! He doesn't understand."

'In an hour or two, Miss Jemima herself opened the door and looked in. She surveyed me where I sat, and then her glance fell on the un- touched slice of bread-and-jam.

' "Ah," said she, "a good man like Mr Wilmot cannot realise the hardness of a stubborn heart. I don't want to be unkind to you, Susan, but I have a duty to perform to your mother and to your poor uncle. You shall not leave this room until you apologise to me for your insolence of this morning, and until you tell me whom you were speaking to in the church."

'The lie that came into my mind—"But I was not speaking to anyone, Miss Jemima"—faded away on my tongue. And I simply looked at her in silence.

' "You have a brazen face, Susan," said she, "and if you grow up as you are now, you will be a very wicked woman." '

'I think,' said Susan, '*that* was a perfectly dreadful thing to say, Grannie.'

'Times change, my dear,' said the old lady. 'And now—well, it is fortunate there is very little more to tell. For this hill has taken nearly all the breath out of my body!'

The two of them were now on the crest of the hill. The light was beginning to die away in the sky, and the mists to grow milkier in the hollows of the flat country that lay around and beneath them. Far, far away, facing them across the wild, a reddish-coloured moon was rising. From low down below, a dog barked—it might be from dead Miss Jemima's farmyard. The little church surrounded by its low wall seemed to have gathered in closer to its scattered stones.

'Yes, Grannie dear?' breathed Susan, slipping her hand into the cotton-gloved one that hung near. 'What then?'

'Then,' replied her grandmother, 'the door was locked again. Anger and hatred filled that silly little body sitting in the bedroom, and towards evening I fell asleep. And I must have dreamed a terrifying dream, though when I awoke I could not remember my dream—only its horror. I was terrified at it in that solitude, and I knew by the darkening at the window that it must be at least nine or ten o'clock. Night was coming, then. I could scarcely breathe at the thought. A second mug of milk had been put beside the plate; but I could not even persuade myself to drink any of it.

'Then in a while I heard Miss Jemima's footsteps pass my room. She made no pause there, and presently after I knew that she was gone to bed. She had not even troubled to look in on her wretched little prisoner. The hardness of that decided me.

'I tiptoed over to the door, and with both hands softly twisted the handle. It was still locked. Then I went to the window and discovered, as if the Fairy Creature herself had magicked it there, that a large hay-wain half full of hay, its shafts high in the air, had been left drawn up within a few feet of my window. It looked dangerous, but it was not actually a very difficult jump even for a child of my age; and I think I might have jumped even if there had been no cart at all. My one thought was to run away. *Anywhere*—so long as there was no chance of Miss Jemima's finding me.

'But even in that excited foolish moment I had sense enough left—before I jumped out of the window—to take a little warm jacket out of my chest-of-drawers, and to wrap my money-box up in a scarf so that it should not jangle too much. I pulled my letter up from its cranny in the wainscot by its thread, and put it on the pink dressing-table. And at that moment, in the half dark I saw my face in the looking-glass. I should hardly have recognised it. It looked nearly as old, Susan, as I do now.'

'Yes, dear Grannie,' said Susan.

'Then I jumped—without the slightest harm to myself. I scrambled down into the yard and, keeping close to the house, crept past the kennel, the old sheep-dog merely shaking her chain with her thumping tail a little as I passed. And then, as soon as I was beyond the tall gate-posts, I ran as fast as my legs would carry me.'

'But *not*,' cried Susan almost with a shout in the still air, '*not* to the churchyard, Grannie. I think that was the most wonderful thing of all.'

'Not so very wonderful, my dear, if you remember that I was now intensely afraid of the Fairy Creature, after seeing that look in her countenance when Miss Jemima was approaching the church. Something in me had all along, as you know, said, *Don't be deceived by her. She means you no well*. I cannot explain that; but so it was. Yet all the time I had been longing to follow where she might lead. Why she should wish to carry off a human child I don't know, but that she really wanted me I soon discovered for certain.

'If you follow the tip of my umbrella, you will just be able to see, Susan, a large meadow on the other side of the farm. But I don't think even your sharp eyes will detect the stones standing up in it. They are called the Dancers, and though I was a little frightened of passing them in the darkness, this was the only way to take. Gradually I approached them, my heart beating beneath my ribs like a drum, until I was come near.

'And there, lovelier than ever, shining as fairly as if with a light of her own, sitting beneath the largest of the Dancers, directly in my path, was She. But this time I knew she was not alone. I cannot describe what passed in my heart. Still I longed to go, still I was in anguish at the thought of it. I didn't dare to look at her, and all I could think to do was to pretend not to see anything. How I had the courage I cannot think. Perhaps it was the courage that comes when fear and terror are almost beyond bearing.

'I put my money-box on to the grass; the scarf was already wet with dew. Then, very slowly, I put my black jacket on and buttoned it up. And then, with face turned away from the stone, I walked slowly on down the path, between the Dancers, towards the one that is called the Fiddler, in their midst. The night air was utterly silent. But as I approached the stone, it seemed as if it were full of voices and footsteps and sounds of wings and instruments, yet all as small as the voices of grasshoppers.

'I just kept saying, "Oh, please, God; oh, please, God," and walked on. And when at last I came to the stone, the whole world suddenly seemed to turn dark and cold and dead. Apart from the ancient stone, leaning up out of the green turf as it had done for centuries, there was not a sign or a symptom, Susan, of anything or anybody there.'

'I think I can *just* see the stone, Grannie, but I would not be there like that in the dark, not for anything—anything in the world . . . I expect it was what you *said* made the Fairy go. And then, Grannie?'

'Then, Susan, my heart seemed to go out of me. I ran on, stumbling blindly for a little way, then lost my balance completely over a tussock of grass or a mole-heap and fell flat on my face. Without any words that I can remember, I lay praying in the grass.

'But even then I did not turn back. I got up at last and ran on more lightly, and without looking behind me, across the field. Its gate leads into a by-road. It was padlocked, and as I mounted to the top my eyes could see just above a slight rise in the ground, for the lane lies beneath a little hill there.

'And coming along the road towards me there were shining the lamps of a carriage. I clambered down and crouched in the hedge-side, and in a few moments the lamps reappeared at the top of the incline and the horse came plod-plodding along down the hill. It was a wonderful mild summer night, the sky all faint with stars. What would have happened if it had been cold or pouring with rain I cannot think. But because it was so warm, the air almost like milk, the hood of the carriage was down.

'And as it came wheeling round by the hedge-side, I saw in the filmy starlight who it was who was sitting there. Neither horse nor coachman could see me. I jumped to my feet and ran after the carriage as fast as my legs could carry me, screaming at the top of my voice, "Mother, Mother!"

'Perhaps the grinding of the wheels in the flinty dust and the noise of the hoofs drowned my calling. But I still held tight to my money-box, and though it was muffled by the scarf in which it was wrapped, at each step it made a dull noise like a bird-scare, and this must at last have attracted my mother's attention. She turned her head, opened her mouth wide at sight of me—I see her now—then instantly jumped up and pulled the coachman's buttoned coat-tails. The carriage came to a standstill . . .

'And that,' said the old lady, turning away her head for one last glance of the countryside around her, 'that is all, Susan.'

Susan gave a last great sigh. 'I can't think what you must have felt, Grannie,' she said, 'when you were safe in the carriage. And I can't——' But at this point she began to laugh very softly to herself, and suddenly stood still. 'And I can't think either,' she went on, 'what Miss Jemima must have thought when you and *Great*-Grannie knocked at the door. You did tell me once that she opened her bedroom window at the sound of the knocking, and looked out in her nightdress. I expect she was almost as frightened as you were amongst those Dancers.'

The two of them were now descending the hill on the side away from the farm and the church. And not only their carriage standing beneath them, but the evening star had come into view. There never was such a peaceful scene—the silver birches around them standing perfectly still, clothed with their little leaves, and the rabbits at play among the gorse and juniper.

'Bless me, Mum,' said the old cabman as he opened the carriage door, 'I was just beginning to think them fairises had runned away with you and the young lady.'

Susan burst completely out laughing. 'Now don't you think, Grannie,' she said, 'that is a very, very curious quincidence?'

ARTHUR MACHEN

Johnny Double

THE worst of it was that Johnny Marchant had nothing particular to complain of. He did not live in a slum in the most miserable part of London. He lived in a beautiful old house in the country. His father did not beat him when he came home drunk, because his father very rarely left his house and therefore he couldn't come home. And besides, his father never got drunk. His old grandmother never thought of shutting him up in dark cupboards. All the cupboards at Johnny's home were full of books and of curious and beautiful things, so there was no room for Johnny. Besides, his grandmother, who came on visits about twice a year, would never have dreamt of doing such a silly thing. In the first place she was as kind as kind could be; and then she was not the sort of woman to take a lot of rare china out of a cupboard for the sake of putting a little boy into it; in fact, as I say, Johnny Marchant had nothing whatever to complain of, and that's a pity. People are not interested in a child who isn't shut up in the dark, starved, or beaten. It is true that Johnny's mother had died when he was a year old. But he never remembered her, and his nurse Mary knew what a boy's feelings are, and generally had gooseberry jam for tea. Or if not, blackberry jelly in the blue Chinese pot with the yellow dragons.

So, since we cannot pretend that Johnny Marchant had a rough time, we may as well make the best of the smooth things that he enjoyed. To begin with, the house that he lived in was old and odd and beautiful. It was in a hollow looking over a quiet bay of a calm blue sea. About it were groves of dark ilex trees, green all the year round; and then there were huge old laurels of a brighter green that blossomed and bore a crimson-purple fruit. There was a lawn in front of the house with fuchsia hedges twenty feet high. On one side was the kitchen garden, where the peaches grew from pale green to yellow, and from yellow to pink, and from pink to crimson all through the spring and summer. On the other side were the dessert apples and pears in an orchard sloping to the south and the sea. Then from the first lawn steps went down to the second lawn, called Johnny Summerhouse Lawn, for here was a summer house that had tried to look like a Chinese temple, before the white roses had grown all over it. And then another flight of steps went down to Well Lawn, where a tall pine tree grew off a red rock, and all manner of green boughs shaded a bubbling well, with white sand always stirring at the bottom of it, as the water rose clear and cold out of the heart of the hill. And, after that, below again was the wild place where all the trees grew thick together and the ground was rich with ferns, and a steep path twisted in and out of the wildness down to the sea.

As for the house; it was about a hundred and twenty years old. There was a ground floor and a first floor, and that was all, and then a thatched roof. The walls were painted white, and the veranda was painted green, and purple clematis covered it. And on the path, in front of the house, were six great green tubs, and in the six great green tubs there were six great green bushes of box, as old as the house. The man who had built it was a captain in the Navy, who had fought in all the fights against Napoleon and had sailed all over the world besides. He had made the builders paint the walls white, and had called his house Casabianca, or White House. But when the box trees in the tubs grew big and round, as they soon did, the country people called the place 'The Bunches,' and at last it was known as Casabianca Bunches, and Johnny never heard the last of it when he went to school and told his best friend where he lived. In fact he was called 'Bunches' at Oxford; and for all I know his fellow-judges call him 'Brother Bunches' to this day—except when they are all dressed in scarlet and white and wear great wigs.

So there were all sorts of nice things outside the house, and one could always get lost in the wild place. And when it rained, there were all sorts of nice things inside the house. There were Chinese monsters and junks and temples made of ivory and lacquer cabinets, rich red and gold and mother-of-pearl, and Japanese pictures in deep fine colours, with people making horrible faces in the front, and blue mountains and rivers and bridges in the distance, and Indian gods with too many arms, and elephants' heads, and serpents and everything a boy can want. As for books, there were plenty everywhere: Baxter's *Saints' Rest*, *The Arabian Nights*, Jeremy Taylor, *Roderick Random*, the Poetical Works of Akenside, the Waverley Novels, *Gil Blas*, *Gulliver's Travels*, all Dickens', Jortin's *Sermons*, and *Don Quixote*. In due time Johnny tried them all— very small bits of some of them, and, as his father said, gave himself a liberal education. And yet his father and his grandmother and his Aunt Letitia were sometimes 'quite uneasy' about him. He was so very odd at times. The old doctor came over from Nantgaron and heard all about it, and looked at Johnny's tongue, and punched him in the proper places, and sent powders; and that was no good. Then Johnny was taken to the doctor at Bristol, who said he must live on cream and mutton chops done pink; and that was no good. Then Johnny was taken to the doctor in London, and he said that raw carrots, finely sliced, with plenty of nuts, would make an immense change for the better; but that did no good. Though his doctor spoke of 'irritability of the nervous system,' 'marked psychological cachexia,' 'idiosyncrasy,' and 'pathogenic' at considerable length.

Johnny's trouble was a very odd one, and for some time his relations didn't think much about it. It began by his telling long stories about where he had been and what he had seen, all the most wonderful things that he hadn't seen and couldn't have seen. Mary, the nurse, heard most of these tales in the morning and at tea-time and at bed-time, and she only said, 'Yes, dear'; 'Of course, darling'; 'I see, Master Johnny'; and 'Well, I'm sure!' not heeding a word of it. So she heard how Johnny had been a long way off to a big town, ever so much bigger than Nantgaron, and there were houses and houses, and then a sort of country in the middle of the houses, full of trees and grass, and there all the wild beasts in the picture-books came alive, elephants and everything. And Mary cut more bread-and-butter, for this was at tea, and said, 'Beautiful, I'm sure.' Another time there was a story of a great place, full of lights, and seats rising one behind another; and then something dark went away, and there was a wood beyond, and people in queer dresses talking and singing. 'That's the way,' said Mary, 'and here's your nightshirt, Master Johnny, nice and warm, as I've aired it myself by the kitchen fire.' Then it was a tale about another country in the middle of the big town, not the country where the beasts in the picture-book came to life, but a different one, and big soldiers in scarlet and gold with bright swords in their hands riding through the country, and a band playing. And Mary went on cutting the bread-and-butter and helping the jam and brushing Johnny's hair, and not putting herself out a bit. Sometimes Johnny would tell his adventures to his father, who let him run on as he liked. Imaginative children, he said to himself, will always 'make up' and 'make believe,' and it is absurd to punish them for lying. So he would listen almost as quietly as Mary; and one night Johnny told him a long and confused story of one of the bright places with rows of seats rising one above another and the dark place getting bright, and then all sorts of wonderful things happening: a man all white and misty, who talked in a deep voice and seemed to frighten everybody very much, and a king and queen sat on thrones, and a man in a black cloak, who seemed very miserable, talked to them, and at last they all killed each other, and so everybody was dead, and it got dark again, and there was a great noise. Mr Marchant went on reading his paper, and said, 'I see,' and 'Very good, and what did they do then?' 'Did you say a churchyard and a rather cross clergyman with a bald head? Dear me! About your bedtime, isn't it?' He thought nothing about it, and he didn't think anything about it when his cousin Anna—one of the 'Dawson girls,' aged fifty-five— wrote to him from London and said amongst many other things: 'Do you think *Hamlet* quite a suitable play for Johnny? He is surely very young for all the horrors. I must say he seemed to be enjoying himself when I saw him two or three weeks ago at the Lyceum. Irving is certainly very fine. Was Johnny staying with the Gascoignes? I did not recognize the lady next to him.' Mr Marchant simply said, 'Tut, tut, tut: Anna talking nonsense as usual,' and paid no more attention to the matter. He had not listened to half Johnny's story of the misty man and the miserable man and the king and queen and the cross clergyman, and he had forgotten all about the rest. And, anyhow, he knew that Johnny had been at Casabianca Bunches all the summer, and Anna had always been a muddlehead.

Mr Marchant only began to get seriously disturbed about the boy one hot day in August, when Johnny was about nine. There was some business to be done at Nantgaron, the market town, eight miles away, and Mr Marchant drove over in the dogcart. As he was lunching in the coffee-room of The Three Salmons, his friend, Captain Lloyd, came in and sat down at another table and began to munch bread and cheese and to drink beer out of a great silver tankard with a lid. At first he talked of the harvest, which, as he said, was the earliest for twenty years, and then he remarked:

'What have you done with Johnny? Turned him loose in the tuck shop?'

'Johnny?' said Mr Marchant. 'What d'you mean? I left him at home. Nothing to amuse him at Nantgaron.'

'Nonsense, I saw him in the High Street ten minutes ago. He was staring at those steeplejacks mending the weathercock on the spire of St Mary's.'

'I left Johnny reading on the veranda at home an hour and a half ago, and I've only just come. He could hardly have walked the distance in the time. You must have mistaken some other boy for him.'

'Well, that's very strange. I was quite close to him. He was wearing a straw hat with a green ribbon and a pheasant's feather stuck in it.'

Mr Marchant looked very oddly at Captain Lloyd.

'Queer things boys will wear,' was all he said, and that was not much to the point. But the fact was that he had noticed the pheasant's feather in the straw hat with the green ribbon on Johnny's head when he said good-bye to him on the veranda, and had told Johnny that that style of hat was very little worn in town just now. Clearly Johnny had managed to get a lift into Nantgaron, and the only thing to do was to ask him what he meant by it. And so when Mr Marchant got home about tea-time, the first thing he did was to ask Mary, the nurse, whether Master Johnny had come back.

'He's not been away, sir. He's reading in the Rose Bower, and I'm just going to call him for his tea.'

'Not been away, Mary? Do you mean he was in to dinner?'

'As usual, sir, at one o'clock. Roast chicken and raspberry tart. And I thought to myself how children can eat so well and the weather so hot.'

Mr Marchant looked hard at the nurse and then said:

'Oh, I see. Thank you, Mary. That's all right, then.'

He didn't see at all. But he thought the matter over, and decided that it was quite possible that some other little boy might have a straw hat with a green ribbon and stick a pheasant's tail feather in it. Soon after tea Mr Marchant was enjoying his hollyhocks and his pipe on the Summer-house Lawn, and Johnny was helping, and putting in a word about the Templar in *Ivanhoe*. And then he said: 'Daddy! weren't those men wonderful to-day, right up on the very top of the church?'

And Mr Marchant's pipe dropped out of his mouth.

It was no good to try to get Johnny to explain. He didn't seem to think that there was anything to explain. He said he wondered what his father was doing at Nantgaron, so he thought he would go and see; and that was all, and that was how all his relations got 'quite uneasy,' as they said. And the doctors' medicines and chopped carrots and nuts made no difference whatever. Till at last the parson said there was nothing for it but school, and the boy was 'packed off,' first of all to a big preparatory school, and then to a bigger public school. Odd things happened once or twice at both places. He began to tell the other boys one of his queer stories and was promptly kicked and clouted as a young liar. Then he got into trouble for being about the town at midnight, and things looked extremely serious. But as he was able to prove that he was fast asleep in the dormitory at the time, his house-master only gave him lines on general principles. Johnny was cured, or so his father and the people at home thought.

But many years afterwards, only three years ago as a matter of fact, and some time after Johnny had become Mr Justice Marchant, it was appointed that he should try Henry Farmer, who was accused of the dreadful Hetton murder. When the court was opened, and the judge and the prisoner faced each other, a few people noticed that the two men in their different places 'looked as if they had seen a ghost.' The prisoner in the dock gasped and shuddered, and muttered something about 'the man in scarlet,' and the judge on the bench turned ghastly white, and his head almost fell on the desk before him. Mr Justice Marchant said in a faint voice that he feared a somewhat severe indisposition would prevent him trying the case. The prisoner was put back: it was another judge who sentenced Farmer to death a few days later. Mr Justice Marchant never told anyone that he had seen the man in the dock before—and with the red knife in his hand.

ELEANOR FARJEON

Elsie Piddock Skips in her Sleep

ELSIE Piddock lived in Glynde under Caburn, where lots of other little girls lived too. They lived mostly on bread-and-butter, because their mothers were too poor to buy cake. As soon as Elsie began to hear, she heard the other little girls skipping every evening after school in the lane outside her mother's cottage. Swish-swish! went the rope through the air. Tappity-tap! went the little girls' feet on the ground. Mumble-umble-umble! went the children's voices, saying a rhyme that the skipper could skip to. In course of time, Elsie not only heard the sounds, but understood what they were all about, and then the mumble-umble turned itself into words like this:

> 'ANdy SPANdy SUGARdy CANdy,
> FRENCH ALmond ROCK!
> Breadandbutterforyoursupper'sallyourmother'sGOT!'

The second bit went twice as fast as the first bit, and when the little girls said it Elsie Piddock, munching her supper, always munched her mouthful of bread-and-butter in double-quick time. She wished she had some Sugardy-Candy-French-Almond-Rock to suck during the first bit, but she never had.

When Elsie Piddock was three years old, she asked her mother for a skipping-rope.

'You're too little,' said her mother. 'Bide a bit till you're a bigger girl, then you shall have one.'

Elsie pouted and said no more. But in the middle of the night her parents were wakened by something going Slap-slap! on the floor, and there was Elsie in her night-gown skipping with her father's braces. She skipped till her feet caught in the tail of them, and she tumbled down and cried. But she had skipped ten times running first.

'Bless my buttons, mother!' said Mr Piddock. 'The child's a born skipper.'

And Mrs Piddock jumped out of bed full of pride, rubbed Elsie's elbows for her, and said: 'There-a-there now! dry your tears, and tomorrow you shall have a skip-rope all of your own.'

So Elsie dried her eyes on the hem of her night-gown; and in the morning, before he went to work, Mr Piddock got a little cord, just the right length, and made two little wooden handles to go on the ends. With this Elsie skipped all day, scarcely stopping to eat her breakfast of bread-and-butter, and her dinner of butter-and-bread. And in the evening, when the schoolchildren were gathered in the lane, Elsie went out among them, and began to skip with the best.

'Oh!' cried Joan Challon, who was the champion skipper of them all, 'just look at little Elsie Piddock skipping as never so!'

All the skippers stopped to look, and then to wonder. Elsie Piddock certainly *did* skip as never so, and they called to their mothers to come and see. And the mothers in the lane came to their doors, and threw up their hands, and cried: 'Little Elsie Piddock is a born skipper!'

By the time she was five she could outskip any of them: whether in 'Andy Spandy', 'Lady, Lady, drop your Purse', 'Charley Parley stole some Barley', or whichever of the games it might be. By the time she was six her name and fame were known to all the villages in the county. And by the time she was seven, the fairies heard of her. They were fond of skipping themselves, and they had a special Skipping-Master who taught them new skips every month at the new moon. As they skipped they chanted:

> 'The High Skip,
> The Sly Skip,
> The Skip like a Feather,
> The Long Skip,
> The Strong Skip,
> And the Skip All Together!
>
> 'The Slow Skip,
> The Toe Skip,
> The Skip Double-Double,
> The Fast Skip,
> The Last Skip,
> And the Skip against Trouble!'

All these skips had their own meanings, and were made up by the Skipping-Master, whose name was Andy-Spandy. He was very proud of his fairies, because they skipped better than the fairies of any other county; but he was also very severe with them if they did not please him. One night he scolded Fairy Heels-o'-Lead for skipping badly, and praised Fairy Flea-Foot for skipping well. Then Fairy Heels-o'-Lead sniffed and snuffed, and said: 'Hhm-hhm-hhm! there's a little girl in Glynde who could skip Flea-Foot round the moon and back again. A born skipper she is, and she skips as never so.'

'What is her name?' asked Andy-Spandy.

'Her name is Elsie Piddock, and she has skipped down every village far and near, from Didling to Wannock.'

'Go and fetch her here!' commanded Andy-Spandy.

Off went Heels-o'-Lead, and poked her head through Elsie's little window under the eaves, crying: 'Elsie Piddock! Elsie Piddock! there's a Skipping-Match on Caburn, and Fairy Flea-Foot says she can skip better than you.'

Elsie Piddock was fast asleep, but the words got into her dream, so she hopped out of bed with her eyes closed, took her skipping-rope, and followed Heels-o'-Lead to the top of Mount Caburn, where Andy-Spandy and the fairies were waiting for them.

'Skip, Elsie Piddock!' said Andy-Spandy, 'and show us what you're worth!'

Elsie twirled her rope and skipped in her sleep, and as she skipped she murmured:

> '*ANdy SPANdy SUGARdy CANdy,*
> *FRENCH ALmond ROCK!*'
> Breadandbutterforyoursupper'sallyourmother'sGOT!'

Andy-Spandy watched her skipping with his eyes as sharp as needles, but he could find no fault with it, nor could the fairies.

'Very good, as far as it goes!' said Andy-Spandy. 'Now let us see how far it *does* go. Stand forth, Elsie and Flea-Foot, for the Long Skip.'

Elsie had never done the Long Skip, and if she had had all her wits about her she wouldn't have known what Andy-Spandy meant; but as she was dreaming, she understood him perfectly. So she twirled her rope, and as it came over jumped as far along the ground as she could, about twelve feet from where she had started. Then Flea-Foot did the Long Skip, and skipped clean out of sight.

'Hum!' said Andy-Spandy. 'Now, Elsie Piddock, let us see you do the Strong Skip.'

Once more Elsie understood what was wanted of her; she put both feet together, jumped her rope, and came down with all her strength, so that her heels sank into the ground. Then Flea-Foot did the Strong Skip, and sank into the ground as deep as her waist.

'Hum!' said Andy-Spandy. 'And now, Elsie Piddock, let us see you do the Skip All Together.'

At his words, all the fairies leaped to their ropes, and began skipping as lively as they could, and Elsie with them. An hour went by, two hours, and three hours; one by one the fairies fell down exhausted, and Elsie Piddock skipped on. Just before morning she was skipping all by herself.

Then Andy-Spandy wagged his head and said: 'Elsie Piddock, you are a born skipper. There's no tiring you at all. And for that you shall come once a month to Caburn when the moon is new, and I will teach you to skip till a year is up. And after that I'll wager there won't be mortal or fairy to touch you.'

Andy-Spandy was as good as his word. Twelve times during the next year Elsie Piddock rose up in her sleep with the new moon, and went to the top of Mount Caburn. There she took her place among the fairies, and learned to do all the tricks of the skipping-rope, until she did them better than any. At the end of the year she did the High Skip so well, that she skipped right over the moon.

In the Sly Skip not a fairy could catch her, or know where she would skip to next; so artful was she, that she could skip through the lattice of a skeleton leaf, and never break it.

She redoubled the Skip Double-Double, in which you only had to double yourself up twice round the skipping-rope before it came down. Elsie Piddock did it four times.

In the Fast Skip, she skipped so fast that you couldn't see her, though she stood on the same spot all the time.

In the Last Skip, when all the fairies skipped over the same rope in turn, running round and round till they made a mistake from giddiness, Elsie never got giddy, and never made a mistake, and was always left in last.

In the Slow Skip, she skipped so slow that a mole had time to throw up his hill under her rope before she came down.

In the Toe Skip, when all the others skipped on their tiptoes, Elsie never touched a grass-blade with more than the edge of her toe-nail.

In the Skip Against Trouble, she skipped so joyously that Andy-Spandy himself chuckled with delight.

In the Long Skip she skipped from Caburn to the other end of Sussex, and had to be fetched back by the wind.

In the Strong Skip, she went right under the earth, as a diver goes under the sea, and the rabbits, whose burrows she had disturbed, handed her up again.

But in the Skip like a Feather she came down like gossamer, so that she could alight on a spider-thread and never shake the dew-drop off.

And in the Skip All Together, she could skip down the whole tribe of fairies, and remain as fresh as a daisy. Nobody had ever found out how long Elsie Piddock could skip without getting tired, for everybody else got tired first. Even Andy-Spandy didn't know.

At the end of the year he said to her: 'Elsie Piddock, I have taught you all. Bring me your skipping-rope, and you shall have a prize.'

Elsie gave her rope to Andy-Spandy, and he licked the two little wooden handles, first the one and then the other. When he handed the rope back to her, one of the handles was made of Sugar Candy, and the other of French Almond Rock.

'There!' said Andy-Spandy. 'Though you suck them never so, they will never grow less, and you shall therefore suck sweet all your life. And as long as you are little enough to skip with this rope, you shall skip as I have taught you. But when you are too big for this rope, and must get a new one, you will no longer be able to do all the fairy skips that you have learned, although you will still skip better in the mortal way than any other girl that ever was born. Good-bye, Elsie Piddock.'

'Aren't I ever going to skip for you again?' asked Elsie Piddock in her sleep.

But Andy-Spandy didn't answer. For morning had come over the Downs, and the fairies disappeared, and Elsie Piddock went back to bed.

If Elsie had been famous for her skipping before this fairy year, you can imagine what she became after it. She created so much wonder, that she hardly dared to show all she could do. Nevertheless, for another year she did such incredible things, that people came from far and near to see her skip over the church spire, or through the split oak-tree in the Lord's Park, or across the river at its widest point. When there was trouble in her mother's house, or in any house in the village, Elsie Piddock skipped so gaily that the trouble was forgotten in laughter. And when she skipped all the old games in Glynde, along with the little girls, and they sang:

> 'ANDy SPANdy SUGARdy CANdy,
> FRENCH ALmond ROCK!
> Breadandbutterforyoursupper'sallyourmother'sGOT!'—

Elsie Piddock said: 'It aren't all *I've* got!' and gave them a suck of her skipping-rope handles all round. And on the night of the new moon, she always led the children up Mount Caburn, where she skipped more marvellously than ever. In fact, it was Elsie Piddock who established the custom of New-Moon-Skipping on Caburn.

But at the end of another year she had grown too big to skip with her little rope. She laid it away in a box, and went on skipping with a longer one. She still skipped as never so, but her fairy tricks were laid by with the rope, and though her friends teased her to do the marvellous things she used to do, Elsie Piddock only laughed, and shook her head, and never told why. In time, when she was still the pride and wonder of her village, people would say: 'Ah, but you should ha' seen her when she was a littling! Why, she could skip through her mother's keyhole!' And in more time, these stories became a legend that nobody believed. And in still more time, Elsie grew up (though never very much), and became a little woman, and gave up skipping, because skipping-time was over. After fifty years or so, nobody remembered that she had ever skipped at all. Only Elsie knew. For when times were hard, and they often were, she sat by the hearth with her dry crust and no butter, and sucked the Sugar Candy that Andy-Spandy had given her for life.

It was ever and ever so long afterwards. Three new Lords had walked in the Park since the day when Elsie Piddock had skipped through the split oak. Changes had come in the village; old families had died out, new families had arrived; others had moved away to distant parts, the Piddocks among them. Farms had changed hands, cottages had been pulled down, and new ones had been built. But Mount Caburn was as it always had been, and as the people came to think it always would be. And still the children kept the custom of going there each new moon to skip. Nobody remembered how this custom had come about, it was too far back in the years. But customs are customs, and the child who could not skip the new moon in on Caburn stayed at home and cried.

Then a new Lord came to the Park; one not born a Lord, who had grown rich in trade, and bought the old estate. Soon after his coming, changes began to take place more violent than the pulling down of cottages. The new Lord began to shut up footpaths and destroy rights of way. He stole the Common rights here and there, as he could. In his greed for more than he had got, he raised rents and pressed the people harder than they could bear. But bad as the high rents were to them, they did not mind these so much as the loss of their old rights. They fought the new Lord, trying to keep what had been theirs for centuries, and sometimes they won the fight, but oftener lost it. The constant quarrels bred a spirit of anger between them and the Lord, and out of hate he was prepared to do whatever he could to spite them.

Amongst the lands over which he exercised a certain power was Caburn. This had been always open to the people, and the Lord determined if he could to close it. Looking up the old deeds, he discovered that, though the Down was his, he was obliged to leave a way upon it by which the people could go from one village to another. For hundreds of years they had made a short cut of it over the top.

The Lord's Lawyer told him that, by the wording of the deeds, he could never stop the people from travelling by way of the Downs.

'Can't I!' snorted the Lord. 'Then at least I will make them travel a long way round!'

And he had plans drawn up to enclose the whole of the top of Caburn, so that nobody could walk on it. This meant that the people must trudge miles round the base, as they passed from place to place. The Lord gave out that he needed Mount Caburn to build great factories on.

The village was up in arms to defend its rights.

'Can he do it?' they asked those who knew; and they were told: 'It is not quite certain, but we fear he can.' The Lord himself was not quite certain either but he went on with his plans, and each new move was watched with anger and anxiety by the villagers. And not only by the villagers; for the fairies saw that their own skipping-ground was threatened. How could they ever skip there again when the grass was turned to cinders, and the new moon blackened by chimney-smoke?

The Lawyer said to the Lord: 'The people will fight you tooth and nail.'

'Let 'em!' blustered the Lord; and he asked uneasily: 'Have they a leg to stand on?'

'Just half a leg,' said the Lawyer. 'It would be as well not to begin building yet, and if you can come to terms with them you'd better.'

The Lord sent word to the villagers that, though he undoubtedly could do what he pleased, he would, out of his good heart, restore to them a footpath he had blocked, if they would give up all pretensions to Caburn.

'Footpath, indeed!' cried stout John Maltman, among his cronies at the Inn. 'What's a footpath to Caburn? Why, our mothers skipped there as children, and our children skip there now. And we hope to see our children's children skip there. If Caburn top be built over, 'twill fair break my little Ellen's heart.'

'Ay, and my Margery's,' said another.

'And my Mary's and Kitty's!' cried a third. Others spoke up, for nearly all had daughters whose joy it was to skip on Caburn at the new moon.

John Maltman turned to their best adviser, who had studied the matter closely, and asked: 'What think ye? Have we a leg to stand on?'

'Only half a one,' said the other. 'I doubt if you can stop him. It might be as well to come to terms.'

'None of his footpaths for us,' swore stout John Maltman. 'We'll fight the matter out.'

So things were left for a little, and each side wondered what the next move would be. Only the people knew in their hearts that they must be beaten in the end and the Lord was sure of his victory. So sure, that he had great loads of bricks ordered; but he did not begin building for fear the people might grow violent, and perhaps burn his ricks and destroy his property. The only thing he did was to put a wire fence round the top of Caburn, and set a keeper there to send the people round it. The people broke the fence in many places, and jumped it, and crawled under it; and as the keeper could not be everywhere at once, many of them crossed the Down almost under his nose.

One evening, just before the new moon was due, Ellen Maltman went into the woods to cry. For she was the best skipper under Mount Caburn, and the thought that she would never skip there again made her more unhappy than she had ever thought she could be. While she was crying in the dark, she felt a hand on her shoulder, and a voice said to her: 'Crying for trouble, my dear? That'll never do!'

The voice might have been the voice of a withered leaf, it was so light and dry; but it was also kind, so Ellen checked her sobs and said: 'It's a big trouble, ma'am, there's no remedy against it *but* to cry.'

'Why, yes, there is,' said the withered voice. 'Ye should skip against trouble, my dear.'

At this Ellen's sobs burst forth anew. 'I'll never skip no more!' she wailed. 'If I can't skip the new moon in on Caburn, I'll never skip no more.'

'And why can't you skip the new moon in on Caburn?' asked the voice.

Then Ellen told her.

After a little pause the voice spoke quietly out of the darkness. 'It's more than you will break their hearts if they cannot skip on Caburn. And it must not be, it must not be. Tell me your name.'

'Ellen Maltman, ma'am, and I do love skipping. I can skip down anybody, ma'am, and they say I skip as never so!'

'They do, do they?' said the withered voice. 'Well, Ellen, run you home and tell them this. They are to go to this Lord and tell him he shall have his way and build on Caburn, if he will first take down the fence and let all who have ever skipped there skip there once more by turns, at the new moon. *All*, mind you, Ellen. And when the last skipper skips the last skip, he may lay his first brick. And let it be written out on paper, and signed and sealed.'

'But ma'am!' said Ellen, wondering.

'No words, child. Do as I tell you.' And the withered voice sounded so compelling that Ellen resisted no more. She ran straight to the village, and told her story to everybody.

At first they could hardly swallow it; and even when they had swallowed it, they said: 'But what's the sense of it?' But Ellen persisted and persisted; something of the spirit of the old voice got into her words, and against their reason the people began to think it was the thing to do. To cut a long story short they sent the message to the Lord next day.

The Lord could scarcely believe his ears. He rubbed his hands, and chortled at the people for fools.

'They've come to terms!' he sneered. 'I shall have the Down, and keep my footpath too. Well, they shall have their Skipping-Party; and the moment it is ended, up go my factories!'

The paper was drawn out, signed by both parties in the presence of witnesses, and duly sealed; and on the night of the new moon, the Lord invited a party of his friends to go with him to Caburn to see the sight.

And what a sight it was for them to see; every little girl in the village was there with her skipping-rope, from the toddlers to those who had just turned up their hair. Nay, even the grown maidens and the young mothers were there; and the very matrons too had come with ropes. Had not they once as children skipped on Caburn? And the message had said 'All.' Yes, and others were there, others they could not see: Andy-Spandy and his fairy team, Heels-o'Lead, Flea-Foot, and all of the rest, were gathered round to watch with bright fierce eyes the last great skipping on their precious ground.

The skipping began. The toddlers first, a skip or so apiece, a stumble, and they fell out. The Lord and his party laughed aloud at the comical mites, and at another time the villagers would have laughed too. But there was no laughter in them tonight. Their eyes were bright and fierce like those of the fairies. After the toddlers the little girls skipped in the order of their ages, and as they got older, the skipping got better. In the thick of the schoolchildren, 'This will take some time,' said the Lord impatiently. And when Ellen Maltman's turn came, and she went into her thousands, he grew restive. But even she, who could skip as never so, tired at last; her foot tripped, and she fell on the ground with a little sob. None lasted even half her time; of those who followed some were better, some were worse, than others; and in the small hours the older women were beginning to take their turn. Few of them kept it up for half a minute; they hopped and puffed bravely, but their skipping days were done. As they had laughed at the babies, so now the Lord's friends jibed at the babies' grandmothers.

'Soon over now,' said the Lord, as the oldest of the women who had come to skip, a fat old dame of sixty-seven, stepped out and twirled her rope. Her foot caught in it; she staggered, dropped the rope, and hid her face in her hands.

'Done!' shouted the Lord; and he brandished at the crowd a trowel and a brick which he had brought with him. 'Clear out, the lot of you! I am going to lay the first brick. The skipping's ended!'

'No, if you please,' said a gentle withered voice, 'it is my turn now.' And out of the crowd stepped a tiny tiny woman, so very old, so very bent and fragile, that she seemed to be no bigger than a little child.

'You!' cried the Lord. 'Who are *you?*'

'My name is Elsie Piddock, if you please, and I am a hundred and nine years old. For the last seventy-nine years I have lived over the border, but I was born in Glynde, and I skipped on Caburn as a child.' She spoke like one in a dream, and her eyes were closed.

'Elsie Piddock! Elsie Piddock!' the name ran in a whisper round the crowd.

'Elsie Piddock!' murmured Ellen Maltman. 'Why, mum, I thought Elsie Piddock was just a tale.'

'Nay, Elsie Piddock was no tale!' said the fat woman who had skipped last. 'My mother Joan skipped with her many a time, and told me tales you never would believe.'

'Elsie Piddock!' they all breathed again; and a wind seemed to fly round Mount Caburn, shrilling the name with glee. But it was no wind, it was Andy-Spandy and his fairy team, for they had seen the skipping-rope in the tiny woman's hands. One of the handles was made of Sugar Candy, and the other was made of French Almond Rock.

But the new Lord had never even heard of Elsie Piddock as a story; so laughing coarsely once again, he said: 'One more bump for an old woman's bones! Skip, Elsie Piddock, and show us what you're worth.'

'Yes, skip, Elsie Piddock,' cried Andy-Spandy and the fairies, 'and show them what you're worth!'

Then Elsie Piddock stepped into the middle of the onlookers, twirled her baby rope over her little shrunken body, and began to skip. And she skipped as NEVER so!

First of all she skipped:

'ANdy SPANdy SUGARdy CANdy,
FRENCH ALmond ROCK!
Breadandbutterforyoursupper'sallyourmother'sGOT!'

And nobody could find fault with her skipping. Even the Lord gasped: 'Wonderful! wonderful for an old woman!' But Ellen Maltman, who *knew*, whispered: 'Oh, mum! 'tis wonderful for *anybody*! And oh mum, do but see—she's skipping in her sleep!'

It was true. Elsie Piddock, shrunk to the size of seven years old, was sound asleep, skipping the new moon in with her baby rope that was up to all the tricks. An hour went by, two hours, three hours. There was no stopping her, and no tiring her. The people gasped, the Lord fumed, and the fairies turned head-over-heels for joy. When morning broke the Lord cried: 'That's enough!'

But Elsie Piddock went on skipping.

'Time's up!' cried the Lord.

'When I skip my last skip, you shall lay your first brick,' said Elsie Piddock.

The villagers broke into a cheer.

'Signed and sealed, my lord, signed and sealed,' said Elsie Piddock.

'But hang it, old woman, you can't go on for ever!' cried the Lord.

'Oh yes, I can,' said Elsie Piddock. And on she went.

At midday the Lord shouted: 'Will the woman never stop?'

'No, she won't,' said Elsie Piddock. And she didn't.

'Then I'll stop you!' stormed the Lord, and made a grab at her.

'Now for a Sly Skip,' said Elsie Piddock, and skipped right through his thumb and forefinger.

'Hold her, you!' yelled the Lord to his Lawyer.

'Now for a High Skip,' said Elsie Piddock, and as the Lawyer darted at her, she skipped right over the highest lark singing in the sun.

The villagers shouted for glee, and the Lord and his friends were furious. Forgotten was the compact signed and sealed—their one thought now was to seize the maddening old woman, and stop her skipping by sheer force. But they couldn't. She played all her tricks on them: High Skip, Slow Skip, Sly Skip, Toe Skip, Long Skip, Fast Skip, Strong Skip, but never Last Skip. On and on and on she went. When the sun began to set, she was still skipping.

'Can we never rid the Down of the old thing?' cried the Lord desperately.

'No,' answered Elsie Piddock in her sleep, 'the Down will never be rid of me more. It's the children of Glynde I'm skipping for, to hold the Down for them and theirs for ever; it's Andy-Spandy I'm skipping for once again, for through him I've sucked sweet all my life. Oh, Andy, even you never knew how long Elsie Piddock could go on skipping!'

'The woman's mad!' cried the Lord. 'Signed and sealed doesn't hold with a madwoman. Skip or no skip, I shall lay the first brick!'

He plunged his trowel into the ground, and forced his brick down into the hole as a token of his possession of the land.

'Now,' said Elsie Piddock, 'for a Strong Skip!'

Right on the top of the brick she skipped, and down underground she sank out of sight, bearing the brick beneath her. Wild with rage, the Lord dived after her. Up came Elsie Piddock skipping blither than ever—but the Lord never came up again. The Lawyer ran to look down the hole; but there was no sign of him. The Lawyer reached his arm down the hole; but there was no reaching him. The Lawyer dropped a pebble down the hole; and no one heard it fall. So strong had Elsie Piddock skipped the Strong Skip.

The Lawyer shrugged his shoulders, and he and the Lord's friends left Mount Caburn for good and all. Oh, how joyously Elsie Piddock skipped then!

'Skip Against Trouble!' cried she, and skipped so that everyone present burst into happy laughter. To the tune of it she skipped the Long Skip, clean out of sight. And the people went home to tea. Caburn was saved for their children, and for the fairies, for ever.

But that wasn't the end of Elsie Piddock; she has never stopped skipping on Caburn since, for Signed and Sealed is Signed and Sealed. Not many have seen her, because she knows all the tricks; but if you go to Caburn at the new moon, you may catch a glimpse of a tiny bent figure, no bigger than a child, skipping all by itself in its sleep, and hear a gay little voice, like the voice of a dancing yellow leaf, singing:

ANdy SPANdy SUGARdy CANdy,
FRENCH ALmond ROCK!
Breadandbutterforyoursupper'sallyourmother'sGOT!'

LUCY BOSTON

The Tiger-Skin Rug

WE really had gone to the view day before the sale at Vale Manor in the hopes of finding some honest chairs and well-made chests of drawers, but from that point of view it was disappointing; the furniture was poor, commonplace stuff. The only interesting feature of the house was the collection of stuffed animals. Big game hunting had been the owner's absorbing passion, for there were horns and antlers, heads and feet of almost every wild beast and several enormous glass cases containing tigers, lions and antelopes that had been mounted with incomparable skill. You stood your stick in an elephant's leg and hung your hat on a stand made out of four Buffalo heads arranged back to back. It was a most imposing piece, and I said, to tease my wife, that I intended to bid for it.

The place looked more like a museum than a sale. Crowds stood gaping at the exhibits but obviously with no intention of buying; though there was a well-stocked wine cellar that might bring many to the actual sale.

In a small room containing a collection of native weapons, the walls bristling with spears, arrows, drums and shields, my wife's eye was taken by a rug of curious and wonderful workmanship. It was composed mainly of a large and very beautiful tiger skin spread fully out, and set into a background of patchwork fur almost as fine as a mosaic; a curving line of flat ivory pieces was cunningly set in to represent its teeth, and its eyes were ringed with white also and stared ferociously. Two skins cut into lifelike silhouettes of monkeys with bright bead eyes were worked in on either side of its head and two young jackals flanked its zig-zag tail.

It was a unique thing, very soft and rich, and I could see at once by my wife's face that she was determined to have it. She is like a spoiled child when she goes shopping and, though I give in to her, I always pretend to the last moment to be obdurate, and she is always taken in. So we were playing out our usual farce when a parson, apparently a guest or next door neighbour for he had no hat on and was drawling along to his companion as one who had known everything intimately, turned his flow of reminiscence towards our rug.

'Ah, yes! dear me!' he said, 'there is something that might interest you; the old Colonel used to be very proud of that; he said it was the finest tiger he ever saw, and he got it single handed without even a beater or gun-boy. The natives would not have anything to do with it because one of their tribesmen had "gone tiger" the week before and they felt superstitious about it. Gone tiger? Oh, yes! Oh, yes! quite common. When a native is turned out of the tribe for some misdeed, or goes mad, or something of that kind, he goes off into the jungle and they say comes back as a tiger to revenge himself. You should hear them beat their gongs when they think there's one about. Shocking! I came across a case when I was at the Mission in Cheieng Kong. The natives say they can tell when it is a tiger-man because the monkeys don't run away from it; they know it's out for man murder and they think themselves safe. That's why he had those monkeys' figures put by its jaws. Yes! rather a boastful idea, I quite agree, these big game hunters get like that. Poor old Colonel! when he was in his cups his boasting was dreadful. Ah me! we are all sinners! He took a dislike to that rug afterwards and had it locked in here. I remember him one night, when he had had too much, standing in here rocking from his heels to his toes and saying, "See, Padre, you can't have too many spears round a tiger." A sad case. Well, he had his good points.'

I had nudged my wife's elbow several times during this dramatic recital for the Parson was obviously enjoying himself. They held up a corner of the rug to examine the workmanship and the beautiful striped golden coat fell into soft moving folds.

I released my wife from her suspense, and we moved off to find someone who would bid for us. I spoke to a burly man in respectable plain clothes, who looked as though he might be a detective or auction-eer's foreman, but he was, he told us, the ex-butler, taking a last look round, and he obligingly offered to pass on to a decent dealer any instructions we cared to give. I gave him my card with 'Lot No. 240, Chinese Tiger Skin with Monkeys' written on it. He read it and handed it back to me.

'Don't you have it, Sir,' he said. 'It's a bad piece of work.'

'What do you mean?' I asked, 'it looks in very good condition.'

'Well, it's had too many stories told about it, and where there's stories there's bother. We have lost good maids over that rug.'

'It did the old Colonel no harm, did it?' said my wife. 'Didn't he die a natural death?'

'Well, if you call it that,' the butler replied. 'A tiger finished him in the end. He couldn't keep away from them; he went back to Mandalay.'

'Well, I am much obliged to you,' I said, 'all the same,' and I gave him my card again and two halfcrowns.

'As you like, Sir,' he said moving off.

In due course a long yielding bundle was delivered to our little station.

'What's this?' said a porter jocosely, as he lugged it out of the van in jerks. 'A body?'

It was lashed with ropes in the oddest way.

My wife and I later unpacked it together, pleased with the anticipation of trying it about the house. I must say I wondered when we first spread it out whether we had not made a mistake in purchasing it. It looked out of place in our very ordinary house, for I was neither a sportsman, nor had my wife any Chelsea notions of decoration. She is a comfortable, comfort-loving woman and all fur appealed to her, whether it was an opossum coat collar for herself or bedside sheepskin mats for the children's feet. This rug she intended for her own room which was large and rather badly lit for its size, the low square windows facing into the wood which surrounded the house at no great distance on three sides.

She set to work at once to adapt the room to her new purchase; the beds had to be pushed aside to make more floor space.

'Something will have to go, that's all,' she said as she surveyed the new effect, but actually all that she ultimately removed was a reproduction of Botticelli's 'Madonna and Child' which had previously always hung over our little girl's bed in its old position. We have one child of our own aged four, whom we named Julia, and my first wife had died leaving me a stepson, Brian, who being deprived of both his natural parents had been adopted by us and took the place of the son of the house. He was now fifteen, a handsome boy, and we were very fond of him.

Our house was situated well away from any main road and at a little distance from the village, so our natural neighbours were foxes, pheasants, owls, woodpigeons and squirrels. Jays and badgers were not uncommon, for the coverts were high with bracken and little trodden, and the hollows dense with willow and willow-herb.

It was the beginning of a sudden July heatwave which grew daily hotter and I was thankful coming back from town in the evening for this cool and informal retreat, where the only urban intrusion was a motor-van from a local store, and an ice-cream cart that had weekly appointments with the scattered farm children and passed our gate every Wednesday ringing a hand-bell.

In this unfrequented spot imagine our surprise one evening when we heard the wheezing and strident notes of a popular air suddenly start up, and there came into sight along our drive, that figure of Victorian childhood, an organ-grinder with his monkey.

Julia ran out full tilt and then stood hesitant in front of him for a shy stare, while the man, who looked like a Malay, turned his machine more rapidly and shifted his wandering gaze up at the windows with that meaningless and idiotic grin so often seen on these hapless aliens.

My wife came out with a banana for the child to give to the monkey. Julia, upbraided by Brian for cowardice, presently advanced to within reach of the chain and held out the banana which the monkey seized, and then, with inverted gratitude, turned and bit her sharply in the finger. My wife darted forward with her hand upraised to strike it, but it took a bound on to the Malay's shoulder and off again; the collar round its waist broke and away it went with its tail in the air across the lawn and up the nearest tree.

Julia, thoroughly hurt in her feelings of right and wrong, was hurried indoors for an application of iodine, while Brian, myself and our gardener, Bibby, helped to coax and chase the monkey. It evaded all our devices and chattered malignantly at us from tree to tree as it worked its way deeper into the wood.

Eventually I had to order the Malay off the premises; we had dismissed him politely at first with a glass of beer and half a crown to console him, but he understood so little of what we said that in the end I had to resort to threatening attitudes most distasteful to me, but I now felt less confidence in his imbecile looks. He was probably a rascal and practised this trick in every country place, coming back at night with the excuse of looking for his monkey and taking away with him whatever it and he could lay their hands on.

He went at last, and as he turned into the lane he shifted his organ on to his back, and intoning some native chant, he punctuated his shuffling steps with rhythmic leaps and stamping, and so passed out of sight. It occurred to me to go in and ring up the police to warn them of a possible pilferer, but perhaps he considered the loss of his monkey had ruined his trade, for he did not pass through the village and no-one else in the district saw him.

The antics of this departing figure with a load of mischief on its back kept recurring as a subject of conversation during the evening. Brian gave a spirited imitation of it to Julia when she was being dried after her bath. My wife said, 'Don't do that, Brian, you'll give the child nightmares,' but she

always said 'Don't do that' to everything; it was the regular accompaniment to our laughter and quite ineffectual. I think often she hardly knew
when she said it herself; but Julia was far from having nightmares; she
played monkey sitting on Brian's shoulder and taking great leaps from
there to the springy bed and exhausted herself with peals of laughter;
then with a biscuit in each hand for her supper she dumped herself down
on the new rug and, pleased with its softness, put her head down to turn
somersaults; the yellow curls on her little head fell forward and lay softly
mingling with the fur so near them in colour. If my wife had bought it
especially to shew off Julia's childish beauty she could not have done
better.

Julia had paused in the first position of the somersault, her eye
attracted by the tiger's ivory teeth over which she began to run her
finger, but my wife snatched her hand away saying 'Don't do that' at
which we all laughed, and she blushed, and said she supposed she was
still thinking of the monkey.

We were all late that night, for there can be few things like a monkey
hunt for wasting time. We were not ready for dinner before nine and it
was nearly twelve when I said to my wife 'Good Heavens! look at the
time.' I yawned and stretched myself and rose to see to the locking up,
when the door bell clanged loudly. I went to open it expecting perhaps
the night constable, but a tall stranger stood there, who, raising his hat
and speaking in an unusually deep and vibrant tone, addressed me in a
manner that left no doubt of his breeding. He apologised for disturbing
me at that time of night, but might he use the telephone as his car had
completely broken down. Our telephone was in the sitting room and so
I led the way there. My wife looked at us enquiringly and smiled
without waiting for my explanation in her habitual frank and friendly
way.

The stranger was dressed with distinction, even elegance, and had
something of military correctness in his bearing. He bowed to my wife
with renewed apologies and while I stood with the receiver at my ear I
listened to his explanation and took stock of his appearance. It was both
striking and vaguely familiar, and I felt it from the start to be as attractive
as it was in some way repellent; and this was my wife's first impression
too, as she told me later. His physique was magnificent and his profile
might have come off an Etruscan Vase so pure was the line from brow
to nose; but his eyes had a cat-like upward tilt at the outer corners and
his sleek hair was in even ripples of the darkest red, a violent colour,
more animal than human. A white streak running backwards through it
from the temple, relic of some former wound or shock, made his head

all the more arresting. Under his short red moustache his mouth had curves that were not reassuring, but when he smiled in reply to my wife's sympathy he drew the corners of his lips back over his teeth in a way that was peculiar and taking.

He was on his way to some friends about 40 miles distant, had been held up by constant engine trouble and now could get no further. He wished to get a taxi to take him to the nearest hotel. But here his bad luck followed him for I could not get any answer from the Exchange for all my ringing, and was wondering how much help one ought to offer to a total stranger of intriguing appearance, when it leaked out in conversation that the family he was on his way to visit were well known to us by name, friends of friends, and at once the whole position was altered. So strong is the social feeling among educated people in the counties that a familiar name acts like a password.

We felt now that it was too late for him to move on anywhere that night and my wife pressed him to let us put him up. I poured him out a whiskey, and as I considered the nuisance it would be to me if I had to get out my car and drive him to the nearest inn, I became as hospitable as she. He demurred very much at putting us to such inconvenience but in the end he acknowledged his gratitude, and when we had pushed his car into shelter and he had hung up his hat and coat in the lobby, we settled down again for another half hour in the new role of hosts and guest. He was at once at his ease and his deep purring voice and alert politeness were pleasant to hear and see. There was a deprecating quality in his attention as if conscious he was not acceptable to all, and yet I felt he was a man who could rarely have been unsuccessful. I judged him to be of frank intention and I enjoyed his presence. I have described him perhaps at greater length than you have patience for, but I tried that night in vain to analyse the very strong impression he made on me.

As we rose to say goodnight my wife reminded him that we did not yet know his name. 'Dr Sathanos,' he replied with a bold frank smile at her as if aware that the extraordinary name fitted him too well. 'A very old name; my father was a Greek and my mother Scotch.' He passed his hand apologetically over his hair with a wry look.

We gave him a bedroom on the ground floor, the only one at liberty in the holidays, and my wife warned him jokingly to close his windows if he was afraid of monkeys; but he replied that it only needed that to make him feel quite at home, he having only just returned from Rangoon.

But it was my wife who on opening her sleepy eyes in the morning saw the monkey squatting on her new rug, briskly turning itself about and clicking with satisfaction and interest. She started up and shooed angrily, but it did not seem frightened. It rose and walked deliberately towards the window its arms hanging and its wicked little face grinning back at us, then slowly swinging itself up on to the sill it sat there a moment, gave a low squawk as if to say it would soon return, and sidled quietly out into the creepers.

I have little time for breakfast on weekdays, and when one is swallowing one's coffee too hot, now or never, manners are reduced to their minimum. But Dr Sathanos with his strange and legendary face made breakfast an art, and rose so easily and so often to wait on us all, and had so many ways of considering everybody that I felt a boor beside him. He talked with charming equality to the children, and Brian was soon entirely under the spell both of his powerful physique and of his polish and experience. As for Julia she did nothing but stare at him, her eating and drinking was mechanical and unconscious. He passed behind her chair as he laid a plate on the sideboard and touched her sovereign gold hair, remarking in his deep vibrant voice 'That is the colour I love more than any other'.

I said goodbye to him in a hurry and commended him to my wife's attention. When I returned that evening he was still there; his car could not be ready for a day or two and his friends, it seemed, had some domestic trouble and could no longer receive him, so my wife had asked him to stay till his car was ready, because he was company for me and so good to Brian. She was a great talker, never so happy as when there was something to say.

Young Dr Wainwright had been in for a drink and a chat and had said there was an outbreak of tropical fever on the river side and warned her to keep the children away from the Cinema. He was worried because he hadn't much experience of it. He is a clever young man and always admits what he doesn't know, but wasn't it an extraordinary coincidence, quite providential, do you know Dr Sathanos is a specialist in just that sort of thing and so kindly offered to give him any help he could. Dr Wainwright was calling for him the next day. Of course one couldn't help thinking of that monkey; nobody knows what ship it came off or anything.

I asked her where everybody was now, for we were having tea in a quiet tête-à-tête, all the windows open wide because of the great heat and not a sound came through but the ring-doves cooing.

Why, she replied, Bibby had come to say there was a circus going past down by the priory gates and Dr Sathanos had strolled down with the children. Should we go and meet them?

We walked along down a little bracken track waving away the flies that rose in hordes, and bye and bye saw Brian swinging on a gate and Dr Sathanos with Julia on his shoulder. Our neighbours, the Bensons, were there too with their enormous dog, a cross between an Alsatian and a Great Dane and a really majestic creature. Piebald ponies were trotting past, a camel and some tiny donkeys. As one of these tried to turn in at the gate Brian asked the man in charge where were the Elephants.

'They've gone by the other way,' he replied. 'Funny thing, we had trouble with them a while back; something in the wind they didn't like and we had to humour them; never known it happen before.'

At this moment the children were distracted from their disappointment by a menagerie van carrying jackals who, as it drew level, suddenly set up a commotion. They thrust themselves against the bars and flinging back their heads the whole lot yelped. The procession had come to a momentary halt and their cage was facing Dr Sathanos, towards whom all their outcry seemed directed. I can see him now standing there chuckling in his deep throat, the corners of his mouth drawn back in a smile which shewed all his teeth, and they were sharp and even.

'Why do they howl like that?' said Julia, who had turned rigid and slipped down off his shoulder to come to me.

'Perhaps they are home-sick,' said Dr Sathanos; 'it's a long time since they followed a hunter,' and he began to spin jungle tales to Brian's ever open ears.

It grew no cooler even by bed time and as I lay awake disturbed by the high treble of the mosquitoes, I heard the wood outside as restless as I: there seemed a perpetual rustle without enough wind to make it; birds would start twittering from their sleep here and there; a nearby jay woke me as I was dozing, then a rabbit screamed—poor little devil, I always hate to hear them—and every leaf outside the window seemed to itch.

Another day as sultry followed. I hate heat myself but our guest came down almost purring with health, cool and obliging as ever. It is no use judging a man by his face or saying his mouth is coarse and bitter when every action he does denies it. He was certainly an original personality, a great character and a really good sort.

We returned from town together, he having been to the fever hospital, and tea was laid in the garden. As we were eating it Brian saw our friend the monkey peering at us from the trees; it ran along a spreading branch which hung over the lawn and great was our surprise to see it had found a companion. The two of them advanced by stages to Dr Sathanos' chair where he sat with his back to them, but seeing us all pointing he looked back and tipped his chair until he could throw one of them a biscuit which it nimbly caught.

'Oh, don't do that,' said my wife, 'they might come again and give us all tropical fever.'

'I beg your pardon,' said the Doctor, 'but if you don't like them we will soon get rid of them, as we learnt to do in the jungle.'

He turned round and rested his hands on the back of the chair, leaning towards the monkeys like a great quadruped, and made a face at them in the horribly realistic manner of a snarling tiger. The monkeys went off in great bounds chattering their teeth at him and Brian laughed uproariously, but Julia, who had run round behind the Doctor's chair in order to get a better view, received this grimace at close quarters and was terrified almost into hysterics. The Doctor tried, with the rest of us, to pacify her, but about his smile perhaps there lingered still in her fancy a trace of fang and she screamed afresh at every advance.

Of course I know that when the heat passes a certain temperature in this country we all get snappy. My wife and I were vexed with Julia and annoyed with each other, but, in the long run, it was the monkeys who got most of the blame for this unfortunate incident. Where on earth could a second one have come from? It increased my wife's fear of tropical fever in as much as illogically she was convinced that an unknown source must be infected. So in the evening when Dr Sathanos had retired to his quiet bedroom to write a report of Dr Wainwright's cases I went into the wood with an old army rifle, the only weapon I had, intending to shoot them.

It was an amazing evening for England, the sky was bright apricot and the level sun filled the wood with stripes and bars of shadow and glare. The midges rose and sank in columns and everything was amazingly silent. I really had quite a jungle feeling as I stalked this strange game, and was completing the circle of my stealthy round near our own gate when at last I saw the pair of them, their arms encircling a big bough and their cheeks laid sideways against it. The light was bad, but I was taking careful aim when a rustle in my wife's bamboo hedge behind me made them look in my direction and sidle to the safer side of the tree. I should have said that it was a large dog's tail I heard brushing backwards and forwards, but, if so, it was a very guilty dog, for, as I swore in my vexation, the sound withdrew from me. The bamboos quivered and stood upright again and nothing broke cover.

I knew I could never get those wily little devils now so I turned in at the gate. Bibby was watering his geraniums by the side door.

'Does the Bensons' dog ever poach up here?' I asked.

He said, well, he couldn't exactly say he had ever seen it to be really sure, but he had seen something that was certainly very big and might have been him down in the willow covert the night before, when he came to look at his traps, but it is so full of willow weed, he said, you couldn't really say, not to be sure, when it was a question of neighbours. But I was vexed by losing my shot and answered that I should want him to take a note down to them in the morning.

That night was the first night on which we heard the howling. Everybody knows how a cat can make one's spine creep, but this was far worse and all the more eerie for being low and searching. It woke us both up; my wife sat bolt upright in bed.

'What's that?'

'It can only be a cat,' I replied; 'what else is there?'

She insisted that I should get up and look. I pulled up the blind; the moon, which was near the full, streamed in and fell on my wife's scared face, and cast a queer light on the tiger skin mottled by the shadows of the wisteria sprays which fringed the windows. I looked out and saw the lawn like satin, and the fir wood that stuck its crests into the sky like so many jet black spears, and stretched its shadow on the grass before it. Below the window each silver slab of the crazy paving was clearly outlined and every little plant had its mat of shadow. All was still and empty.

I turned back to get into bed and as, in crossing the floor, I put my bare foot on the tiger skin I swore and stumbled forward. There must have been a mouse under it for it moved as if it were alive.

'I wish that damned cat was in here instead of outside,' I said; 'the place is alive with mice.'

I was annoyed with my wife for making too much of a tale about that cat, for what else can it possibly have been? I could see Sathanos was laughing at her; his smile was too polite to be spontaneous, but, I felt, too bold to be quite polite.

After all she was his hostess; I flattered myself I was rather his sort, we had a great deal in common, but you have to know a man very well before you laugh at his wife. That grin of his shewing all his teeth was unnecessary, and it rather jarred; besides, though things looked different in the morning, I didn't like that howling myself, either that night or the next; in fact it was abominable, and the more I thought the less I liked it. I could only think of two causes; either it was a natural sound, made by an animal, in which case it was certainly one I did not care to have about, or else it was a supernatural one; it was diabolical enough, God knows, but a sane family man can't come down to breakfast and say that he thinks the devil's in the garden. I could see my wife had thoughts she didn't like to say and, of course, if she had said what I was thinking I should have answered with sarcasm, so she kept her thoughts to herself; but she was jumpy and said 'Don't do that' oftener than usual, even when Julia ran across the lawn.

The next thing was that the cook left, refusing to give either reason or notice, and my wife was much upset at such a contretemps with a visitor in the house whom she so much wished to please. But as he had been most appreciative of her regime before, so he became the easiest to please now. Camp life suited him down to the ground, he said, and insisted on trying his hand as cook. Brian followed him, for the first time in his life seeing the kitchen as an adventure.

I wrote a rather strong note to the Bensons, asking them to keep their dog up, and took it upstairs to my wife to see if she thought they would be offended. It was a Saturday and she was counting the sheets with the housemaid.

'If you please, Ma'm,' the girl was saying, 'might we have Bibby in to put a piece of felt along the bottom of your door? There must be a draught blowing in, because your new rug won't lie flat. I can't keep it straight. It gave me such a start when I went in last night to see it heave up like.'

'My good girl,' I interrupted sharply, handing my wife the note, 'it's as hot as an oven and there's no wind at all. Do talk sense.'

'Well, sir,' she finished lamely, 'I didn't say wind, I said draught.'

'I don't think I like it in here anyway,' said my wife. 'Not this hot weather—you don't want fur in your room. Take it down with you, Keith, if you're going, and put it over the couch in the sitting room.'

I did so, and sent Bibby off to the Bensons with my note. The sun was torrid. For nearly a week it had been getting steadily hotter. After lunch even Sathanos seemed to feel it, though not uncomfortably.

He settled himself down on the fur covered couch full length with his hands behind his head, the embodiment of strength and ease, and his deep magnetic voice was most soothing.

'Julia must go for her rest,' said my wife—the invariable signal for disturbance—and Julia of course protested.

'Let her stay down and lie here,' said Sathanos drowsily, rising from the couch and leaving an almost perfect mould of his head, shoulders and hips in the soft rug.

He bent down with a strange smile to pick her up and lay her in his place, but Julia turned mulish. She didn't want to lie down at all, she wouldn't be put on the couch; she tugged with sudden shyness at the wrist by which he held her. Meanwhile Brian, intolerant at the disturbance and annoyed to see his idol occupied with a baby, bounced on to the vacant couch and wrapping the rug round him, said provokingly 'Right. Then you can go upstairs. It will be all the better for us, we shan't have to talk baby talk.'

At this point something rather shocking occurred. Dr Sathanos, as if giving way to an uncontrollable fit of irritation, crouched down and putting his face close to Julia's, directed at her his beastly murderous snarl. Perhaps it was only meant as an object lesson and a moral against naughtiness, or perhaps only as a bachelor's clumsy joke, but it looked like real malice and made a most unpleasant impression.

Her mother with a red face snatched her up as she fought for breath in choking terror, and hurried her out of the room.

'I'm sorry you did that,' I said to the doctor, who had walked to the mantelpiece and turned his back on us. Every man is touchy about his daughters, and I felt quite outraged.

'Camp jokes don't go down in the nursery, I'm afraid,' he answered with a shrug; 'I apologise.'

He lit himself a cigarette and in the mirror I saw his pointed fingernails silhouetted against the window, and his slanting eyes fixed darkly on the unconscious reflection of Brian wrapped in the tiger skin.

I chiefly remember the rest of the day for the heat. There was no respite from it. The Doctor had atoned for his lapse of temper by doing more than his share of the work, and before long my wife was smiling her gratitude.

How could one not like him for his jovial adaptability? He was an amiable and proficient cook and butler, his footfall as silent as a native's. As the sultry day drew to a close, more and more his tall figure and enigmatical vitality dominated the house, and more and more a dread and presentiment closed in upon us with the night. Brian particularly seemed restless and wan, especially when the Doctor was absent. I remember we teased him for it.

In bed my wife talked and turned, wanted me to throw back the blankets, alter the blinds, open the door, anything but settle to sleep. I knew quite well what it was that kept her in suspense. I rather thought I heard a slight noise downstairs too, and I determined to keep watch; so lifting Julia into my wife's bed—an instinctive action, there was no sense in it—I slipped between the blind and the window, armed with my rifle.

The moon was at the full, riding among high clouds that travelled slowly on the hot wind; it blew in gusts through the window. Two owls called and answered across the garden, their ghostly too-whoo's tracing the direction of their flitting. All else was silent, and set as if for a crisis.

Frequent meteors fled across the sky, their journey never finished. The leaves rustled in my ears and a spider's thread trailed across my face. Suddenly a Jay's harsh note rang out across the wood, tearing the silence with warning. We knew the signal, and I waited in agonising tension, for what seemed an age; and still too soon that wild and howling cry swelled out from somewhere close below the window—enough to draw the very soul out of a man, and my heart stopped beating when I heard it. Again and again it came, from here and there, and presently I realised that a slight figure had come out on to the lawn and was standing alone, the moonlight falling full on his face and rumpled hair. It was Brian, walking slowly in a dazed way, and looking helplessly round as if someone had been calling him. I leant out to shout to him, but he seemed not to hear; he had started back a step and was staring as if fascinated into the bushes below me. Now he turned and began to run, looking backwards towards the house as the object of his terror now drew its long body out of the shadows. Two or three relentless bounds across the lawn overtook him, and with an infernal cry it bore him down. I fired convulsively. Cry and shot re-echoed through the wood and the heaving mass was still.

My wife lay sobbing through her chattering teeth as I rushed out of the room, stumbling down the stairs in the dark till I stopped to put my hand out to feel for the electric switch at the bottom. Then I saw with a shock of new fear that I had almost run into a silent unexpected presence, for the moon shone through the fanlight in the hall, and fell on the red hair and pockmarked face of Dr Sathanos bent close to mine, his lips drawn back nearly to his ears in a hateful smile at my undisguised fear.

'Sathanos!' I shouted as I switched on the light—but there was no one there.

'Sathanos! Sathanos! What a name to echo down one's hall in the dead of night! But no one came. I turned on all the lights and ran from room to room, but his had a disused look, and all were empty. Outside I saw Bibby, roused no doubt by my shot, and hurrying out from his cottage. He was on the lawn before me. He looked strangely at me as I came up, and I saw that what lay at his feet was the tiger-skin rug, wet with dew, and under it we found the body of Brian, dead, with a bullet-wound through his head.

It was days after this tragedy before I spoke to my wife of Dr Sathanos' disappearance, but she too looked queerly at me and seemed to shrink from me, as if I had said something unforgivable or opened one of those subjects whose existence can never be acknowledged.

WILLIAM PÈNE DU BOIS

Elisabeth the Cow Ghost

IN a town in Switzerland lived a man named Paul who had a calf named Elisabeth.

Elisabeth was a cream-coloured calf and everybody who saw her would say, 'What a gentle calf! What dreamy eyes!'

And when she grew older into a big cream-coloured cow, everybody who saw her would say, 'Such a gentle cow! And what dreamy eyes!'

And when she grew very old into an aged cream-coloured cow, everybody who saw her would say, 'What a gentle old cow! And what beautiful dreamy old eyes!'

UNTIL

Elisabeth grew tired of being called so gentle and became quite angry.

After a while she grew awfully old and was ready to die, but just before she died, she heard Paul say, 'Isn't it a shame? She is such a gentle cow with such dreamy eyes!'

This made Elisabeth so mad that she decided to come back in the form of a ghost after she died to show everybody how fierce she really was.

She died the next morning and Paul felt awfully sad. He was so sad that he almost forgot his birthday which was only three days off.

Suddenly Paul had an idea. 'I shall have a big birthday party,' said he, 'and invite all my friends and have a big celebration.'

He hoped this way to forget Elisabeth who made him feel so sad.

That night Paul sat up very late thinking about his party. Suddenly he heard a strange noise in the dining-room. He ran downstairs and found the ghost of a cow floating over the dining-room table.

Then he heard the ghost speak. It said, 'I am the ghost of a fierce cow. I shall come and haunt you and scare you every night.'

But Paul looked at it carefully and said, 'Oh, cow ghost, I can see by your gentle look that you are the ghost of poor Elisabeth, the most gentle cow that ever lived.'

At this it was so mad that it floated very fast out of the window, mooing loudly.

The next morning, Paul went to see his friends Yvonne, Jacques and Claude in a nearby village.

He asked them to his party which was now only two days away. They all said they would come so he went home and soon it was night.

That night at the same time as the night before he heard a strange noise in the living-room. He ran downstairs and found the ghost of a cow with a big hood over its head and a great spear on its tail.

It was floating over the mantelpiece. It said, 'I am the ghost of the fiercest cow that ever existed. I shall haunt you and scare you day and night.'

But Paul looked at it carefully and said, 'I can see by your cream-coloured body that you are the ghost of poor Elisabeth, the most gentle cow I have ever known.'

At this it was so angry that it floated with great speed through a crack in the wall and disappeared, mooing and sobbing very sadly.

The next day Paul went to a town which was many miles away. There he saw his friends Pierre, Suzanne and Jeanne and invited them to his party which was to be the next day. He then returned home, arriving late at night.

When he entered the house he heard strange noises in the kitchen so he ran in and found the ghost of a cow. It was all covered with sheets, except for little holes for its eyes to see through, and it was floating over the kitchen stove.

Then he heard the ghost speak. It said, 'I am the ghost of a cow so fierce that even as a calf I was feared for miles around.'

But Paul looked at it with great care and said, 'I see by your dreamy eyes that you are the ghost of poor, poor Elisabeth, the most gentle, most kind and playful cow that ever grazed in Switzerland.'

At this it snorted, mooed loudly, sobbed sadly and disappeared through a very small hole down the sink.

The next day there was a big party and Yvonne, Claude, Pierre, Jacques, Suzanne and Jeanne all were there.

Everybody had a wonderful time until late at night
WHEN
SUDDENLY
there was a strange noise in the kitchen and then it moved to the living-room, and in the living-room there were grunts, snorts and moo sounds.

Claude was puzzled.
Suzanne was frightened.

Pierre was worried.
Yvonne was curious.
Jacques was startled.
Jeanne was afraid.

But Paul was all these things and also awfully angry because it was his birthday party.

And then an extraordinary looking ghost entered. It was all covered with sheets, with a hood over its eyes and a spear on its tail, and it snorted very loudly.

It floated over the table and said, 'I am the ghost of a cow famous for fierceness and cruelty. I shall haunt and scare you all every moment of your lives.'

At this everybody was so scared that they all ran away in all directions, yelling and screaming. They went home feeling very frightened.

Paul was afraid to go home because he was afraid of this terrifying ghost.

He finally walked up to the house and peeked in one window, and then in all the other windows, and seeing no ghost he went in and cautiously went to bed.

He was just going to sleep when he heard a soft mooing downstairs. At this he was furious, so furious that he grabbed a big stick and decided to beat up whatever he met. He ran downstairs, threw open the door, put on the lights, and yelled in his deepest voice, 'Who goes there?'

But there before him was floating the ghost of the good cow Elisabeth. Then he heard the ghost speak. It said, 'It was I who scared you tonight, Paul. Did I really scare you?'

'Yes,' said Paul.

'Did I *really* scare you?' said Elisabeth.

'You certainly did,' said Paul.

'Then I am awfully sorry,' said Elisabeth, 'and I shall never do it again, never never again.'

And before Paul could say a thing, it floated out of the window and disappeared into the night.

And this was because Elisabeth was really a very gentle cow with very dreamy eyes.

R O B E R T   B R I G H T

Georgie

IN a little village there stood a little house which belonged to Mr and Mrs Whittaker. Up in the little attic of this little house there lived a little ghost. His name was Georgie. Every night at the same time he gave the loose board on the stairs a little creak. And the parlour door a little squeak. And then Mr and Mrs Whittaker knew it was time to go to bed. And Herman, the cat, knew it was time to prowl. And Miss Oliver, the owl, she knew it was time to wake up and say, 'Whoo-oo-oo!'

And so it went, with everything as it should be, until Mr Whittaker took it into his head to hammer a nail into the loose board on the stairs. And to oil the hinges of the parlour door. And so the stairs wouldn't creak anymore. And the door wouldn't squeak anymore. And Mr and Mrs Whittaker didn't know when it was time to go to bed anymore. And Herman, the cat, didn't know when it was time to begin to prowl anymore. And poor Miss Oliver, she didn't know when to wake up anymore and went on sleeping. And Georgie sat up in the attic and moped.

That was a fine how-do-you-do!

Pretty soon, though, Georgie decided to find some other house to haunt. But although he ran to this house and then to that house, each house already had a ghost.

The only house in the whole village which didn't have a ghost was Mr Gloam's place. But that was so awfully gloomy! The big door *groaned* so! And the big stairway *moaned* so! And besides, Mr Gloam himself was such a crotchety old man, he came near to frightening Georgie half to death.

So Georgie ran away to a cow-barn where there lived a harmless cow. But the cow paid no attention to Georgie. She just chewed her cud all the time, and it wasn't much fun.

Meanwhile, a lot of time went by and it rained a good deal. And during the winter it snowed to beat the band. And out at the cow-barn Georgie was terribly cold and uncomfortable.

BUT what with the dampness from the rain and the coldness from the snow, something happened to that board on the Whittaker stairs and to the hinges on the Whittaker parlour door.

It was Herman who discovered it and told Miss Oliver. And she woke up with a start. Miss Oliver flew right over to the barn to tell Georgie that the board on the stairs was loose again, and that the hinges on the parlour door were rusty again.

What glad tidings that was for Georgie! He ran home lickety-split.

And so, at the same old time the stairs creaked again. And the parlour door squeaked again. And Mr and Mrs Whittaker knew when it was time to go to sleep again. And Herman knew when to begin to prowl again. And as for Miss Oliver, she knew when it was time to wake up again and say 'Whoo-oo-oo!'

Thank goodness!

DAVID SEVERN

All in the Night's Work

'I DON'T mind *what* you say,' Clare insisted. 'The place is haunted! Nobody's lived there since the Jennings left.'

'Too big,' said her brother. 'Who wants a house that size, nowadays?'

'I don't *care*! Whatever you say, you wouldn't spend a night there, so why not believe me?'

'Because I don't believe in ghosts,' said Frank, flatly. 'And no more does Tony. Do you?'

'Well,' I hedged, 'I'm not sure.'

'Oh, yes, you are,' said Frank, making up my mind for me. 'All tommy-rot. You've never seen one, have you?'

I had to shake my head.

'Give Tony a chance,' Clare said, and I felt her eyes on me. 'I believe he thinks there's something in it.' And then, as I made no reply, she turned to her brother. 'You haven't answered my question, anyway. You're not afraid, are you?'

'Afraid of what? Of spending a night at the Manor? Of course not. But what a mad idea!'

'Why?' inquired Clare sweetly. 'Because of the ghost?'

Frank exploded. 'Look here, what's all this? Some scheme of yours and Tony's? What's the game, eh? D'you think you're going to get me . . .'

'I think you'll have to, now,' said Clare. 'Or admit the place is haunted. You can see he doesn't want to,' she added triumphantly, for my benefit. 'Not one little bit. I must say I wouldn't care to face the ghost myself.'

Frank turned and put his elbows on the mantelshelf. He looked down on us, his face flushed.

'You know it's nothing to do with that,' he said. 'But a whole night in an empty house, beastly uncomfortable and dirty . . .'

Clare leaned back in her chair and laughed.

'About the craziest way of spending a night you could think of,' Frank continued, his voice edging over into anger. 'If you want me to go, you'll have to come too. One or other of you!'

'All right! I'll go with him,' I said, struggling to sit up in my chair. 'I'll spend a night with Frank at the Manor.'

I wondered, afterwards, what had made me say it. I think I sensed that Clare was set on taking her brother down a peg or two. And then, of course, I wanted badly to win her praise; to do something she would admire. I certainly succeeded in this and for the moment the price was easy enough. Later on that same night I realised, a great deal more clearly, what I had let myself in for.

As soon as Frank was convinced that I was serious and meant to force the issue, he settled down with typical thoroughness to plan the night's work. Since I was going to share the hardships he soon stopped grumbling about them, but wherever he could he made things awkward. To-night it had to be. No postponement would suit him. 'Let's get the ridiculous business over and done with,' was his point of view. 'No use putting it off.' And so we went upstairs and wriggled into extra jerseys and muffled ourselves up to the eyes in scarves and greatcoats. 'No central heating at the Manor,' as Frank put it. And the December night was cold; not far from freezing.

Now that it came to the point, Clare didn't want us to go. 'You'll keep together, won't you? And do be careful.' She was getting herself quite worked up.

'We'll do no such thing!' exclaimed Frank. 'We're out to lay the ghost—or the rumours of a ghost. We'll keep watch in different parts of the house. That widens our chance of seeing it!'

I thought this was sheer bravado, just to impress his sister. I might have known that Frank usually meant what he said. Clare did her best to dissuade him, but of no avail, and ten minutes after saying good night to her we were passing through the Manor gates. Our shoes crunched on the gravel and the park spread into misty dimness on each side of us, gently rolling and faintly silvered under the moon. We seemed outrageously conspicuous, striding up the drive as if we owned the place. We were trespassing, of course. I mentioned this to Frank, but he only laughed. 'Who's going to mind?' he said.

'But Frank, how are we going to get into the house?' I had suddenly realised that we were not coming armed with the key of the front door!

'Wait and see,' he grinned.

Dimly, the long shape of the Manor formed in front of us, unsubstantial as stage scenery. As we approached nearer, tiny blades of moonlight glanced from the upper windows; blank black panes staring at nothing. Once across the terrace, the pillars of the vast portico towered over us like smooth beech trunks. I had not realised how big the place was.

'This way,' Frank murmured, and I think he, too, was overawed by the size, the stillness of the great house.

We crept along close to the wall, until Frank stopped by one of the tall, narrow windows looking out on to a sunken stone court that once, I suppose, had been a rose garden. I heard the small click as he opened his penknife. He stooped, his bulk covering his actions, but my heart began to race with powerful excitement. A grating noise was followed by the stealthy squeak of a window pushed up inch by inch. There was no need for such caution, but I would defy anyone in our position to act noisily or with less care. Ducking his head, Frank wormed through the opening, and I followed him. A moment later we were standing together inside the Manor.

'Got your torch?'

I nodded, and felt the reassuring shape of it in my pocket. Frank flashed his own around the dark, hollow shell of the room and took a creaking step or two across the floor-boards. Then he turned, as if to shut the window. That was more than I could bear.

'Leave it open,' I exclaimed. 'We may want to get out of here in a hurry.'

He looked at me oddly, and laughed—not very convincingly I thought. 'We're not leaving till the morning,' he said. 'But have it your own way. Let's take a look round.'

The great rooms and halls were vast caverns in the semi-darkness. Our quiet steps echoed through them, noisily hollow, and our slightest exchange of whispers seemed to reach to the farthest extremities. The musty smell of the place began to sicken me. I thought of the cheerful, warm room we had left; armchairs drawn up to the fire. Why couldn't I have kept quiet? We might have been there now! Or settling into comfortable beds for a good night's sleep.

Frank took it for granted that we were to watch in different parts of the house. In the end he decided to post himself in the passage between two of the larger downstairs rooms, while I had to watch the great hall and the staircase, a distance away from him of about twenty yards. Though a corner of wall hid us, one from the other, we would be able to call out and be heard without difficulty. Frank was rather scornful about these precautions, but he accepted them readily enough. I believe, if I had pressed him hard, he would have agreed to stay with me.

'Well, I'm going to try and get some sleep,' he declared. 'If the ghost wants to be seen, he'll have to wake me up. *Lot of tommy-rot!*' I heard him mutter this last under his breath as we parted and walked to our stations, and envied him his complete assurance.

I reached the entrance to the great hall and sat myself down on the dusty floor, leaning back against the door-post. The boards were hard— I was to feel them a great deal harder as the hours passed—and I heard Frank shuffling about round the corner and finally settling himself.

'All right?' he called, and I answered and said that I was. And then followed silence, if you can call by this name an innumerable number of infinitesimal sounds.

I suppose our ears, in a long and unbroken period of hush, become vastly more sensitive than usual and register smaller and smaller noises. At any rate, as the moments went by the complete quiet of the house was constantly broken, sometimes violently interrupted, by sounds that raised the prickles on the back of my neck. And it was not only the mice. Boards creaked, as if under a meant-to-be-silent tread. Little things snapped, scuffled, squeaked. A vague, impossible-to-define rustling and murmuring swept along the passages and through the rooms, dying away like a breeze on a fine evening in June. Once, someone seemed to sigh, right close against my ear. I kept straining my eyes, staring through the dusk in the direction of every new sound. Frank was keeping very quiet and I wondered if he had already dropped off to sleep. Lucky dog if he had!

I yawned and shone my torch on the dial of my wrist-watch—and then promptly wished I hadn't! Ten minutes to twelve! Nearly midnight, and Clare had said the Manor was haunted. Just on twelve o'clock and we were sitting up for the ghost. I had to clench my teeth to stop them from chattering, but I'm sure it was only the cold. And it *was* cold, too, with a penetrating dampness that chilled me to the marrow. What was I expecting to see? Did I believe in ghosts? Did I believe . . . My forehead broke out in a clammy sweat, but it was only one of the many noises of the night. Nothing new. Nothing had happened. And my fingers tightened involuntarily round the butt of my torch.

Rigid with fear, I suppose I must have dozed off. Immediately I found myself in the middle of vivid dreams, wild and confused. I can only remember for certain that Frank came into them, and that he was in danger. I was terrified for him and helpless—you know the sensation— unable to stir an inch to assist him in any way. I saw his face looking up at me, as if from some pit of darkness; Frank's face, recognisable, but twisted with terror. Why and of what he was frightened I could not tell, only that I shared his fear. He seemed to be trying to call out, trying to make himself heard. And then I did hear him. He was shouting my name, and I woke up with his voice ringing clearly in my ears.

'*Tony! You all right?*'

I understood, then, that it was Frank's real voice I must have heard, and his words had become part of my dream. I called back, wondering if he had seen anything. But no! Evidently he had taken it into his head that I might want reassuring. There was nothing to worry about, he added, and I thanked him, a little mystified by the sudden move on his part. Perhaps I had cried out in my sleep. I tried to settle myself, but was still haunted with the dream-terror and could not shake off the terrible urgency of Frank's demand. I was shivering quite uncontrollably with mingled fear and cold, and felt weak and sick. Now that I had woken up I could not get comfortable again and found it impossible to relax.

Propped in the doorway, my body stiff as a ramrod, I lay braced, from moment to moment imagining the worst. After looking for a long time towards the wide staircase that rose up into the darkness, hard to see, I lacked the courage to turn my head and gaze in any other direction. I sat, frozen in a sort of horror, my mind leaping from one tiny sound to the next, spanning the gulfs of blackness between. Hours seemed to pass in this way. How late was it? Had I dozed for long, or had I woken up almost immediately? Was it midnight, or long past? I fought down my rising panic, but my terrors refused to be subdued. I stifled and throttled myself, fists clenched, bracing my body against the door-post. And then I could stand it no longer. Something seemed to burst inside my head. If I could have found my voice, I would have shrieked and yelled. If I could have moved, I would have run madly through the echoing rooms. But I was a prisoner. Some power I could not resist held me gagged and bound, and for the first time in my life I knew what it was to be *really* afraid.

I shrank into myself, huddled down there by the doorway, cowed as if by a savage blow. I could feel my heart pumping in my ears and my breath came in gusts, hard and irregular. I dared not look up. I dared not even open my eyes. I lay helpless, as if in the grip of another appalling nightmare—and yet this was no dream.

And then I lifted my head, drawn up from a centre of horrifying blackness within the dusk of the Manor, and saw Frank walking away from me, treading very softly, passing by the dim sweep of the stairs. I saw him fairly clearly in the moonlit hall, and felt a new flood of warmth at the sight of him. Without stopping or looking back he disappeared round the corner, returning to his former position. I nearly called out, but somehow, to shatter the silence was very very difficult. I did not call spontaneously, and once I had thought about it I found it hard to summon up the words. I wanted better to preserve the quiet.

He must have tiptoed in, and found me, as he thought, asleep, head sunk on my chest, and so had crept away without disturbing me. I wondered if he, too, had been disturbed and had suddenly wanted company. He could not have seen anything. We had arranged our signal: a short whistle to attract the other's attention. No, he must have paid me a visit, just to find out how I was getting on. The knowledge that he was so near, and awake and watchful was most reassuring. I moved stiffly, to ease my aching back, and saw that the pattern of light had shifted over the floor of the great hall; the moon wheeling on her course across the clear night sky.

My panic had passed. I shivered in the grip of the cold and hunched myself into my muffler. I could not feel my feet and my fingers were icy inside my gloves. I tried to bang my shoes together, but was so sleepy and tired that my muscles failed to respond. The night yawned ahead of me. To imagine the drawn-out hours of darkness; hours that must be passed before it would be morning, was like looking down into a black, fathomless well. Oh, I was so cold—so shivering, shivering cold! And as I turned and tried to ease myself on the hard boards, it seemed to me that the night would never end. A century crawled by. I dozed, half-waking, ever-watchfully. Would I never sleep? Never get comfortable? Never sleep . . .

And almost at once, as it seemed, Frank was shaking me by the shoulders. It was already past seven o'clock, and growing slowly lighter.

I could not get up from the floor without his help, and my legs felt so shaky that at first I could scarcely walk. He supported me, and one after the other we managed to crawl through the open lower half of the window. As we stood on the terrace, we heard steps behind us. We turned, and there was Clare!

'Oh, good! Oh, good!' she exclaimed, running towards us and catching us each by a hand. 'I *am* so glad! I didn't sleep last night for worrying about you. You are all right? And nothing happened? Nothing horrible?'

'Of course not,' laughed Frank. 'And I think Tony's quite disappointed about it!'

Stiffly we walked along to the portico. Clare, between us, pushed her arms through ours. Three abreast, we lurched down the steps. For all my aches and pains I was treading on air! Frank was crowing like a cock. We'd done it and escaped unscathed.

Clare caught and shared our exhilaration and we laughed and talked excitedly as we strode along the drive.

'But didn't you feel afraid, Frank? Not at all?' Clare was asking her brother.

'Once, yes,' he admitted. 'Early on, I did get a bit panicky. Nerves of course.'

'By the way,' I said, 'thanks for coming along in the night. You must have thought I was asleep. Tell the truth I'd been feeling very windy, and the sight of you did me good.'

'Tommy-rot!' exclaimed Frank indignantly, 'I never moved. You were the one to be walking about. I remember calling out after you.'

'But I didn't . . .' I said, and we came to a faltering stop. Clare drew in her breath sharply and she saw us staring at each other with sudden, horrified understanding. And, as if instinctively, we all turned and gazed back at the great house behind us: sightless windows facing into the dawn.

CHRISTOPHER WOODFORDE

Richard

IT is often said that this county or that has been spoilt by tourist traffic, but it is not always true. The family party in the little four-seater saloon car does not venture far, if at all, from the main road in order to eat its picnic luncheon. The motor-coaches on their 'mystery tours' follow their accustomed routes throughout the summer months. The market towns through which these vehicles pass during a fine week-end, and the villages which have been awarded the unhappy status of 'beauty-spots,' continue to live their own lives all unseen by and unknown to the passer-by. If you are like me in finding endless interest and unfailing refreshment in the parish churches of England and their ancient furnishings, you will know that you can turn off any main road and in only a few minutes reach a village where a visitor is still subject to careful scrutiny because he is a stranger.

There is a cluster of such villages on the Cotswolds. None of them receives more than half a dozen lines of description in the guide-books. The tourist has not been instructed to find them. Even the ardent young ladies from the provincial universities who claim to have walked over every yard of this part of the country have not visited them, perhaps because their names are not romantic or because they have never produced even a minor literary or historic figure. I sought out one of these villages because I remembered that its church contained an object which I thought was beautiful. I had not seen it for more than twenty years and I was young when I first discovered it. In my experience one of two things may happen in such a case. Either I am disappointed because the thing has not the merit which, in my youthful enthusiasm, I thought it had, or it more than fulfils my expectations and offers me increased satisfaction and delight. In this instance, the second visit was rewarding: a lovely example of seventeenth-century altar rails, beautifully proportioned and in an excellent state of preservation.

My companion was not interested in them. As he was fourteen years of age, I did not ask him to be so. He had been excused his afternoon's games and the first part of his evening's work because it was his birth-

day, and I had obtained permission to take him with me on my expedi-
tion. The break in the school routine, the car ride, and tea were the treat,
and the churches had to be politely endured. Here, after a cursory glance
at the monuments, he had settled down in a pew to read the guide-book.
After a few minutes he looked up.

'Sir, what is a serpent?'

'Surely you know that, Richard?'

'Yes, sir,' he said, 'a snake. But this book says that there is an old one
hanging on the wall of the tower of the church in the next village.'

'Oh, that means a kind of musical instrument which they used in
church when they had orchestras instead of organs,' I explained.

'Do you think, sir, that we might go and look at it?'

It had been a lovely February day, but my diary said 'Sun rises 6.57,
sets 5.40.' We had eaten an early tea, and I had intended that only one
more church should be visited after it, so that the boy could be delivered
at his school well within the latest time allowed for his return. Still, the
homeward journey lay through the village that had preserved its serpent
and the boy had been very patient with my own activities.

'All right, Richard,' said I. 'We will look at it, but we must not be too
long about it.'

The church was locked. Its incumbent, when eventually he answered
our ringing of his front-door bell, insisted on accompanying us to the
church and then proceeded to pour out a stream of information about it
and its contents. At last we disentangled ourselves, partly because it was
too dark to see more and partly by promises that one day we would
return and spend a longer time over the many points of interest which,
we were assured, remained to be appreciated.

'Well, did you like him, Richard?' I asked, as we set out again.

'He was jolly nice, sir,' he replied. 'I've never seen a thing like that
before. I wish I could have played it.'

'It seemed to be very firmly fixed to the wall.'

'Was that stained glass really Norman, sir?'

'No, it was painted in about the year 1500.'

'Yes, sir. We're on the wrong road, aren't we, sir?'

We were. In my anxiety to get away from the voluble rector I had
taken another road out of the village. In the ordinary way I would have
turned my car round, but I thought it probable that if I went on there
would be a road turning to the left and so leading us back to the main
road. When we had travelled about a mile and a half the hoped-for
signpost appeared. It was an ancient structure. One of its arms pointed
to the left. The lettering on it was well-nigh indecipherable, but we

made out that it directed the traveller to some farm. There was no arm pointing to the village we had lately visited, but a second arm pointed to the small town through which we had to pass on our way home.

By this time it was nearly dark. We started off again, but had not gone more than fifty yards before an exclamation from Richard made me turn my head.

'What is the matter?' I asked.

'Did you see that money on the road, sir? It looked like a half-crown and some shillings.'

'Go back and pick it up,' I said, bringing the car to a standstill, 'but be as quick as you can: it is getting late.'

I switched off the headlights and lit a cigarette. The moon was rising and Richard would be able to see well enough. A wide valley separated us from the main road. The way which we had taken appeared to run parallel with it on a rather higher level. On the main road there was a considerable amount of traffic. The lights of the cars lit up the beech-trees which lined it on its further side. Sometimes when the cars approached one another, the lights dipped as if in courteous greeting. Down in the darkness of the valley there were a few lights. Their disposition suggested that there was a farm, probably the nameless farm which the signpost had indicated, with two or three labourers' cottages near it.

Richard was taking his time. I wondered if I ought to point out to him on his return that 'Finding is keeping' is neither a legal nor a moral maxim. In any case, he had had a quite long enough time in which to pick up the money. I got out of the car and strolled back. I could not see him.

'Come along, Richard,' I called. 'We must go on now.'

There was no reply.

'Bother the child,' I thought. 'I suppose that he has walked back to see if there is any more.'

I passed the signpost. There was no trace of him.

'Richard,' I called again.

There was no answering call. The wind soughed in the grasses at the sides of the road and in the distance a car's horn sounded. A low hedge separated the grass verge from the fields on the valley side of the road. I walked along it as far as the car. I looked into the car, which was empty. I walked back down the other grass verge, stumbling once into a trench which had been cut to allow the rain-water to drain off the road. There was only a foot-high bank on that side. The boy was nowhere to be seen.

Some people fear the countryside after nightfall. I suppose that the fear is bred partly of stories heard or read in childhood and partly of inheritance from that very distant past when the creatures of darkness might well be hostile. I have not got this fear, but I believe that I know whether there is another human being near me in the darkness or not. I felt then that Richard, and perhaps someone else, were near by: and I felt too that there was an atmosphere of tension and, for want of a better word, restraint. Above all, it was being borne in upon me that there was urgent need to take some quick action, but I had no inkling of what that action ought to be. There was one place where I had not looked for Richard, on the roadway leading down to the farm. Again, there was no one. The only thing to do was to go back to the car and to drive it down to the farm and seek help. As I reached the road and started towards the car, the signpost caught my eye. It had turned partly black. My heart began to pound violently, although a moment passed before my mind grasped the significance of what was before me. Then I saw quite distinctly that the signpost had folded its two arms round Richard and had drawn him up against itself so that his feet were several inches off the ground. The top of it was bending over his head in a very horrid way.

I do not know what others would have done in such a case. I heard myself say, as if to a dog which has seized a glove:

'Drop him at once! Do you hear me? At once!'

On those words it turned and began to move off over the bank and across the field, still holding the boy and going with a jolting gait like a puppet moved with strings.

I gave chase. The field was ploughed and heavy. My raincoat impeded me. My head throbbed violently. I felt that at all costs I must not lose sight of the Thing in front of me. Then I fell headlong. As I picked myself up, I found that I had fallen over Richard's body. The Thing lay on the ground beyond him. Overcome by a fit of ungovernable rage, I went up to it and stamped upon it. I expected to feel the solid impact of my shoe upon wood. Instead it gave way and bulged upon each side of my foot like a half-filled air-cushion. I turned from it and picked up the boy. It seemed to be a long way back to the road. Curiously I now had no fear of the Thing that we left behind us. Richard was no light weight and the sticky earth clung to my shoes. At last we were by the car. I laid Richard on the grass and felt inside his coat. His heart was beating soundly and regularly, but he showed no signs of consciousness. I knocked the heavy clods from my shoes and then sat Richard on the seat beside me. It may seem foolish that I did not lay him on the back seat, but I felt that it would be better that he should be near me.

I decided not to stop and seek a doctor on the way back. The best plan was to get Richard into bed as soon as possible. I had driven about fifteen miles when I received the last shock of the evening.

'Sir, are we nearly home?'

'About ten miles to go,' I replied, and was surprised to find that my voice was normal. 'How are you feeling?'

'Quite all right, sir. I think I've been asleep,' said he. 'Gosh! I am stiff. Why does going to sleep in the daytime make you stiff, sir?'

'Perhaps your muscles do not relax properly?' I suggested. 'Would you like a sweet?'

'Yes, sir, please.'

He sucked contentedly for the remainder of the journey and said nothing.

I stopped at the school entrance and he got out.

'Thanks awfully for the outing and the tea, sir; it's been wizard.'

'I am glad you enjoyed yourself. Good-bye.'

'Good-bye, sir.'

I went round to the headmaster's front door and reported our return. I apologized to him for cutting the time rather fine, saying that I had visited one more church than I had originally intended to do.

'Did you have to reach it by way of a ploughed field?' he asked, looking at my shoes and the bottoms of my trousers.

I lied blandly and, I think, convincingly.

'No, but it was locked and I attempted a short cut to the rectory which landed me in the rector's vegetable garden.'

During the following weeks I was laid up with a poisoned foot. The doctor said that it had become poisoned through a bite or sting in the heel, and asked me how I had come by such a thing in February. I could think of only one explanation, which I did not feel able to give to him. In Genesis iii. 15 I read that the Lord God said to the serpent: 'Thou shalt bruise his heel.' As Richard had truly remarked, it had been a wizard outing.

By way of postscript I must place on record the result of a small experiment which I subsequently made. About six months later Richard was again my companion in the car. It was a brilliant summer afternoon and we were travelling along a great arterial road. Stopping the car a few yards beyond a signpost, I said:

'Richard, will you go back and see how far it is to Stratford on Avon?'

After a moment's silence he replied: 'If you don't mind, sir, I'd rather you backed the car.'

I put the car into reverse, read the mileage, and set off again.

'I hope I wasn't rude about not getting out, sir,' said Richard.

'Not at all,' I said.

'You see, sir, it's queer, but signposts make me feel sick. I asked matron about it and she said that I'd probably felt ill by one when I was a little boy. Do you think that's true?'

'Quite possibly, Richard,' I answered. 'Shall we have tea in Stratford on Avon?'

'I'd love to, sir,' he answered. 'Are you going to visit any churches after tea?'

'No,' I said decisively, 'I am not.'

ALISON UTTLEY

The Wee Ghostie

ONCE there was a little girl-ghost who lived in the cupboard under the stairs, in an old house. She had lived there for many years, but she never got any older. Her pale little face kept its charming oval, her curved lips smiled and her eyes looked calmly down on the world her body had left long before.

She liked the little cupboard, where she dreamed and slept all day, only coming out at night when everyone was asleep. Then the planks in the cupboard floor squeaked, and the door rattled, and there was a sigh and a tiny moan as she slipped through a crack and walked in the house.

'It's only the ghostie,' explained the grandfather, who lived in the house with his daughter and her children. 'Take no notice of her and she won't take any notice of you. There's been a ghostie ever since I remember, but she's only a wee lassie.'

The children opened wide their eyes, but Judy, the youngest, sat very still, listening. She thought once that she heard a voice high and far away, crying, 'Oh-oh-oh, I can't find her. Oh-oh-oh.' It was like an owl calling in the trees, wailing and lost.

'The ghostie has lost something,' said Judy solemnly. 'She's lonely.'

'I dare say she has lost something,' answered her grandfather, 'but she lost it so long ago nobody can find it.'

'Let's turn out the cupboard and look,' said Judy. 'Then we can see the ghostie sleeping there.'

'You won't see her. She's invisible,' said the grandfather. 'I don't think she sleeps there, she goes to a land in the air. But you can turn out the cupboard for it is in a mess, I can never find anything I want. Your mother will be glad to see it straightened.'

So the next wet day the three children turned out the deep cupboard under the stairs, and they found many things which might have been lost and might not. Old tennis racquets with strings broken, a cricket bat and stumps, a broken old basket, a heap of mildewed books with old-fashioned pictures, a folding chair, a child's cot, and some shoes, all lay under a pile of newspapers, and in them was a mouse's nest.

'That's the ghostie's house,' laughed Jane to Judy. 'That's what made the squeak and cry you heard.'

'I don't think so,' whispered Judy. 'It was a real voice, not an owl's or a mouse's.'

They carried the ball of feathers and papers away and then returned to look at the empty cupboard. Nothing was left except dust and dirt and bits of plaster.

The hall was full of rubbish and Mother gasped when she saw it.

'What a terrible mess!' she cried. 'I had no idea we had so much stuff buried here.'

'We are looking for the ghostie,' explained Judy. 'And all we found was a mouse nest, and this rubbish.'

'I used to think a ghostie lived here when I was little,' said her mother. 'I was shut here in the darkness when I was naughty, and I heard little moans and rustles.'

'Poor Mother,' said Judy. 'I'm glad you don't put us there. Were you very frightened?'

'No, I was rather afraid of the dark but I liked the little murmurs and the sounds. Now I never hear them. I had forgotten all about my little wee ghostie girl,' said her mother.

'Leave everything as it is,' she continued. 'Miranda will scrub out the cupboard and make it all clean. Then I will sort out the things not worth keeping, and there will be much more room in this old cupboard.'

Miranda brought her brushes and her pail of hot water. She sighed at the dusky hole, and laughed at the tale of a ghostie, but she scrubbed and rubbed the boards and the walls, till the cupboard was clean as a new pin. One board was loose and when she put her pail on it, it squeaked and moaned.

'There's your ghostie,' she said to Judy who stood watching her. 'It wants a nail.'

She gave a tug of the loose board and it came away. A space was disclosed, and in it lay a little wooden box all smothered in cobwebs. She lifted it out and she saw the lid was held by a tiny brass latchet. She raised the latchet and the lid fell back on its brass hinges. Inside lay a small wooden doll, whose face was worn and rubbed with age. The black hair was painted on its head, and its blue eyes looked out with astonishment from the small carved little face. The nose was nearly flat and the cheeks were pale pink. Curved red lips seemed to smile, as Miranda held up the doll for Judy to see. The white cotton dress sprigged with lilac was long and full, pleated and ruffled with tiny stitches, and its folds reached to the top of the black painted boots on the doll's legs. Round the doll's waist was a sash of lilac silk, splitting into streamers. At the waist from the sash hung a little lilac bag, and inside was something hard, as Miranda pinched it.

'Oh, Miranda, let me look,' squealed Judy, holding out her hands for the discovery.

She grasped the doll and raced to her mother.

'Mother! Mother! Look what Miranda found, in a box under the floor,' she cried.

'It must have belonged to one of my great aunts,' pondered her mother, looking closely at the doll, examining the long drawers and the petticoat.

'What's in the pocket?' cried Judy, and she untied the little bag, and took out a silver groat dated 1836, and a minute pocket handkerchief edged with tiny lace.

'Oh, Judy. How lovely,' said her mother. 'I'll wash the dress and make a new sash and you can have your great-great-aunt's doll for your very own. She must have loved it. I wonder why she put it under the floor.'

'Perhaps she was going away,' said Judy.

'Perhaps she didn't put it there herself, but someone else hid it and forgot it. Perhaps she died and the doll was forgotten,' said Mother sadly.

'I'll take the doll to bed with me and comfort her,' said Judy, and she kissed the faded little face, and stroked the doll.

That night the doll lay in Judy's arms in bed, it was kissed and comforted and sung to, but it seemed restless. It was not possible, of course, but Judy felt it move by itself. She took it out and laid it on the oak table by the bed, on a shawl for warmth.

'Lie there,' she whispered, and she stretched out her hand and touched the little figure in the darkness. Then she fell asleep, and she dreamed and dreamed of the doll. She was wakened suddenly by a slight sound, a little thud, and when she put out her fingers the doll had fallen to the carpet. She leaned over to pick it up, but the shawl was empty. The doll was walking stiffly on its little painted boots, and a shining light seemed to come from it, a halo surrounded the little creature. The light came not from the doll but from a child's hand which held it and guided its feet across the room. As Judy stared she could see the dim outline of a child in a long white nightdress gliding along the carpet, holding the doll's hand.

'Oh, my baby! I've got thee again. I've found thee, my love, my sweeting,' whispered a tiny voice soft as a dream, and the wind howled outside and thumped at the window and the owl in the fir tree hooted and called.

'Husha-by, my baby. Hush thee, my dear one,' crooned the little voice, and then it began to sing a lullaby.

Judy sat up in bed, shivering with excitement, half with fear and half with joy, for she could hear the tiny thuds of the doll's wooden feet pattering over the carpet, and see the faint light which went by the doll, outlining the shape of the little girl who led it away.

Then the doll disappeared, the light faded, and there was silence, except for the faint voice in the distance sighing 'Oh, my dear one. Oh, my sweeting. I've found thee and we will never be parted again.'

Sighing with happiness which flooded the room and made her heart beat wildly, her mind singing like the little ghostie's voice, Judy fell asleep. Had she been dreaming, she wondered next day? The empty shawl lay on the floor, the doll had gone.

'The wee ghostie took back her doll last night,' she told her mother. 'She came for it and took it away. Oh, she was so glad, and I was glad too. I saw her, Mummy, in her white nightgown.'

'So that is what the poor little thing wanted,' said Judy's mother. 'She has been hunting for a hundred years or more, and now she has found her treasure. I'm so happy about her. She won't come back any more, Judy. She will sleep now.'

But the mother was wrong. Judy saw her once again, walking across the room with her doll clasped in her arms, and her face smiling. Then, swinging the little wooden doll, dandling it gently, the ghostie faded and all was silent.

ROBERT ARTHUR

The Haunted Trailer

It was inevitable, of course. Bound to happen some day. But why did it have to happen to me? What did *I* do to deserve the grief? And I was going to be married, too. I sank my last thousand dollars into that trailer, almost. In it Monica and I were going on a honeymoon tour of the United States. We were going to see the country. I was going to write, and we were going to be happy as two turtle-doves.

Ha!

Ha ha!

If you detect bitterness in that laughter, I'll tell you why I'm bitter.

Because it had to be me, Mel—for Melvin—Mason who became the first person in the world to own a haunted trailer!

Now, a haunted castle is one thing. Even an ordinary haunted house can be livable in. In a castle, or a house, if there's a ghost around, you can lock yourself in the bedroom and get a little sleep. A nuisance, yes. But nothing a man couldn't put up with.

In a trailer, though! What are you going to do when you're sharing a trailer, even a super-de-luxe model with four built-in bunks, a breakfast nook, a complete bathroom, a radio, electric range, and easy chair, with a ghost? Where can you go to get away from it?

Ha!

Ha ha!

I've heard so much ghostly laughter the last week that I'm laughing myself that way now.

There I was. I had the trailer. I had the car to pull it, naturally. I was on my way to meet Monica in Hollywood, where she was living with an aunt from Iowa. And twelve miles west of Albany, the first night out, my brand-new, spic-and-span trailer picks up a hitch-hiking haunt!

But maybe I'd better start at the beginning. It happened this way. I bought the trailer in New England—a Custom Clipper, with chrome and tan outside trim, for $2,998. I hitched it on behind my car and headed westwards, happier than a lark when the dew's on the thorn. I'd been saving up for this day for two years, and I felt wonderful.

I took it easy, getting the feel of the trailer, and so I didn't make very good time. I crossed the Hudson river just after dark, trundled through Albany in a rainstorm, and half an hour later pulled off the road into an old path between two big rocks to spend the night.

The thunder was rolling back and forth overhead, and the lightning was having target practice with the trees. But I'd picked out a nice secluded spot and I made myself comfortable. I cooked up a tasty plate of beans, some coffee, and fried potatoes. When I had eaten I took off my shoes, slumped down in the easy chair, lit a cigarette, and leaned back.

'Ah!' I said aloud. 'Solid comfort. If only Monica were here, how happy we would be.'

But she wasn't, so I picked up a book.

It wasn't a very good book. I must have dozed off. Maybe I slept for a couple of hours. Maybe three. Anyway, I woke with a start, the echo of a buster of a thunderbolt still rattling the willow pattern tea set in the china cupboard. My hair was standing on end from the electricity in the air.

Then the door banged open, a swirl of rain swept in, and the wind—anyway, I thought it was the wind—slammed the door to. I heard a sound like a ghost—there's no other way to describe it—of a sigh.

'Now this,' said the voice, 'is something like!'

I had jumped up to shut the door, and I stood there with my unread book in my hand, gaping. The wind had blown a wisp of mist into my trailer and the mist, instead of evaporating, remained there, seeming to turn slowly and to settle into shape. It got more and more solid until—

Well, you know. It was a spectre. A haunt. A homeless ghost.

The creature remained there, regarding me in a decidedly cool manner.

'Sit down, chum,' it said, 'and don't look so pop-eyed. You make me nervous. This is my first night indoors in fifteen years, and I wanta enjoy it.'

'Who—' I stammered—'who—'

'I'm not,' the spectre retorted, 'a brother owl, so don't who-who at me. What do I look like?'

'You look like a ghost,' I told him.

'Now you're getting smart, chum. I *am* a ghost. What *kind* of a ghost do I look like?'

I inspected it more closely. Now that the air inside my trailer had stopped eddying, it was reasonably firm of outline. It was a squat, heavy-set ghost, attired in ghostly garments that certainly never had come to it new. He wore the battered ghost of a felt hat, and a stubble of ghostly beard showed on his jowls.

'You look like a tramp ghost,' I answered with distaste, and my uninvited visitor nodded.

'Just what I am, chum,' he told me. 'Call me Spike Higgins. Spike for short. That was my name before it happened.'

'Before what happened?' I demanded. The ghost wafted across the trailer to settle down on a bunk, where he lay down and crossed his legs, hoisting one foot encased in a battered ghost of a shoe into the air.

'Before I was amachoor enough to fall asleep riding on top of a truck, and fall off right here fifteen years ago,' he told me. 'Ever since I been forced to haunt this place. I wasn't no Boy Scout, so I got punished by bein' made to stay here in one spot. Me, who never stayed in one spot two nights running before!

'I been gettin' kind of tired of it the last couple of years. They wouldn't even lemme haunt a house. No, I hadda do all my haunting out in th' open, where th' wind an' rain could get at me, and every dog that went by could bark at me. Chum, you don't know what it means to me that you've picked this place to stop.'

'Listen,' I said firmly, 'you've got to get out of here!'

The apparition yawned.

'Chum,' he said, 'you're the one that's trespassin', not me. This is my happy hunting ground. Did I ask you to stop here?'

'You mean,' I asked between clenched teeth, 'that you won't go? You're going to stay here all night?'

'Right, chum,' the ghost grunted. 'Gimme a call for six a.m.' He closed his eyes, and began snoring in an artificial and highly insulting manner.

Then I got sore. I threw the book at him, and it bounced off the bunk without bothering him in the least. Spike Higgins opened an eye and leered at me.

'Went right through me,' he chortled. 'Instead of me goin' through it. Ha ha! Ha ha ha! Joke.'

'You—' I yelled, in a rage. 'You—stuff!'

And I slammed him with the chair cushion, which likewise went through him without doing any damage. Spike Higgins opened both eyes and stuck out his tongue at me.

Obviously I couldn't hurt him, so I got control of myself.

'Listen,' I said, craftily. 'You say you are doomed to haunt this spot forever? You can't leave?'

'Forbidden to leave,' Spike answered. 'Why?'

'Never mind,' I gritted. 'You'll find out.'

I snatched up my raincoat and hat and scrambled out into the storm. If that ghost was doomed to remain in that spot forever, I wasn't. I got into the car, got the motor going, and backed out of there. It took a lot of manoeuvring in the rain, with mud underwheel, but I made it. I got straightened out on the concrete and headed westwards.

I didn't stop until I'd covered twenty miles. Then, beginning to grin as I thought of the shock the ghost of Spike Higgins must have felt when I yanked the trailer from underneath him, I parked on a stretch of old, unused road and then crawled back into the trailer again.

Inside, I slammed the door and—

Ha!

Ha ha!

Ha ha ha!

Yes, more bitter laughter. Spike Higgins was still there, sound asleep and snoring.

I muttered something under my breath. Spike Higgins opened his eyes sleepily.

'Hello,' he yawned. 'Been having fun?'

'Listen,' I finally got it out. 'I—thought—you—were—doomed— to—stay—back—there—where—I—found—you—forever!'

The apparition yawned again.

'Your mistake, chum. I didn't say I was doomed to stay. I said I was forbidden to leave. I didn't leave. You hauled me away. It's all your responsibility and I'm a free agent now.'

'You're a what?'

'I'm a free agent. I can ramble as far as I please. I can take up hoboing again. You've freed me. Thanks, chum. I won't forget.'

'Then—then—' I sputtered. Spike Higgins nodded.

'That's right. I've adopted you. I'm going to stick with you. We'll travel together.'

'But you can't!' I cried out, aghast. 'Ghosts don't travel around! They haunt houses—or cemeteries—or maybe woods. But—'

'What do you know about ghosts?' Spike Higgins' voice held sarcasm. 'There's all kinds of ghosts, chum. Includin' hobo ghosts, tramp ghosts, ghosts with itchin' feet who can't stay put in one spot. Let me tell you, chum, a 'bo ghost like me ain't never had no easy time of it.

'Suppose they do give him a house to haunt? All right, he's got a roof over his head, but there he is, stuck. Houses don't move around. They don't go places. They stay in one spot till they rot.

'But things are different now. You've helped bring in a new age for the brotherhood of spooks. Now a fellow can haunt a house and be on the move at the same time. He can work at his job and still see the country. These trailers are the answers to a problem that's been bafflin' the best minds in the spirit world for thousands of years. It's the newest thing, the latest and best. Haunted trailers. I tell you, we'll probably erect a monument to you at our next meeting. The ghost of a monument, anyway.'

Spike Higgins had raised up on an elbow to make his speech. Now, grimacing, he lay back.

'That's enough, chum,' he muttered. 'Talking uses up my essence. I'm going to merge for a while. See you in the morning.'

'Merge with what?' I asked. Spike Higgins was already so dim I could hardly see him.

'Merge with the otherwhere,' a faint, distant voice told me, and Spike Higgins was gone.

I waited a minute to make sure. Then I breathed a big sigh of relief. I looked at my raincoat, at my wet feet, at the book on the floor, and knew it had all been a dream. I'd been walking in my sleep. Driving in it too. Having a nightmare.

I hung up the raincoat, slid out of my clothes, and got into a bunk.

I woke up late, and for a moment felt panic. Then I breathed easily again. The other bunk was untenanted. Whistling, I jumped up, showered, dressed, ate, and got under way.

It was a lovely day. Blue sky, wind, sunshine, birds singing. Thinking of Monica, I almost sang with them as I rolled down the road. In a week I'd be pulling up in front of Monica's aunt's place in Hollywood and tooting the horn—

That was the moment when a cold draught of air sighed along the back of my neck, and the short hairs rose.

I turned, almost driving into a hay wagon. Beside me was a misty figure.

'I got tired of riding back there alone,' Spike Higgins told me. 'I'm gonna ride up front a while an' look at th' scenery.'

'You—you—' I shook with rage so that we nearly ran off the road. Spike Higgins reached out, grabbed the wheel in tenuous fingers, and jerked us back on to our course again.

'Take it easy, chum,' he said. 'There's enough competition in this world I'm in, without you hornin' into th' racket.'

I didn't say anything, but my thoughts must have been written on my face. I'd thought he was just a nightmare. But he was real. A ghost had moved in with me, and I hadn't the faintest idea how to move him out.

Spike Higgins grinned with a trace of malice.

'Sure, chum,' he said. 'It's perfectly logical. There's haunted castles, haunted palaces, and haunted houses. Why not a haunted trailer?'

'Why not haunted ferryboats?' I demanded with bitterness. 'Why not haunted Pullmans? Why not haunted trucks?'

'You think there ain't?' Spike Higgins' misty countenance registered surprise at my ignorance. 'Could I tell you tales! There's a haunted ferryboat makes the crossing at Poughkeepsie every stormy night at midnight. There's a haunted private train on the Atchison, Sante Fé. Pal of mine haunts it. He always jumped trains, but he was a square dealer, and they gave him the private train for a reward.

'Then there's a truck on the New York Central that never gets where it's going. Never has yet. No matter where it starts out for, it winds up some place else. Bunch of my buddies haunt it. And another truck on the Southern Pacific that never has a train to pull it. Runs by itself. It's driven I dunno how many signalmen crazy, when they saw it go past right ahead of a whole train. I could tell you—'

'Don't!' I ordered. 'I forbid you to. I don't want to hear.'

'Why, sure, chum,' Spike Higgins agreed. 'But you'll get used to it. You'll be seein' a lot of me. Because where thou ghost, I ghost. Pun.' He gave a ghostly chuckle and relapsed into silence. I drove along, my mind churning. I had to get rid of him. *Had* to. Before we reached California, at the very latest. But I didn't have the faintest idea in the world how I was going to.

Then, abruptly, Spike Higgins' ghost sat up straight.

'Stop!' he ordered. 'Stop, I say!'

We were on a lonely stretch of road, bordered by old cypresses, with weed-grown marshland beyond. I didn't see any reason for stopping. But Spike Higgins reached out and switched off the ignition. Then he slammed on the emergency brake. We came squealing to a stop, and just missed going into a ditch.

'What did you do that for?' I yelled. 'You almost ditched us! Confound you, you ectoplasmic, hitch-hiking nuisance! If I ever find a way to lay hands on you—'

'Quiet, chum!' the apparition told me rudely. 'I just seen an old pal of mine. Slippery Samuels. I ain't seen him since he dropped a bottle of nitro just as he was gonna break into a bank in Mobile sixteen years ago. We're gonna give him a ride.'

'We certainly are not!' I cried. 'This is my car, and I'm not picking up any more—'

'It may be your car,' Spike Higgins sneered, 'but I'm the resident haunt, and I got full powers to extend hospitality to any buddy ghosts

I want, see? Rule II, subdivision c. Look it up. Hey, Slippery, climb in!'

A finger of fog pushed through the partly open window of the car at his hail, enlarged, and there was a second apparition on the front seat with me.

The newcomer was long and lean, just as shabbily dressed as Spike Higgins, with a ghostly countenance as mournful as a Sunday School picnic on a rainy day.

'Spike, you old son of a gun,' the second spook murmured, in hollow tones that would have brought goose-flesh to a statue. 'How've you been? What're you doing here? Who's he?'— nodding at me.

'Never mind him,' Spike said disdainfully. 'I'm haunting his trailer. Listen, whatever became of the old gang?'

'Still hoboing it,' the long, lean apparition sighed. 'Nitro Nelson is somewhere around. Pacific Pete and Buffalo Benny are lying over in a haunted jungle somewhere near Toledo. I had a date to join 'em, but a storm blew me back to Wheeling a couple of days ago.'

'Mmm,' Spike Higgins' ghost muttered. 'Maybe we'll run into 'em. Let's go back in my trailer and do a little chinning. As for you, chum, make camp any time you want. Ta ta.'

The two apparitions oozed through the back of the car and were gone. I was boiling inside, but there was nothing I could do.

I drove on for another hour, went through Toledo, then stopped at a wayside camp. I paid my dollar, picked out a spot, and parked.

But when I entered the trailer, the ghosts of Spike Higgins and Slippery Samuels, the bank robber, weren't there. Nor had they shown up by the time I finished dinner. In fact I ate, washed, and got into bed with no sign of them.

Breathing a prayer that maybe Higgins had abandoned me to go back to 'boing it in the spirit world, I fell asleep. And began to dream. About Monica—

When I woke, there was a sickly smell in the air, and the heavy staleness of old tobacco smoke.

I opened my eyes. Luckily, I opened them prepared for the worst. Even so, I wasn't prepared well enough.

Spike Higgins was back. Ha! Ha ha! Ha ha ha! I'll say he was back. He lay on the opposite bunk, his eyes shut, his mouth open, snoring. Just the ghost of a snore, but quite loud enough. On the bunk above him lay his bank-robber companion. In the easy chair was slumped a third apparition, short and stout, with a round, whiskered face. A tramp spirit, too.

So was the ghost stretched out on the floor, gaunt and cadaverous. So was the small, mournful spook in the bunk above me, his ectoplasmic hand swinging over the side, almost in my face. Tramps, all of them. Hobo spooks. Five hobo phantoms asleep in my trailer!

And there were cigarette butts in all the ash trays, and burns on my built-in writing desk. The cigarettes apparently had just been lit and let burn. The air was choking with stale smoke, and I had a headache I could have sold for a fire alarm, it was ringing so loudly in my skull.

I knew what had happened. During the night Spike Higgins and his pal had rounded up some more of their ex-hobo companions. Brought them back. To *my* trailer. Now—I was so angry I saw all five of them through a red haze that gave their ectoplasm a ruby tinge. Then I got hold of myself. I couldn't throw them out. I couldn't harm them. I couldn't touch them.

No, there was only one thing I could do. Admit I was beaten. Take my loss and quit while I could. It was a bitter pill to swallow. But if I wanted to reach Monica, if I wanted to enjoy the honeymoon we'd planned, I'd have to give up the fight.

I got into my clothes. Quietly I sneaked out, locking the trailer behind me. Then I hunted for the owner of the trailer camp, a lanky man, hard-eyed, but well dressed. I guessed he must have money.

'Had sort of a party last night, hey?' he asked me, with a leering wink. 'I seen lights, an' heard singing, long after midnight. Not loud, though, so I didn't bother you. But it looked like somebody was havin' a high old time.'

I gritted my teeth.

'That was me,' I said, 'I couldn't sleep. I got up and turned on the radio. Truth is, I haven't slept a single night in that trailer. I guess I wasn't built for trailer life. That job cost me $2,998 new, just three days ago. I've got the bill-of-sale. How'd you like to buy it for fifteen hundred, and make two hundred easy profit on it?'

He gnawed his lip, but knew the trailer was a bargain. We settled for thirteen-fifty. I gave him the bill-of-sale, took the money, uncoupled, got into the car, and left there.

As I turned the bend in the road, heading westwards, there was no sign that Spike Higgins' ghost was aware of what had happened.

I even managed to grin as I thought of his rage when he woke up to find I had abandoned him. It was almost worth the money I'd lost to think of it.

Beginning to feel better, I stepped on the accelerator, piling up miles between me and that trailer. At least I was rid of Spike Higgins and his friends.

Ha!

Ha ha!

Ha ha ha!

That's what I thought.

About the middle of the afternoon I was well into Illinois. It was open country, and monotonous, so I turned on my radio. And the first thing I got was a police broadcast.

'All police, Indiana and Illinois! Be on the watch for a tan-and-chrome trailer, stolen about noon from a camp near Toledo. The thieves are believed heading west in it. That is all.'

I gulped. It couldn't be! But—It sounded like my trailer, all right. I looked in my rear-vision mirror, apprehensively. The road behind was empty. I breathed a small sigh of relief. I breathed it too soon. For at that moment, round a curve half a mile behind me, something swung into sight and came racing down the road after me.

The trailer.

Ha!

Ha ha!

There it came, a tan streak that zipped round the curve and came streaking after me, zigzagging wildly from side to side of the road, doing at least sixty—without a car pulling it.

My flesh crawled, and my hair stood on end. I stepped on the accelerator. Hard. And I picked up speed in a hurry. In half a minute I was doing seventy, and the trailer was still gaining. Then I hit eighty—and passed a motorcycle cop parked beside the road.

I had just a glimpse of his pop-eyed astonishment as I whizzed past, with the trailer chasing me fifty yards behind. Then, kicking on his starter, he slammed after us.

Meanwhile, in spite of everything the car would do, the trailer pulled up behind me and I heard the coupling clank as it was hitched on. At once my speed dropped. The trailer was swerving dangerously, and I had to slow. Behind me the cop was coming, siren open wide, but I didn't worry about him because Spike Higgins was materializing beside me.

'Whew!' he said, grinning at me. 'My essence feels all used up. Thought you could give Spike Higgins and his pals the slip, huh? You'll learn, chum, you'll learn. That trooper looks like a tough baby. You'll have fun trying to talk yourself out of this.'

'Yes, but see what it'll get *you*, you ectoplasmic excrescence!' I raged at him. 'The trailer will be stored away in some country garage for months as evidence while I'm being held for trial on the charge of stealing it. And how'll you like haunting a garage?'

Higgins' face changed.

'Say, that's right,' he muttered. 'My first trip for fifteen years, too.'

He put his fingers to his lips, and blew the shrill ghost of a whistle. In a moment the car was filled with cold, clammy draughts as Slippery Samuels and the other three apparitions appeared in the seat beside Higgins.

Twisting and turning and seeming to intermingle a lot, they peered out at the cop, who was beside the car now, one hand on his gun butt, trying to crowd me over to the shoulder.

'All right, boys!' Higgins finished explaining. 'You know what we gotta do. Me an' Slippery'll take the car. You guys take the trailer!'

They slipped through the open windows like smoke. Then I saw Slippery Samuels holding on to the left front bumper, and Spike Higgins holding on to the right, their ectoplasm streaming out horizontal to the road, stretched and thinned by the air rush. And an instant later we began to move with a speed I had never dreamed of reaching.

We zipped ahead of the astonished cop, and the speedometer needle began to climb again. It took the trooper an instant to believe his eyes. Then with a yell he yanked out his gun and fired. A bullet bumbled past; then he was too busy trying to overtake us again to shoot.

The speedometer said ninety now, and was still climbing. It touched a hundred and stuck there. I was trying to pray when down the road a mile away I saw a sharp curve, a bridge, and a deep river. I froze. I couldn't even yell.

We came up to the curve so fast that I was still trying to move my lips when we hit it. I didn't make any effort to take it. Instead I slammed on the brakes and prepared to plough straight ahead into a fence, a stand of young poplars, and the river.

But just as I braked, I heard Spike Higgins' ghostly scream, 'Allay-OOP!'

And before we reached the ditch, car and trailer swooped up in the air. An instant later at a height of a hundred and fifty feet, we hurtled straight westwards over the river and the town beyond.

I'd like to have seen the expression on the face of the motorcycle cop then. As far as that goes, I'd like to have seen my own.

Then the river was behind us, and the town, and we were swooping down towards a dank, gloomy-looking patch of woods through which ran an abandoned railway line. A moment later we struck earth with a jouncing shock and came to rest.

Spike Higgins and Slippery Samuels let go of the bumpers and straightened themselves up. Spike Higgins dusted ghostly dust off his palms and leered at me.

'How was that, chum?' he asked. 'Neat, hey?'

'How—' I stuttered— 'how—'

'Simple,' Spike Higgins answered. 'Anybody that can tip tables can do it. Just levitation, 'at's all. Hey, meet the boys. You ain't been introduced yet. This is Buffalo Benny, this one is Toledo Ike, this one Pacific Pete.'

The fat spook, the cadaverous one, and the melancholy little one appeared from behind the car, and smirked as Higgins introduced them. Then Higgins waved a hand impatiently.

'C'm on, chum,' he said. 'There's a road there that takes us out of these woods. Let's get going. It's almost dark, and we don't wanna spend the night here. This used to be in Dan Bracer's territory.'

'Who's Dan Bracer?' I demanded, getting the motor going, because I was as anxious to get away from there as Spike Higgins' spook seemed to be.

'Just a railway dick,' Spike Higgins said, with a distinctly uneasy grin. 'Toughest bull that ever kicked a poor 'bo off a freight.'

'So mean he always drank black coffee,' Slippery Samuels put in, in a mournful voice. 'Cream turned sour when he picked up the jug.'

'Not that we was afraid of him—' Buffalo Benny, the fat apparition, squeaked. 'But—'

'We just never liked him,' Toledo Ike croaked, a sickly look on his ghostly features. 'O' course, he ain't active now. He was retired a couple of years back, an' jes' lately I got a rumour he was sick.'

'Dyin',' Pacific Peter murmured hollowly.

'Dyin'.' They all sighed the word, looking apprehensive. Then Spike Higgins' ghost scowled truculently at me.

'Never mind about Dan Bracer,' he snapped. 'Let's just get goin' out of here. And don't give that cop no more thought. You think a cop is gonna turn in a report that a car and trailer he was chasin' suddenly sailed up in the air an' flew away like a aeroplane? Not on your sweet life. He ain't gonna say nothing to nobody about it.'

Apparently he was right, because after I had driven out of the woods, with some difficulty, and on to a secondary highway, there was no further sign of pursuit. I headed westwards again, and Spike Higgins and his pals moved back to the trailer, where they lolled about, letting my cigarettes burn and threatening to call the attention of the police to me when I complained.

I grew steadily more morose and desperate as the Pacific Coast, and Monica, came nearer. I was behind schedule, due to Spike Higgins' insistence on my taking a roundabout route so they could see the Grand Canyon, and no way to rid myself of the obnoxious haunts appeared. I couldn't even abandon the trailer. Spike Higgins had been definite on that point. It was better to haul a haunted trailer around than to have one chasing you, he pointed out, and shuddering at the thought of being pursued by a trailer full of ghosts wherever I went, I agreed.

But if I couldn't get rid of them, it meant no Monica, no marriage, no honeymoon. And I was determined that nothing as insubstantial as a spirit was going to interfere with my life's happiness.

Just the same, by the time I had driven over the mountains and into California, I was almost on the point of doing something desperate. Apparently sensing this, Spike Higgins and the others had been on their good behaviour. But I could still see no way to get rid of them.

It was early afternoon when I finally rolled into Hollywood, haggard and unshaven, and found a trailer camp, where I parked. Heavy-hearted, I bathed and shaved and put on clean clothes. I didn't know what I was going to say to Monica, but I was already several days behind schedule, and I couldn't put off ringing her.

There was a telephone in the camp office. I looked up Ida Bracer—her aunt's name—in the book, then put through the call.

Monica herself answered. Her voice sounded distraught.

'Oh, Mel,' she exclaimed, as soon as I announced myself, 'where have you been? I've been expecting you for days.'

'I was delayed,' I told her, bitterly. 'Spirits. I'll explain later.'

'Spirits?' Her tone seemed cold. 'Well, anyway, now that you're here at last, I must see you at once. Mel, Uncle Dan is dying.'

'Uncle Dan?' I echoed.

'Yes, Aunt Ida's brother. He used to live in Iowa, but a few months ago he was taken ill, and he came out to be with Aunt and me. Now he's dying. The doctor says its only a matter of hours.'

'Dying?' I repeated again. 'Your Uncle Dan, from Iowa, dying?'

Then it came to me. I began to laugh. Exultantly.

'I'll be right over!' I said, and hung up.

Still chuckling, I hurried out and unhitched my car. Spike Higgins stared at me suspiciously.

'Just got an errand to do,' I said airily. 'Be back soon.'

'You better be,' Spike Higgins' ghost said. 'We wanta drive around and see those movie stars' houses later on.'

Ten minutes later Monica herself, trim and lovely, was opening the door for me. In high spirits, I grabbed her round the waist, and kissed her. She turned her cheek to me, then, releasing herself, looked at me strangely.

'Mel,' she frowned, 'what in the world is wrong with you?'

'Nothing,' I carolled. 'Monica darling, I've got to talk to your uncle.'

'But he's too sick to see anyone. He's sinking fast, the doctor says.'

'All the more reason why I must see him,' I told her, and pushed into the house. 'Where is he, upstairs?'

I hurried up, and into the sickroom. Monica's uncle, a big man with a rugged face and a chin like the prow of a battleship, was in bed, breathing stertorously.

'Mr Bracer!' I said, breathless, and his eyes opened slowly.

'Who're you?' a voice as raspy as a shovel scraping a concrete floor growled.

'I'm going to marry Monica,' I told him. 'Mr Bracer, have you ever heard of Spike Higgins? Or Slippery Samuels? Or Buffalo Benny, Pacific Pete, Toledo Ike?'

'Heard of 'em?' A bright glow came into the sick man's eyes. 'Ha! I'll say I have. And laid hands on 'em, too, more'n once. But they're dead now.'

'I know they are,' I told him. 'But they're still around. Mr Bracer, how'd you like to meet up with them again?'

'Would I!' Dan Bracer murmured, and his hands clenched in unconscious anticipation. 'Ha!'

'Then,' I said, 'if you'll wait for me in the cemetery the first night after—after—well, anyway, wait for me, and I'll put you in touch with them.'

The ex-railway detective nodded. He grinned broadly, like a tiger viewing its prey and eager to be after it. Then he lay back, his eyes closed, and Monica, running in, gave a little gasp.

'He's gone!' she said.

'Ha ha!' I chuckled. 'Ha ha ha! What a surprise this is going to be to certain parties.'

The funeral was held in the afternoon, two days later. I didn't see Monica much in the interim. In the first place, though she hadn't known her uncle well, and wasn't particularly grieved, there were a lot of details to be attended to. In the second place, Spike Higgins and his pals kept me on the jump. I had to drive around Hollywood, to all the stars' houses, to Malibou Beach, Santa Monica, Laurel Canyon, and the various studios, so they could sightsee.

Then, too, Monica rather seemed to be avoiding me, when I did have time free. But I was too inwardly gleeful at the prospect of getting rid of the ghosts of Higgins and his pals to notice.

I managed to slip away from Higgins to attend the funeral of Dan Bracer, but could not help grinning broadly, and even at times chuckling, as I thought of his happy anticipation of meeting Spike Higgins and the others again. Monica eyed me oddly, but I could explain later. It wasn't quite the right moment to go into details.

After the funeral, Monica said she had a headache, so I promised to come round later in the evening. I returned to the trailer to find Spike Higgins and the others sprawled out, smoking my cigarettes again. Higgins looked at me with dark suspicion.

'Chum,' he said, 'we wanta be hitting the road again. We leave tomorrow, get me?'

'Tonight, Spike,' I said cheerfully. 'Why wait? Right after sunset you'll be on your way. To distant parts. Tra la, tra le, tum tum te tum.'

He scowled, but could think of no objection. I waited impatiently for sunset. As soon as it was thoroughly dark, I hitched up and drove out of the trailer camp, heading for the cemetery where Dan Bracer had been buried that afternoon.

Spike Higgins was still surly, but unsuspicious until I drew up and parked by the low stone wall at the nearest point to Monica's uncle's grave. Then, gazing out at the darkness-shadowed cemetery, he looked uneasy.

'Say,' he snarled, 'whatcha stoppin' here for? Come on, let's be movin'.'

'In a minute, Spike,' I said. 'I have some business here.'

I slid out and hopped over the low wall.

'Mr Bracer!' I called. 'Mr Bracer!'

I listened, but a long freight rumbling by half a block distant, where the Union Pacific lines entered the city, drowned out any sound. For a moment I could see nothing. Then a misty figure came into view among the headstones.

'Mr Bracer!' I called as it approached. 'This way!'

The figure headed towards me. Behind me Spike Higgins, Slippery Samuels and the rest of the ghostly crew were pressed against the wall, staring apprehensively into the darkness. And they were able to recognize the dim figure approaching before I could be sure of it.

'Dan Bracer!' Spike Higgins choked, in a high, ghostly squeal.

'It's him!' Slippery Samuels groaned.

'In the spirit!' Pacific Pete wailed. 'Oh oh oh oh OH!'

They tumbled backwards, with shrill squeaks of dismay. Dan Bracer's spirit came forward faster. Paying no attention to me, he took off after the retreating five.

Higgins turned and fled, wildly, with the others at his heels. They were heading towards the railway line, over which the freight was still rumbling, and Dan Bracer was now at their heels. Crowding each other, Higgins and Slippery Samuels and Buffalo Benny swung on to a passing truck, with Pacific Pete and Toledo Ike catching wildly at the rungs of the next.

They drew themselves up to the top of the trucks, and stared back. Dan Bracer's ghost seemed, for an instant, about to be left behind. But one long ectoplasmic arm shot out. A ghostly hand caught the rail of the guard's van, and Dan Bracer swung aboard. A moment later, he was running forward along the tops of the trucks, and up ahead of him, Spike Higgins and his pals were racing towards the engine.

That was the last I saw of them—five phantom figures fleeing, the sixth pursuing in happy anticipation. Then they were gone out of my life, heading east.

Still laughing to myself at the manner in which I had rid myself of Spike Higgins' ghost, and so made it possible for Monica and me to be married and enjoy our honeymoon trailer trip after all, I drove to Monica's aunt's house.

'Melvin!' Monica said sharply, as she answered my ring. 'What are you laughing about now?'

'Your uncle,' I chuckled. 'He—'

'My uncle!' Monica gasped. 'You—you fiend! You laughed when he died! You laughed all during his funeral! Now you're laughing because he's dead!'

'No, Monica!' I said. 'Let me explain. About the spirits, and how I—'

Her voice broke.

'Forcing your way into the house—laughing at my poor Uncle Dan—laughing at his funeral—'

'But Monica!' I cried. 'It isn't that way at all. I've just been to the cemetery, and—'

'And you came back laughing,' Monica retorted. 'I never want to see you again. Our engagement is broken. And worst of all is the *way* you laugh. It's so—so ghostly! So spooky. Blood-chilling. Even if you hadn't done the other things, I could never marry a man who laughs like that. So here's your ring. And good-bye.'

Leaving me staring at the ring in my hand, she slammed the door. And that was that. Monica is very strong-minded, and what she says, she means. I couldn't even try to explain. About Spike Higgins. And how I'd unconsciously come to laugh that way through associating with five phantoms. After all, I'd just rid myself of them for good. And the only way Monica would ever have believed my story would have been from my showing her Spike Higgins' ghost himself.

Ha!

Ha ha!

Ha ha ha ha!

If you know anyone who wants to buy a practically unused trailer, cheap, let them get in touch with me.

SORCHE NIC LEODHAS

The House that Lacked a Bogle

THERE once was a house that lacked a bogle. That would be no great thing for a house to be wanting in the ordinary way, but it happened that this house was in St Andrews. That being a town where every one of the best houses has a ghost or a bogle, as they call it, of its own, or maybe two or even more, the folk who lived in the house felt the lack sorely. They were terribly ashamed when their friends talked about their bogles, seeing that they had none of their own.

The worst of it was that they had but lately come into money and had bought the house to set themselves up in the world. They never thought to ask if it had a bogle when they bought it, just taking it for granted that it had. But what good was it to be having a fine big house if there was no bogle in it? In St Andrews, anyway!

The man of the house could be reckoned a warm man with a tidy lot of money at his banker's, while his neighbour MacParlan had a hard time of it scraping enough to barely get by. But the MacParlans had a bogle that had been in the family since the time of King Kenneth the First, and they had papers to prove it.

The woman of the house had two horses to her carriage, and Mrs MacNair had no carriage at all. But the MacNairs had *three* bogles, being well supplied, and Mrs MacNair was so set up about them that it fair put one's teeth on edge to hear her going on about them and their doings.

Tammas, the son of the house, told his parents that he couldn't hold up his head when chaps talked about their bogles at his school, and he had to admit that there weren't any at his house at all.

And then there was Jeannette, the daughter of the house (her name was really Janet but she didn't like the sound of it, it being so plain). Well, *she* came home one day, and banged the door to, and burst into tears. And when they all asked her what was amiss, she said she'd been humiliated entirely because they hadn't a bogle, and she'd never show her face outside the house again until her papa got one for her.

Well, it all came to this. Without a bogle, they could cut no figure at all in society, for all their money.

They did what they could, of course, to set the matter right. In fact, each one of them tried in his own way, but not letting on to the others, however, lest they be disappointed if naught came of it.

The man of the house kept an eye on MacParlan's house and found out that MacParlan's bogle liked to take a stroll by nights on the leads of MacParlan's roof. So one night, when all the MacParlans had gone off somewhere away from home, he went over and called up to Mac-Parlan's bogle. After a bit of havering, the man got down to the point. 'Do you not get terrible tired of haunting the same old place day in and day out?' he asked.

'What way would I be doing that?' the bogle asked, very much surprised.

'Och, 'twas just a thought I had,' said the man. 'You might be liking to visit elsewhere maybe?'

'That I would not,' said the bogle flatly.

'Och well,' said the man, 'should you e'er feel the need o' a change of scene, you'll find a warm welcome at my house any time and for as long as you're liking to stay.'

The bogle peered down at him over the edge of the roof.

'Thank you kindly,' said he, 'but I'll bide here wi' my own folks. So dinna expect me.' And with that he disappeared.

So there was naught for the man to do but go back home.

The woman of the house managed to get herself asked to the Mac-Nairs' house for tea. She took with her a note to the MacNairs' bogles, telling them she was sure the three of them must be a bit cramped for room, what with there being so many of them and the MacNairs' house being so small. So she invited any or all of them to come over and stay at her house, where they'd find plenty of room and every comfort provided that a bogle could ever wish.

When nobody was watching, she slipped the note down behind the wainscoting in the MacNairs' drawing room, where she was sure the MacNairs' bogles would be finding it.

The MacNairs' bogles found it all right, and it surprised them. They didn't know exactly what to make of the note when they'd read it. But there was no doubt the woman meant it kindly, they said to each other. Being very polite bogles, they decided that she deserved the courtesy of an answer to the note, and since none of them was very much for writing, the least they could do was to send one of themselves to decline the invitation. The woman had paid them a call, so to speak. So one of them went to attend to it that same night.

The bogle met up with the woman of the house just as she was coming out of the linen press with a pile of fresh towels in her arms. The

maids had left that day, being unwilling to remain in a house so inferior
that it had no bogle to it. She'd have been startled out of her wits had she
not been so glad to see the bogle.

'Och then!' said she, "tis welcome you are entirely!'

'Thank ye kindly,' said the bogle.

'You'll be stopping here I hope?' questioned the woman eagerly.

'I'm sorry to be disappointing you,' said the bogle, 'but I'm not
staying. I'm needed at home.'

'Och now,' said the woman, 'and could they not make do without
you just for a month or two? Or happen even a fortnight?'

But she could see for herself that the bogle was not to be persuaded.
In fact, none of them could accept her invitation. That's what the bogle
had come to tell her. With their thanks, of course.

"Tis a sore thing,' complained the woman, 'what with all the money
paid out for the house and all, that we have no bogle of our own. Now
can you be telling me why?'

'I would not like to say,' said the bogle.

But the woman was sure he knew the reason, so she pressed him until
at last the bogle said reluctantly, 'Well, this is the way of it. The house
is too young! Losh! 'Tis not anywhere near a hundred years old yet, and
there's not been time enough for anything to have happened that would
bring it a bogle of its own. And forbye . . . ' The bogle stopped talking at
that point.

'Och! What more?' urged the woman.

'W-e-e-ell,' said the bogle slowly, 'I'd not be liking to hurt your
feelings, but your family is not, so to speak, distinguished enough. Now
you take the MacParlans and the Macphersons and the MacAlistairs—
their families go back into the far ages. And the MacAlpines is as old as
the hills and rocks and streams. As for the MacNairs,' he added proudly,
'och, well, the MacNairs *is* the MacNairs. The trouble with your family
is that there is nothing of note to it. No one knows exactly where it
would be belonging. There's no clan or sept o' the name. Losh! The
name has not even a "Mac" at the front of it.'

'Aye,' said the woman slowly, 'I can see that fine.'

And so she could. For the truth was that they had come from Wig-
town and were not a Highland family at all.

'Well,' said the bogle, 'that's the way it is. So I'll bid you good night.'
And away he went like a drift of mist, leaving the poor woman of the
house alone and uncomforted.

The daughter of the house had taken to her bed and spent her time
there, weeping and sleeping, when she wasn't eating sweeties out of a

pink satin box and reading romantic tales about lovely ladies who had adventures in castles just teeming with ghosts and handsome gentlemen in velvet suits of clothes.

So there was no one left to have a try but the son, Tammas. It must be admitted he did the best he could, even if it turned out that he was maybe a little bit too successful.

Tammas had got to the place where he kept out of the way of his friends on account of the shame that was on the family; he being young and full of pride. He only went out by night, taking long walks in lonely places all by himself.

One night he was coming back from one of these walks, and he came along by a kirkyard. It was just the sort of spot that suited his gloomy thoughts, so he stopped and leaned over the wall to look at the long rows of gravestones.

'All those graves lying there,' he thought, 'with many a bogle from them stravaging through the town and not a one of them for us. 'Tis not fair on us.'

He stopped to think about the injustice of it, and then he said out loud, 'If there's a bogle amongst you all who's got no family of his own, let him just come along with me. He can bide with us and welcome.' And with a long, deep sigh he turned back up the road and started for home.

He'd not gone more than twenty paces past the end of the kirkyard, when of a sudden he heard a fearful noise behind him. It was so eerie that it near raised the hair right off from his head. It sounded like a cat yowling and a pig squealing and a horse neighing and an ox bellowing all at one and the same time.

Tammas scarcely dared turn and look, with the fright that was on him, but turn he did. And he saw 'twas a man coming towards him. He was dressed in Highland dress with kilt and sporran, jacket and plaid showing plain, and the moonlight glinting off his brooch and shoe buckles and off the handle of the dirk in his hose. He carried a pair of bagpipes under his arm and that was where the noise was coming from.

'Whisht, man,' called Tammas, 'leave off with the pipes now. The racket you're making's enough to wake the dead.'

''Twill do no such thing,' said the piper. 'For they're all awake already and about their business. As they should be, it being midnight.'

And he put his mouth at the pipes to give another blow.

'Och, then ye'll wake all the folks in St Andrews,' protested Tammas. 'Give over now, that's a good lad!'

'Och nay,' said the piper soothingly. 'St Andrews folk will pay us no heed. They're used to us. They even like us.'

By this time he had come up to Tammas where he stood in the middle of the road. Tammas took another look at him to see who the piper was. And losh, 'twas no man at all. 'Twas a bogle!

''Tis a strangely queer thing,' said the piper sadly. 'I've been blowin' on these things all the days of my mortal life till I plain blew the life out o' my body doing it. And I've been blowing on them two or three hundred years since then, and I just cannot learn how to play a tune on them.'

'Well, go and blow somewhere else,' Tammas told him. 'Where it's lonely, with none to hear you.'

'I'd not be liking that at all,' said the piper. 'Besides, I'm coming with you.'

'With me!' Tammas cried in alarm.

'Och aye,' said the piper, and then he added reproachfully, 'you asked me, you know. Did you not?'

'I suppose I did,' Tammas admitted reluctantly. 'But I'd no idea there'd be anyone there listening.'

'Well, *I* was there,' the piper said, 'and I was listening. I doubt that I'm the only bogle in the place without a family of my own. So I accept the invitation, and thank ye kindly. Let's be on our way.'

And off he stepped, with his kilt swinging and his arms squared just so and the pipes going at full blast.

Tammas went along with him, because there was nowhere else he could go at that hour but back to his home.

When they got home, Tammas opened the door and into the house the two of them went. All the family came running to see what was up, for the pipes sounded worse indoors than out since there was less room there for the horrible noise to spread.

'There!' Tammas shouted at them all, raising his voice over the racket of the bagpipes. 'There's your bogle for you, and I hope you're satisfied!'

And he stamped up the stairs and into his room, where he went to bed with his pillow pulled over his ears.

Strange to tell, they really were satisfied, because now they had a bogle and could hold their own when they went out into society. Quite nicely as it happened, for they had the distinction of being the only family in the town that had a piping ghost—even if he didn't know how to play the pipes.

It all turned out very well, after all. The daughter of the house married one of the sons of the MacNairs and changed her name back to

Janet, her husband liking it better. And she had a 'Mac' at the front of her name at last, as well as her share of the three MacNair bogles, so she was perfectly happy.

The mother and father grew a bit deaf with age, and the piping didn't trouble them at all.

But Tammas decided he'd had all he wanted of bogles and of St Andrews as well. So he went off to London where he made his fortune and became a real Sassenach. In time, he even got a 'Sir' before his name, which gave him a lot more pleasure than he'd ever have got from a 'Mac'.

The bogle never did learn to play the bagpipes, though he never left off trying. But nobody cared about that at all. Not even the bogle.

PAMELA ROPNER

The January Queen

THE classroom was cold, a bitter, gnawing cold that stiffened our fingers and made our feet ache so that we shifted them constantly with little scraping sounds like mice. Outside the wind blew in fierce, spasmodic gusts, slapping the rain against the high, uncurtained windows, tearing at the leafless trees, and rattling the bare branches.

Time was numb and the minutes of the algebra lesson ticked by with an almost unendurable sloth. There was nothing that we could do except stare at Miss Murdoch's back. Miss Murdoch seemed at first to be all knitting, a broad expanse of irregular brown like a ploughed field. Her shapeless brown jumper reached far below the line of her bulging hips and merged imperceptibly with her baggy brown, tweed skirt. She wore brown stockings and flat walking-shoes, the heels badly scuffed. Her hair, too, was brown, and hung dispiritedly to her collar. We watched dispassionately as Miss Murdoch wrote busily on the blackboard. She seemed entirely absorbed in what she was doing, for the blackboard was to her a refuge. When she could no longer face our bored, hostile faces, she would turn and cover the flat black surface with a storm of white ciphers. She wrote very fast, almost hysterically, and the squeaking chalk set our teeth on edge. She built a pyramid of ciphers, then a square, then the square was a tower, and soon the whole expanse of board was covered with delicate frost figures, like a forest of rimy trees. But we were lost in the forest, to us it seemed impenetrable. Only Ursula, who sat next to me, could find her way. Her mind was like a light that led her easily down the narrow frosted paths. She rested her chin on her hands and her alert, eager blue eyes followed Miss Murdoch's swift running chalk, and as understanding dawned, a smile curled the corners of her mouth.

The rest of the class shifted noisily, but Ursula sat silent. I reached over to touch her on the arm. 'Ursula,' I whispered. She did not look at me.

'Ursula,' I said again. Then my elbow struck my pencil-box, which fell with a deafening clatter on to the bare wooden floor where it spilled open and all the pencils and pens rolled noisily out. The class giggled, softly at first, then unchecked, loudly, challenging. The flying chalk paused and slowly, reluctantly Miss Murdoch turned round. It was almost a shock to see that her face was not brown but white like the chalk she still held raised in her right hand. She had a thin, dull face, and behind her spectacles, pink like a white mouse's eyes, she blinked regretfully. She opened her mouth to say something, but no words came. Someone at the back shouted, 'We are cold,' and then the stamping began. Thirty pairs of feet banging remorselessly on the floor like drums. Ursula sprang round in her chair; her cheeks were flushed and her fair hair swung angrily. 'Shut up,' she yelled. But as if encouraged by this, the stamping grew louder and the laughter was like a pack of dogs. I glanced round at the algebra mistress, but Miss Murdoch was turned to stone, her hands held up defiantly but more in fear than authority, and I knew that beneath the brown knitted jersey she was trembling. The noise rose to a crescendo. I was flushed and prickling with embarrassment, for we in the front row could see the helpless tears swim in Miss Murdoch's misty eyes.

'Girls. Girls.' Her voice was thin. She clapped her hands but no one paid attention, and she shook her head in despair, lumbered over to the desk and thumped it. 'Please, girls, I must have a little quiet.' Her ineffectual voice was lost in the thunderous stamping. Again she struck the desk, but this time a pile of algebra books swayed, toppled, and crashed down to the ground, and the black bottle of ink unwisely balanced on top of them rolled cruelly over, splashing blue-black tears on to the floor. Miss Murdoch stooped down, drawing in her breath in dismay, but as she did so, she caught her side on the corner of the desk, and I saw her wince with pain.

'Gosh she is clumsy,' Susan whispered scornfully on my other side.

'This is awful.' Ursula's voice was tight and strained.

The bell saved Miss Murdoch. It rang, loud, blessedly impersonal. Almost before it had died away, the class had trooped out giggling. Only Ursula and I were left. Miss Murdoch did not look up from her pool of ink. Ursula left her desk and crept forward until she stood in front of Miss Murdoch's bending form.

'Shall I help you mop it up?' But there was silence, and in that deserted classroom, where the chalk atoms danced furiously in a sudden shaft of pale sunshine, I saw the shadow of Miss Murdoch's humiliation. Poor Miss Murdoch, poor clumsy Murdoch who couldn't keep order, who couldn't teach, who finding life too hostile had retreated into an abstract world of dancing, tormenting figures. She began to cry soundlessly, and unable to bear it any longer I ran from the room.

The next morning, the long-expected frost struck. Even after the bell for school had rung, I looked from my dormitory window to a world grown suddenly old; grey trees, grey grass like hair, grey stones, aged as if from the first beginning of the world. Then the wandering clouds parted and a silver winter sun came out brilliant and uncompromising, and then again was the world transformed, for the dull grass glistened and the rimy trees shone like sticks of sugar icing, and down the long fields, through the glittering wood, the flashing mere was sealed with a film of ice. Shivering and blowing on her fingers, Ursula came across the floor and stood beside me.

'Do you think it will freeze the mere hard?' she asked.

'I don't know,' I said, and wished very deeply that I was not at school, not in dormitory 2 of St Luke's School for Girls. I could be out in this magic, sparkling world. I could run through the frosted grass and feel the hard earth jar my knees and the cutting wind bring tears to my eyes. Ursula left me, but I did not immediately follow her. I don't know how long I stood there. I suppose I must have been day-dreaming, because I did not hear the second bell until after it had rung, for it sounded late in my head. I ran down the stairs and started off down the long corridor that led past the staff room and eventually to our classroom. But as I reached the staff room, the door opened and Miss Murdoch came out and began to walk slowly towards our classroom. I followed her, treading delicately, so that she would not hear me. Outside the door she paused. She seemed to stiffen her whole body, raised her head boldly, flung back her shoulders so that she had a fleeting appearance of confidence, but I saw that her thick hands were tightly clenched and I knew then beyond all doubt that Miss Murdoch was afraid. There was a terrible quiet in the classroom; it was a tangible thing, and the cold of it reached out and touched me. Miss Murdoch stepped quite briskly. I hesitated, meaning to slip in to my desk as she reached the blackboard. I heard her slow heavy feet on the uncarpeted floor. The class was tense and a sudden sick feeling of apprehension caught at my stomach. I waited, uncertain what to do. Then I heard Miss Murdoch draw in her breath in a deep gasp. I heard her running feet and she brushed past me sobbing like a wounded animal. There was a splatter of uneasy laughter. I ran into the classroom. Ursula was up on the platform holding the chalk duster. She held it poised over foot-high letters crudely printed on the blackboard as if she could not believe the cruelty of them. On it someone had written 'MURDOCH IS A CLUMSY ASS'. No one spoke as

Ursula rubbed out the hateful letters, evaporating them in a cloud of flying chalk. It was as if they had never been, but I knew that the mocking ghost of them would always haunt me through the forest of figures like teeth.

For two days the frost drove into the ground like iron. On the third night it was so cold that I couldn't sleep. I tossed and turned, jerking the confining blankets so that soon my feet were icily cold. Outside the moon floated high and brilliant and a counterfeit window gleamed on the floor. I slipped out of bed and crept over to the window and looked down at the wood. Like the trees of Miss Murdoch's forest they stood; shining, silver trees, creatures of fantasy, wraiths of summer, suddenly free, dancing, mysterious and wild.

I was about to return to my cold bed when I heard the door beneath the window softly open and someone came stealthily out. The figure moved slowly forward and I could hear its footsteps crunch faintly on the frozen earth. I peered down and saw with a sudden jerk of surprise that it was Miss Murdoch. She had her back to me and she was bent forward. I thought that she held something in her right hand, but I could not make out what it was. She walked steadily away over the icy grass. I ran to Ursula's bed. Ursula looked beautiful when she was asleep. Her fair hair splayed in careless tendrils over her dreaming face.

'Ursula.' I shook her gently by the shoulder. She stirred, but she did not open her eyes.

'Ursula, wake up.' My voice was urgent.

'What's the matter?' She sounded cross.

'Wake up,' I implored, and she sat up, staring up at me in the crystal darkness.

'What on earth is the matter?'

'It is Miss Murdoch,' I whispered urgently.

Ursula stiffened. 'Miss Murdoch?'

'Come and see by the window. She is out there and I don't know where she is going.'

When we looked out again Miss Murdoch was hurrying down through the wood. She was almost running and there was something purposeful in her gait that frightened me. She was heading straight for the mere.

'Quick——' Ursula's voice was tight and small. 'We must go after her.'

'Shouldn't we wake the others?' I whispered.

'No.' And there was a decisive ring in her voice, so afraid though I was, I did not argue.

We dressed as quickly as we could, pulling thick woollen jerseys over our heads. Then we put on our navy-blue school dressing-gowns, and regulation scarlet felt slippers. We crept noiselessly out into the passage, where we stood listening. Then we slipped gently down the creaking wooden stairs, but nothing stirred. Miss Murdoch had left the door unbolted, but it squeaked disturbingly as we opened it and then we stood holding our breath, poised for flight, but no one came, and we ran out unobserved into that bright, moonlight night. I dashed forward. 'Not too fast,' Ursula clutched at my arm. 'We don't want her to see us.'

'But——' I protested, for a dark fear hung in my mind.

'Please,' Ursula pleaded. 'We mustn't. We really mustn't.'

I was ready to answer her, but her face was turned away from me.

Silently we crept quite close behind Miss Murdoch. Once I trod on a stick and it cracked sharply through the close echoing wood, but she did not pause or glance back. It seemed as if she did not hear us. She seemed conscious of nothing round her; she might have been walking in a dream.

She reached the very edge of the mere, where she stopped. Down the ice the moon shone a brilliant pathway, and in the centre of the mere, the island was dark and hunched. An owl hooted and a light wind rustled the crisp icicled branches of the wood.

I don't know how long Miss Murdoch stood there, then she gave a sigh of the purest pleasure. Ursula pulled me down behind a prickly thorn bush. 'We have just got to wait and see,' she whispered. I didn't argue, but, then, I did not know what else to do.

Quite suddenly Miss Murdoch sat down. She had her back to us and we could not clearly see what she was doing. A shadow came over the moon and in the sudden dark, we waited breathless for it to pass. Then Miss Murdoch stood up and beside me Ursula gasped, for she suddenly seemed immensely tall. She gave a curious little flick of her arms like a bird testing its wings and I heard her crunch over the little stones that edged the lake, with a sound like a sword drawn from its scabbard. In the next instant, Miss Murdoch glided on to the lake, her feet tightly laced in a pair of black skating boots with high old-fashioned blades curved like scimitars. Relief made us giggle.

'She is skating.'

'Fancy Murdoch skating!'

We felt warm. We felt free. We could afford to laugh, but we must not be heard. It would spoil everything. We stuffed our fists into our mouths in an effort to suppress our almost hysterical mirth. Behind us something stirred. Ursula and I sprang round, our hearts beating, but there was no one there. When we looked again, Miss Murdoch had reached the very centre of the mere. For a moment she paused like a dancer at the prelude of the dance and then she began to skate. For as long as I live I shall never forget what I saw on that moonlight night. She was a swallow and a swift. She was a swan. She was Ariel, she was Mercury with wings on her feet, light and deft as a dragonfly, her thin arms held out like wings. Gaily as a spinning top she whirled until there were six Miss Murdochs with six spinning faces. Like a deer she leapt and I saw her skate blades flash as she held her arms to the kindly moon.

Almost without knowing it we crept from our hiding-place and crunched down until we stood on the very edge of the mere. But Miss Murdoch did not see us. She looked towards us, but she did not see us. Merrily, merrily, she spun, intoxicated by the sliding ice beneath her dancing feet. She wove herself a cobweb world, light as air, and like a crust the bitter years fell away; the tyranny of the classroom, the jumbled figures, the blackboard, the chalk, the giggling and shifting of feet, the cruelty and the mocking laughter. Here alone on the spinning ice she was free.

'Wherever did she learn to skate like that?' I could not take my eyes off Miss Murdoch. Round and round she flew like a feather in the wind, higher and higher she leapt. If she had in some magical way floated right off the ice I would not have been surprised, for she was quite transformed.

'Poor, poor Murdoch,' murmured Ursula, but I did not understand why she said that; and I thought it rather strange.

The skates hummed over the ice and its tensile surface slashed by the cutting edge of the skates vibrated like a plucked string. As Miss Murdoch passed, the echo of her dazzling leaps and turns lingered on and Ursula and I, unconscious of the gripping cold, watched her spellbound. She began to circle in ever widening sweeps, but suddenly it seemed as if the ice took on a new note. I felt Ursula's fingers in mine tense. Her voice was high with fear. 'She is going too near the island. The ice is thin under the trees.' She put up her hands to her mouth, cupping them around her lips. Again the ice cried out.

'Miss Murdoch!' Ursula's voice echoed through the winter air, but the dancing figure paid no heed, for into her giddy world no human voice could penetrate.

For yet a third time Miss Murdoch swooped around the island and I heard the ice moan again in protest, and there was an ominous gurgling sound deep down in those dark waters.

Ursula heard it too. She turned to me and before I could stop her, she was away, half stumbling, half sliding over the ice. As she ran she shouted, 'Go back!'

'Ursula.' I didn't know what to do. I stood there paralysed with awful indecision. Miss Murdoch swooped round the corner of the island and as if in a dream I saw it all. The ice cracked wide open. Ursula screamed and Miss Murdoch went into the water quite silently, almost as if she had been expecting it.

Ursula dashed forward. All around her the ice was talking. A few yards short of the gaping hole she stopped short. When she spoke her voice was quite steady and in the still air carried to me quite clearly.

'Behind you, Miss Murdoch, reach behind you. There is an overhanging branch.' There was a convulsive heave in the water and an arm flung up. Miss Murdoch was very near the island.

'I can't reach it.' Her voice was blurred with water, high and desperate.

'Behind you, Miss Murdoch. You are not in very deep water. Reach behind you.'

For a sudden curious moment, she sounded just like the headmistress. The white clutching fingers stretched up for the branch, snatched at it convulsively, missed, snatched again, then tightened around it. The wet branch bent, creaked, but held. Now Ursula was stripping off her jumper. I started off towards her across the ice. I had nearly reached her when she whipped round.

'Don't come too near or we will both go in.' She was still talking in that calm, controlled way. 'Throw me your jumper.' I wrenched off my dressing-gown and pulled my jumper over my head, feeling the wool scrape my face.

'Throw it to me.'

I threw it clumsily. Ursula caught the jumper, knotted the two arms together and twisted them into a rough rope. Then she flung herself face downwards on to the treacherous ice and began to crawl towards where Miss Murdoch still clung for her life to the branch. She crawled quite steadily and slowly and I stood there praying, and I found that I was crying silently and the moon made pale rainbows in my eyelashes.

'Now, Miss Murdoch,' said Ursula in her headmistress's voice.

'Ursula.' The answering cry was faint and tremulous, the voice of a girl.

'I am going to throw you this rope. Hold on to it with your other hand, support yourself and see if you can pull yourself to the island.'

'I can't. I can't. Help me. Help me!' Her voice was very faint now and despair turned up the edge of her words into a shriek.

'You must.' Ursula spoke quite coldly, like the ice.

She clenched her body and threw one end of the makeshift rope, but it fell with a splash into the black water. Somehow Miss Murdoch put up her other hand and gripped it.

'Come on, Miss Murdoch. Come on,' I cried. Slowly, agonisingly, Miss Murdoch pulled herself up.

'Get help quickly.' Ursula flung the words back over her shoulder and I turned and ran back over the ice, up through the glittering wood towards the school, and fear like a dark shadow followed me. I flung myself gasping into the hall. I called for them. Lights snapped on and they came running to me. I was sobbing and shaking. The words spilled out incoherently, but somehow I managed to tell them what had happened. I fought out those words and they seemed to understand, for in a moment, they were gone from me, running out of the school, down through the wood, back towards the ice and that awful gaping hole where poor Miss Murdoch clung for her life. I turned to run after them, but they would not let me go.

Matron took me upstairs, put me firmly to bed where I lay shivering, thinking of Miss Murdoch and brave, kind Ursula.

'What I can't understand,' said Matron over and over again, 'is what you were all doing on the ice,' but I did not tell her. I turned away hugging my secret to myself, trying to shut out the memory that crowded in on me, giving me no relief.

At dawn Ursula came into the room. Shock had set her face so that suddenly she looked much older. She was very pale and she walked over to the window, where she stood with her back to me staring out. I knew then what she had to tell me. I didn't know what to say to her, so I said nothing. Eventually she spoke.

'I couldn't get her out.'

'I know that.'

'You did your best,' said Matron inadequately, but her words sounded lame, and Ursula seemed not to hear them.

For a long time she remained standing there and I heard her whisper, half to herself, 'She was like a queen, a January Queen.' Then she began to shake all over, her head dropped to her hands and the room was full of harsh, bitter sobbing.

For a week or two we all thought about Miss Murdoch, although we did not say much. The headmistress gave us a warning about going down to the mere, and we all contributed to a wreath. Then quite suddenly, like a book that has been read, the subject of Miss Murdoch was dropped, finished, not to be mentioned again. We shut her out of our minds as if she had never been, and prepared ourselves to enjoy the holidays.

In the summer term we had a new algebra mistress. Miss Abigail was small and shy. Where Miss Murdoch had been slow and clumsy, Miss Abigail was deft and quick as a bird. She had a great air of confidence, yet there was something in her manner, a way of turning her head from side to side, an unaccountable stiffening, a tenseness in her voice, that told us surely, inevitably that the cord of discipline that bound us to her was thin and might at any given time snap. I knew this and Ursula knew it and we feared for Miss Abigail.

One afternoon when the classroom was full of the smell of summer and the wayward flight of honeybees, we sat enduring our algebra lesson. Wishing to be out on the sunlit grass, the class was very restless. They began to mutter and a spasm of giggling broke out. It was quite quickly suppressed, but almost immediately broke out again. Miss Abigail turned repeatedly from the blackboard.

'Settle down now, girls,' she said, but her voice lacked conviction. The giggling continued, and they began to shift their feet, and when Miss Abigail turned her back paper notes flicked through the air like snowflakes.

I whirled round in my chair. 'Stop it, stop it,' I shouted.

A big girl at the back of the class imitated me in a high falsetto voice. 'Stop it, stop it do.' And there was a gale of laughter. Miss Abigail faced us and I saw humiliation darken her blue eyes.

I glanced at Ursula.

She would intervene. But to my surprise she did not speak or move. I shook her by the elbow. 'Ursula,' but she was deaf to me. Yet there was something in the stiff way in which she sat that disturbed me. Her head was tilted to one side so that her fair hair swung away from her small close ear. She was listening. Ursula was listening intently to something. But to what? Not to the mindless laughter nor to the jeers. And then I heard a new sound, a curious distant hollow humming, faint at first, then growing louder and louder until it filled the whole room with a rhythmic scraping sound like a saw.

Miss Abigail stared down at us; a new suspicion sharpened her features. 'Whatever is that strange noise?' but no one answered her. And now the dreadful relentless waspish sound was in all the room in all our ears. One by one the noisy class sat silently down and I saw their faces blanch, for we knew, all of us, what it was; it was the sound of skates.

We all knew how the mere would be that afternoon, how it would look under a summer sun, dragonflies twinkling in the standing reeds and the water-boatmen sculling in the green water. It was deadly cold in the classroom and we were aching and shivering. Bitterly the skates sang until the ink in the inkwells stirred and the pencils rattled in the desks with the vibration of their passing. Then quite suddenly Ursula stood up, gripping the sides of the desk as though the solid scarred wood was to her an anchor. She held herself so quiet and stiff that for an unreasoning instant I wondered if she still breathed. Then as I watched, a fleeting smile lit her pale face.

Abruptly as it had begun, the sound of skates ceased, warmth crept back into the atmosphere, the stiffness went out of Ursula and gently almost fluidly she sank down into her chair. Miss Abigail was puzzled. 'Well,' she remarked brightly, 'that horrid noise has gone.' Holding us responsible she smiled at us gratefully and I saw her hands relax. 'That's good, girls.' Her voice was bright. 'I'll hurry through the lesson, I'm sure you are all wanting to run outside.' We didn't answer her. Then there was nothing, only the wind, the distant bark of a dog, the shouts of Class 3 on their way to play tennis, and the screech of Miss Abigail's chalk on the blackboard.

R. CHETWYND-HAYES

Brownie

THE house was built of grey stone, and stood on the edge of a vast moor; an awesome, desolate place, where the wind roared across a sea of heather and screamed like an army of lost souls.

Our father drove into a muddy, weed-infested drive, then braked to a halt. He smiled over his shoulder at Rodney and me, then said cheerfully: 'You'll be very happy here.'

We had grave doubts. On closer inspection the stonework was very dirty, the paintwork was flaking, and generally the house looked as unrelenting as the moor that lay beyond. Father opened the door and got out, his face set in that determinedly cheerful expression parents assume whenever they wish to pretend that all is well, even though appearances suggest otherwise.

'Fine people, Mr and Mrs Fairweather.' He gripped Rodney's arm, then mine, and guided us up a flight of stone steps towards a vast, oak door. 'You'll love 'em. Then, there are all those lovely moors for you to play on. Wish I was staying with you, instead of going back to India. But duty calls.'

He was lying, we both knew it, and perhaps the knowledge made parting all the more sad. He raised a bronzed hand, but before he could grasp the knocker, the door creaked open and there stood Mrs Fairweather.

'Major Sinclair.' She stood to one side for us to enter. 'Come in, Sir, and the young 'uns. The wind's like a knife, and cuts a body to the bone.'

The hall was large, bare, lined with age-darkened oak panels; doors broke both walls on either side of a massive staircase, and there was an old, churchy smell.

'Come into the kitchen with you,' Mrs Fairweather commanded, 'that being the only room that's livable in on the ground floor. The rest is locked up.'

The kitchen lay behind the staircase; a grandfather of all kitchens, having a red tiled floor, a spluttering iron range that positively shone from frequent applications of black lead, and an array of gleaming copper saucepans hanging on brass hooks over the mantelpiece.

A tall, lean old man was seated behind a much-scrubbed deal table. He rose as we entered, revealing that he wore a dark blue boiler suit and a checked cloth cap.

'Fairweather,' his wife snapped, 'where's yer manners? Take yer cap off.'

Mr Fairweather reluctantly, or so it appeared to me, took off his cap, muttered some indistinguishable words, then sat down again. Mrs Fairweather turned to Father.

'You mustn't mind him, Sir. He's not used to company, but he's got a heart. I'll say that for him. Now, Sir, is there anything you'd like to settle with me before you leave?'

'No,' Father was clearly dying to be off, 'the extra sum we agreed upon will be paid by Simpson & Brown on the first of every month. The girl I engaged as governess will arrive tomorrow. Let me see,' he consulted a notebook, 'Miss Rose Fortesque.' He put the notebook away. 'I think that's all.'

'Right you are, Sir,' Mrs Fairweather nodded her grey head, 'I expect you'll want to say a few words to the little fellows before you leave, so me and Fairweather will make ourselves scarce. Fairweather . . .' The old man raised his head. 'Come on, we'll make sure the chicken are bedded down.'

Mr Fairweather followed her out through the kitchen doorway, muttering bad temperedly, and we were left alone with Father, who was betraying every sign of acute discomfort.

'Well, boys,' he was still determined to appear cheerful, 'I guess this is goodbye. You know I'd have loved to have taken you with me, but India is no place for growing boys, and now your mother has passed on there'd be no one to look after you. You'll be comfortable enough here, and Miss Fortesque will teach you all you need to know before you go to school next autumn. O.K.?'

I felt like choking, but Rodney, who had a far less emotional nature, was more prepared to deal with events of the moment.

'Do we own this house, Father?'

'I own this house,' Father corrected gently, 'and no doubt you will one day. As I told you, Mr and Mrs Fairweather are only caretakers, and they are allowed to cultivate some of the ground for their own use. Back before the days of Henry the Eighth, the house was a monastery, but since the Reformation it's been a private house. Your great uncle Charles was the last of our family to live here. I've never found the time to bring the old place up to scratch, so it has stood empty, save for the Fairweathers, since he died.'

'Pity,' said Rodney.

'Quite,' Father cleared his throat. 'Well, I expect the old . . . Mrs Fairweather has a good hot meal waiting for you, so I'll push off.' He bent down and kissed us lightly on the foreheads, then walked briskly to the kitchen door. 'Mrs Fairweather, I'm off.'

The speed with which the old couple reappeared suggested the chicken must be bedded down in the hall. Mr Fairweather made straight for his seat behind the table, while his wife creased her stern face into a polite smile.

'So you'll be going, Sir. I hope it won't be too long before we see you again.'

'No indeed.' Father shook her hand, his expression suddenly grave. 'No time at all. 'Bye, boys, do what the good Mrs Fairweather tells you. Goodbye, Fairweather.' He could not resist a bad joke. 'Hope it keeps fine for you.'

The old man half rose, grunted, then sat down again. Mrs Fairweather preceded Father into the hall. We heard the front door open, then the sound of Father's car; the crunch of gravel as he drove away. He was gone. We never saw him again. He was killed on the Indian North West Frontier fighting Afghanistan tribesmen, and, had he been consulted, I am certain that is the way he would have preferred to die. He was, above all, a soldier.

As Mrs Fairweather never failed to stress, food at Sinclair Abbey was plain, but good. We ate well, worked hard, for Mr Fairweather saw no reason why two extra pairs of hands should not be put to gainful employment, and above all, we played. An old, almost empty house is an ideal playground for two boys. The unused rooms, whenever we could persuade Mrs Fairweather to unlock the doors, were a particular joy. Dust-shrouded furniture crouched like beasts of prey against walls on which the paper had long since died. In the great dining room were traces of the old refectory where medieval monks had dined before Henry's henchmen had cast them out. One stained-glass window, depicting Abraham offering up Isaac as a sacrifice, could still be seen through a veil of cobwebs; an oak, high-backed chair, surmounted by a crucifix, suggested it had once been the property of a proud abbot. For young, enquiring eyes, remains of the old monastery could still be found.

Rose Fortesque came, as Father had promised, the day after our arrival. Had we been ten years older, doubtless we would have considered her to be a slim, extremely pretty, if somewhat retiring girl. As it was, we found her a great disappointment. Her pale, oval face, enhanced by a pair of rather sad blue eyes, gave the impression she was always on the verge of being frightened, the result possibly of being painfully shy.

Where Father had found her I have not the slightest idea. More than likely at some teachers' agency, or wherever prospective governesses parade their scholastic wares, but of a certainty, she was not equipped to deal with two high-spirited boys. It took but a single morning for us to become aware of this fact, and with the cruelty of unthinking youth, we took full advantage of the situation. She was very frightened after finding a frog in her bed, and a grass snake in her handbag, and from then onwards, she watched us with sad, reproachful eyes.

It was fully seven days after our arrival at Sinclair Abbey when we first met Brownie. Our bedroom was way up under the eaves, a long, barren room, furnished only by our two beds, a wardrobe, and two chairs, Mrs Fairweather having decided mere boys required little else. There was no electricity in that part of the house. A single candle lit us to bed, and once that was extinguished, there was only the pale rectangle of a dormer window which, in the small hours, when the sky was clear, allowed the moon to bathe the room in a soft, silver glow.

I woke suddenly, and heard the clock over the old stables strike two. It was a clear, frosty night, and a full moon stared in through the window, so that all the shadows had been chased into hiding behind the wardrobe, under the beds, and on either side of the window. Rodney was snoring, and I was just considering the possibility of throwing a boot at him, when I became aware there was a third presence in the room. I raised my head from the pillow. A man dressed in a monk's robe was sitting on the foot of my bed. The funny thing was, I couldn't feel his weight, and I should have done so, because my feet appeared to be underneath him.

I sat up, but he did not move, only continued to sit motionless, staring at the left hand wall. The cowl of his robe was flung back to reveal a round, dark-skinned face, surmounted by a fringe of black curly hair surrounding a bald patch that I seemed to remember was called a tonsure. I was frightened, but pretended I wasn't. I whispered:

'Who are you? What do you want?'

The monk neither answered nor moved, so I tried again, this time a little louder.

'What are you doing here?'

He continued to sit like a figure in a wax museum, so I decided to
wake Rodney—no mean task for he slept like Rip van Winkle. My
second shoe did the trick and he woke protesting loudly:

'Wassat? Young Harry, I'll do you.'

'There's a man sitting on the foot of my bed, and he won't move.'

'What!' Rodney sat up, rubbed his eyes, then stared at our silent
visitor. 'Who is he?'

'I don't know. I've asked him several times, but he doesn't seem to
hear.'

'Perhaps he's asleep.'

'His eyes are open.'

'Well,' Rodney took a firm grip of my shoe, 'we'll soon find out.' And
he hurled the shoe straight at the brown-clad figure.

Neither of us really believed what our eyes reported: the shoe went
right through the tonsured head and landed with a resounding smack on
a window pane. But still there was no response from the monk, and now
I was so frightened my teeth were chattering.

'I'm going to fetch Mrs Fairweather,' Rodney said after a while, 'she'll
know what to do.'

'Rodney,' I swallowed, 'you're not going to leave me alone with—
him, are you?'

Rodney was climbing out of the far side of the bed.

'He won't hurt you, he doesn't move, and if he does you can belt
under the bed. I say, chuck the candle over, and the matches, I've got to
find my way down to the next floor.'

Left alone, I studied our visitor with a little more attention than formerly,
for, as he appeared to be harmless, my fear was gradually subsiding.

I knew very little about monks, but this one seemed to be a rather
shabby specimen; his gown was old, and there was even a small hole in
one sleeve, as if he indulged in the bad habit of leaning his elbows on the
table. Furthermore, on closer inspection—and by now I had summoned
up enough courage to crawl forward a short way along the bed—he was
in need of a shave. There was a distinct stubble on his chin, and one
hand, that rested on his knee, had dirt under the finger nails. Altogether,
I decided, this was a very scruffy monk.

Rodney had succeeded in waking the Fairweathers. The old lady
could be heard protesting loudly at being disturbed, and an occasional
rumble proclaimed that Mr Fairweather was not exactly singing for joy.
Slippered feet came padding up the stairs, and now Mrs Fairweather's
unbroken tirade took on recognisable words.

'I won't have him lurking around the place. It's more than I'm prepared to stand, though why two lumps of boys couldn't have chased him out, without waking a respectable body from her well-earned sleep, I'll never know.'

'But he doesn't move,' Rodney's voice intervened.

'I'll move him.'

She came in through the doorway like a gust of wind, a bundle of fury wrapped in a flowered dressing gown, and in one hand she carried a striped bath towel.

'Get along with you.' She might have been shooing off a stray cat. 'I won't have you lurking around the house. Go on—out.'

The words had no effect, but the bath towel did. Mrs Fairweather waved it in, or rather through, the apparition's face. The figure stirred, rather like a clockwork doll making a first spasmodic move, then the head turned and a look of deep distress appeared on the up to now emotionless face. The old lady continued to scold, and flapped the towel even more vigorously.

'Go on, if I've told you once, I've told you a hundred times, you're not to bother respectable folk. Go where you belong.'

The monk flowed into an upright position; there is no other word to describe the action. Then he began to dance in slow motion towards the left hand wall, Mrs Fairweather pursuing him with her flapping towel. It was a most awesome sight; first the left leg came very slowly upwards, and seemed to find some invisible foothold, then the right drifted past it, while both arms gently clawed the air. It took the monk some three minutes to reach the left hand wall; a dreadful, slow, macabre dance, performed two feet above floor level, with an irate Mrs Fairweather urging him on with her flapping towel, reinforced by repeated instructions to go, and not come back, while her husband, ludicrous in a white flannel nightgown, watched sardonically from the doorway.

The monk at last came to the wall. His left leg went through it, then his right arm, followed by his entire body. The last we saw of him was the heel of one sandal, which had a broken strap. Mrs Fairweather folded up her bath towel and, panting from her exertions, turned to us.

'That's got shot of him, and you won't be bothered again tonight. Next time he comes, do what I did. Flap something in his face. He doesn't like that. Nasty, dreamy creature, he is.'

'But . . .' Rodney was almost jumping up and down in bed with excitement, '. . . what . . . who is he?'

'A nasty old ghost, what did you imagine he was?' Mrs Fairweather's face expressed profound astonishment at our ignorance; 'one of them old monks that used to live here, donkey's years ago.'

'Gosh,' Rodney eyed the wall through which the monk had vanished, 'do you mean he'll come back?'

'More than likely.' The old lady had rejoined her husband in the doorway. 'But when he does, no waking me out of a deep sleep. Do as I say, flap something in his face, and above all, don't encourage him. Another thing,' she paused and waved an admonishing finger, 'there's no need to tell that Miss Fortesque about him. She looks as if she's frightened of her own shadow as it is. Now go to sleep, and no more nonsense.'

It was some time before we went to sleep.

'Harry,' Rodney repeated the question several times, 'what is a ghost?'

I made the same answer each time.

'I dunno.'

'It seems a good thing to be. I mean, being able to go through walls and dance in the air. I'd make Miss Fortesque jump out of her skin. I say, she must sleep like a log.'

'Her room is some distance away,' I pointed out.

'Still, all that racket I was making . . .' He yawned. 'Tomorrow, we'll ask her what a ghost is.'

'Mrs Fairweather said we were not to tell her about the ghost.'

'There's no need to tell her we've seen one, stupid. Just ask her what it is.'

Rodney tacked the question on to Henry the Eighth's wives next morning.

'Name Henry the Eighth's wives,' Miss Fortesque had instructed. Rodney had hastened to oblige.

'Catherine of Aragon, Anne Boleyn, Jane Seymour, Anne of Cleves, Catherine Howard, and Catherine Parr who survived him, but it was a near thing. Please, Miss Fortesque, what is a ghost?'

'Very good,' Miss Fortesque was nodding her approval, then suddenly froze. 'What!'

'What is a ghost?'

The frightened look crept back into her eyes, and I could see she suspected some horrible joke.

'Don't be silly, let's get on with the lesson.'

'But I want to know,' Rodney insisted, 'please, what is a ghost?'

'Well,' Miss Fortesque still was not happy, but clearly she considered it her duty to answer any intelligent question, 'it is said, a ghost is a spirit who is doomed to walk the earth after death.'

'Blimey!' Rodney scratched his head, 'a ghost is dead?'

'Of course—at least, so it is said. But it is all nonsense. Ghosts do not exist.'

'What!' Rodney's smile was wonderful to behold, 'you mean—you don't believe ghosts exist?'

'I know they don't,' Miss Fortesque was determined to leave the subject before it got out of hand. 'Ghosts are the result of ignorant superstition. Now, let us get on. Harry this time. How did Henry dispose of his wives?'

I stifled a yawn.

'Catherine of Aragon divorced, Anne Boleyn beheaded, Jane Seymour died, Anne of Cleves divorced, Catherine Howard beheaded, Catherine Parr . . .'

'I say, Harry,' Rodney remarked later that day, 'I bet Brownie was the odd man out.'

'Who?'

'Brownie, the monk. There's always one in big establishments. You remember at prep school last year, that chap Jenkins. He was lazy, stupid, never washed. The chances are, Brownie was the odd man out among the other monks. Probably never washed or shaved unless he was chivvied by the abbot, then when he died he hadn't the sense to realise there was some other place for him to go. So, he keeps hanging about here. Yes, I guess that's it. Brownie was the stupid one.'

'I don't think one should flap a towel in his face,' I said, 'it's not polite.'

'You don't have to be polite to a ghost,' Rodney scoffed, 'but I agree it's senseless. Next time he comes we'll find out more about him. I mean, he's not solid, is he? You saw how the towel went right through his head.'

It was several weeks before Brownie came again, and we were a little worried that Mrs Fairweather had frightened him away for good. Then one night I was awakened by Rodney. He was standing by my bed, and as I awoke he lit the candle, his hand fair shaking with excitement.

'Is he back?' I asked, not yet daring to look for myself. 'Yep,' Rodney nodded, 'on the foot of your bed, as before. Come on, get up, we'll have some fun.'

I was not entirely convinced this was going to be fun, but I obediently clambered out of bed, then with some reluctance turned my head.

He was there, in exactly the same position as before, seated sideways on the bed, the cowl slipped back onto his shoulders, and staring at the left hand wall.

'Why does he always sit in the same place?' I asked in a whisper.

'I expect this was the room he slept in, and more than likely his bed was in the same position as yours. I say, he does look weird. Let's have a closer look.'

Holding the candlestick well before him, Rodney went round the bed and peered into the monk's face. Rather fearfully, I followed him.

The face was podgy, deeply tanned, as though its owner had spent a lot of time out of doors, and the large brown eyes were dull and rather sad.

'I told you so,' Rodney said with a certain amount of satisfaction, 'he's stupid, spent most of his time day dreaming while the other monks were chopping wood, getting in the harvest, or whatever things they got up to. I bet they bullied him, in a monkish sort of way.'

'I feel sorry for him,' I said, 'he looks so sad.'

'You would.' Rodney put the candle down. 'Let's see what he's made of. Punch your hand into his ribs.'

I shook my head. 'Don't want to.'

'Go on, he won't hurt you. You're afraid.'

'I'm not.'

'Well, I'm going to have a go. Stand back, and let the dog see the rabbit.'

He rolled up his pyjama sleeve, took a deep breath, then gently brought his clenched fist into contact with the brown robe.

'Can't feel a thing,' he reported. 'Well, here goes.'

Fascinated, I saw his arm disappear into Brownie's stomach; first the fist, then the forearm, finally the elbow.

'Look round the back,' Rodney ordered, 'and see if my hand is sticking out of his spine.'

With a cautious look at Brownie's face, which so far had displayed no signs that he resented these liberties taken with his person, I peered round the brown-covered shoulders. Sure enough, there was Rodney's hand waving at me from the middle of the monk's back.

I nodded. 'I can see it.'

'Feels rather cold and damp,' Rodney said, and brought his arm out sideways. 'As I see it, nothing disturbs him unless something is flapped in his face. I expect the monks used to flap their robes at him, when they wanted to wake him up. Now you try.'

With some misgivings, I rolled up my sleeve and pushed my arm into Brownie's stomach, being careful to close my eyes first. There was an almost indefinable feeling of cold dampness, like putting my arm out of a window early on a spring morning. I heard Rodney laugh, and opened my eyes.

It is a very disturbing experience to say the least, to see your arm buried up to the elbow in a monk's stomach. I pulled it out quickly, determined to have nothing more to do with the entire business, but Rodney had only just begun.

'I'm going in head first,' he announced.

Before I had time to consider what he intended to do, he had plunged his head through Brownie's left ribs, and in next to no time I saw his face grinning at me from the other side. It was really quite funny and, forgetting my former squeamishness, I begged to be allowed to have a go.

'All right,' Rodney agreed, 'but you start from the other side.'

We played happily at 'going through Brownie' for the next twenty minutes. Sideways, backwards, feet first, we went in all ways—the grand climax came when Rodney took up the same position as Brownie, and literally sat inside him. But there was one lesson we learnt; Brownie was undisturbed by our efforts, as long as his head was not touched. Once Rodney tried to reach up and sort of look through the phantom's eyes. At once the blank face took on an expression of intense alarm, the eyes moved, the mouth opened, and had not Rodney instantly withdrawn, I'm certain the ghost would have started his slow dance towards the left hand wall.

But there is a limit to the amount of amusement one can derive from crawling through a ghost. After a while we sat down and took stock of the situation.

'I wonder if he would be disturbed if we jumped in him,' Rodney enquired wistfully.

I was against any such drastic contortion. 'Yes, it would be worse than flapping a towel in his face.'

'I suppose so,' Rodney relinquished the project with reluctance, then his face brightened. 'I say, let's show him to Miss Fortesque.'

'Oh no!' My heart went out to that poor, persecuted creature.

'Why not? In a way we would be doing her a service. After all, she doesn't believe in ghosts. It does people good to be proved they're wrong.'

'I dunno.'

'I'm going to her room,' Rodney got up, his eyes alive with mischievous excitement. 'I'll say there is someone in our room—no, that won't do—I'll say you've got tummy ache.'

'But that's a lie,' I objected.

'Well, you might have tummy ache, so it's only half a lie. You stay here, and don't frighten Brownie, in fact don't move.'

Thankfully, he left me the lighted candle, having thoughtfully provided himself with a torch, for there was no moon, and being alone in the dark with Brownie was still an alarming prospect. I sat down at the phantom's feet and peered up into that blank face. Yes, it was a stupid face, but can a person be blamed for being stupid? Apart from that, his eyes were very sad, or so they appeared to me, and I began to regret the silly tricks we had played on him. Minutes passed, then footsteps were ascending the stairs; Rodney's voice could he heard stressing the gravity of my mythical stomach ache, with Miss Fortesque occasionally interposing with a soft-spoken enquiry.

Rodney came in through the doorway, his face shining with excitement. Miss Fortesque followed, her expression one of deep concern. She stopped when she saw Brownie. Her face turned, if possible, a shade paler, and for a moment I thought she would faint.

'Who . . . ?' she began.

'Brownie,' Rodney announced. 'He's a ghost.'

'Don't talk such nonsense. Who is this man?'

'A ghost,' Rodney's voice rose. 'He is one of the monks who lived here ages ago. Look.'

He ran forward, stationed himself before the still figure and plunged his arm into its chest. Miss Fortesque gasped: 'Oh,' just once before she sank down on to the bed and closed her eyes. The grin died on Rodney's face, to be replaced by a look of alarmed concern.

'Please,' he begged, 'don't be frightened, he won't hurt you, honestly. Harry and I think he's lost. Too stupid to find his way to . . .' he paused, 'to wherever he ought to go.'

Miss Fortesque opened her eyes and took a deep breath. Though I was very young, I admired the way she conquered her fear, more, her abject terror, and rose unsteadily to her feet. She moved very slowly to where Brownie sat, then stared intently at the blank face.

'You have done a dreadful thing,' she said at last, 'to mock this poor creature. I am frightened, very frightened, but I must help him. Somehow, I must help him.'

'How?' inquired Rodney.

'I don't know.' She moved nearer and peered into the unblinking eyes. 'He looks like someone who is sleep-walking. How do you rouse him?'

'Touch his head. Mrs Fairweather flaps a towel in his face.'

Miss Fortesque raised one trembling hand and waved it gently before Brownie's face. He stirred uneasily, his eyes blinked, then, as the hand was waved again, flowed slowly upwards. Miss Fortesque gave a little cry and retreated a few steps.

'No.' She spoke in a voice only just above a whisper. 'Please, please listen.'

Brownie was already two feet above floor level, but he paused and looked back over one shoulder, while a look of almost comical astonishment appeared on his face.

'Please listen,' Miss Fortesque repeated, 'you can hear me, can't you?'

A leg drifted downwards, then he rotated so that he was facing the young woman, only he apparently forgot to descend to floor level. There was the faintest suggestion of a nod.

'You shouldn't be here,' Miss Fortesque continued. 'You, and . . . all your friends, died a long time ago. You ought to be . . . somewhere else.'

The expression was now one of bewilderment and Brownie looked helplessly round the room; his unspoken question was clear.

'Not in this house,' she shook her head, 'perhaps in heaven, I don't know, but certainly in the place where one goes to after death. Can't you try to find it?'

The shoulders came up into an expressive shrug, and Rodney snorted.

'I told you, he's too stupid.'

'Will you be quiet,' Miss Fortesque snapped, 'how can you be so cruel?' She turned to Brownie again. 'Forgive them, they are only children. Surely the other monks taught you about . . . Perhaps you did not understand. But you must leave this house. Go—' she gave a little cry of excitement, 'Go upwards! I'm sure that's right. Go up into the blue sky, away from this world; out among the stars, there you'll find the place. Now, I'm absolutely certain. Go out to the stars.'

Brownie was still poised in the air; his poor stupid face wore a perplexed frown as he pondered on Miss Fortesque's theory. Then, like the sun appearing from behind a cloud, a smile was born. A slow, rather jolly smile, accompanied by a nod, as though Brownie had at last remembered something important he had no business to have forgotten.

He straightened his legs, put both arms down flat with his hips, and drifted upwards, all the while smiling that jolly, idiotic grin, and nodding. His head disappeared into the ceiling, followed by his shoulders and then his hips. The last we saw were those two worn sandals. Miss Fortesque gave a loud gasp, then burst into tears. I did my best to comfort her.

'I'm sure you sent him in the right direction,' I said, 'he looked very pleased.'

'I bet he finishes up on the wrong star,' Rodney commented dourly. I turned on him.

'He won't, I just know he won't. He wasn't so dumb. Once Miss Fortesque sort of jolted his memory he was off like a shot.'

'Now, boys,' Miss Fortesque dried her eyes on her dressing gown sleeve, 'to bed. Tomorrow we must pretend this never happened. In fact,' she shuddered, 'I'd like you to promise me you'll never mention the matter again—ever. Is that understood?'

We said, 'Yes,' and Rodney added, 'I think you're quite brave, honestly.'

She blushed, kissed us both quickly on our foreheads, then departed. Just before I drifted into sleep, I heard Rodney say:

'I wouldn't mind being a ghost. Imagine being able to drift up through the ceiling, and flying out to the stars. I can't wait to be dead.'

Miss Fortesque's theory must have been right. We never saw Brownie again.

MICHAEL KENYON

The Ghost of Top Wood

'I DON'T believe in ghosts,' Sam said.

'I don't believe in ghosts either,' said Old John, and he snipped with his shears. A leaf dropped from the hedge.

'I don't believe in goats,' said Nell, who was three.

'Ghosts, stupid,' said big brother Sam.

'I'm only sayin' what the stories are.' Old John snipped. 'Top Wood is haunted, that's what they say. Anyone goes there alone at night, he'll see things. See things and hear things.'

'What things?'

Sam pinched a leaf off the hedge, leaving one leaf fewer for Old John to snip. Old John was not only old, he was very slow. He did odd jobs in the village: trimming hedges, painting fences. He had mended Sam's roller skates when Sam's dad had been away. He'd come to the rescue of Sam's mum when a water-pipe had burst in the kitchen.

Sam said, 'Is it moans and groans? Or sighing? Or clanking chains?'

'All sorts of things. Ghost things.'

'Well, what do they see then?'

'Things.' Snip went the shears. A leaf fell. 'Shapes. Lights. I dunno. Ghosts of dead people. People dead and forgotten.'

'Thought you didn't believe in ghosts,' Sam said.

'I'm only sayin' what the stories are.' Snip.

'I'm hungry,' said Nell.

'Dad?'

'Mm?'

'D'you believe in ghosts?'

'What? No. I don't know.' Sam's dad was reading the football results in the newspaper, or trying to. 'I've never seen one.'

'Old John says there are ghosts in Top Wood. He doesn't believe in them but he says that's what the stories are. Shapes and things. I think ghosts should moan and have big clanking chains on their feet. I mean, real ghosts. Or like sort of floating sheets with eyes . . . Dad! No!'

Sam's dad had jumped from his chair and was chasing Sam round the room. His shoulders were hunched, his arms flapping. He fluttered his newspaper and moaned.

'Boogie boogie boogie!' moaned Sam's dad.

'It's a goat, it's a goat!' Nell shrieked, hopping up and down with delight.

Sam became excited about secret codes and forgot about ghosts. His friend Alec had been given a book on codes, and the boys sent each other messages written in numbers and invisible inks. When next Sam and Old John happened to meet, Old John was laying turf on the green outside the Rose and Crown. They talked about codes, bicycles, how to make tea out of mint leaves, and the time Old John had been to France.

In the spring when the mint sprouted in the garden Sam remembered about mint tea and plucked a sprig of mint leaves. He made mint tea, but Nell helped, so the tea was upset over the kitchen floor.

'Best place for it. It looks terrible,' their mum said. 'Mop it up, please.'

Only when Sam became lost one evening did he remember about ghosts.

The place where he lost himself was Top Wood.

Top Wood straggled across a hill near the village. Parts of the wood were known to Sam because sometimes he played there with Alec, tracking and being tracked and climbing trees. Alec lived on the far side of the hill, beyond the wood.

The boys were playing Monopoly on the floor of Alec's bedroom when Alec's mother came in to say Sam must start off home, it was evening, his mum and dad would worry, and all the things mothers say at the end of the day. Sam didn't mind leaving because he'd just been sent to gaol and would have to miss three goes anyway.

The road home was empty, the light was already dim, but Sam had a lamp on his bicycle and he switched it on, even though he'd be able to see well enough all the way home.

He had not cycled far when the back wheel began to bump. 'Blast!'

To ride a bicycle with a puncture might ruin the wheel. Sam knew that. So he walked, pushing the bicycle.

The bicycle was heavy, Sam's feet were tired. Pushing a bicycle, not riding it, was stupid. But he daren't ride it. To his left, gloomy in the fading light, loomed Top Wood.

I can leave the bike here by Farmer Mason's field and pick it up in the morning, Sam thought. If I cut straight through Top Wood instead of staying on the road, I'll be home in half the time.

Leaving the bicycle, Sam ran up the slope towards Top Wood.

It was a terrible mistake.

For a long time Sam would not admit to himself that he was lost.

How long is a long time? Ten minutes? Half an hour? Half the night? The wood was dark. But it had been dark when he had plunged into it.

If he walked in a straight line he surely would find a way out somewhere. But to keep straight was not easy. There'd been a pit with a dead tree in the bottom and he'd gone round that, or part of the way round it.

Then he'd tried to go back, the way he had come.

Now he didn't know where he was.

A branch stabbed the side of his head. The wood was as black as a Bible. His foot went into a shallow hole and he stumbled.

Stupid, stupid, not to have brought the lamp from his bike!

Sam knelt among leaves and moss and twigs, shivering and crying.

'Go away, ghosts!' Sam shouted into the blackness.

He was walking again, stumbling, groping with arms stretched out in front of him. Twigs creaked under his shoes. He stood still, listening.

Silence.

Then the sound again. He had thought it might be his own breathing, or the leaves under his feet, but it was further away. A snuffling sound.

'I don't believe in you!' shouted Sam.

Silence.

A badger perhaps. Or a mouse. There were no such things as ghosts.

Sam stumbled on, trying to go faster. He glanced round. Something had glimmered in the dark.

Hadn't it?

'Go away,' he whimpered in a small voice.

The light ahead twinkled and he went towards it. Whether the light was shining close to his nose or deep in the wood, hours away, Sam could not tell. Was it from the window of a cottage at the edge of Top Wood?

Sam groped forwards, hurrying towards the light, frightened of losing it. He had lost a shoe. Though he'd felt for his shoe over the black ground he had given up the search.

Ahead the light twinkled, beckoned, always ahead of him, as though leading him from the wood.

Or leading him round in circles inside the wood? Sam wondered, crying again, whether there were ghosts which played tricks.

'I don't believe in ghosts,' he said aloud.

He wanted to lie down and cover his head but he kept on, following the light.

Suddenly to either side was open space. Sam looked behind him and saw the gloom of Top Wood. In front the fields sloped down to the village.

There was a moon and the night was blue-grey, not black as it had been in the wood. He could see the lights of the Rose and Crown and the village street, and moving away from him, towards the village, the twinkling light which had led him out of the wood.

Sam wanted to shout and laugh. Instead he chased down the fields, gaining on the twinkling light. Near the Rose and Crown he saw that the light was from a lantern held by a man.

Old John.

Old John turned and waved to Sam. Then he walked round the corner of the Rose and Crown.

When Sam ran round the corner, Old John was gone. There was no one. The door of the Rose and Crown was locked.

Sam looked across the green and up the street but Old John had vanished. I'll thank him tomorrow, Sam thought. In his one shoe he raced along the street for home.

There were cars outside Sam's house, and inside were the village policeman, neighbours, and Alec's dad. His own dad was driving through the countryside, searching for him.

'Sam!' his mother cried.

'I was lost—in Top Wood! It was so black! I lost my shoe! Old John showed me the way out!'

The grown-ups looked at each other, and at Sam.

'Old John?' said Sam's mum. 'Old John died yesterday.'

DOROTHY EDWARDS

The Old White Ghost and the Old Grey Granddad

THERE was once an old white ghost who lived behind a water-pipe in an old-fashioned scullery in an old, old house. In this scullery was a big stone sink and a great copper boiler for washing clothes.

For many years this old white ghost haunted the scullery. He made terrible noises in the water-pipes, and after dark, when someone came downstairs to iron the clothes by candlelight he would slip inside the clothes basket and ruffle the washing and then shoot up suddenly in a sheet, or creep across the floor in an old black sock.

Some nights he would blow feathers from the pillow-slips in front of the candle to make strange shadows on the wall; and sometimes— sometimes he would drip a cold-water drop on the neck of the person who was ironing. One cold drop. Aaaah!

AND THEN HE'D BLOW THE CANDLE OUT. OOOOH!

People hated his tricks. They became very frightened. Soon they refused to go into the scullery at all.

They stopped using it for washing, and over the years it got filled up with all the things no one wanted to throw away.

At last a very large family came to live in that old house. There was a father and a mother and their seven children and an old grey granddad. Now there was a battered pram and an old push-bike, an old clothes wringer with wooden rollers for crushing water out of the washing, and several old tubs, and a great bundle of comics on the scullery floor. In the stone sink stood a pile of old gramophone records and an old-fashioned gramophone with a tin horn and a handle to wind it up with. Perched on top of the copper was an old basket-chair. And over and under and between all these things were broken toys and rags and rubbish.

The mother took all her washing to the launderette up the road, and as all her family wore drip-dry clothes no ironing was needed. So nobody ever went into the scullery.

All these things that nobody wanted got dustier and dustier, under a great grey cobweb blanket.

At night the old white ghost came out from behind the water-pipe and made ghostly noises. He moaned and sighed until the cobwebs rocked and shivered and the basket-chair creaked. But there was no one to hear him. No one to tremble with fear or run away shrieking. 'I might as well not bother,' the old white ghost said mournfully.

One reason why no one heard him was because there were so many noises in the house anyway. The family never stopped making noises of one kind or another: shouting, hammering, sawing, sewing-machining, vacuuming, and quarrelling. And the radio, TV, and hifi were always switched on, all at the same time.

Only the old grey granddad was quiet. He sat in a chair in the corner of the sitting-room, with his hands over his ears to keep out the din.

One day this old grey granddad felt he couldn't stand the racket any longer, so he got out of his chair and began to prowl about the house. Every room was filled with people, their things, and their noise!

'If only I could find somewhere quiet,' the poor old man said. 'If only I could find a quiet place for myself.'

At last he crept down the kitchen steps and found himself in the scullery. The spiders had woven so many webs that only a dim light crept through the window, but the old man peered around in the gloom and took a fancy to what he saw.

'Why,' he said, 'I could make myself a snug little place down here. I could get them upstairs to help me clear out the rubbish, and, with a lick of whitewash here and a dab of paint there, it would come up a treat!'

'After all,' said the old grey granddad, 'I more than pay my way, so they owe me something!'

And all the time he stood there, talking to himself, the old white ghost watched him from behind the water-pipe in the corner. The old white ghost was interested, but he didn't show himself, he just waited and bided his time.

The old grey granddad went back upstairs and he began to shout— louder than the loudest child to make himself heard.

'I pay my way,' he yelled, 'so I've got my rights. I want that scullery downstairs for my own private place and I'd thank you all to help me clear it out and make it homelike.'

And because his family were very fond of him, and because they knew he had justice on his side, they all stopped their hammering, banging, sawing, machining, shouting and making all the other noises, and got together to clear out the old-fashioned scullery.

What a time they had—carrying all the old things out into the yard and stacking them up by the dustbins.

Sometimes the old grey granddad would shout, 'Not that! Not that! I could do with that!'

In that way he saved the basket-chair for himself. He got the two youngest children scrubbing it clean, and the mother upstairs looking out a cushion for it. 'I always liked to sit in a basket-chair,' the old grey granddad said.

He found an old folding-table behind the wringer, and enough planks of wood to make himself some shelves—as for the old gramophone with the tin horn—he went mad with joy when that turned up, and he looked at the pile of records. 'All those old songs—all those old bands!' he said. 'They don't make music like that nowadays. I can listen to my heart's content.'

And when they began to clear out the bundles of old comics he said, 'Weary Willie and Tired Tim! Why, that takes me back to my boyhood! They'll be just the thing for me to read when I'm sitting in my basket-chair with my table at my elbow.'

And all this time the old white ghost made never a sound nor a movement, he just watched from behind the water-pipe. He watched while they cleared the scullery. He watched while they whitewashed and painted and hung shelves. He watched while the father laid a carpet that the mother had found in a second-hand shop. He watched and waited until at last the old grey granddad was alone in his nice new quarters. Until he was sitting in his basket-chair with his pile of old comics on the table and the freshly oiled gramophone and the well-dusted records to hand in the nicely scrubbed sink.

He waited till the old man had switched on the electric lamp that the father had wired for him, and spread out his toes to the electric fire the eldest grandson had fixed in place of the old copper-fire, and reached for the first copy of *Chips* before 'Uuuggh-Ah-h-h-h,' he said in the water-pipe. 'Uh, uh, uh, uh!'

He looked hard at the old grey granddad, but the old man didn't stir. After all the family racket he had put up with for so long, he wasn't to be upset by ghostly water-pipes. Instead he smiled sweetly, and leaning forward, he wound the handle of the gramophone, and the scullery was full of the gay and scratchy sound of a long-ago band of the Grenadier Guards. It was as if the ghosts of the old dead bandsmen filled the little warm scullery as they listened to their music. The old grey granddad welcomed them with pleasure.

The old white ghost was puzzled.

Presently, however, he grew bold again, and he began to rustle the pile of comics, but the old grey granddad didn't seem to mind a bit. He just picked up a big flat-iron that he was using for a door-stop and put it on top of the pile. 'Draughts,' he said.

The old white ghost remembered his trick with the water, and loosed a drop on the old man's neck. 'Condensation,' said that happy old man. 'It's the old pipes warming up.'

The old white ghost tried to blow out the light, as he'd blown out candles in the old haunting days. But the electric bulb never flickered, and the old grey granddad went on to read *Comic Cuts*.

The old white ghost was baffled. He began to moan from sheer despair. 'I want to haunt you,' he said. 'Please let me frighten you.'

The old grey granddad looked up over his spectacles and saw the flickering outline of the old white ghost. 'It's no good,' he said, 'I know all about you. Everyone knows about you. You think you're a ghastly spectre and so did a lot of other people. I know you're just draught, and air-locks in the pipes, and condensation—I know you can be rats or mice or imagination, so don't ask me to be afraid of you.

'I tell you what,' said the old grey granddad, 'there's an old stool over in that corner, I'll bring it up near to the fire here, and you can sit yourself down beside me and listen to the music. You can take a peek over my shoulder at these comics, they're good for a laugh any time. In that way—I won't worry you and you won't worry me.'

And that's just what the old white ghost did. He perched himself on the stool and listened to the long-dead voices of comic singers and mournful singers, and the long-lost strains of forgotten bands. Sometimes he took a peek over the old granddad's shoulder and they laughed together over old jokes.

And if sometimes the old white ghost got up from his stool and made ghostly noises in the pipes, or moaned and wailed for old times' sake, the old grey granddad only said: 'Ah—but if it's real noise you're after—that lot upstairs can beat you hollow.'

MARGARET MAHY

Looking for a Ghost

RUNNING along the footpath, fire in his feet, came Sammy Scarlet. He ran on his toes, leaping as he ran, so that he seemed to dance and spin through the twilight like a grey, tumbling bird learning to fly. Sammy leaped as he ran to keep himself brave. He was going to a haunted house. That evening he was going to see a ghost for the first time in his life.

The haunted house was along a city street. It was the last house left in the street, falling to pieces in the middle of a garden of weeds. The glass in the windows was broken, and some of them were crossed over with boards. There was a tall fence round it, but in some places the fence was tumbling down.

'They'll put a bulldozer through that old place soon,' said the man in the shop at the corner. 'That's a valuable section, a commercial section.'

'Haunted?' Sammy had asked.

'They say there's a ghost, but it only comes out in the evening after the shops have shut up and most people have gone home. I've never seen it,' said the man in the corner shop, 'and I'm not hanging around here after five-thirty just to watch some ghost. Only a little one too, they say.'

'A twilight ghost,' Sammy said to himself, and felt as if something breathed cold on the back of his neck, and whispered with cold lips in his ear.

Now he ran swiftly through the early evening. Sammy had chosen his time carefully . . . not so dark that his mother would worry about him, not too light for a small, cold ghost.

'Just a quick prowl around!' thought Sammy, as he ran and leaped to keep away the fear which ran beside him like a chilly, pale-eyed dog.

'If I go back now, I'm a coward,' thought Sammy, and leaped again. 'I've promised myself to see a ghost and I'm *going* to see a ghost.'

He knew the street well, but evening changed it. It took him by surprise, seeming to have grown longer and emptier. And at the end of the street the haunted house was waiting. Sammy could see its gate and its tired tumbledown fence. By the gate something moved softly. Sammy leaped in his running, matching his jump to the jump of his heart. But the shadow by the gate was only a little girl bouncing a ball with a stick. She looked up as Sammy came running towards her.

'Hello,' she said. 'I thought no one ever came here in the evening.'

'I've come,' Sammy answered, panting. 'I'm going to see the ghost.'

The little girl looked at him with shadowy black eyes. 'A real ghost?' she asked. 'What ghost?'

'A ghost that haunts this house,' Sammy replied. He was glad of someone to talk to, even a girl with a striped rubber ball in one hand and a stick in the other. She looked back at the house.

'Is this house haunted?' she asked again. 'I suppose it looks a bit haunted. It's got cobwebs on it, and thistles in the garden. Aren't you frightened of the ghost, then?'

'I'm not scared of ghosts,' said Sammy cheerfully. (He hoped it sounded cheerful.) 'They can be pretty scary to some people but, I don't know how it is, somehow they don't scare me. I'm going through the fence to take a look. They say it is only a little one.'

'Why don't you try the gate?' suggested the girl, pushing at the gate with her stick. It creaked open. Sammy stared.

'That's funny,' he said. 'I looked at the gate earlier and it was locked.'

'I'll come with you,' said the girl. 'My name is Belinda, and I would like to see a ghost too.'

'I don't think you'd better,' replied Sammy, frowning, 'because ghosts can be pretty horrible, you know . . . with sharp teeth and claws and cackling laughs. Bony too!'

'There's nothing wrong with being bony,' said Belinda.

She was very thin with a pale, serious face and long brown hair. Though she did not smile she looked friendly and interested. Her heavy shoes made her legs look even thinner, and her dress was too big for her, Sammy thought. Certainly it was too long, giving her an old-fashioned look.

'If it's scary to be bony,' said Belinda, 'I might frighten the ghost. Anyway the gate is open and I can go in if I want to.' She stepped into the old garden and Sammy stepped after her, half cross because she was coming into his private adventure, half pleased to have company. As he came through the gate Sammy felt a cold breath fall on the back of his neck. Turning round slowly he saw nothing. Perhaps it was just a little cool wind sliding into the empty garden with them.

'A garden of thistledown and dandelions,' Belinda cried. 'A garden all for birds and beetles and ghosts.' She seemed to like what she saw. 'The lawn is almost as tall as my shoulder. A ghost could easily be in that long grass, and just rise up beside us like smoke.'

Sammy glanced thoughtfully at the grass, half expecting a smoky shape to billow up and wave its arms at him. But—no smoke, no sound. It was all very still. He could hear cars out on the main road, but they seemed like thin dreams of sound, tiny flies buzzing far away. He walked up the brick path and stood on the front steps of the haunted house, looking at its sad veranda. One of the carved posts was crumbling down and the veranda sagged with it.

'You'd feel cruel just standing on this veranda,' Sammy remarked. 'It looks so limp and sick.'

'Cruelty to verandas!' said Belinda seriously. 'Stand on it lightly, Sammy, and we'll go inside. I think a ghost would be more likely to be inside, don't you?'

'The door will be locked, won't it?' Sammy said. Then, 'How did you know my name?' he asked, looking puzzled.

'You *look* like a Sammy,' was all she said. She pushed the door and it slowly opened, like a black mouth opening to suck them into its shadows.

'I might stay out here,' Sammy said. 'The floor could cave in or something.' His voice was quiet and squashed small by the heavy silence of the whole house and garden.

'You don't have to be afraid,' Belinda told him kindly. 'It's just an old, empty house, and old houses were made of good wood.' Through the dark door she slid and vanished. Sammy *had* to follow her. Then he got the most terrible fright. He was standing in a hall so dim and dusty that he could see almost nothing. But what he *could* see was a dim and dusty figure at the other end of the hall moving slowly towards him.

'The ghost!' cried Sammy.

Belinda looked back at him. He could not see her face properly, but for some reason he thought she might be smiling.

'It isn't a ghost,' she told him. 'It's a looking-glass. There's a tall cupboard at the end with a looking-glass in its door. It's your own reflection that's frightening you.'

Sammy blinked and saw that what she said could be true. They walked cautiously up the hall. The looking-glass reflected the open doorway behind them. It was so dark inside that the evening outside looked bright and pearly.

Sammy rubbed his finger across the looking-glass.

The looking-glass moved and they heard a low moaning.

'The ghost!' gasped Sammy again, but it was just the cupboard door. It was a little bit open, and creaking when Sammy touched it.

'Come upstairs!' Belinda said. 'They were nice, once, these stairs. They used to be polished every day.'

'How can you tell?' asked Sammy, looking up the dark stairway.

'They are smooth under the dust,' Belinda replied, 'smooth with feet walking, and hands polishing. But that was a long time ago.'

'How can you see your way upstairs?' Sammy asked. 'It's so dark.'

'There's enough light,' she answered, already several steps above him. Sammy came after her. Out of the dark came a hand, soft and silent as the shadows, and laid silken fingers across his face.

'The ghost!' cried Sammy for the third time.

'Cobwebs, only cobwebs!' called Belinda back to him. Sammy touched his face. His own fingers, stiff with fright, found only cobwebs, just as Belinda had said. He stumbled and scrambled up after her onto the landing. There was a window boarded over. It was easy to peep through the cracks and look over the thistly garden and down the empty street.

'There used to be grass there,' Belinda whispered, peering out. 'Grass and cows. But that was a long time ago.' She straightened up. 'Come through *this* door,' she said in her ordinary voice.

Sammy did not want to be left behind. They went through the door into a small room. The boards had partly slipped away from the windows. Evening light brightened the walls and striped the ceiling. There were the remains of green curtains and a rocking-chair with one rocker broken. Sitting in the chair was a very old doll. It looked as if someone had put it down and had gone out to play for a moment. The doll seemed to expect someone to be back to play with it. Sammy looked over to the doll and around the room, and then out through the window. 'There's no ghost,' he said, 'and it's getting late. I'll have to be going.'

The ghost did not seem as important as it had a moment ago, but Sammy thought he would remember the silent, tumbling house and its wild garden, long after he had stopped thinking about ghosts.

They went down the stairs again and Sammy did not jump at the cobwebs. They went past the looking-glass and he creaked the cupboard door on purpose this time. Now the sound did not frighten him. It was gentle and complaining, not fierce or angry.

'It only wants to be left alone,' Belinda said, and that was what it sounded like.

They walked down the hall and Sammy turned to wave goodbye to his reflection before he shut the door. The reflection waved back at him from the end of a long tunnel of shadow. Outside, the evening darkened. Stars were showing.

'No ghost!' said Sammy, shaking his head.

They walked to the gate.

'Will you be coming back some other night to look for the ghost?' Belinda asked.

'I don't think so,' Sammy answered. 'I don't really believe in ghosts. I just thought there might be one. I've looked once and there isn't one and that's enough.'

He turned to run off home, but something made him stop and look sharply at Belinda.

'Did you see *your* reflection in that looking-glass?' he asked curiously. 'I don't remember your reflection.'

Belinda did not answer his question. Instead she asked him one of her own.

'Everyone has a reflection, don't they?' It was hard to see her in the late evening, but once again Sammy thought she might be smiling.

'You went up the stairs first,' he went on. 'Why didn't you brush the cobwebs away?'

'I'm not as tall as you,' Belinda said.

Sammy peered at her, waiting for her to say something more. Just for a moment, very faintly, he felt that chilly breeze touch the back of his neck again.

'No ghost!' he said at last. 'No such things as ghosts!' Then, without a goodbye, he ran off home, rockets in the heels of his shoes.

Belinda watched him go.

'The question is,' she said to herself, 'whether he would recognize a ghost, supposing he saw one.'

She went back through the gate and locked it carefully after her. She was already faint and far off in the evening, and as she pushed the bolt home she disappeared entirely.

PHILIPPA PEARCE

At the River-Gates

LOTS of sisters I had (said the old man), good girls, too; and one elder brother. Just the one. We were at either end of the family: the eldest, my brother John—we always called him Beany, for some reason; then the girls, four of them; then me. I was Tiddler, and the reason for that was plain.

Our father was a flour miller, and we lived just beside the mill. It was a water-mill, built right over the river, with the mill-wheel underneath. To understand what happened that wild night, all those years ago, you have to understand a bit about the working of the mill-stream. About a hundred yards before the river reached the mill, it divided: the upper river flowed on to power the mill, as I've said; the lower river, leaving the upper river through sluice-gates, flowed to one side of the mill and past it; and then the upper and lower rivers joined up again well below the mill. The sluice-gates could be opened or shut by the miller to let more or less water through from the upper to the lower river. You can see the use of that: the miller controlled the flow of water to power his mill; he could also draw off any floodwaters that came down.

Being a miller's son, I can never remember not understanding that. I was a little tiddler, still at school, when my brother, Beany, began helping my father in the mill. He was as good as a man, my father said. He was strong, and he learnt the feel of the grain, and he was clever with the mill machinery, and he got on with the other men in the mill—there were only ten of them, counting two carters. He understood the gates, of course, and how to get just the right head of water for the mill. And he liked it all: he liked the work he did, and the life; he liked the mill, and the river, and the long river-bank. One day he'd be the miller after my father, everyone said.

I was too young to feel jealousy about that; but I would never have felt jealous of Beany, because Beany was the best brother you could have had. I loved and admired him more than anyone I knew or could imagine knowing. He was very good to me. He used to take me with him when you might have thought a little boy would have been in the way. He took me with him when he went fishing, and he taught me to fish. I learnt patience, then, from Beany. There were plenty of roach and dace in the river; and sometimes we caught trout or pike; and once we caught an eel, and I was first of all terrified and then screaming with excitement at the way it whipped about on the bank, but Beany held it and killed it, and my mother made it into eel-pie. He knew about the fish in the river, and the little creatures, too. He showed me fresh-water shrimps, and leeches—'Look, Tiddler, they make themselves into cro-quet-hoops when they want to go anywhere!' and he showed me the little underwater cottages of caddis-worms. He knew where to get good watercress for Sunday tea—you could eat watercress from our river, in those days.

We had an old boat on the river, and Beany would take it upstream to inspect the banks for my father. The banks had to be kept sound: if there was a breach, it would let the water escape and reduce the water-power for the mill. Beany took Jess, our dog, with him in the boat, and he often took me. Beany was the only person I've ever known who could point out a kingfisher's nest in the river-bank. He knew about birds. He once showed me a flycatcher's nest in the brickwork below the sluice-gates, just above where the water dashed and roared at its highest. Once, when we were in the boat, he pointed ahead to an otter in the water. I held on to Jess's collar then.

It was Beany who taught me to swim. One summer it was hotter than anyone remembered, and Beany was going from the mill up to the gates to shut in more water. Jess was following him, and as he went he gave me a wink, so I followed too, although I didn't know why. As usual, he opened the gates with the great iron spanner, almost as long in the handle as he was tall. Then he went down to the pool in the lower river, as if to see the water-level there. But as he went he was unbuttoning his flour-whitened waistcoat; by the time he reached the pool he was naked, and he dived straight in. He came up with his hair plastered over his eyes, and he called to me: 'Come on, Tiddler! Just time for a swimming lesson!' Jess sat on the bank and watched us.

Jess was really my father's dog, but she attached herself to Beany. She loved Beany. Everyone loved Beany, and he was good to everyone. Especially, as I've said, to me. Just sometimes he'd say, 'I'm off on my own now, Tiddler,' and then I knew better than to ask to go with him. He'd go sauntering up the river-bank by himself, except for Jess at his heels. I don't think he did anything very particular when he went off on his own. Just the river and the river-bank were happiness enough for him.

He was still not old enough to have got himself a girl, which might have changed things a bit; but he wasn't too young to go to the War. The War broke out in 1914, when I was still a boy, and Beany went.

It was sad without Beany; but it was worse than that. I was too young to understand then; but, looking back, I realize what was wrong. There was fear in the house. My parents became gloomy and somehow secret. So many young men were being killed at the Front. Other families in the village had had word of a son's death. The news came in a telegram. I overheard my parents talking of those deaths, those telegrams, although not in front of the girls or me. I saw my mother once, in the middle of the morning, kneeling by Beany's bed, praying.

So every time Beany came home on leave, alive, we were lucky.

But when Beany came, he was different. He loved us as much, but he was different. He didn't play with me as he used to do; he would sometimes stare at me as though he didn't see me. When I shouted 'Beany!' and rushed at him, he would start as if he'd woken up. Then he'd smile, and be good to me, almost as he used to be. But, more often than he used to, he'd be off all by himself up the river-bank, with Jess at his heels. My mother, who longed to have him within her sight for every minute of his leave, used to watch him go, and sigh. Once I heard her say to my father that the river-bank did Beany good, as if he were sickening for some strange disease. Once one of the girls was asking Beany about the Front and the trenches, and he was telling her this and that, and we were all interested, and suddenly he stopped and said, 'No. It's hell.' And walked away alone, up the green, quiet river-bank. I suppose if one place was hell, then the other was heaven to him.

After Beany's leaves were over, the mill-house was gloomy again; and my father had to work harder, without Beany's help in the mill. Nowadays he had to work the gates all by himself, a thing that Beany had been taking over from him. If the gates needed working at night, my father and Beany had always gone there together. My mother hated it nowadays when my father had to go to the gates alone at night: she was afraid he'd slip and fall in the water, and, although he could swim, accidents could happen to a man alone in the dark. But, of course, my father wouldn't let her come with him, or any of my sisters, and I was still considered much too young. That irked me.

Well, one season had been very dry and the river level had dropped. The gates were kept shut to get up a head of water for the mill. Then clouds began to build up heavily on the horizon, and my father said he was sure it was going to rain; but it didn't. All day storms rumbled in the distance. In the evening the rain began. It rained steadily: my father had already been once to the gates to open the flashes. He was back at home, drying off in front of the fire. The rain still drove against the windows. My mother said, 'It can't come down worse than this.' She and my sisters were still up with my father. Even I wasn't in bed, although I was supposed to have been. No one could have slept for the noise of the rain.

Suddenly the storm grew worse—much worse. It seemed to explode over our heads. We heard a pane of glass in the skylight over the stairs shatter with the force of it, and my sisters ran with buckets to catch the water pouring through. Oddly, my mother didn't go to see the damage: she stayed with my father, watching him like a lynx. He was fidgeting up and down, paying no attention to the skylight either, and suddenly he said he'd have to go up to the gates again and open everything to carry all possible floodwater into the lower river. This was what my mother had been dreading. She made a great outcry, but she knew it was no use. My father put on his tarpaulin jacket again and took his oil lamp and a thick stick—I don't know why, nor did he, I think. Jess always hated being out in the rain, but she followed him. My mother watched him from the back door, lamenting, and urging him to be careful. A few steps from the doorway and you couldn't see him any longer for the driving rain.

My mother's lingering at the back door gave me my chance. I got my boots on and an oilskin cape I had (I wasn't a fool, even if I was little) and I whipped out of the front door and worked my way round in the shelter of the house to the back and then took the path my father had taken to the river, and made a dash for it, and caught up with my father and Jess, just as they were turning up the way towards the gates. I held on to Jess's tail for quite a bit before my father noticed me. He was terribly angry, of course, but he didn't want to turn back with me, and he didn't like to send me back alone, and perhaps in his heart of hearts he was glad of a little human company on such a night. So we all three struggled up to the gates together. Just by the gates my father found me some shelter between a tree-trunk and a stack of drift-wood. There I crouched, with Jess to keep me company.

I was too small to help my father with the gates, but there was one thing I could do. He told me to hold his lamp so that the light shone on the gates and what he was doing. The illumination was very poor, partly because of the driving rain, but at least it was better than nothing, and anyway my father knew those gates by heart. Perhaps he gave me the job of holding the light so that I had something to occupy my mind and keep me from being afraid.

There was plenty to be afraid of on that night of storm.

Directing what light I could on to my father also directed and concentrated my attention on him. I could see his laborious motions as he heaved the great spanner into place. Then he began to try to rack up with it, but the wind and the rain were so strong that I could see he was having the greatest difficulty. Once I saw him stagger sideways nearly into the blackness of the river. Then I wanted to run out from my shelter and try to help him, but he had strictly forbidden me to do any such thing, and I knew he was right.

Young as I was, I knew—it came to me as I watched him—that he couldn't manage the gates alone in that storm. I suppose he was a man already just past the prime of his strength: the wind and the rain were beating him; the river would beat him.

I shone the light as steadily as I could, and gripped Jess by the collar, and I think I prayed.

I was so frightened then that, afterwards, when I wasn't frightened, I could never be sure of what I had seen, or what I thought I had seen, or what I imagined I had seen. Through the confusion of the storm I saw my father struggling and staggering, and, as I peered and peered, my vision seemed to blur and to double, so that I began sometimes to see one man, sometimes two. My father seemed to have a shadow-self besides himself, who steadied him, heaved with him, worked with him, and at last together they had opened the sluice-gates and let the flood through.

When it was done, my father came back to where Jess and I were, and leant against the tree. He was gasping for breath and exhausted, and had a look on his face that I cannot describe. From his expression I knew that he had *felt* the shadow with him, just as I had seen it. And Jess was agitated too, straining against my hold, whining.

I looked past my father, and I could still see something by the sluice-gates: a shadow that had separated itself from my father, and lingered there. I don't know how I could have seen it in the darkness. I don't know. My father slowly turned and looked in the direction that he saw me looking. The shadow began to move away from the gates, away from us; it began to go up the long river-bank beyond the gates, into the darkness there. It seemed to me that the rain and the wind stilled a little as it went.

Jess wriggled from my grasp and was across the gates and up the river-bank, following the vanished shadow. I had made no move, uttered no word, but my father said to me, 'Let them go!' I looked up at him, and his face was streaming with tears as well as with rain.

He took my hand and we fought our way back to the house. The whole house was lit up, to light us home, and my mother stood at the open back door, waiting. She gave a cry of horror when she saw me with my father; and then she saw his face, and her own went quite white. He stumbled into her arms, and he sobbed and sobbed. I didn't know until that night that grown men could cry. My mother led my father indoors, and I don't know what talk they had together. My sisters looked after me, dried me, scolded me, put me to bed.

The next day the telegram came to say that Beany had been killed in action in Flanders.

It was some time after that that Jess came home. She was wet through, and my mother thought she was ill, for she sat shivering by the fire, and for two days would neither eat nor drink. My father said: 'Let her be.'

I'm an old man: it all happened so many years ago, but I've never forgotten my brother Beany. He was so good to us all.

RUTH PARK

Somebody Lives in the Nobody House

SOME people can tell you a ghost story that happened to their great-grandfather, or their neighbour's aunt in Moonee Ponds. But my spooky story happened to me, Sally Gavin, and only last year. On the day after my eleventh birthday, as a matter of fact.

I still often think of that late afternoon—the Ferryman's Arms beside the weedy river, its windows red with a sunset that wasn't really happening. And then, later on, when Fenella and I were alone in that dim cobwebby room, and time had become tangled up somehow, and we heard that croaky old man's voice coming from nowhere. The memory still makes me shiver, and Fenella feels the same way.

My sister Fenella was nine at the time of the ghost. Mum must have been round the twist when she gave her that romantic name, for Fenella at nine was as romantic as a mixmaster. A bossy, know-all kid, with a tongue hung in the middle. Around home she was known as The Blob, or Orrible, or Dr No. She's different now, a cheerful tearaway, and we all like her much more.

Dad and Fenella and I were driving along this clay horror stretch in the Northern Rivers country. Mum had intended to come, but our brother Robbie had burst out with chickenpox, and so she was home with him, no doubt very pleased to be spared the inevitable hardships of Dad's expeditions.

Dad is a pernikety driver, and when he saw a police cycle coming up fast on his right, he looked offended. He pulled over, and this Martian did a wheelie through the puddles and showered the car with dirt. He took off his helmet and stuck a brown face into the window, grinning. Rather nice. He said he was Constable Fiddler from Burangie, the tiny township we'd zizzed through some five kilometres or so back.

'Dan Gavin,' said Dad civilly.

'Dad was NOT speeding,' said Fenella in her loud, set-down voice. 'I was personally keeping an eye on the dial.'

The young constable laughed. 'It's just that Des Harris at the service station told me you'd mentioned you were going through to the old Ferryman pub tonight.'

'Dad may buy it and turn it into a motel,' announced Orrible. Dad gave her one of his belt-up looks and explained to the officer that he was just going to look the place over. He had never as much as seen a good photograph of it.

The constable pensively scratched the red welt the helmet had left on his forehead. 'I was just thinking,' he said. 'Maybe you don't know the place is derelict, nothing but rats and dry rot. It hasn't been occupied for forty years or more. People around here called it the Nobody House.'

'I suppose they say it's haunted!' said Fenella scornfully.

Dad explained that we didn't intend actually dossing in the old building. Our car has a camping body, and anyway, Dad has this junior-school love for sleeping under a tree in his old sleeping-bag. You could see he wasn't going to be done out of that.

He listened impatiently to the young constable, as he said: 'Just the same, Mr Gavin, I wish you'd reconsider. It's getting dark quickly, the road's a shocker, the bridge at the ferry's nothing to write home about, and after all the rain we've had lately there'll be mud in all directions. Why not drive back and spend the night at Burangie pub and come out this way again tomorrow?'

Of course Constable Fiddler knew that area better than we did, and what he said made sense. But instantly Fenella put on a demo. She had not only been promised she could camp in the car; she was also chief cook for the trip and had brought sausages and tomatoes to fry on the portable stove, and Dad was not being just, and justice was needed in the world of today, because just look at Rhodesia, and aboriginal land rights and Zoos. Well, actually, just before she got to Zoos Dad became bored with the whole thing and said he'd drive on a few kilometres and if the weather turned worse, he'd return to Burangie.

'Your decision. Okay?' said Constable Fiddler, a bit sharply, I thought, and he turned once more into a Martian and did another wheelie that spattered our car from head to tail. Dad drove on in a temper.

The countryside looked soaked to the skin. In the foothills ahead of us silky-oaks were blooming, custard yellow against the storm clouds. You could see rainshowers tearing themselves away, spinning into willywillies of drops and then petering out in mid-air. The road was less rutted now, but it had a slick, yukky surface and Dad drove very carefully. All at once I noticed someone standing beside the road, waving. In that sodden, lonely landscape another human being was the last thing I had expected to see. Dad stopped.

'Need a lift, mate? We're only going as far as the old Ferryman, though.'

'That'll do grand. Much obliged, mister.'

It was a boy three or four years older than myself, dressed in worn overalls. He had a grain sack over his shoulders as though he expected a downpour any minute. As he slid into the back seat he half-smiled at me. He had one of those shy clean country faces and crooked teeth.

Naturally Fenella turned around at once and treated our passenger to a recountal of how we lived in the Blue Mountains outside Sydney; her teacher believed she was going to amount to something with the violin (she hasn't yet); Dad specialised in ferreting out old properties and doing them up for a motel chain; Robbie had the chickenpox, and she was going to fry the sausages as soon as we camped because she was ravishing. She meant ravenous, of course, and I saw a grin flit over the boy's face.

'Lonesome out there,' said the boy. 'Better to spend the night in town, I reckon.'

'Why?' asked Fenella. The boy didn't answer so Dad asked if the bridge were dangerous.

'I guess she's all right,' said the boy. 'Used to be dangerous when the river ran a banker, got carried away once and someone got drowned. No, I was just thinking, there's heavy weather on the way and you might get bogged and that.'

'We'll chance it,' said Dad. I could see he was testy because of all the discouragement he was getting. Before Orrible could launch into her speech about how sport was for dummos and she was learning chess, I asked the boy where he lived.

'Not far,' he said. I was going to ask how he got into Burangie to school, when we came to the top of the hill, and there before us was the river, and willows and casuarinas, and amongst them the most picturesque old inn, like something out of a Victorian book. It was a Georgian building, with tiny-paned windows, and a rounded veranda curving about the house to shelter the lower storey. There were half a dozen chimneys of yellow brick, topped with twisty chimney pots, and to one side a stableyard with a high arched gateway of stone. Of course I knew that the Ferryman's Arms had once been a staging-post for Cobb and Co coaches, and I imagined them sweeping down this very hill, jingling and creaking, the coachman blowing his horn, the passengers looking forward to supper of roast mutton and boiled currant pudding in the parlour and then a night's sleep between clean sheets.

'I suppose they drove right on to a big ferry punt?' asked Dad.

'That's so, mister,' replied the boy, pointing. 'Down there by the she-oaks and where the bridge is now. The ferrymen pulled the punt over with ropes and weights. But the river's nearly all silted up now. It only runs at times like that, after weeks of heavy rain.'

'Just look at the way the sunset is reflected in those old windows,' I said. 'You'd swear people lived there. That's not a Nobody House.'

I couldn't take my eyes off the place. It looked so homely, so cosy in the shelter of the big dark hills. We drove down the grade and Dad crept over the bridge in second gear. But it seemed solid enough.

It was true what the boy had said—the river was almost swamp. The bed had been taken over by reeds and coarse grass, and the water was muddy, with crusts of yellow bubbles. When we drove into the stable-yard, it was full of mouldy rubbish—broken casks and iron wheelrims and rotten timber. Moss grew between the paving stones, and there was a pump with an iron handle red with rust. Beyond were stables, their half-doors hanging, their interiors dark and forbidding.

But Dad didn't seem to find it disagreeable. 'I think we'll camp right here,' he said. 'What do you say, Sally? There's a bit of overhang from the veranda if the rain comes down again.'

As he spoke there was a long roll of thunder as though someone had run a stick around a huge bell. The boy shivered. Fenella spiked him with her inquisitive glance.

'You're scared! Do you think it's haunted?'

The boy looked away in his shy way. 'There's talk of a ghost, all right.'

He was going to say something else but off went Fenella, in her best Orrible manner, hammering that poor boy into the ground with scoffings. He looked embarrassed. Dad and I stood there looking at the inn, and I knew he was thinking the same thing as I was, how welcoming it was, with its broken windows shining crimson in the sunset. Then all at once I realised something. The sun had set half an hour or more before.

'Well then,' said Fenella, who was now beside us, 'the lights have been put on. The poor old ghost who lives in the Nobody House is afraid of the dark!'

But the power poles had finished on the other side of the river; I had noticed particularly. And though the daylight hadn't quite gone, and frogs were blurting down in the reeds and mosquitoes were whining around, I began to feel a bit queer.

Dad and I think alike. He said, as though to himself, 'Of course there are such things as generators.' Then he said loudly and cheerfully, 'Must be someone here after all. I'll just go and see. Start unpacking the grub, kids. I won't be long.'

I had this impulse to say: 'No, Dad, don't!' But he leaped on the veranda and marched along to the big front door, which stood wide open, half off its hinges. Its pretty shellshaped fanlight was shattered to bits. I heard Dad call: 'Hello in there, anyone at home?'

Just then all the lights went out. In the moment before my eyes became used to the twilight, I saw the lightning blinking in the mountains of cloud above. Fenella said severely: 'What a dumb thing for Dad to do! The floor might be all rotten and he didn't even take the torch.'

The torch was in the glove-box, so I stuck my head inside the car and said: 'Hand me the torch, will you. You'll find it inside the . . .'

But the car was empty. I got the torch myself and shone it around the stableyard but there was no sign of the boy. He must have slipped out of the car and gone off to wherever he lived. I felt a bit disgusted that he hadn't even said thanks to Dad for the lift, but I supposed he was keen to get back to the pigfarm or whatever it was before the storm broke. Orrible, however, thought he'd got peeved because she rubbished him about ghosts.

'He looked pretty sore,' she said triumphantly.

'Oh, shut up,' I said, 'and let's go and find Dad. He must be bashing around inside there in the dark.'

The front-door steps were overgrown with fennel and half-dead hydrangeas, and slimy with wet and decay. I called: 'Dad, we've got the torch,' and shone it round inside the door. The interior was just like a cave, huge and dark and full of rubbish. Something twinkled, and both Fenella and I jumped, but it was only a sliver of broken mirror with golden writing on it, behind an immense half-wrecked timber counter.

'This must have been the bar,' I said.

Fenella shouted rudely: 'Okay, parent, no jokes, where are you?'

Then I saw a line of footprints in the dust which lay on the floor like grey down. They led to a half-open door beside the bar. I knew Dad wasn't one to play jokes—not on us, anyway—and I couldn't imagine why he would have gone straight into that little room. I imagined him fallen down a hole in the floor boards, fractured skull, and goodness knows what else. So I was annoyed when I felt Fenella pressing uneasily against me.

'I don't like all those mirrors, Sally,' she whispered, and indeed the effect of those unexpected flashes, dim and cobwebby as they were, as I turned the torch this way and that, was so scarey that I growled: 'Stop telling me what you don't like!'

We went over to the half-open door and pushed and it opened with the regulation T.V. haunted house creak. Fenella giggled halfwittedly. I called: 'You in here, Dad? Dad?'

He wasn't. It was a sort of little office, with a tottery desk piled with dirty old account books and an old-fashioned black telephone on the wall. Vandals had been in, I suppose: there were torn papers and footmarks all over the floor. Fenella said in a voice that was actually shaky: 'Maybe he went upstairs.'

I thought that unlikely in the dim light and all, but I felt so jumpy that I gladly agreed: 'That's it. We'll go back into the bar and look for the stairs.'

Right then, sudden as a gunshot, a voice said: 'Go away! Go away! No peace anywhere!'

They talk about being paralysed with shock. Well, Fenella and I really were. Then Fenella gave a quavering snort.

'Sssssh!' I whispered. I knew the voice wasn't Dad's, or the boy's, either.

'I can't help it,' gasped Orrible. She grabbed me with a grip like a wrestler's.

All I could think of was getting out of there. And all the time this croaky old voice was sort of breathing, somewhere beyond the office door: 'A man can't find peace anywhere. That's all I want, peace . . .'

The lightning went off like a photoflash, and both of us saw someone was standing in the doorway. It was the figure of an old, old man, the queerest, raggiest old man I ever saw. He had a beard and a tattered hat that kept the rest of his face in shadow. I was petrified. I couldn't even point the torch at him. Fenella bored her head into my neck. She was shaking like a leaf. Then the old man kind of faded back into the shadows, and we heard that complaining voice getting fainter.

'Why don't they go away and leave me in peace?'

We clung to each other like two monkeys. My sister was sobbing out loud now. 'It must be the ghost that haunts the hotel. And it's done something awful to Daddy.'

I think my blood stopped circulating then, for now I heard footsteps out in the empty bar room. Fenella gave a terrifying squawk, and then Dad's voice called: 'That you, Sally? Where the heck ARE you kids?'

The next moment he was in the office, as mad as a hornet. 'Why the devil didn't you stay by the car, you young twits?'

'We came in to look for you, of course,' hiccupped Fenella, 'after the lights went out.'

'But that was only a moment ago,' protested Dad.

'It certainly was not,' I said, angry now. 'It must have been twenty minutes. We've been walking around, searching and calling. We thought maybe you'd fallen through the floor.'

'Queer,' murmured Dad. 'Now that I come to think of it, everything seemed extraordinarily silent, almost uncanny. Then I heard young Orrible snort or something.'

Fenella began to cry again, while I told Dad what we'd seen and heard. He didn't rubbish me.

Fenella blurted: 'That boy we picked up, HE ran away. He was scared because he knew all the while that this nasty place is haunted.'

Dad gave us both a hug. 'Whatever it was you saw, I've had enough of it. We'll clear out for Burangie right away. The rain's started and I'm blowed if I'm going to spend a miserable wet night with two kids both babbling about spooks.'

The phone rang. Fenella jumped and shrieked. Dad said tetchily: 'Oh, turn it up, Blob. It's probably only that Constable Thing ringing to say the river's rising or something.'

He took the receiver off its hook. 'Hello, hello? Dan Gavin here. Who's that? Hello? Can you hear me?'

I had stopped being terrified. I was just awed. I kept saying: 'Dad. Dad.'

He shushed me. 'Damn these country exchanges, can't make out more than a word here and there. Oh, shut UP, Sal! WHAT? Speak louder, man!'

'Dad,' I said. 'The phone isn't connected. Look at the wires, Dad, not connected for years.'

'Ah, what's the use,' he said. He put the phone back on the hook. 'All I could make out was something about the river coming up, and some babble about the bridge. Sally, what's the matter, you're as white as paper.'

I showed him the corroded ends of the wires.

Well, he took the torch and had us out of that place and into the car in four seconds flat. The rain was pelting down. The engine wouldn't start. Dad said: 'Oh, dear heavens, not now.' He pulled out the choke and she fired. We backed out of the stableyard, and the headlamps cast a yellow fan over the debris. It looked so sad and lonely, the way the old ghost had sounded.

Fenella had her head out the window, directing Dad as he turned to get on to the bridge. She squealed: 'There he is, the ghost, standing in the doorway!'

The lights showed him up like a figure in a faded old photo. Dad put the car in gear with the kind of grind he'd murder poor Mum for, and we clattered over the bridge. All the reedy part was now under water, and the lowest boughs of the trees were awash. I knew any moment now the river would be over the bridge decking. I kept thinking about the disconnected phone, someone had warned us, but who, and why? Then Fenella, who was kneeling on the rear seat looking through the back window, croaked: 'Dad, he's following us across the bridge. The ghost, Daddy!'

Dad jammed on the brakes. I shouted: 'Don't stop! He might catch us up, he's halfway across the bridge already.'

'Be quiet, Sally,' said Dad curtly. 'I've had enough of this. I'm ashamed of myself.'

He opened the door and the rain stabbed in.

'He'll get you!' shrieked Fenella. Dad slammed the door. By the dim light of the rearlights and the occasional flash of lightning we saw him run towards the ghost, who was staggering and splashing through water already kneehigh. We saw Dad grab the figure.

'It's not a ghost at all, it's just a poor fallen-down old man,' shouted Fenella and in a flash she was out of the car and splashing through the rain to help Dad drag the man along. So I was the one who saw what happened.

First of all there was a long deep low roar, away off, in the hills, it seemed. And all the lights in the Ferryman's Arms went on. Every window shone; light poured out the open door and lit up the stableyard, the trees. It was beautiful, the very picture of an old inn waiting to welcome weary travellers. Then I saw the shape of the hill behind it changing. For a moment I couldn't believe it, then my sense came back to me and I, too, leaped out of the car and raced to help Dad and Fenella.

'It's a landslide,' I shouted. 'The whole hill's coming down on the Ferryman!'

The roar was fearsome, like surf.

Somehow we pushed and pulled the old man into the back seat. Dad drove like fury maybe six or seven hundred metres from the river. Then we stopped and just looked, mesmerised, as that hill came down on the building. It was no use speaking; nothing could be heard over the grinding, grating thunder of the avalanche. The old inn crumpled up, slid towards the flooding river with all its lights blazing. It was pushed like a toy in front of a torrent of mud. Then the lights went out, and we couldn't see anything. The roar had stopped, there were only rushing glugging sounds.

It was a terrible drive back to Burangie. The old man seemed almost unconscious. It was a relief when we saw headlights coming towards us. Not only Constable Fiddler in a car, but two other vehicles with several men in each, including the police sergeant.

'We should have listened to you, Constable,' said Dad. He looked knocked-out, and like the rest of us he was as wet as a sponge. The sergeant said that the river was running a banker at Burangie too, and he'd thought perhaps the bridge would go and we'd be marooned. Dad was about to explain what had happened when the old man on the back seat stirred and said feebly: 'Saved me life they did, saved me life.'

The men gathered around. 'It's Pop Trivett, what d'you know? Where'd you spring from, Pop?'

'Saved me life,' whispered the old man. 'I come down from me claim when the big wet started and holed up in the old ruin, snug as a bug. Woke up and heard folk talking and thought they was ghosts.'

'Silly,' said Fenella. 'It was us.'

'I was pretty riled,' said the old man. 'Ghosts mooning around, waking a man up. A man needs his peace and quiet. Then when I heard the car start I knew I'd made a bloomer. Lucky I got woke up though, because then I heard the landslide beginning up in the hills and I went for me life. But I couldn'ta made it without the gent and the girls here.'

You're thinking that I've tricked you, that this isn't a ghost story but a we-thought-it-was-a-ghost story. But you're wrong.

That night in the Burangie pub we slept like logs. After breakfast next morning Constable Fiddler called. He had already been out to see the wreckage of the Ferryman's Arms. The river was blocked and had flooded the whole valley. Mr Trivett, we now learned, was a pensioner who fossicked for gold up in the hills. He was in the hospital, chirpy as a cricket.

'We were sure he was the ghost who lived in the Ferryman!' said Fenella.

'Nobody House was supposed to be haunted all right,' said the Constable, 'though I didn't want to say so, straight out, in case you thought I was around the twist or something. But it wasn't haunted by an oldtimer like Pop. The ghost was a boy of fourteen or so. Usually he was seen on the road before you reached the bridge.'

Fenella and I just gulped. Dad said in a low kind of voice: 'How . . . how did he become a ghost, if I may put it that way?'

So Constable Fiddler told us about the original Old Man Flood which, some forty years before, caused the Ferryman's Arms to fall into disuse. The boy had lived up in the hills on a farm. His people saw heavy water coming down the river, and they thought the Ferryman might be in danger. They tried to phone, but it was a bad line and they couldn't make themselves understood. So they sent the lad down with a message, but as he was crossing the bridge it collapsed and he was drowned.

I think it was our experience that night that changed Orrible to Fenella, an agreeable kind of person. Maybe it changed me, too. I wonder about things, though. Did we drive into the past that night, with the inn all lit up to welcome late travellers? And then the phone message which didn't quite get through but told us enough to frighten us and make us get out and save all our lives. Did that belong to the past, too? Because there WAS something queer about the time factor. Dad thought he was in the Nobody House for only a moment or so, but Fenella and I absolutely know it was much longer than that.

And that boy. He wasn't a bit like a ghost. In the car I touched his hand by accident, and it was as warm as mine. He was just—ordinary. It does make you wonder how many more of them there are about.

J. S. LEATHERBARROW

The Ghostly Goat of Glaramara

THE four of us were sitting in the parlour of a little inn in Borrowdale. It was a welcome Christmas relaxation after the stiff academic chores of a final degree year.

The days were occupied with strenuous tramping along Lakeland roads and the ascent of the more accessible mountain slopes; the evenings with desultory reading of the lighter sort of paperback and with much smoking and talk. The prospect of a stiff climb over Scafell into Wasdale inclined me to hope for an early night and a long rest. But the others would not agree.

Thompson, who was an indefatigable talker and at times was not averse to listening, had, as usual, a lively suggestion. 'I vote,' he said, 'that one of us tells a yarn, and the obvious candidate is Philip, who will certainly soon be asleep unless we make him oblige.' Deeming and Heap supported him and I could see there was no escape.

I heard the landlord stumbling upstairs to bed and then Deeming put a few more pieces of wood on the fire. It was no use arguing for he was well aware that I had been versed in uncanny stories through the influence of a scoutmaster who, round the camp fire, had given us a taste for Lord Halifax and M. R. James. I sat up in my chair and resolutely knocked out my pipe in the grate.

It was John Burton who told me this story, and I had no reason to think that it wasn't true. Burton and I had been friends at school, but he had had more brains than the rest of us and had gone to Oxbridge. When he came home on vacations he used to tell us about his college friends and the eccentric dons whom he had met, and this is one of the strange stories which he told me.

The professor of geology at Burton's University was rather an odd sort of fellow whom no one ever understood nor certainly tried to like. He kept to himself a good deal and had few friends, but Burton got to know him fairly well because they shared the same hobby. Both were enthusiasts for classical archaeology and they used to go out together at week-ends to take part in the excavation of the site of a Roman villa not far from the University city.

Morton, as the professor was called, was a bachelor with strange religious beliefs which forbade him celebrating such occasions as Christmas and Easter.

He made a habit of going to some remote place for a holiday at such festival times, taking with him for study some long and abstruse books on geology and archaeology.

Burton recommended him to try the Lake District for a quiet few days, and Morton began to enquire for suitable lodgings for the Christmas week. Burton, of course, was always keen on this place in Borrowdale, but Morton said that he didn't want a Christmas holiday in a pub. He wanted a quiet place where he could study. So our landlady here fixed him up in a farmhouse a bit further down the valley. It was a place that quite suited him and he was sure that he would get the quiet there that he needed to study his books.

Morton arrived at Brownthwaite Farm on the day before Christmas. The air was sharp and frosty and as he stalked around the farmyard in heavy coat and fur gloves he surveyed the valley, where the towering bulk of Glaramara and Scafell seemed to build a massive barrier between Borrowdale and Wastwater.

The nearest building to the farm was this inn, about half a mile down the valley and away from the mountain block. Beyond the inn was the church and the village, consisting of a score of houses and a shop. The professor blessed the happy solitude and looked forward to an interesting evening with his geology.

After tea he returned to his room on the first floor and sat down before the log fire that his hostess had made for him. He opened his bag and took out a large volume called *The Borrowdale Series of Volcanic Eruptions* which he handled lovingly and laid open on his knee. The first chapter gave him immense pleasure.

As he got well into the middle of the second, he heard such a crash from below as made him wonder whether the house was falling down. After the crash came screams of laughter interspersed with the tinkling of a piano. Poor Morton could not concentrate on the Borrowdale eruptions any longer. It seemed as though they had invaded the house. He managed to stumble through to the end of the second chapter, but when he had finished it he knew little of what it contained. As the noise became louder, he became more angry and closed the tome with a furious bang.

In a little while he heard the farmer's wife coming up the stairs and, as she entered his room, spoke to her severely. 'Well, what is it,

Mrs Stokes?' he said. 'There certainly is rather a row going on down-stairs, isn't there?'

'There is indeed,' said Mrs Stokes, 'but being as it's Christmas Eve we thought you wouldn't mind. The children are having a party downstairs and my little boy wants to know whether you'll come down and tell them a ghost story as they're tired of playing musical flops.'

Morton rose in a rage at the mention of Christmas Eve and musical flops and ghost stories and, thinking of the solitary situation of the farm and the fascination of the Borrowdale eruptions, he turned fiercely on Mrs Stokes. 'Tell them ghost stories!' he shouted, 'I'll see them in hell first!' Mrs Stokes retired haughtily and disdainfully, passing remarks as she descended the stairs upon the manners and morals of University gentlemen in general.

Morton tried to settle down to geology again but the eruptions proceeded with increased violence beneath him and, deprived of their ghost story, the merrymakers put more energy into their musical flops. The professor wearily gave up his attempts to read geology and looked around for something else to do.

His glance fell upon a shelf of books in a recess in a corner of the room and he selected one book at random. It was called *Strange Tales from the Lake Country* and had been written by some parson of the neighbour-hood in the last century. Unpromising as it looked, Morton opened the book at the first story and began to read. Surprisingly to himself, he became interested and settled down to read in earnest, oblivious now of the noise below.

The second story was about a strange happening which had disturbed the good people of Borrowdale in 1770. In a cottage high up on Glara-mara lived an old woman whom all the valley said was a witch, who poisoned their sheep, addled their eggs and caused their new-born children to be born with hare lips. The old woman came down to the village once a week to buy her provisions, but no one ever spoke to her nor had the least idea where she got her money. Her only friend was an ancient goat which trotted behind her on these expeditions and carried some of her parcels in its mouth.

The expression on the goat's face was what frightened the people most. Some called it a devilish leer, some said they heard it laugh and that its laugh was like that of a malevolent child. A little bell hung round its neck and people could hear it ringing as the old woman went up and down the mountain and around the village. Some villagers said that they had looked out of their bedroom windows at night and had seen the old woman and her goat standing in their gardens below. The sheep continued to be poisoned, the eggs addled and the children born with hare lips in the Borrowdale Valley.

At last the desperate villagers waited on the parson, beseeching him to admonish the old woman in the name of the Church. He, at any rate, should know how to deal with a witch's spell. He preached learned sermons against her from the three-decker pulpit of his newly built church, plentifully laced with quotations from the best classical and contemporary authors. His eloquence had no effect.

His people insisted that he should solemnly abjure the old woman in person, so one Christmas Eve, a frosty night, the Vicar of Borrowdale buttoned up his great coat and, thinking sadly of that newly cut copy of Locke's *Reasonableness of Christianity* which he had left on the table near the warm fire in his parlour, strode up the valley in the direction of the slopes of Glaramara.

Half way up the mountain he saw the light of the old woman's cottage and strode vigorously in that direction, determined to finish with the unpleasant business as quickly as he could. Locke's admission as to the existence of an intellectual world, wherein were an infinite number and degrees of spirits out of the reach of our ken and guess, was rather too fresh in his mind. But the climb was long and steep, and when the parson reached the door of the cottage he was exhausted and the lights of the vicarage down in the valley seemed very tiny and far away.

He knocked but received no answer. He opened the door and walked in, but there was no sign of the old woman. In the fireplace, however, was a cauldron of simmering stew, and watching it steadfastly sat the goat. The parson shivered, though it was hot in the cottage, and drew his great coat closer about him. The goat turned and fixed its eyes upon him steadfastly. He could have sworn that it smiled at him cynically. The parson then began to call aloud the old woman's name, but there was no response.

After shouting several times and receiving no answer the parson made up his mind to give up the errand, and with a sigh of relief he turned to go. As he reached the door, he stopped abruptly and turned around, for he was sure that he had heard a cynical laugh from the middle of the room. But there was no one there; only the goat still engrossed in its occupation of watching the stew.

The parson made his way out of the old woman's garden and found the path which led down Glaramara in the direction of Seathwaite village. Thankfully he quickened his steps and as he drew near to the bottom of the valley he began to sing to himself one of Watts' hymns, for he was pleased that he had been able to evade an interview with the old woman and at the same time to have done his best to fulfil his duty to his parishioners. The lights of the vicarage looked much nearer now.

The vicar paused for a moment to take breath, for he had long passed his sixtieth birthday and was growing stout and slow moving. Then he gave a start and dislodged a stone. An irrational impulse of fear possessed him. From the distant height of Glaramara above him he heard, quite distinctly, the tinkling of a bell. He looked round nervously and saw in the distance a yellow light moving regularly from side to side.

The parson quickened his pace and hurried on; behind him the bell tinkled incessantly. He was well down the valley now and walking as fast as his breath would let him. Occasionally he glanced over his shoulder, heard the tinkling becoming louder and saw the yellow light growing larger and brighter. He saw the lamp in the vicarage window shining near ahead in the distance.

Again he looked round and this time in the darkness dimly made out the shape of the old woman carrying her lantern and her goat trotting obediently at her side. The sound of the tinkling bell swelled into a torrent of noise. The parson broke into a frenzied run. The vicarage gate was now only a few yards ahead, but the goat was at his heels and the loud tinkling of the bell and the noise of his breath seemed to the parson to drown his cries for help.

After one last frantic burst of speed, he reached his gate, flung it open, rushed through and slammed it in the faces of the old woman and her goat. The parson sank down exhausted on the vicarage lawn and fainted. The goat, however, claimed its reward in the shape of a jagged piece of cloth which it tore from the tail of his greatcoat as he was flinging open the vicarage gate.

This was the tale the parson told his servant, who found him there in the garden a few minutes later. To be sure, the servant saw neither the old woman nor the goat, but there was the evidence of the piece of cloth missing from her master's coat, a fine new garment bought from Kendal only that winter, and snow which fell later in the night covered up the imprints which he was certain he would have found in the mud outside the garden gate.

Then there was the evidence of the little scared maidservant, who vowed that before she went downstairs to help to revive her master, she happened to look through the landing window which gave on Glaramara and there she saw a speck of light moving upwards and from side to side as though someone carrying a lantern were climbing the mountain. It was all so obvious.

Superstitions died hard in country places in those days and, although the event was never recorded in the annals of Carlisle castle, Borrowdale saw one of the last witch burnings of history. The old woman died, it was said, protesting her innocence, but she refused any spiritual help from the parson when he visited her and cursed horribly at the country folk who piled on the faggots. In her cottage were found many little plaster images stuck all over with pins and these the simple Borrowdale people, who had never heard of or at any rate never understood what the parson meant by 'the age of reason', burnt in the same fire as their modeller, murmuring at the same time prayers that they should be preserved ever after from the wiles of the Evil One. But they felt no certainty about it.

When, later on, the parson related his experience to his scholarly neighbour at Crosthwaite the vicar retorted by reaching down the learned Bishop Sprat's History of the Royal Society which assured him that *'From the time in which the real philosophy has appeared, there is scare any whisper remaining of such horrors; every man is unshaken at those tales at which his ancestors trembled. The course of things goes quietly along in its own true channel of natural causes and effects.'* But the vicar of Borrowdale was not convinced. On the whole, he said, he was more inclined to trust the words of Locke.

Professor Morton closed the book and shivered. The house was quiet and the fire had gone out. He pondered for some time over the story he had read and began to speculate as to its truth. The villagers, he thought, were a set of credulous fools. The parson was either a madman or a knave. Or perhaps he was a drunkard. This suggestion pleased him. He had probably stumbled home from the village pub after a Christmas Eve jollification and torn his coat on the garden gate and fallen in a drunken stupor in the garden. Those 18th century parsons were not particularly scrupulous about their habits. The more he thought about it the more he pitied the lonely old woman and her pet animal.

After a while he got up and tried to fan the embers of the fire but he could not arouse it. Then he went to the door of his room and looked out on to the landing, but the house was all dark and silent. He remembered the children's party and assumed that it must now be over and the family in their beds. He determined that he, too, would go to bed. He undressed and blew out the oil lamp which was lighting his room. A flood of moonlight lit the bedroom until it seemed as light as the late afternoon of a winter's day.

Going to the window, he saw that the sky was ablaze with stars and the trees glistening with frost. The professor had a little of the poet in his nature and, as he did not yet feel particularly tired, he put on his dressing gown and drew a chair close to the window. There he sat, gazing out at Glaramara, bathed in silver moonlight and the Borrowdale beck murmuring over its stones.

He continued thus for a few minutes and then something happened which made him lean forward and peer more intently into the night. For, coming slowly down the mountain, he thought he saw a tiny yellow light, and borne across the frosty air he thought he heard the tinkling of a bell. Impatiently he got up from his chair and strode across the room, flung off his dressing gown, climbed into bed and buried himself in a mass of bedclothes. But try as he would, he could not sleep but lay awake thinking of the winking light and the tinkling bell.

As he dozed towards slumber there reached his ears again the tinkling, louder and more insistent. Louder and louder it sounded until it seemed to thunder in his ears and the professor could endure it no longer. He leapt out of bed and rushed across to the window. An impulse he could not resist forced him to fling it wide open. He peered out.

What he saw did not surprise him. He had expected it ever since he had heard the sound of the bell. There below in the garden stood the old woman and her goat. She stretched out her arm and pointed at him whilst the goat stood silently watching. The appearance of the couple fixed itself for the rest of his life in the professor's mind. Where the woman's face should have been was what resembled a clotted mass of singed brown roots such as a gardener might have turned up from a diseased bush and tried to burn. The goat had a bearded face which registered its image on the professor's mind with appalling clarity. Its bloodshot eyes seemed to burn with fire and to reflect an infinitude of evil.

In loathing and horror the professor was drawn towards the couple with an irresistible magnetic compulsion. He screamed aloud and leaned out of the open window. The old woman was beckoning him and even the terror that possessed him could not restrain him. He felt that he must follow her and her goat. Further and further he leaned, with arms outstretched in her direction. Further and further. Strong hands clutched his shoulders and he felt himself pulled back into the room with rough force.

The farmer and his wife said that on Christmas Eve they had taken home to Seathwaite village some of the children who had been at their party, and returning to their farm had been horrified to see the old professor, their guest, hanging far out of his bedroom window, shrieking with terror. The farmer had rushed up to the professor's room, just in time to prevent him falling headlong.

The professor, he told his friends, had been altogether unreasonable and on Christmas morning had told him that he could not stay at the farm an hour longer and asked him to get a trap to take him back to Keswick. This the farmer said he could only do at great expense, but the professor replied that he would pay anything if only he could get out of Borrowdale that morning. Mrs Stokes was not pleased; it seemed to cast aspersions on their hospitality. The professor, she said, was by no means a reasonable man.

Nevertheless, very early on Christmas morning, a trap drew up before the front door of the farm to convey the professor via Rosthwaite and Grange to Keswick station and after the most tortuous and slow Christmas Day journey, to Oxbridge University. There followed tremendous speculation as to why old Morton had chosen to eat his very late Christmas dinner at Oxbridge instead of in the quietude of the Lake District. But John Burton knew, and if ever he finds out that I've told the tale to you three, there'll be the very devil to pay.

The other three continued to smoke without speaking when my story was finished. I got up and pushed back my chair in a resolute way. 'Now I'm really going to bed,' I insisted. The others paid no attention to my remark but continued to gaze, ruminating, into the fire.

I moved resolutely towards the door and stairs. I was determined not to be involved in discussion as to the rights and wrongs and probabilities of the story. I had no clear ideas myself.

Two sizeable beds stood in the spacious inn bedroom. It was not long before I heard Heap, who was my partner, coming up. Deeming and Thompson soon followed and we heard them enter their room opposite ours. Heap and I were soon snuggling deep in our comfortable beds. Soon he was asleep and snoring loudly.

In another minute I too was dozing on the borderland between sleep and waking. In another I too would have been asleep. Suddenly I started and called out, so violently that I wakened Heap. For across the clear mountain air floated distinctly the silvery tinkle of a bell.

JOAN AIKEN

She was Afraid of Upstairs

MY cousin Tessie, that was. Bright as a button, she was, good as gold, neat as ninepence. And clever, too. Read anything she would time she were five. Papers, letters, library books, all manner of print. Delicate little thing, peaky, not pretty at all, but, even when she was a liddle un, she had a way of putting things into words that'd surprise you. 'Look at the sun a-setting, Ma,' she'd say. 'He's wrapping his hair all over his face.' Of the old postman, Jumper, on his red bike, she said he was bringing news from Otherwhere. And a bit of Demarara on a lettuce leaf—that was her favourite treat—a sugarleaf, she called it. 'But I haven't been good enough for a sugarleaf today,' she'd say. 'Have I, Ma?'

Good she mainly was, though, like I said, not a bit of harm in her.

But upstairs she would not go.

Been like that from a tiny baby, she had, just as soon as she could notice anything. When my Aunt Sarah would try to carry her up, she'd shriek and carry on, the way you'd think she was being taken to the slaughterhouse. At first they thought it was on account she didn't want to go to bed, maybe afraid of the dark, but that weren't it at all. For she'd settle to bed anywhere they put her, in the back kitchen, the broom closet under the stairs, in the lean-to with the copper, even in the coalshed, where my Uncle Fred once, in a temper, put her cradle. 'Let her lie there,' he said, 'if she won't sleep up in the bedroom, let her lie there.'

And lie there she did, calm and peaceable, all the livelong night, and not a chirp out of her.

My Aunt Sarah was fair put about with this awkward way of Tessie's, for they'd only the one downstairs room, and, evenings, you want the kids out of the way. One that won't go upstairs at night is a fair old problem. But, when Tessie was three, Uncle Fred and Aunt Sarah moved to Birmingham, where they had a back kitchen and a little bit of garden, and in the garden my Uncle Fred built Tessie a tiny cabin, not much bigger than a packing-case it wasn't, by the back kitchen wall, and there she had her cot, and there she slept, come rain, come snow.

Would she go upstairs in the day?

Not if she could help it.

'Run up, Tessie, and fetch me my scissors—or a clean towel—or the hair brush—or the bottle of camomile,' Aunt Sarah might say, when Tessie was big enough to walk and to run errands. Right away, her lip would start to quiver and that frantic look would come in her eye. But my Aunt Sarah was not a one to trifle with. She'd lost the big battle, over where Tessie was to sleep. She wasn't going to have any non-sense in small ways. Upstairs that child would have to go, whether she liked it or not. And upstairs she went, with Aunt Sarah's eye on her, but you could hear, by the sound of her feet, that she was having to drag them, one after the other, they were so unwilling, it was like hauling rusty nails out of wood. And when she was upstairs, the timid tiptoeing, it was like some wild creature, a squirrel or a bird that has got in by mistake. She'd find the thing, whatever it was, that Aunt Sarah wanted, and then, my word, wouldn't she come dashing down again as if the Militia were after her, push the thing, whatever it might be, into her mum's hands, and then out into the garden to take in big gulps of the fresh air. Outside was where she liked best to be, she'd spend whole days in the garden, if Aunt Sarah let her. She had a little patch, where she grew lettuce and cress, Uncle Fred got the seeds for her, and then people used to give her bits of slips and flower-seeds, she had a real gift for getting things to grow. That garden was a pretty place, you couldn't see the ground for the greenstuff and flowers. Narcissus, bluebells, sweet-peas, marigolds.

Of course the neighbours used to come and shove their oar in. Neighbours always will. 'Have a child that won't go upstairs? I'd not allow it if she was mine,' said Mrs Oakley that lived over the way. 'It's fair daft if you ask me. *I'd* soon leather her out of it.' For in other people's houses Tessie was just the same—when she got old enough to be taken out to tea. Upstairs she would not go. Anything but that.

Of course they used to try and reason with her, when she was old enough to express herself.

'Why don't you go, Tessie? What's the matter with upstairs? There's nothing bad up there. Only the beds and the chests-of-drawers. What's wrong with that?'

And Aunt Sarah used to say, laughing, 'You're nearer to heaven up there.'

But no, Tessie'd say, 'It's bad, it's bad! Something bad is up there.' When she was very little she'd say, 'Darkwoods. *Darkwoods*,' and 'Grandfather Moon! I'm frightened, I'm frightened!' Funny thing that, because, of the old moon itself, a-sailing in the sky, she wasn't scared a bit, loved it dearly, and used to catch the silvery light in her hands, if she were out at night, and say it was like tinsel falling from the sky.

Aunt Sarah was worried what would happen when Tessie started school. Suppose the school had an upstairs classroom, then what? But Uncle Fred told her not to fuss herself, not to borrow trouble; very likely the child would have got over all her nonsense by the time she was of school age, as children mostly do.

A doctor got to hear of her notions, for Tessie had the diptheery, one time, quite bad, with a thing in her throat, and he had to come ever so many times.

'This isn't a proper place to have her,' he says, for her bed was in the kitchen—it was winter then, they couldn't expect the doctor to go out to Tessie's little cubbyhole in the garden. So Aunt Sarah began to cry and carry on, and told him how it was.

'I'll soon make an end of that nonsense,' says he, 'for now she's ill she won't notice where she is. And then, when she's better, she'll wake up and find herself upstairs, and her phobia will be gone.' That's what he called it, a phobia. So he took Tessie out of her cot and carried her upstairs. And, my word, didn't she create! Shruk! You'd a thought she was being skinned alive. Heads was poking out of windows all down the street. He had to bring her down again fast. 'Well, she's got a good strength in her, she's not going to die of the diptheery, at all events,' says he, but he was very put out, you could see that. Doctors don't like to be crossed. 'You've got a wilful one there, Missus,' says he, and off he goes, in high dudgeon. But he must have told another doctor about Tessie's wilfulness, for a week or so later, along comes a Doctor Trossick, a mind doctor, one of them pussycologists, who wants to ask Tessie all manner of questions. Does she remember this, does she remember that, when she was a baby, and *why* won't she go upstairs, can't she tell him the reason, and what's all this about Grandfather Moon and Darkwoods? Also, what about when her Ma and Pa go upstairs, isn't she scared for them too?

'No, it's not dangerous for them,' says Tessie. 'Only for me.'

'But *why* is it dangerous for you, child? What do you think is going to happen?'

'Something dreadful! The worst possible thing!'

Dr Trossick made a whole lot of notes, asked Tessie to do all manner of tests on a paper he'd brought, and then he tried to make her go upstairs, persuading her to stand on the bottom step for a minute, and then on the next one, and the one after. But by the fourth step she'd come to trembling and shaking so bad, with the tears running down, that he hadn't the heart to force her any further.

So things stood, when Tessie was six or thereabouts. And then one day the news came: the whole street where they lived was going to be pulled down. Redevelopment. Rehousing. All the little two-up, two-downs were to go, and everybody was to be shifted to high-rise blocks. Aunt Sarah, Uncle Fred, and Tessie were offered a flat on the sixteenth floor of a block that was already built.

Aunt Sarah was that upset. She loved her little house. And as for Tessie—'It'll kill her for sure,' Aunt Sarah said.

At that, Uncle Fred got riled. He was a slow man, but obstinate.

'We can't arrange our whole life to suit a child,' he said. 'We've been offered a Council flat—very good, we'll take it. The kid will have to learn she can't have her own way always. Besides,' he said, 'there's lifts in them blocks. Maybe when she finds she can go up in a lift, she won't take on as much as if it was only stairs. And maybe the sixteenth floor won't seem so bad as the first or second. After all, *we'll* all be on one level—there's no stairs in a flat.'

Well, Aunt Sarah saw the sense in that. And the only thing she could think of was to take Tessie to one of the high-rise blocks and see what she made of it. Her cousin Ada, that's my Mum, had already moved into one of the tower blocks, so Aunt Sarah took Tessie out in her pushchair one afternoon and fetched her over to see us.

All was fine to start with, the kid was looking about her, interested and not too bothered, till the pushchair was wheeled into the lift and the doors closed.

'What's this?' says Tessie then.

'It's a lift,' says Aunt Sarah, 'and we're going to see your Auntie Ada and Winnie and Dorrie.'

Well, when the lift started going up, Aunt Sarah told us, Tessie went white as a dishclout, and time it got up to the tenth, that was where we lived, she was flat on the floor. Fainted. A real bad faint it was, she didn't come out of it for ever so long, and Aunt Sarah was in a terrible way over it.

'What have I done, what have I done to her,' she kept saying.

We all helped her get Tessie home again. But after that the kid was very poorly. Brain fever, they'd have called it in the old days, Mum said. Tossing and turning, hot as fire, and delirious with it, wailing and calling out about Darkwoods and Grandfather Moon. For a long time they was too worried about her to make any plans at all, but when she began to mend, Aunt Sarah says to Uncle Fred:

'*Now* what are we going to do?'

Well, he was very put out, natural, but he took his name off the Council list and began to look for another job, somewhere else, where they could live on ground level. And at last he found work in a little seaside town, Topness, about a hundred miles off. Got a house and all, so they was set to move.

They didn't want to shift before Tessie was middling better, but the Council was pushing and pestering them to get out of their house, because the whole street was coming down; the other side had gone already, there was just a big huge stretch of grey rubble, as far as you could see, and half the houses on this side was gone too.

'What's *happening?*' Tessie kept saying when she looked out of the window. 'What's happening to our world?'

She was very pitiful about it.

'Are they going to do that with my garden too?' she'd say. 'All my sweetpeas and marigolds?'

'Don't you worry, dearie,' says Aunt Sarah. 'You can have a pretty garden where we're going.'

'And I won't have to sleep upstairs?'

'No, no, Dad'll fix you a cubbyhole, same as he has here.'

So they packed up all their bits and sticks and they started off. Sam Whitelaw lent them his grocery van for the move, and he drove it too.

It was a long drive—over a hundred miles, and most of it through wild, bare country. Tessie liked it all right at first, she stared at the green fields and the sheep, she sat on Aunt Sarah's lap and looked out of the window, but after a few hours, when they were on the moor, she began to get very poorly, her head was as hot as fire, and her hands too. She didn't complain, but she began to whimper with pain and weakness, big tears rolled down, and Aunt Sarah was bothered to death about her.

'The child wasn't well enough to shift yet. She ought to be in a bed. What'll we do?'

'We're only halfway, if that,' says Mr Whitelaw. 'D'you want to stop somewhere, Missus?'

The worst of it was, there weren't any houses round there—not a building to be seen for miles and miles.

On they went, and now Tessie was throwing herself from side to side, delirious again, and crying fit to break her mother's heart.

At last, ahead of them—it was glimmery by then, after sunset of a wintry day—they saw a light, and came to a little old house, all by itself, set a piece back off the road against a wooded scarp of hill.

'Should we stop here and see if the folk will help us?' suggested Mr Whitelaw, and Aunt Sarah says, 'Oh, yes. Yes! Maybe they have a phone and can send for a doctor. Oh I'm worried to death,' she says. 'It was wicked to move the child so soon.'

The two men went and tapped at the door and somebody opened it. Uncle Fred explained about the sick child, and the owner of the house— an old, white-haired fellow, Aunt Sarah said he was—told them, 'I don't have a phone, look'ee, I live here all on my own. But you're kindly welcome to come in and put the poor little mawther in my bed.'

So they all carried Tessie in among them—by that time she was hardly sensible. My poor aunt gave a gasp when she stepped inside, for the house was really naught but a barn or shippen, with a floor of beaten earth and some farm stuff, tumbrils and carts and piles of turnips.

'Up here,' says the old man, and shows them a flight of stone steps by the wall.

Well, there was nothing for it; up they had to go.

Above was decent enough, though. The old fellow had two rooms, fitted up as bedroom and kitchen, with an iron cooking-stove, curtains at the windows, and a bed covered with old blankets, all felted-up. Tessie was almost too ill to notice where she'd got to. They put her on the bed, and the old man went to put on a kettle—Aunt Sarah thought the child should have a hot drink.

Uncle Fred and Mr Whitelaw said they'd drive on in the van and fetch a doctor, if the old man could tell them where to find one.

'Surely,' says he, 'there's a doctor in the village—Wootten-under-Edge, five miles along. Dr Hastie—he's a real good un, he'll come fast enough.'

'Where is this place?' says Uncle Fred. 'Where should we tell him to come?'

'He'll know where it is,' says the old man. 'Tell him Darkwoods Farm.'

Off they went, and the old man came back to where Aunt Sarah was trying to make poor Tessie comfortable. The child was tossing and fretting, whimpering and crying that she felt so ill, her head felt so bad!

'She'll take a cup of my tansy tea. That'll soothe her,' said the old man, and he went to his kitchen and brewed up some green drink in an old blue-and-white jug.

'Here, Missus,' said he, coming back. 'Try her with a little of this.'

A sip or two did seem to soothe poor Tessie, brung her to herself a bit, and for the first time she opened her eyes and took a look at the old man.

'Where is this place?' she asked. She was so weak, her voice was no more than a thread.

'Why, you're in my house,' said the old man. 'And very welcome you are, my dear!'

'And who are you?' she asked next.

'Why, lovely, I'm old Tom Moon the shepherd—old Grandfather Moon. I lay you never expected you'd be sleeping in the moon's house tonight!'

But at that, Tessie gave one screech, and fainted dead away.

Well, poor Aunt Sarah was that upset, with trying to bring Tessie round, but she tried to explain to Mr Moon about Tessie's trouble, and all her fears, and the cause of her sickness.

He listened, quiet and thinking, taking it all in.

Then he went and sat down by Tessie's bed, gripping hold of her hand.

She was just coming round by then, she looked at him with big eyes full of fright, as Aunt Sarah kneeled down by her other side.

'Now, my dearie,' said Mr Moon. 'You know I'm a shepherd, I never hurt a sheep or a lamb in my life. My job is to look after 'em, see? And I'm certainly not a-going to hurt *you*. So don't you be frit now—there's nothing to be frightened of. Not from old Grandfather Moon.'

But he could see that she was trembling all over.

'You've been scared all your life, haven't you, child?' said he gently, and she nodded, Yes.

He studied her then, very close, looked into her eyes, felt her head, and held her hands.

And he said, 'Now, my dearie, I'm not going to tell ye no lies. I've never told a lie yet—you can't be lying to sheep or lambs. Do ye believe that I'm your friend and wish you well?'

Again she gave a nod, even weaker.

He said, 'Then, Tessie my dear, I have to tell you that you're a-going to die. And *that's* what's been scaring you all along. But you were wrong to be in such a fret over it, lovey, for there's *naught to be scared of*. There'll be no hurt, there'll be no pain, it be just like stepping through a door. And I should know,' he said, 'for I've seen a many, many sheep and lambs taken off by weakness or the cold. It's no more than going to sleep in one life and waking up in another. Now do ye believe me, Tessie?'

Yes, she nodded, with just a hint of a smile, and she turned her eyes to Aunt Sarah, on the other side of the bed.

And with that, she took and died.

ISAAC BASHEVIS SINGER

The Extinguished Lights

IT was the custom to light the Hanukkah candles at home, rather than in a synagogue or studyhouse, but this particular studyhouse in Bilgoray was an exception. Old Reb Berish practically lived there. He prayed, studied the Mishnah, ate, and sometimes even slept on the bench near the stove. He was the oldest man in town. He admitted to being over ninety, but some maintained that he was already past one hundred. He remembered the war between Russia and Hungary. On holidays he used to visit Rabbi Chazkele from Kuzmir and other ancient rabbis.

That winter it snowed in Bilgoray almost every day. At night the houses on Bridge Street were snowed under and the people had to dig themselves out in the morning. Reb Berish had his own copper Hanukkah lamp, which the beadle kept in the reading table with other holy objects—a ram's horn, the Book of Esther written on a scroll, a braided Havdalah candle, a prayer shawl and phylacteries, as well as a wine goblet and an incense holder.

There is no moon on the first nights of Hanukkah, but that night the light from the stars made the snow sparkle as if it were full of diamonds. Reb Berish placed his Hanukkah lamp at the window according to the law, poured oil into the container, put a wick into it, and made the customary benedictions. Then he sat by the open clay stove. Even though most of the children stayed at home on Hanukkah evenings, a few boys came to the studyhouse especially to listen to Reb Berish's stories. He was known as a storyteller. While he told stories he roasted potatoes on the glowing coals. He was saying, 'Nowadays when snow falls and there is a frost, people call it winter. In comparison to the winters of my times the winters of today are nothing. It used to be so cold that oak trees burst in the forests. The snow was up to the rooftops. Bevies of hungry wolves came into the village at night, and people shuddered in bed from their howling. The horses neighed in their stables and tried to break the doors open from fear. The dogs barked like mad. Bilgoray was still a tiny place then. There was a pasture where Bagno Street is today.

'The winter I'm going to tell you about was the worst of them all. The days were almost as dark as night. The clouds were black as lead. A woman would come out of her kitchen with the slop pail and the water turned to ice before she could empty it.

'Now hear something. That year the men blessed the Hanukkah lights on the first night as they did every year, but suddenly a wind came from nowhere and extinguished them. It happened in every house at the same time. The lights were kindled a second time, but again they were exitinguished. In those times there was an abundance of wood to help keep the houses warm. To keep the wind out, cracks in the windows were plugged up with cotton or straw. So how could the wind get in? And why should it happen in every house at the same moment? Everybody was astonished. People went to the rabbi to ask his advice and the rabbi's decision was to continue rekindling the lights. Some pious men kept lighting the candles until the rooster crowed. This happened on the first night of Hanukkah, as well as on the second night and on the nights after. There were non-believers who contended that the whole thing was a natural occurrence. But most of the people believed that there was some mysterious power behind it all. But what was it—a demon, a mocker, an imp? And why just on Hanukkah?

'A fear came over the town. Old women said that it was an omen of war or an epidemic. Fathers and grandfathers were so disturbed that they forgot to give Hanukkah money to the children, who couldn't play games with the dreidel. The women did not fry pancakes as they had in former years.

'It went on like this until the seventh night. Then, after everyone was asleep and the rabbi was sitting in his chamber studying the Talmud, someone knocked on his door. It was the rabbi's custom to go to sleep early in the evening and to get up after midnight to study. Usually his wife served him tea, but in the middle of the night the rabbi poured water into the samovar himself, lit the coals, and prepared the tea. He would drink and study until daybreak.

'When the rabbi heard the knocking on the door, he got up and opened it. An old woman stood outside and the rabbi invited her to come into his house.

'She sat down and told the rabbi that last year before Hanukkah her little granddaughter Altele, an orphan, died. She had first gotten sick in the summer and no doctor could help her. After the High Holidays, when Altele realized that her end was near, she said, "Grandmother, I know that I'm going to die, but I only wish to live until Hanukkah, when Grandpa gives me Hanukkah money and I can play dreidel with the girls." Everybody in Bilgoray prayed for the girl's recovery, but it so happened that she died just a day before Hanukkah. For a whole year after her death her grandparents never saw her in their dreams. But this night the grandmother had seen Altele in her dreams three times in a row. Altele came to her and said that because the people of the town had not prayed ardently enough for her to see the first Hanukkah candle, she had died angry and it was she who extinguished the Hanukkah lights in every house. The old woman said that after the first dream she awakened her husband and told him, but he said that because she brooded so much about her grandchild, she had had this dream. The second time when Altele came to her in her dream, the grandmother asked Altele what the people of the town could do to bring peace to her soul. The girl began to answer, but the old woman woke up suddenly before she could understand what Altele was saying. Only in the third dream did the girl speak clearly, saying it was her wish that on the last night of Hanukkah all the people of Bilgoray, together with the rabbi and the elders, should come to her grave and light the Hanukkah candles there. They should bring all the children with them, eat pancakes, and play dreidel on the frozen snow.

'When the rabbi heard these words, he began to tremble, and he said, "It's all my fault. I didn't pray enough for that child." He told the old woman to wait, poured some tea for her, and looked in the books to see if what the girl asked was in accordance with the law. Though he couldn't find a similar case in all the volumes of his library, the rabbi decided on his own that the wish of that grieved spirit should be granted. He told the old woman that on a cold and windy night there is very little chance for lights to burn outdoors. However, if the ghost of the girl could extinguish all the lights indoors, she might also have the power to do the opposite. The rabbi promised the old woman to pray with all his heart for success.

'Early in the morning, when the beadle came to the rabbi, he asked him to take his wooden hammer and go from house to house, knock on shutters, and tell the people what they must do. Even though Hanukkah is a holiday, the rabbi had ordered the older people to fast until noon and ask forgiveness of the girl's sacred soul—and also pray that there should be no wind in the evening.

'All day long a fierce wind blew. Chimneys were blown off some roofs. The sky was overcast with dark clouds. Not only the unbelievers, but even some of the God-fearing men, doubted lights could stay lit in a storm like this. There were those who suspected that the old woman invented the dream, or that a demon came to her disguised as her late grandchild in order to scoff at the faithful and lead them astray. The town's healer, Nissan, who trimmed his beard and came to the synagogue only on the Sabbath, called the old woman a liar and warned that the little ones might catch terrible colds at the graveyard and get inflammation of the lungs. The blizzard seemed to become wilder from minute to minute. But suddenly, while the people were reciting the evening prayer, a change took place. The sky cleared, the wind subsided, and warm breezes wafted from the surrounding fields and forests. It was already the beginning of the month of Teveth and a new moon was seen surrounded with myriads of stars.

'Some of the unbelievers were so stunned they couldn't utter a word. Nissan the healer promised the rabbi that scissors would never touch his beard again and that he would come to pray every day of the week. Not only older children, but even the younger ones, were taken to the graveyard. Lights were kindled, blessings were recited, the women served the pancakes with jam that they had prepared. The children played dreidel on the frozen snow, which was as smooth as ice. A golden light shone over the little girl's grave, a sign that her soul enjoyed the Hanukkah celebration. Never before or after did the graveyard seem so festive as on that eighth night of Hanukkah. All the unbelievers did penance. Even the Gentiles heard of the miracle and acknowledged that God had not forsaken the Jews.

'The next day Mendel the scribe wrote down the whole event in the parchment Community Book, but the book was burned years later in the time of the First Fire.'

'When did this happen?' one of the children asked.

Reb Berish clutched his beard, which had once been red, then turned white, and finally became yellowish from the snuff he used. He pondered for a while and said, 'Not less than eighty years ago.'

'And you remember it so clearly?'

'As if it took place yesterday.'

The light in Reb Berish's Hanukkah lamp began to sputter and smoke. The studyhouse became full of shadows. With his bare fingers the old man pulled three potatoes out of the stove, broke off some pieces, and offered them to the children. He said, 'The body dies, but the soul goes up to God and lives forever.'

'What do all the souls do when they are with God?' one of the boys asked.

'They sit in Paradise on golden chairs with crowns on their heads and God teaches them the secrets of the Torah.'

'God is a teacher?'

'Yes, God is a teacher, and all the good souls are His pupils,' Reb Berish replied.

'How long will the souls go on learning?' a boy asked.

'Until the Messiah comes, and then there will be the resurrection of the dead,' Reb Berish said. 'But even then God will continue to teach in His eternal yeshiva, because the secrets of the Torah are deeper than the ocean, higher than heaven, and more delightful than all the pleasures the body could ever enjoy.'

JAN MARK

Who's a Pretty Boy, Then?

RACHEL's house had a very small garden. The people on the end of the terrace had a big one, round the side as well as at the back, but Rachel's house was in the middle, so there was only a small strip of garden behind, and none at all in front. Once Rachel had travelled right to the top of Debenham's, on the escalators, to where they kept all the furniture and carpets. Some of the carpets were laid out on the floor, as if they were in a real house, and there was one carpet that was as big as Rachel's whole garden; well, almost. Two of those carpets would definitely have been bigger than Rachel's garden.

Rachel's mum could have done with a bit more room because she liked growing things, and there was not much scope for gardening on a carpet, but she made the most of what space there was. Along the back fence, by the alley, there were sprouts and cabbages, with fringes of radishes and spring onions in between, and the lusty rhubarb that was trying to get out, through the palings. In the middle was a grass plot that had to be cut with shears because there wasn't enough to buy a mower for, and down either side were flowers. Mum even had little bushes growing in old buckets, on the concrete up by the back door, and there was a stringy sort of vine that did not look at all well, and that had come over the wall from Mrs Sergeant's.

'For a bit of peace,' said Mum, pruning it tenderly. So the whole garden was a carpet of grass and plants except for one threadbare patch, the size of a large hearthrug, right next to the house. Nothing grew there.

Mum couldn't understand it. It was a good sunny spot, sheltered from the wind, but it made no difference what she planted, nothing came up. She tried carrots and lettuce first, and when they failed she put in onions, then beetroot, then marrows and finally nasturtiums which are difficult *not* to grow, but by now it was getting late in the year, and nothing was growing anywhere. Next spring she set bedding plants instead of seeds, but after a few days the plants looked poorly and lay down limp. Then she got silly and planted dandelions. 'They'll grow if nothing else does,' she said, but they didn't. Even fireweed would not grow there.

'It must be the drains,' Gran said. 'You ought to get the council to have a look. It might be typhoid.'

'I'd have thought bad drains would be good for plants,' said Mum.

'Ever see a carrot with typhoid?' Gran sniffed.

By the time they had lived in the house for three years Rachel's little sister Donna had been born, Gran had moved to Maidstone, Rachel was at the Junior school and Dad suddenly started to be interested in budgerigars. Gran had kept a blue budgerigar called Pip in a cage on the sideboard, but Dad did not approve of birds like that.

'Is it cruel to keep them in cages then?' Rachel asked. She thought it probably was cruel.

'I don't know about cruel,' said Dad, 'but it doesn't look natural to me, a full-grown bird standing on one leg with a bell on its head saying, "Who's a pretty boy, then?" and kissing itself in the mirror. If we have any birds they're going to behave like birds'; and on the bald patch where nothing grew, he built an aviary.

First he put down concrete, and over this went a tall enclosure of wire netting on a frame of battens, in the angle of the house and the garden wall. At one end was a wooden sentry box with perches, where the birds could sleep safe from draughts and passing rats.

'There aren't any rats round here,' said Mum.

'Livestock attracts them,' said Dad, and made all the joints and angles rat-proof. Rachel hoped there would be rats.

At the weekend Dad and Rachel took the bus out past the M2 flyover and spent the afternoon looking in the woods for good sound branches so that the birds would have somewhere to sit, like wild birds, and afterwards they went up on to the downs to find lumps of chalk, essential for healthy feathers. They had a bit of trouble on the way home with what the bus conductor referred to as half a dead tree. 'I ought to sell you a ticket for it,' he said, and there was some unpleasantness with a woman who complained that Dad had tried to put her eye out, but they brought it home safely and it was set up in the flight, which was what Dad called the open part of the aviary.

'Why's it called an aviary, Dad?' Rachel asked.

'Look it up,' said Dad, as he always did when Rachel wanted to know what words meant. She was never sure whether this was because he thought it was good for her to look things up, or because he did not know the answer. She took care not to ask him which it was. This time she fetched the dictionary and learned that the Latin word for bird was *avis*. She was pleased to know some Latin.

For a long time the dictionary had been the only book on the shelf, but now it had been joined by magazines and illustrated books about budgerigars. The birds in the pictures were brightly coloured and when Rachel leafed through the pages her eye was captured by succulent names; Lutinos, Opalines and Satinettes, Cobalts, Cinnamons and Visual Violets; glassy, glossy words with rare flavours. She imagined the dead branch in the aviary brilliant with expensive sweets like a fabulous Christmas tree.

Then the budgerigars arrived. There were six of them and they came in little cardboard boxes with holes in the sides. Dad took them into the aviary and let them loose; then he left, without the birds following him, because he had built the aviary with double doors. There was a space between them which was, he said, the air-lock. Rachel looked up air-lock and decided that he must be joking.

'What are we going to call them?' Rachel said.

'We're not going to call them anything,' Dad said. 'They don't need names. And another thing,' he said, sternly, to Rachel and Mum and Donna who had come out to watch, 'I don't want anyone trying to teach them to talk. These budgerigars are going to be as near wild as tame birds can be. There's going to be trouble if I catch any of them creeping up to me and saying, "Who's a pretty boy, then?" And no wolf-whistles.'

Mum went indoors to give Donna her lunch, but Rachel stayed close up against the wire and watched the budgerigars ('I don't want to hear anyone calling them budgies') exploring their new home, bouncing on the branches and tidying their feathers, investigating seed trays, grit pans and water pots. There was no doubt that they looked much more impressive in their aviary than Pip had done in his cage, but she could not help wondering if they wouldn't be happier with a bell or two, and a mirror.

'They don't need mirrors,' said Dad, 'they've got each other to look at.'

When the birds had settled in they began to purr and chirrup in the sunshine.

'See,' said Dad, 'they can talk to each other. There's no point in making them learn words, those squawks are all the language they need. They mean something.'

'So do words,' Rachel said.

'Not to budgerigars,' Dad said, firmly. 'You can teach a budgerigar to say the Lord's Prayer. You can teach him to sing *God Save the Queen*. You can teach him to count to a hundred backwards, but he'll never know what he's saying. They don't really *talk*, they just copy sounds.'

Rachel remembered Pip, looking sideways into his mirror and saying coyly, 'Who's a pretty boy, then?' He had always sounded as though he knew exactly what it meant, and very pleased with himself; but then, budgerigars usually did sound pleased with themselves, and they looked smug, too. Rachel thought it might be something to do with having no neck.

It was a fine warm August, that year. Donna sat in her pram in the middle of the grass, and squawked when the birds squawked. She would watch them for hours as they bowed and curtseyed, turned somersaults and hung by one leg. Rachel liked spying on them when they went to sleep in the shelter, with their heads turned right round and their beaks buried in their back feathers. It gave her a furry feeling in her front teeth; little kittens had the same effect, and baby rabbits.

The budgerigars had been in residence for almost six weeks when Dad came home from work one evening in a bad mood. They could tell he was in a bad mood by the way he shut the kitchen door. He always came in through the back gate and paused to have a look at the birds on his way past the aviary, before coming indoors. Tonight he didn't stop in the kitchen; he went straight through to the front room where Rachel and Mum were watching television.

'Own up, then,' he said. 'Who did it?'

'Who did what?' said Mum. 'Keep your voice down or we shall have old mother Sergeant banging on the wall.'

'Who's been at those birds?'

Mrs Sergeant thumped on the wall.

'Have they got out, then?' Mum looked alarmed. 'Rachel, have you been fiddling . . .?'

'Oh, they're all there,' said Dad, *'and one of them's talking.* Who did it?'

'What did it say?' Rachel asked. She hoped that it had not said hello. She always said it herself as she passed the aviary on her way to school; not to teach them, just to be friendly.

'I say "Good morning, ladies and gentlebirds" when I put the seed in,' Mum said. Rachel was surprised. It was not the kind of joke that Mum went in for. 'Don't tell me that *they've* been saying "Good morning, ladies and gentlebirds" too,' said Mum.

'Stop acting innocent,' said Dad. 'Come out here and listen.'

They went out to the aviary. One of the birds was white, more noticeable than the others and more sociable. Rachel thought of it as Snowball, although she was careful never to say so. When the white bird saw the family standing round, it flew up to a branch and sidled along, until it was close to the wire.

'Pretty me,' it said.

'Hear that?' Dad demanded. 'Pretty me! I'll give it pretty me. Who's been saying "Pretty me" to that bird?'

'No,' said Rachel. 'I haven't.' She was not quite sure if this was, in fact, what the bird had said. The words had come out muffled and rather subdued, not at all like Pip's self-satisfied croak. She wished it would speak again but it only sat there on its branch, the little wrinkled eyelids crimping up and down.

'If any of those birds says another word, *one* other word, there'll be trouble,' said Dad. He was looking at Rachel.

'I never,' said Rachel.

'I suppose it was Donna, then.'

Donna hadn't even got around to saying ma-ma yet.

'Well, it wasn't me,' Mum said. 'Why don't you sell up and get canaries instead? They don't have much to say for themselves.' She went indoors.

After tea, when Dad had gone to play darts at the *Man of Kent*, Rachel slipped out to the aviary again. The white bird was still sitting on its twig, next to the wire. Rachel went and stood close, sucking her teeth as Gran used to do with Pip, to indicate that she was ready for a chat. The white bird opened its eyes, and its beak.

'Pity me,' it said, in its sad, hoarse voice. 'Pity me. Pity me.'

Rachel's first thought was, 'Good; it isn't copying anything I've said.' Then she began to wonder who it was copying. Surely no one would deliberately teach a budgerigar to say 'Pity me'? Perhaps Mum had said it without thinking—no; people didn't say things like that without thinking. Perhaps the bird had *tried* to say 'Pretty me' but couldn't talk very well? Perhaps Mrs Sergeant had been having a go at it, over the wall.

Rachel sucked her teeth again.

'Pity me,' said the white bird. One of the green budgerigars, there were two of them, fluttered down from the topmost twig and clung with beak and claws to the wire netting. It turned its head sideways to look at her.

'Pity me,' said the green bird.

The two yellow birds clambered up from below. 'Pity me. Pity me. Pity me.' Rachel shivered. She had not noticed that the sun was down below the roofs of the houses in the next street. The aviary was in shadow and she could only just make out the shape of the blue budgerigar, hunched on its perch in the shelter, in silence, while the white, the green and the yellow birds pressed against the netting and repeated dully, 'Pity me. Pity me.'

The next day was Saturday, mild and still, and in the morning the budgerigars swung and fluttered in the aviary with never a word to say. They nibbled at chickweed, honed their beaks on cuttlefish bones and chucked millet seeds about, very busy being budgerigars; but as the day wore on an uneasy silence settled over the aviary. Birds sang in other gardens but the budgerigars fluffed themselves up, drew their spare feet into their feathers and closed their eyes. They looked, to Rachel, not so much tired as depressed. She went over to the netting, carrying Donna, and said, 'Come on, boys, cheer up.'

A yellow budgerigar opened one eye and said, 'Oh, I'm so cold. Oh, I'm so cold.'

'Pity me,' said the white bird. The others ruffled their feathers and were motionless again.

'Cross my heart,' Rachel gabbled, that evening. 'Cross my heart and cut my throat, it wasn't me.'

'None of that nonsense,' said Dad. 'I want a straight answer, yes or no. Did you or didn't you?'

'No!' Rachel yelled. She was shocked. People didn't yell at Dad. 'I never did. Anyway, if I had, I wouldn't have taught them to say things like that. I'd have taught them "Give us a kiss" and—and—'

'Who's a pretty boy, then?'

'Yes. But I *didn't*.'

It was raining on Sunday. The budgerigars stayed in their shelter and looked at the weather with their small eyes half shut, and said nothing all day. Dad was on late turn the following week, from four till midnight, so he saw the birds only in the daytime when it was bright, and they were bright, but it seemed to Rachel that they were not so bright as they had been, and after Dad left for work, wheeling his bicycle away down the alley, she visited the aviary. The birds, that had stopped flying and gibbering, settled on their twigs and shuffled towards her; all of them, all six. They looked furtive and unwell.

'Pity me,' said the white bird.

'Oh, I'm so cold,' said the two yellow birds.

'Pity me.'

'Cold as clay,' said the blue bird that had never spoken before.

'*What?*'

Rachel jumped and turned round. Mum was standing behind her, lips pressed together tight and frightened.

'What did that bird say?'

'I don't know, Mum.' She did know, but she did not want to tell.

'Don't say anything to your dad. I'm going to watch out, this evening. Someone must be coming into the garden after dark and doing this.'

Mum watched every evening that week, and caught no one, heard nothing, even though she kept up her vigil until Dad came home at midnight. By the weekend the birds had stopped squawking and flying from twig to twig. The chickweed withered untouched; the millet sprays hung neglected from the branches. On Saturday morning Dad and Mum and Rachel stood round the aviary and listened to the listless little voices droning, 'Oh, I'm so cold.' 'Pity me.' 'Oh, I'm so cold.' 'Cold as clay.' 'Pity me. Pity me.'

'This is getting beyond a joke,' Dad said, and talked of calling the police.

'Come off it,' said Mum, 'you can't call the police because your budgies are talking daft.'

'You call that talking daft?'

'No, not really, but they aren't damaged, are they? They haven't been stolen.'

'Not damaged? Look at them.'

They all looked at the bedraggled birds, with their feathers poking out at odd angles like bristles on a bottle brush, and their dreary eyes. The white budgerigar, once the most beautiful of all, had pulled out its tail feathers and slouched on its perch with all the grace of an old shuttle-cock.

'What could the police do?' Mum said. 'Question them?'

Dad scowled and went to consult his budgerigar books. Later he went shopping and came home with cod-liver oil and fortified seed and a mineral block like a lump of grey Edinburgh rock.

'To cheer them up,' he said.

'They'd probably fancy a nip of whisky, sooner,' said Mum. 'Wouldn't you?'

They had not cheered up by Sunday evening, and on Monday, the last day of October, Dad was back at work. He was on the night shift now, and did not leave home until twenty to twelve. Rachel heard him go, kept awake by the continual opening and closing all evening of the back door, as Mum and Dad took turns to leap out on the intruder; but they didn't catch anyone. When Dad's rear light had turned left at the end of the alley, Rachel crept downstairs. Mum was clearing up, before going to bed, but she sat down at the table when Rachel padded into the kitchen. She sighed.

'I don't know.'

'I'm sorry, Mum. I couldn't sleep. The back door . . .'

'I didn't mean you, it's those blooming budgies. We've been in and out a dozen times this evening, and we haven't heard anyone.'

'I don't think there's anyone to hear,' said Rachel.

'You get along to bed,' Mum said, crossly. 'You'll be having me see things, next.'

Rachel said, 'I don't think there's anything to see, either. I don't think there's anything at all, and only the birds can hear it. Are you going out to look?'

'No,' said Mum. 'Not on your life—and neither are you.'

When Dad came home from work next morning, he found Mum and Rachel standing by the aviary, watching the budgerigars that drooped on their branches.

'Oh, I'm so cold,' said one.

'I shall always be very cold,' said another, 'cold as clay.'

'I shall always be here,' said a third.

'I shall never go away,' said the white bird.

'Pity me.'

'Pity me.'

'No,' said Dad, for the twentieth time. 'No!' he shouted. 'We are not moving. I never heard such nonsense. We're staying here.'

'Right,' said Mum, 'then it's up to you. Either those birds go or I do.'

The budgerigars were sold to good homes and went to live in cages with bells and mirrors. Donna missed them very much, so instead of the budgerigars they got a Hertz Roller canary that lived up to its name by standing on its toes all day and yelling 'Rrrrrrrrrrrrrrrrrrr' on a very high note. Dad broke up the aviary and on the place where nothing would grow he put down crazy paving in five different cheerful colours with a little pond in the middle. He called it a patio and to decorate it he bought a plastic orange tree in a pot and a plaster stork to stand by the pond. Rachel didn't much like the look of the patio, but the orange tree did not die, and the stork never said a word.

PENELOPE LIVELY

Uninvited Ghosts

MARIAN and Simon were sent to bed early on the day that the Brown family moved house. By then everyone had lost their temper with everyone else; the cat had been sick on the sitting-room carpet; the dog had run away twice. If you have ever moved you will know what kind of a day it had been. Packing cases and newspaper all over the place . . . sandwiches instead of proper meals . . . the kettle lost and a wardrobe stuck on the stairs and Mrs Brown's favourite vase broken. There was bread and baked beans for supper, the television wouldn't work and the water wasn't hot so when all was said and done the children didn't object too violently to being packed off to bed. They'd had enough, too. They had one last argument about who was going to sleep by the window, put on their pyjamas, got into bed, switched the lights out . . . and it was at that point that the ghost came out of the bottom drawer of the chest of drawers.

It oozed out, a grey cloudy shape about three feet long smelling faintly of woodsmoke, sat down on a chair and began to hum to itself. It looked like a bundle of bedclothes, except that it was not solid: you could see, quite clearly, the cushion on the chair beneath it.

Marian gave a shriek. 'That's a ghost!'

'Oh, be quiet, dear, do,' said the ghost. 'That noise goes right through my head. And it's not nice to call people names.' It took out a ball of wool and some needles and began to knit.

What would you have done? Well, yes—Simon and Marian did just that and I daresay you can imagine what happened. You try telling your mother that you can't get to sleep because there's a ghost sitting in the room clacking its knitting-needles and humming. Mrs Brown said the kind of things she could be expected to say and the ghost continued sitting there knitting and humming and Mrs Brown went out, banging the door and saying threatening things about if there's so much as another word from either of you . . . .

'She can't see it,' said Marian to Simon.

' 'Course not, dear,' said the ghost. 'It's the kiddies I'm here for. Love kiddies, I do. We're going to be ever such friends.'

'Go away!' yelled Simon. 'This is our house now!'

'No it isn't,' said the ghost smugly. 'Always been here, I have. A hundred years and more. Seen plenty of families come and go, I have. Go to bye-byes now, there's good children.'

The children glared at it and buried themselves under the bedclothes. And, eventually, slept.

The next night it was there again. This time it was smoking a long white pipe and reading a newspaper dated 1842. Beside it was a second grey cloudy shape. 'Hello, dearies,' said the ghost. 'Say how do you do to my Auntie Edna.'

'She can't come here too,' wailed Marian.

'Oh yes she can,' said the ghost. 'Always comes here in August, does Auntie. She likes a change.'

Auntie Edna was even worse, if possible. She sucked peppermint drops that smelled so strong that Mrs Brown, when she came to kiss the children good night, looked suspiciously under their pillows. She also sang hymns in a loud squeaky voice. The children lay there groaning and the ghosts sang and rustled the newspapers and ate peppermints.

The next night there were three of them. 'Meet Uncle Charlie!' said the first ghost. The children groaned.

'And Jip,' said the ghost. 'Here, Jip, good dog—come and say hello to the kiddies, then.' A large grey dog that you could see straight through came out from under the bed, wagging its tail. The cat, who had been curled up beside Marian's feet (it was supposed to sleep in the kitchen, but there are always ways for a resourceful cat to get what it wants), gave a howl and shot on top of the wardrobe, where it sat spitting. The dog lay down in the middle of the rug and set about scratching itself vigorously; evidently it had ghost fleas, too.

Uncle Charlie was unbearable. He had a loud cough that kept going off like a machine-gun and he told the longest most pointless stories the children had ever heard. He said he too loved kiddies and he knew kiddies loved stories. In the middle of the seventh story the children went to sleep out of sheer boredom.

The following week the ghosts left the bedroom and were to be found all over the house. The children had no peace at all. They'd be quietly doing their homework and all of a sudden Auntie Edna would be breathing down their necks reciting arithmetic tables. The original ghost took to sitting on top of the television with his legs in front of the picture. Uncle Charlie told his stories all through the best programmes and the dog lay permanently at the top of the stairs. The Browns' cat became quite hysterical, refused to eat and went to live on the top shelf of the kitchen dresser.

Something had to be done. Marian and Simon also were beginning to show the effects; their mother decided they looked peaky and bought an appalling sticky brown vitamin medicine from the chemists to strengthen them. 'It's the ghosts!' wailed the children. 'We don't need vitamins!' Their mother said severely that she didn't want to hear another word of this silly nonsense about ghosts. Auntie Edna, who was sitting smirking on the other side of the kitchen table at that very moment, nodded vigorously and took out a packet of humbugs which she sucked noisily.

'We've got to get them to go and live somewhere else,' said Marian. But where, that was the problem, and how? It was then that they had a bright idea. On Sunday the Browns were all going to see their uncle who was rather rich and lived alone in a big house with thick carpets everywhere and empty rooms and the biggest colour television you ever saw. Plenty of room for ghosts.

They were very cunning. They suggested to the ghosts that they might like a drive in the country. The ghosts said at first that they were quite comfortable where they were, thank you, and they didn't fancy these new-fangled motor-cars, not at their time of life. But then Auntie Edna remembered that she liked looking at the pretty flowers and the trees and finally they agreed to give it a try. They sat in a row on the back shelf of the car. Mrs Brown kept asking why there was such a strong smell of peppermint and Mr Brown kept roaring at Simon and Marian to keep still while he was driving. The fact was that the ghosts were shoving them; it was like being nudged by three cold damp flannels. And the ghost dog, who had come along too of course, was car-sick.

When they got to Uncle Dick's the ghosts came in and had a look round. They liked the expensive carpets and the enormous television. They slid in and out of the wardrobes and walked through the doors and the walls and sent Uncle Dick's budgerigars into a decline from which they have never recovered. Nice place, they said, nice and comfy.

'Why not stay here?' said Simon, in an offhand tone.

'Couldn't do that,' said the ghosts firmly. 'No kiddies. Dull. We like a place with a bit of life to it.' And they piled back into the car and sang hymns all the way home to the Browns' house. They also ate toast. There were real toast-crumbs on the floor and the children got the blame.

Simon and Marian were in despair. The ruder they were to the ghosts the more the ghosts liked it. 'Cheeky!' they said indulgently. 'What a

cheeky little pair of kiddies! There now . . . come and give uncle a kiss.'
The children weren't even safe in the bath. One or other of the ghosts
would come and sit on the taps and talk to them. Uncle Charlie had
produced a mouth organ and played the same tune over and over again;
it was quite excruciating. The children went around with their hands
over their ears. Mrs Brown took them to the doctor to find out if there
was something wrong with their hearing. The children knew better
than to say anything to the doctor about the ghosts. It was pointless
saying anything to anyone.

I don't know what would have happened if Mrs Brown hadn't happened to make friends with Mrs Walker from down the road. Mrs
Walker had twin babies, and one day she brought the babies along for
tea.

Now one baby is bad enough. Two babies are trouble in a big way.
These babies created pandemonium. When they weren't both howling
they were crawling around the floor pulling the tablecloths off the tables
or hitting their heads on the chairs and hauling the books out of the
bookcases. They threw their food all over the kitchen and flung cups of
milk on the floor. Their mother mopped up after them and every time
she tried to have a conversation with Mrs Brown the babies bawled in
chorus so that no one could hear a word.

In the middle of this the ghosts appeared. One baby was yelling its
head off and the other was glueing pieces of chewed up bread onto the
front of the television. The ghosts swooped down on them with happy
cries. 'Oh!' they trilled. 'Bless their little hearts then, diddums, give
auntie a smile then.' And the babies stopped in mid-howl and gazed at
the ghosts. The ghosts cooed at the babies and the babies cooed at the
ghosts. The ghosts chattered to the babies and sang them songs and the
babies chattered back and were as good as gold for the next hour and
their mother had the first proper conversation she'd had in weeks.
When they went the ghosts stood in a row at the window, waving.

Simon and Marian knew when to seize an opportunity. That evening
they had a talk with the ghosts. At first the ghosts raised objections.
They didn't fancy the idea of moving, they said; you got set in your
ways, at their age; Auntie Edna reckoned a strange house would be the
death of her.

The children talked about the babies, relentlessly.

And the next day they led the ghosts down the road, followed by the
ghost dog, and into the Walkers' house. Mrs Walker doesn't know
to this day why the babies, who had been screaming for the last half
hour, suddenly stopped and broke into great smiles. And she has never

understood why, from that day forth, the babies became the most tranquil, quiet, amiable babies in the area. The ghosts kept the babies amused from morning to night. The babies thrived; the ghosts were happy; the ghost dog, who was actually a bitch, settled down so well that she had puppies which is one of the most surprising aspects of the whole business. The Brown children heaved a sigh of relief and got back to normal life. The babies, though, I have to tell you, grew up somewhat peculiar.

FARRUKH DHONDY

The Bride

So you're still teaching down at the old school then? Yeah, thanks I will take a pew this time. Can I say straight up, I'm sorry about last time I came round. Three years almost to the day. Been in Morocco and Spain and India, on the trail like. I'm not rich any more. Three years old these Levis, bought the shirt out there. Have a butchers through the window, no E-Type Jag. Shanks Pony and London Transport, guv.

Must admit, came round that time to come flash, show off, because I remembered something you used to say to us kids in school. What was it? You goes, 'You don't get rich by working hard, you get rich by making other people work hard.' And I come to tell you that I'd done it on my own. Wasn't true and I knew you wouldn't like it, but I thought I'd make you feel a mug, because you had a prejudice, like, you were always going on at us about how we was working class and would never be loaded.

Nah, not any more. What happened to it? That's what I've come to tell you, chief. It's a funny story, but on my mother's life it's true. How did I get poor again? You started it. When? That day three years ago when you showed me that newspaper cutting. You had me well sussed.

Where to start? With Jaswinder, of course. You won't believe this, but it was her made me rich. She gave it me, laid it on me, I'll tell you how in a minute, hang on.

Begin with when I left school. I got these dead beat jobs. Thirty, maybe forty sheets a week. Hey, you remember that half-caste geezer what used to teach us basketball? I met him in a pub down Kew, about two years after I left school. He always pulled tasty birds, didn't he? He comes up to me and he says, 'How you doing, Les?'

'Tony,' I says.

'Yeah, Tony,' he says. Now you wouldn't have made that kind of mistake, would you, as a teacher I mean.

'I'm on the sales side of IPC and Thompson Newspaper groups,' I said.

Very impressed he was, till John, remember John, he was with me, says, 'Yeah, Tone's got a paper pitch down Camberwell. "Evening Standard".'

That's what I was doing till I met Carrots, remember her. Turned snobbish, goes with this art school teacher guy, but I got talking to her and her old man was trying to flog jewellery what he made himself and he's looking for lads to fifty-fifty with him for taking it round. So I left the pitch and started in for him.

'Venetian chain, box chain, Boston chain, one, two three four silly money in the store.' Diddled him too. Used to go down with his stuff to the Portobello and up the Lock and that kind of market with pseuds buying junk from con artists like me. Struck it rich with Arabs outside hotels who'd give you a twenty and ask you to keep the change for a bracelet worth eighty pence. Not bad.

Slap the box, lay out the bracelets, necklaces, rings, stuff that I got from this geezer and then from my uncle, knocked-off clobber, genuine articles that were as hot as grandma's fresh fried chips, souvenirs that had been on police five, the lot, you name it.

I was making a small whack and having a good time, until I began to realise that being happy is looking hard for what you want, not having what you've got, if you get my meaning. You do? First one. Most people don't. You may have been my English teacher, but you never got me to say things like I meant them, but you were watching me, all those years, so you know what I'm on about.

At least you know who I'm on about. Dead right, guv. I carried a picture of her tattooed on my brain. I thought of her a lot, Jaswinder. What do you expect. I grew up with them Pakis. What else can a poor boy from Southall do? I'll admit it, I was brought up to think white. My dad's a racialist. Still, yeah. When I was young, I mean little, he was always going on about moving because the picture houses had been taken over by Indian films.

It was daft, right, because my old man never saw no films, just watched telly, and my mum used to tell him that the last thing he'd seen was when he took her to Gone with the Wind. And that would start him off.

I knew you used to think I was right prejudiced, but that's because you only joined our school in the fourth year and I was a skin at the time. We had to do it. I'll tell you, I don't think you teachers knew what was going on down there. We was in the minority, right, and it was our country, but you wouldn't allow us to say it. And the Asian kids, they came flash. 'Sikhs rule' and all this, and there was so many of them you only opened your mouth if you wanted a taste of knuckle sand-wich.

I fancied her something rotten, guv, but in the junior years I didn't let on, because it would have shamed me up bad, guy. But then it started. You think them Asian kids are straight, but what they used to get up to, mate, was nobody's business. Just like kids anywhere, I suppose. But not Jaswinder. Her dad was mad strict, wouldn't even allow her on to the Broadway. I knew that on Saturdays she'd go shopping with her mum so I used to hang about the cafe, the only white cafe going, and check her on her way there and she'd be shy or cautious or whatever, and hardly say hello when she was with her mum and give you a total blank if she was with her dad, a big turbanned geezer. Enough to frighten the daylights out of you, mate. Nah? Out of me, then.

The only Asian kid who hung around with us whites after school was Junaid. He was your favourite, wasn't he? Couldn't do nothing wrong. Butter wouldn't melt in his mouth, except he only got margarine down at the social services where he lived. He only got around with us because he was brought up in care all his life and had to go in with the tough nuts, mostly white kids, down the orphan shop. I know that all of you felt sorry for him, poor kid, teacher's pet. He was nasty, you know. How? I'll tell you. The lads didn't feel sorry for him. He had more money any day of the week than all of us put together, because them kids down that centre used to pull jobs. Remember when they cleaned out the electronics shop by going in through the roof and cutting the plasterboard ceiling? That was Junaid and his mates. He didn't care that it was an Asian shop, he just came all that Asian shit because he wanted sympathy. And he got it too.

Cry? I could have laughed. The girls, they'd wet their pillows for him, if not their knickers. 'Aw poor fellow, poor Junaid,' the super-runt of Battersea Dogs' Home. Dr Barnardo was invented for him. On my life, he lived on it. And they brought him presents and food and that. He loved it. You could have exchanged my mum, dad and the budgie for half the clobber he got off his tear-jerking violins trip.

All right, that doesn't mean he was nasty, but I didn't much care for him because I knew, from the fourth year up, there was something going on between him and Jaswinder.

And I'd made a fool of myself. On parents' day I followed her around when she was with her dad and chose all the subjects for my fourth year options that she'd chosen. Ended up doing needlework and cookery and bloody Geography. And Junaid done the same, but you teachers thought he done that to be with the girls because he was a bit like that wasn't he? Not a poof, but kind of soft and wimpish.

When I asked her, at the end of the fifth year whether she was going to the school disco, she replied that her dad was too strict. But she made it in the end and she was necking with Junaid in a dark corner till I couldn't stand it no more. You remember that night? When I smashed up the turntable and you lot had to throw me out? You never reckoned what that was all about, did you? A fair idea? Yeah, well, it was because she was kissing him in the corner and I couldn't take it no more so I shouted, 'Lights out at the orphanage at eight, homeless mongrels should pack it in.'

He came for me and I smashed him one before going for the record he had requested three times. It was Jaswinder stopped him and came between us, and then I was thrown out. I knew I shouldn't have said that but a red haze sort of knocked me out, come in front of my eyes, I couldn't stop myself. She came after me into the winter night.

'Why did you say that to him?' she goes. 'You're not like that, Tony.'

'You know why,' I goes.

'You're like my brother,' she goes.

'Some bleedin' brother, I know what you think of whites.'

'Not me,' she goes, 'I'm not . . .'

'Then how come you turn up when you said you wasn't coming when I ask you?'

'My dad, he kicked up a fuss, he wouldn't let me go and I've just come, I don't know what he'll do when he finds out . . .'

I tell you what I did then. I grabbed hold of her and I kissed her. I felt her pulling away and she says, 'Tony, please,' like something out of a stupid love story and I was thinking it's my only chance, the only time I'd be with her in the dark.

Anyway her dad come round, you remember it? Takes her away and abuses all the teachers.

I went home with my head singing. It was worth it. And as I walked home by the yellow sulphur light, I was that dopey with that kiss I thought 'Romeo, Romeo, where art thou,' or whatever it was. Pure Shakespeare, guy. But next morning I knew it was no good. Straight up, have you ever loved somebody, I mean fancied her, that it made you sick?

After that I used to hang about netball practice when she was there, the only boy in the gym and I used to hold her purse and her bracelets and that because she didn't want to leave them in the changing room with all the thieving kids about.

I know you knew him well, but I knew him too, guv, Junaid. Remember the time you was reading his story to the class? You'd set us some wimpy English essay on ourselves or something and hardly none of us had done it and Junaid turns up with twenty-eight pages, guy. My Life of Sorrow, he'd called it and even before you took it in for homework, he was handing it round and all the girls were asking him if it was all true and softness like that. She had the bloody nerve to give it to me to read.

'Junaid's story of his life. It should be on telly. You read it, Tony, maybe you'll understand how lonely he is.'

I took it off her. Garbage it was. So I told the lads that you'd probably be so chuffed to get some homework back for a change that you'd read it to the class and I filled in them bits. Two pages of filth. Gave it back to Jaswinder, keeping a straight face. Yeah, you remember that, but you sussed it. When she handed it to you, you read it straight, pornography and all till Junaid couldn't stand it no longer and he thought Jaswinder had done the trick on him or at least helped with it and he grabbed the sheets from you and tore them up in front of the class and all the kids were splitting themselves. Junaid came in the next morning blind drunk. He was pretending he'd tried to commit suicide. Bloody joke. And you and Jaswinder fell for it and walked him up and down the corridor to get him over it.

I felt bad, to tell you the truth. But I wished he'd done it. Funny, isn't it?

And he wasn't really Indian, Junaid. He was brought up like us by the social workers and that. He didn't know about their customs like. You remember the next time he began this suicide lark? You don't know what happened. I'll tell you.

I wrote Jaswinder a letter. I finally got up the courage and did it. It was stupid, confessing, but I'd tried everything else. That's why I used to come flash about getting rich one day because I reckoned girls fancy fellers who say they're going to reach the top, any top, and I wasn't good at nothing else. I waited for a reply, but she never sent me one. Instead she came to me at break-time with her mates and she tied this bracelet round my wrist. It was kind of blue and red and gold tinsel, like one of them cloth badges you wear if you support a team. And she gives me a kiss on the cheek.

Then her mate says to me, 'It's an Indian custom.'

'What's it mean?'

'You got to give her a present first, anything, a bar of Kit Kat.'

'Yeah,' I said. 'I'll get J something.'

I got her a teddy bear and I put my gold sovereign round its neck.

'Now tell me,' I said to her and my heart was thumping.

'It means you're my brother now and you've sworn to protect me.'

'Yeah?' I goes. 'How?'

'Like a brother. I really like you Tony, but not in that way, you understand?'

I understood, guv. The hollow in my stomach understood. She wants me out of the running. I was a fool to think I could beat it.

But that evening I got up to mischief. I was down the cafe wearing this damn bracelet and Junaid turned up with his thieving mates and they were all taking the mick out of my bracelet, so I told them it was an old Indian custom and Jaswinder had given it me.

'What's it mean?' Junaid said, going serious.

'What's an engagement ring mean, mate?'

He never said nothing but that was when they found him.

She had to explain to him after they'd pumped his stomach out at the hospital and again her dad came and dragged her away and threatened Junaid for messing with his daughter. Right Indian film stuff.

Then school was over and I thought I'd never see her again because I moved down Stockwell with my brother-in-law. I was wrong, of course. I saw her.

It must have been a Thursday night, 22nd of December. I was down an antique market in North London and the lads had lit lamps on their stalls. I didn't have a stall, but I traded off of a lamp of a geezer what sold old records and that. It couldn't have been late, because it was dark early then and when the market packed up at seven or so, we used to go off for a drink. The barrows would be left out in the cold and the fog with their lamps on till the market boys came and dismantled them. I went off to the pub like, I'd done enough trade in the last half hour and the market began to empty. When I finished boozing I noticed the strap for my box was missing, so I thought I'd go back and get it.

The street was littered with cardboard boxes and junk. It was foggy. Dark too. I found my strap and was lacing it to my box when I looked down the street and I thought I saw in the fog a figure of a woman standing by a lit barrow.

'Hello,' I says to myself, rubbing my hands for cold, 'some punter's trading late.'

There was no mistaking it. It was a lit barrow piled with show cases and that and I shifted my head and couldn't see no one attending it. But there was this wrapped figure standing in front of it.

'One of the lads left his stuff,' I thought, and helpful as ever, I went down the street.

There was no one about and this figure, a lady, turns to me. I thought I'd say something cheeky, like, so I wandered up. I couldn't recall this particular barrow and I would have, 'cause it was in my trade, it was loaded with cases of jewellery, a naked bulb hanging from the wire, plugged in to the junction box on the lamppost. The light was throwing shadows on her face so I had to get close up before I saw it was Jaswinder. She was wearing a cape and when she turned to me I saw she was in a saree.

'Stap me dead,' I said. 'What're you doing here?'

'Looking,' she said. 'Where's the man who sells these things?'

'Is that all you've got to say to me?'

'I'm in a hurry,' she goes.

Then I see she has tears rolling down her cheeks. 'I was to be married today, it's my wedding night,' she goes.

'Don't spring that on me,' I said. 'What's the matter? You don't look happy about it.'

'Same old story, Tony,' she said. 'My father arranged a marriage with my neighbour's cousin.'

'So why are you alone on a night like this?'

'Alone?' she goes. 'There's you.'

'Don't talk stupid. What're you doing about it? I thought you'd end up with Junaid.'

'He's dead,' she said and she began to howl.

'*What?*'

'And now I'm to be married to a stranger.'

'When?'

'But I can't find the jewellery I'd like to wear. He's very particular. He is a jeweller and a goldsmith himself.'

'Why are you doing it?' I said. I was pleading with her. 'This is bloody England. You don't have to marry this geezer. Your dad can't tell you what to do.'

'No, he can't,' she said, 'but I'm to meet my bridegroom and I must have something to wear. Going without jewellery is a kind of pitiable nakedness.'

'Didn't your father get you none? How did you end up here?'

'You were here,' she said. 'I tied a bracelet on your arm three years ago.'

'I know,' I said. 'And I promised. I'll do anything you want, just name it, and if I can do it, you can have it.'

'It's England and I can do what I like,' she said and her tears seemed to disappear and she laughed.

I don't know whether I was stoned or what, but it was weird. I was thinking to myself that something funny was going on.

'I've got some jewellery. I'm in the trade,' I said. 'Jaswinder, it's just trinkets, but you can have it if that's all you want.'

'It's all I want,' she said. 'An anklet of gold, a bride should have a golden anklet.'

'That's tall,' I said. 'Not my order,' but I opened up my case and dragged out the most expensive chains and that I had. 'Maybe not perfect, but it's something. Fourteen carat.'

'You were always a bit gone on me, weren't you Tony?'

'Not a bit,' I said. 'A lot.'

'I knew you'd help,' she said. 'Goodbye Tony.'

'Wait a bit,' I said, 'let me get you a cab. I'll go with you, see you're all right.'

But she didn't wait. She didn't even raise a hand. She just turned and walked into the fog, out of the circle of light. I left my case and I ran shouting after her. I thought she must have dodged down one of the lanes but she wasn't nowhere.

I didn't go home that night. I went to the park, climbed over the railings and walked on the frozen grass and threw stones at the ice on the ponds. I didn't do any selling for the next few days. Just hung about.

Then the next time I was down the same market where I'd met her, I left my box and went for a cup of tea with one of the barrow boys. Left the box on Frank's barrow where he said he'd keep a beady on it for me. Come back and open it to set my stuff out on a mat. Started shouting already, 'See what I've got here, darling,' all the palaver. Jesus creepers, it caught me short that. You can't guess it. I opened the box and my stuff had gone. Instead there was real hard clobber in it. I couldn't believe my eyes. Solid gold bracelets, earrings with diamonds, rings with sapphires, the metal work done like old designs.

Hullo, I thought, Frank's having a giggle on the side. I looked up at him but he was doing his own trade, poker face.

'Oi, Frank,' I said. 'What's this lark then.'

He didn't know what I was on about. I was that shocked, bits of me froze.

'What're you complaining about,' Frank said, cool and wily.

I figures to myself, he must be trying to pin something on me, he and his mates, fit me up like. So I said I'm taking the lot down the bull-ring, hand the lot in and report my trinkets stolen.

'It's your life,' he said, not concerned. He swore nobody had touched that box, though he'd been selling steady and had a crowd.

I took the stuff round to my uncle's who knows gold when he tastes it. He thought they were knocked off too and they looked hot, more carrots than a rabbit's freezer, and the bill would be round eventually, but maybe I could get a reward for the lot. They were too big to keep, he said, so I went down the cop shop and I couldn't tell them the true story so I said I found them. They took my particulars, but the sergeant there he looked at me as though I'd made a run from Cain Hill.

Three months later the cops tell me, the stuff's clean. No reports of it stolen or missing. I could have it.

I couldn't believe it. My uncle takes it down with me to this collector geezer he knows and he says give him three days, he'll trace it. I come back to him and he says it's Indian jewellery, but no mark on it to show who owned it or made it. That's what set me thinking. She done it. Jaswinder. I remembered every word she said that night and it was a jeweller she was being married off to. And I was sure because in the collection there was one of them brother–sister bracelets, only this time in gold and with stones, not a cloth one. But how had she got them to me? I went back to Frank and asked him if there was any Indians hovering about his stall that day.

'Yeah,' he says, 'Tonto came by. How do you expect me to remember?'

'All right,' I said. 'No skin off my nose, I'm bleedin' rich.'

That's how, guv, that's the story. Flogged all the stuff except the bracelet to this collector and set up shop with my uncle. That's where I got the Jag and the suit you saw me in last time. Spent a year like that. Travelled a bit—Majorca, Costa, you know the circuit. Then I thought I'd find her. I'd go to India and find her even though I was scared. Putting an end to a mystery is always a bit scary for me, I don't know about you. But I made up my mind and I drove down to Southall to check her family. I'd hung about that street a thousand times, walking down past the corner in the evenings when I was still at school, hoping she'd come out. I rung the bell and this Indian lady, oldish come out. I asked for Jaswinder. I said I knew she was in India, but could I have her address?

'No Jaswinder,' she says and shakes her head. I couldn't get her to understand what I was after.

Then this little girl in the garden, an Indian girl, comes up and says, 'They've gone. That family's gone. My daddy knows them,' she says. 'That lady doesn't speak English and neither does my mum.'

'Where's your daddy?'

'Office,' she says.

That's when I come round to you. I thought maybe you'd know. And you told me Jaswinder was dead.

I couldn't live with that. I still had the bracelet. I raced back that evening to Southall and waited for the neighbour, the little girl's father to get home and I stepped up to him out of my Jag.

I asked him about Jaswinder.

'Whole family gone. One year ago. Gone back to India.'

He didn't look as though he wanted to talk. I had to tell him some lie. I was thinking on my feet.

'You've got to tell me what you know about it,' I said. 'Listen, please, I was . . .' I don't know what came into me, I said, 'I was her husband.'

'Husband?' He looked stunned. 'But she was loving muslim boy.'

'Which muslim boy? Junaid? I know all about him. Look, we got secretly married but then she went off with this boy she knew from school. I left her alone, I don't know what happened to her then.'

He took me inside his house. He was wondering about me, but he was willing to talk after I told him that.

He brought out this newspaper cutting from the local paper. He'd kept it. 'Sad business,' he said. 'Her father was forcing her. Very rich man but too old, he found for her. Jeweller in India. Father was very broken when she kill herself with the muslim boy.'

I looked at the date of the newspaper cutting. It was the 22nd of December. The story was dated the 21st.

'This can't be possible,' I said. 'I saw her on the 22nd.'

'You went to funeral? Very sad,' he said.

'Look, I wasn't her husband or anything. I was just lying to make you tell me about it,' I confessed.

'What does it matter,' he said. 'But you shouldn't tell these kind of lies. You look a decent gentlemans.'

'I was her brother,' I said, almost to myself and I could see I confused him even more. But I couldn't spend my time sorting him out, if you know what I mean.

I got back home and looked for the bracelet. I kept it in my drawer with my underwear and that. It was gone.

As I went home, I was sure it would still be there, but it wasn't. She would have left me that, I thought, but then I hadn't acted like a brother, I'd been a bit frantic like, I'd blown it.

GEORGE MACKAY BROWN

Ivor

TEN years ago, my mother rented a house in Hamnavoe in the Orkneys
for the whole summer. My mother was a serious archaeologist; there
were plenty of ancient monuments for her to explore. And there was a
'dig' on that summer, a thousand-year-old Viking farm.

(My parents were divorced. My father doesn't come into this
story.)

North we went, by train and ferryboat, my mother, three sisters older
than me, and my frightened sea-sick self. The ferry-boat, *St Ola*, passed
under the immense red cliffs of Hoy, the highest perpendicular cliffs in
Britain.

The house we were to live in was built on a stone jetty, or pier, that
jutted into the harbour of the little port—an old eighteenth-century
stone house of three storeys.

We shared the pier with an old couple who lived in another house.
The old man with the sailor's cap looked at us with open curiosity as we
humped our baggage indoors. The old woman, after one shy look,
disappeared indoors.

'I bet,' said I, as we were finishing our tea, 'there's a ghost in this house.'

'Rubbish,' said my mother. 'I've lived forty years, in prehistoric
houses and in new bungalows, and I've never had one supernatural
experience.'

'An old sailor with a wooden leg,' I said. 'He must have been a pirate. He
has a patch on one eye. Under that flagstone is buried his chest of gold!'

'None of this talk!' cried Matilda. 'I won't sleep tonight.'

'There's a ghost all right,' said Maud. 'A tall dark lady. She died of
love. She appears out there when the moon's full.' (And Maud pointed
to the little yard of the house, built over the sea.)

Matilda covered her ears and ran out of the house, leaving the rem-
nants of her egg and chips on the plate.

'I said, that's enough!' said my mother, quite sharply. 'I want no
fighting on this holiday.'

After a brief silence my eldest sister Maria, who all that year had been immersed in the poems of Shelley, said, 'No *individual* ghosts—of course not. There is the One Spirit of the Universe, out of which we came and to which we shall return.'

My mother poured us all another cup of tea.

After the third day, I said to myself, 'This is the very lousiest holiday I've ever had! It is, it is!' And I threw another lonely stone into the lonely sea.

My mother was away all day, from 9 a.m. till near sunset, digging up old Viking stones as if they were jewels.

My sisters went their own ways. Maria did water-colours; pale insipid things with too much of the 'spirit of the universe' in them for my taste. Matilda and Maud were forever with ponies and pony lovers at a farm across the bay.

For three days there was no one on the pier but myself and the old neighbour man who glared at me from his wicker chair beside the door.

(It was high summer—all the boys of Hamnavoe, it seemed, had gone south to the cities on holiday—or to youth camps, or conferences, or a music school.)

I got tired of speaking to gulls and the old man's black cat (though it was a nice creature that rubbed its head on my knuckles, and sang to me).

I summoned courage one morning to speak to the wicked-looking old man. I approached him diagonally and deviously, with many lingerings and turnings, and brief examinations of clouds and buttercups.

At last the confrontation could not be delayed. He puffed at his pipe and spat. He smelt of rum.

'Tell me,' I stammered, 'about the ghost on this pier, the old pirate.'

He glared at me. One eye was grey and one was green. His face was bristly as a thistle for want of a shave.

'Ghost!' he yelled. 'What ghost? What nonsense is this! What does a whipper-snapper like you know about ghosts!' (He gave a snort and a puff at his pipe and a spit.) 'There's plenty of trouble in the world without ghosts, believe you me. There's old women, for example—always nagging and grousing. . . . That barman, he refused me a last glass of rum because I was a shilling short . . . me, his best customer! That barman's worse than any ghost. Ghosts are good compared to living folk, if you ask me!'

He took three mighty puffs of his pipe, and spat such a gob it half drowned a daisy growing between the flagstones of the pier in tobacco poison.

At this point I was aware that a third party had joined the dialogue (if you could call it that).

It was old Betsy, the misanthrope's wife. She was holding a white plate with a slice of gingerbread on it. 'Here,' she said, smiling. 'It's good.'

She was a good old lady, Betsy.

Old Fred glared malevolently into silence; his pipe crackled and reeked; he stank of stale rum.

At last, on the fifth day, I found a friend!

I was sitting at the edge of the pier, my feet dangling over the water, trying to catch those small silver-grey fish they call 'sillocks'.

I caught nothing. There were plenty of sillocks in the water—shoals of them—legions. But they ignored my baited hook.

I turned. There was a boy sitting a metre away from me, his brown legs dangling, looking deep into the water that flung up into his face a web of shifting gleams.

'O hullo,' I said, surprised.

He smiled, but said nothing.

As if this strange boy's appearance had put a kind of spell on the sillocks, one after another they bit on bait and barb and I swung them on to the pier, little glittering flashes. I had never been so excited! These were the first fish I had ever caught.

Soon I had a score of sillocks beside me on the edge of the pier—some tarnished in death, a few feebly slithering, the newest-caught ones twisting and gleaming still in the sun.

There, all of a sudden, was the black cat Tinker. Tinker was like a miser with bars of silver, over that scattering of sillocks. How Tinker sang!

But the boy with the corn-coloured hair, he was no longer there. He had vanished as silently as he had come.

I took the sillocks to show to old Fred who was of course sitting outside in his chair.

'Pretty good, boy,' he said. 'You're learning. We'll make a fisherman of you yet.'

Old Betsy was suddenly in the door, this time with a glass of ginger ale in her hand.

'Pier sillocks,' said the old man. 'No good. Poor things. You want to try dropping a line out there, at the mouth of the harbour. There you haul the big ones you can fry for your supper. Those things—pooh!— only fit for cats.'

Betsy said, 'You can use our rowing boat, on the slip down there, any time you want. But don't go too far out. It's dangerous—the tide-race. . . .'

'It's funny,' I said, handing the empty glass back,'the fish only started to bite after that boy came and sat beside me.'

'Boy?' said old Fred. 'What boy? I've been here all morning and I saw no boy. I don't like boys. Boys aren't welcome here.'

The weather continued fine. At last I got tired of fishing for sillocks.

I availed myself of the offer to use the old man's rowing boat, *Sheena*. After a few splashes and zigzags along the harbour front, I found I could handle the oars quite well.

There are two uninhabited little green islands across the water from the town. The idea occurred to me that I would, after breakfast next morning, take a parcel of egg and cheese and tomato sandwiches, and a few bottles of lemonade, and row to the outer island and have there a little private picnic to myself.

My mother had gone with a trowel to her ancient stones twenty kilometres away. My sisters were busy with horses, or trying to inter-pret 'the spirit of the universe' by means of water-colours.

Old Fred sat in his chair, puffing furiously—a sign that he was in a bad mood this morning.

Tinker the cat eyed me from the garden wall with golden eyes.

I had hardly got the *Sheena* into the water, when I was aware of the strange boy sitting in the stern. I fixed the oars into the rowlocks and turned the *Sheena* round.

'Hello,' I said, 'how on earth did you get on board?'

Again, no words: only that enchanting smile, as if all the freshness and transient beauty of a summer were gathered into one young face.

I cannot say how glad I was that he was there, sharing the boat with me.

On that green islet we passed the happiest day of my life. We bathed in the sea, on the far side of the islet. We ran about in the sun and wind till we were dry. Those sandwiches—no venison, no royal swan, no sturgeon have ever (I believe) tasted so marvellous, with silver sound-less sea music all around! Nor was any champagne or vintage claret like our three shared bottles of lemonade.

Meantime, the ferry boat from the south isles entered the harbour, and a blue fishing boat and a white fishing boat came from the Atlantic with screaming tumults of gulls at the stern of each.

We rowed back through the bow waves of the larger ferry from Scotland, the *St Ola*. The *Sheena* dipped and soared so alarmingly that for a second or two I feared we would be swamped. I knew my face was blanched! My friend laughed delightedly. Soon we were in quiet water again, making oar-swirls and oar-plangencies on the mirror gleams of the bay.

As soon as the *Sheena* touched the slipway, the boy was up and off. . . .

Old Fred had dropped off to sleep in his chair. His cold pipe was in his hand.

I knocked at the door. I told Betsy what a wonderful day it had been. I thanked her for the loan of the boat. 'But I wouldn't have had such a fine time,' I said, 'if it hadn't been for that boy.'

'What boy?' said the kind old lady. 'Weren't you alone?'

It struck me that he had never told me his name. He had never in fact uttered a single word. (The strangeness of it came on me suddenly.)

'I don't know,' I said. 'He has kind of corn-coloured hair.'

Old Betsy looked at me wonderingly.

The old man snored and snored like a blunt saw going through wood.

'There are no boys like that hereabouts,' said Betsy. 'Not that I know about.' (There was, I thought, a slight tremor about her gentle withered mouth.)

'He's dumb,' I said. 'I'm sure he's dumb.'

She went on shaking her head.

'I think,' said Betsy a week or so later, 'I've never seen such a good summer as this, no, not even when I was a small girl. You're lucky. Some summers can be cold bleak times, believe me.'

My mother and my three sisters, coming home each evening from their various avocations, looked increasingly like gypsies. The sun had soaked deeply, too, into the backs of my hands and into my long lean legs. Drying my face each morning, a kind of wild Indian face flashed back at me from the mirror.

There was no more talk of ghosts in our house. The freedom of the four living elements was enough for us.

Only the old man in his basket chair seemed to be unhappy. 'Rheumatics!' he snarled. 'Rheumatics is in my shoulder this year—first time I've had rheumatics there. Like a piece of rusty barbed wire going back and fore, back and fore, through the bones.'

I murmured that I hoped he'd soon be better.

'Believe me, boy,' said he, 'never wish to be an old man like me. It's not desirable—it's by no manner of means to be wished for. If it wasn't for my rum and my pipe, I couldn't carry on another week.'

'You're not half thankful enough,' said Betsy. She appeared briefly at the door, threw a handful of crumbs to the birds, then turned to go indoors again. 'You're a selfish ungrateful old man, and you always have been.'

Fred snarled and cut some black twist tobacco into his palm with a blunt shiny knife blade.

'There's only one thing worse than age,' he said, 'and that's to be cut off in your youth—yes, to be taken suddenly, the way some ignorant yokel tears a rose from a bush in passing.'

I could have sworn there were two tear-drops then, one in each wicked old eye. But it might only have been those worn prisms quivering in the sun.

I even got bored with the *Sheena*, after a week or ten days of puttering about in the harbour alone. My silent friend, the handsome golden-haired one, had not come back since the picnic on the island.

Why should I feel forsaken, almost bereaved, because a boy whose name I did not know was as rare and unpredictable as a shower of rain or a sunburst on water?

Those days when he wasn't there were at last bleak and empty, however the great red jar of the sun tilted its splendours of light and warmth over the summer islands.

A week passed; ten days. Still he didn't come. I might have taken the opportunity to explore the little town and the shores and hills round about; but I felt that if I were away from the pier, even for an hour, he might have come and gone again.

So, day after golden day, I lingered about the pier and endured the grumblings of the old man.

Sometimes he came back from the inn reeking of rum, and then he was more awkward and bad-tempered than ever. And it didn't make a whit of difference to him whether Betsy chided him or spoke kindly to him.

Always she had (smiling) a handful of sweets for me, or a glass of her homemade lemonade.

'It's lonely for you here,' she said. 'Nobody to speak to but Tinker and the gulls and that old drunken thing. You should take the bus to Kirkwall some morning and see St Magnus Cathedral. Or the ferryboat that goes through Scapa Flow to the south isles. It isn't good for boys to be lonely.'

I couldn't tell this nice old lady what kept me at the stone pier, day after day.

At nights I dreamed often about my friend whose name I had never got to know. They were such strange beautiful dreams as I have never had before or since. Always, in those dreams, the gold-headed boy brimmed over with happiness—I had never known such joy and excitement in my own life. And in every dream he was urging me to join him. 'Come!' he'd cry. 'Come now, quickly!' And I longed to go with him, along the shores and the bird-haunted lochs and hills; but in the dreams I could not go, I seemed to be enchanted like the knight-at-arms to this one small area of wave-washed stones, the pier, and the slipway, and the yard, and our empty house.

In one dream he was carrying a zinc bucket, and it was half full of shellfish that he'd gathered from the rock pools: winkles, mussels, limpets. 'Look!' he cried. 'Look at this lot—if you were with me we'd have twice as many.' (I longed to be with him—I could not move—it was as if I stood drenched in honey.)

Once he was on a hillside, in the dream—he had been gathering flowers: lupins, meadowsweet, marigolds, ox-eye daisies, iris. His face was mysterious and veiled with the fragrant shadows. 'There's more here than I can carry!' he shouted into the wind. 'I've got the whole of summer in my arms—look, too much; there's a marigold fallen! You must come and help me. Please. . . .'

I was shackled as always, to my grey ordinary world.

Was it dew on his face, or tears?

The strange thing is that, though the boy had never uttered a word to me in our few daytime encounters, in the dreams his voice rang like a new, sweet, wind-hung bell, vibrant with the joy of being alive in that high bounteous summer between boyhood and youth: the one golden time, I have learned since, that knows no shame or guilt. 'Come,' he cried. 'Do you want to grow old and ugly like old Skipper Fred?'

In the last dream, I was walking on a desolate beach. I was miserable. I was in search of my mother and sisters. I wanted them home with me, for a strange reason: I felt threatened without them. (This was unusual—generally, I was glad when they kissed me goodbye and went to their horses, old stones, water-colours, once the breakfast dishes had been stacked away.) In the dream—as I walked on the wet sand—I longed bitterly for them.

The boy was suddenly there, in the dream. He was carrying in his arms a great white silent sea bird. 'In a few days,' he said, and his words were heartbreakingly beautiful among the sea sounds, the Atlantic crashings and whisperings and lullings—'Next week, some morning, you and I are going to the crags. Look at that cliff there, to the north— the Black Crag—that's where we'll go, you and I, just the two of us. There's nothing finer in the world, boy, than to hang there between the clouds and the waves. You go from niche to niche, up and down, and across, and the birds are a white shrieking choir all about your head! Promise you'll come.'

'I'll try,' I said, 'but I find it hard to get away.'

He laughed. 'You'll come,' he said. 'We'll be free as the birds for ever.'

Then the white bird in his arms began to thrash and struggle. It shrieked in the boy's face! It half broke from him. One of its wings covered his mouth. . . . In that moment of lyrical brutishness, I woke up to a desolation of spirit I had never known before. . . .

Three more days passed. I hung about the pier more discontented than ever. Still the sun was a great loom of brightness in the south. Three barren dreamless nights passed. I rose to breakfast with four chattering coffee-swilling letter-reading women.

The old man Fred was grumpier than ever. Even old Betsy seemed subdued as the first days of August came in.

I decided, suddenly, that I'd had enough of hanging blankly about this pier. I would take Betsy's advice and do a bit of exploring.

I left the pier after breakfast. The women of the house had already gone. Tinker the cat chased a butterfly under the washing line.

I took the road round the shore of Hoy Sound. There are two islands lying to the south across a ramping turbulent tide-race—Graemsay, a small green island with a scatter of crafts and two lighthouses, and Hoy with its soaring blue-scarred glacier-rounded hills. Betsy had told me about the beach called Warbeth that was nice for picnics and bathing and rock-pool rifling, and about the Black Crag, a dangerous place, that lay beyond. 'Keep well back from the Black Crag!' she had warned me, shaking a finger.

On I walked, among the sea gleams and the lulling sea sounds.

What Betsy hadn't told me was that the road led past the local cemetery, or kirkyard, or (as the oldest people had called it in their quaint way) 'God's acre'.

This black honeycomb of death made me pause. The yard of a thousand stones: I couldn't bring myself to skirt the outer wall of it, even, though the Atlantic lay on the far side, open and free. The marvellous ocean music was already in my ears.

I was in the act of turning back when I saw the boy in the kirkyard, all alone. He seemed to be lingering round one stone in particular. I called out to him. He paid no attention. There was a most astonishing expression on his face: wonderment, fear, a kind of dawning joy. Once he reached out with his finger and touched the stone.

I called out to him again. He paid no attention. I ran—I stumbled in my hurry—I bruised my knee on a kerb—to get through the gate and be with him. 'Wait, I'm coming! Here—it's me! I'll go wherever you want. . . .'

He was not there. There was no one there, in the kirkyard on this beautiful summer morning, but myself.

I searched everywhere for him. He had fled like a shadow—it seemed he might have merged into the stone.

I returned at last to the tomb he had been lingering at. Under a list of ancient worn Victorian names, this was cut:

IVOR SINCLAIR
Died aged 11 years
as the result of an accident
5th August 1911

Butterflies tumbled silently among the graves. From the rocks below came the Atlantic whisper, again and again. The ripening cornfield on the slope above sent its multitudinous whisperings among the stones of the God-acre.

It was early afternoon when I got back to our pier. There was no sign of old Fred. I didn't have to wait long for an explanation. 'Drunk!' said Betsy. 'He went to the inn at opening time and he spent all his pension money before dinner—every last penny! Two fishermen carted the old villain home. *I don't want him*, I said to them. *Throw him on the bed there. He'll come to in his own time. Silly old fool!—I hope he has a splitting headache. . . .*'

I had never seen Betsy so upset. But, upset or not, she hastened indoors to fetch me shortbread and ginger ale.

'He always gets drunk on the fifth of August,' she said. 'That's to say, he gets ten times drunker on the fifth of August than he is most days. Something happened—oh, a long time ago—when he was just about the age you are now. I don't suppose you want to hear about it—why should you? Well, I'll tell you all the same. Fred had a twin brother, and by all accounts they were very close. They went everywhere together. They were inseparable. They fished together and they flew kites together. At Hallowe'en they lit fires and they did all sorts of mischief. . . . Well, then, it was the summer holidays. One morning they decided to go to the crags. In those days, seventy years ago, it was nothing for men and boys to go to the cliffs. All that great crag knowledge is lost now. Fred and this brother of his, they had done it hundreds of times before. Nobody worried about them. . . . Well, this very day seventy years ago—fifth of August in the year 1911—Fred came back from the Black Crag alone. Late in the evening he came back, to this very house on this very pier, grey as a ghost, and not able to speak. At last he managed to say that a great white bird had flown at his brother and knocked him off a ledge.

'They found Ivor's body next day at the foot of the crag, all broken.'

A week later, my mother and sisters and I left Orkney.

The sea gateway out of Orkney is guarded by two immense crags, one on each side, the Kame of Hoy and Black Crag.

I sat on the deck of the *St Ola* with Maria. Of my three sisters she was the one I had got to know best over the last few days. We were muffled in thick coats and bonnets and scarves; for at last the golden idyll had broken, and wind whined in the rigging and spindrift was blown from the crests of the waves.

I told Maria the story of the boy Ivor who had suffered a cliff death so long ago: without, of course, mentioning my own dealings with that ghost and dream creature. 'Life is cruel,' I declared. 'It isn't fair. I'll never understand it. . . .'

Maria quoted some poetry (Shelley, of course):

> He is made one with Nature; there is heard
> His voice in all her music, from the moan
> Of thunder, to the song of night's sweet bird.
> He is a presence to be felt and known
> In darkness and in light, in herb and stone,
> Moving itself where'er that Spirit doth move
> Which hath withdrawn his being to its own,
> Which wields the world with never-wearied love,
> Sustains it from beneath, and kindles it above.

The boat moved to the open colder waters. A thong of spindrift lashed my face; it left a marvellous taste of salt.

VIVIEN ALCOCK

Siren Song

1 AUGUST 1981
Dear Tape Recorder,
   This is me. My name's Roger and I'm nine years old today. You're my birthday present.
   Happy birthday to me,
   Happy birthday to you,
   Happy birthday, dear both-of-us . . .

1 August 1982
   R for Roger. R for Roger. This is Roger, mark ten, calling. I'm not going to bore you with a bite-by-bite account of my birthday tea, like last year. This time I'll only record the exciting moments in my life. Over and out.

1 August 1983
   My name is Roger Kent. I am eleven years old. I want to get this down in case anything happens to me.
   I hate this village. I wish we hadn't come to live here. There's something funny about it.
   For one thing, there are no other children here. Except Billy Watson, and he's weird. He's a thin, white-faced boy who jumps when you speak to him. Mum says he's been ill, and I must be kind. I was. I asked him to come to my birthday tea today. He twitched like I'd stabbed him in the back, and his eyes scuttled about like beetles. Then he mumbled something and ran off.
   The grown-ups are peculiar, too. They're old and baggy-eyed, as if they'd been crying all night. When they see me, they stop talking. They watch me. It's a bit scary.
   At first I thought they didn't like me. But it's not that. They look as if they know something terrible's going to happen to me, and are sorry about it.
   Mrs Mason's the worst. I hate the way she looks at me. Her eyes are . . . I dunno . . . sort of hungry. I don't mean she's a cannibal. It's more like . . .

D'you know why gerbils sometimes eat their own babies? It's because they're afraid they're in danger, and think they'll be safer back inside.

That's just how Mrs Mason looks at me. As if she'd like to swallow me to keep me safe. But what from?

This morning, when she heard it was my birthday, she hugged me. I jerked away. I didn't mean to be rude. I honestly thought she was going to start nibbling my ear. That's the sort of state I'm in.

'Never go out at night,' she said. (That's nothing. Mum's always telling me that nowadays. It's what came next.) 'Never go out at night, *whatever sounds you hear!*'

Funny thing to say, wasn't it? 'Whatever sounds you hear.'

I've been thinking and thinking, but I can't imagine what she meant. If we lived by the sea, I'd think of smugglers. You know, like that poem—'Watch the wall, my darling, while the gentlemen go by.'

Perhaps they're witches! I'm not being silly. There *are* witches nowadays. It was in the papers once. COVEN OF WITCHES EXPOSED, it said. They certainly were exposed! There was this photograph of men and women with nothing on. Not that you could see much, only their backs. They didn't look wild and exciting at all. Just stupid. And cold—you could almost see the goosepimples. Still, they were witches.

D'you think it's that?

Full moon tonight. I'm going to stay awake and listen. It must be happening somewhere near enough for me to hear, or she wouldn't have said that.

Supposing they use our garden?

Suppose Mum's joined them! She's been a bit strange lately. No, that's silly.

10.30 p.m. I'm sitting by the window. Nothing's happened yet. Just the usual night noises, and not many of those. This village dies after ten o'clock. A dog barking. An owl getting on my nerves, can't the stupid thing say anything else?

It's boring. I think I'll go to bed for a bit.

0.00. I've got a digital clock and that's what it says. Like Time's laid eggs in a row. No time. Nothing point nothing nothing time. Don't count your minutes before they're hatched.

What's that?

Only an owl. The window's wide open, and it's cold. The moon is round and bright. There are shadows all over the garden. I can't see anything. It's very quiet now. No wind.

Listen!
Children! I can hear children laughing. I can hear their voices calling softly . . .

I think they're in Billy Watson's garden. He must be having a midnight party, and he hasn't asked me! Pig! No wonder he ran off when I invited him to tea.

I wish I could see them. There're too many trees. Too many shadows.
Listen!

This microphone's too small. I held it out of the window, but I didn't get anything.

They were singing. Their voices were high and clear. I could hear every word. It was a funny little tune. Sort of sad, but nice. There's a chorus where they all hoot softly like baby owls. I think I can remember the words—

'Little ghost, all dressed in white,
Walking on a summer's night,
(Hoooo, hooo,)
Calling to her childhood friend,
Asking him to come and play,
But his hair stands up on end.
Billy Watson runs away.'

Billy Watson! So they arc friends of his! I suppose they're playing a game . . .
Listen . . .

It was a girl singing alone this time. I'm sure it was a girl. Her voice was so high and sweet and sad, it made me ache. This is what she sang—

'Don't you love me any more?
I'm as pretty as before.
(Hooo, hooo,)
Though my roses all are gone,
Lily-white is just as sweet.
Stars shine through me now, not on
Flesh that's only so much meat.'

I wish I could see her . . .

   'Coo-ee! Over here!'

They heard me. I know they did. They're whispering. Now they're coming nearer. I can hear the bushes rustling by our wall. Look! I think one of them's slipped over into our garden. It's difficult to be sure. There are so many shadows. I'm going to dangle the microphone out of the window . . .

   Listen!

> 'Billy, see the moon is bright.
> Won't you play with me tonight?
> (Hooo, hooo,)
> Billy Watson's now in bed,
> With his fingers in his ears,
> And his blankets hide his head,
> And his face is wet with tears.'

I got it that time! It's very faint, but you can just make out the words. I don't think they can be friends of Billy's after all. They sounded as if they were mocking him. I wonder who they are?

Oh, they're going away now! I can hear them running through the bushes. Laughing. They've gone!

No. There's still one standing in the shadow of the lilac tree. Just below my window. I'm sure it's the girl. I can see her white frock gleaming . . . unless it's just moonlight. She's all alone now. Waiting for me.

   Listen!

> 'Little ghost all dressed in white
> Singing sadly in the night,
> (Hooo, hooo,)
> Who will play with me instead?
> Must I be lonely till the end?
> Is there any child abed
> Brave enough to be my friend?'

I'm coming! Wait for me! I know I promised Mum I'd never go out at night, but . . . The moon is shining bright as day. Someone is singing in the garden below. Softly. Sweetly. Surely it won't matter if I go out just once?

The rest of the tape is blank. Roger Kent was never seen again.

AIDAN CHAMBERS

The Tower

'SURELY you understand now,' Mr Phelps said, patient and smiling. 'I've explained it to you three times, Martin.'

His son sighed and stared at the Ordnance Survey map spread out on the caravan table.

'I know,' he said. 'It's just that I'm sure there was a tower exactly where I've marked it.'

'You've got it wrong, nitwit. I keep telling you, there's a pond there, that's all.' The smile had gone now.

'I suppose.'

'What do you mean, you suppose!'

'But the map could be wrong. Or you could be wrong yourself.'

Mr Phelps drew in his breath. 'Martin, there are times when I wonder if you have any brains at all. I've told you—I've seen it. The map is accurate and *I am not wrong*!'

'Don?' Mrs Phelps was lying face down on a travelling rug spread on the grass just outside the caravan door. 'Remember, dear, we're on holiday.' Though pretending to sleep as she sunbathed in her bikini, she had been eavesdropping on the conversation, half expecting it to end in a row.

Mr Phelps shuffled from his seat behind the table and went to the door, his walking boots clumping on the floor and his angry weight making the caravan tremble.

'Well,' he chuntered, 'he really is stupid as well as stubborn sometimes, Mary. I've explained till I'm blue in the face but he just doesn't seem capable of taking it in.'

'Maybe he has a blind spot for maps.'

'A blind spot for maps! Mary, you can't have a blind spot for maps. You can, perhaps, for French or maths. But not for *maps*. They're designed so any fool can understand.'

He stared across the heat-hazed field to the woods beyond and wondered why he hadn't gone off on his walk alone instead of listening to his son blathering about a tower that wasn't there and the map being wrong.

Mrs Phelps flopped on to her back, put her sunglasses on and patted the rug at her side.

'Come and sit here for a few minutes,' she said.

Her husband obeyed, squatting cross-legged, his arms hugging his knees.

'I wouldn't mind,' he said, more in regret than anger now, 'if he just listened a bit more carefully. But he argues. Doesn't try to learn first.'

'It's his age,' Mrs Phelps said. 'I bet you were just the same when you were fourteen.'

'Never!'

His wife laughed, gently. 'Course you were, everybody is.'

'Not me. I was keen to know about things. Everything. Information, that's what it's about. You don't get to know things by arguing the toss with someone who knows more than you do. You listen. Question. Pick their brains.'

Mrs Phelps stroked her husband's knee. 'Well, you aren't in school now. Just relax. Enjoy yourself. That's what holidays are for.'

Mr Phelps edged his legs out of range of his wife's hand.

The summer afternoon sang.

'Maybe,' Mrs Phelps said after a while, but quietly so that Martin wouldn't hear, 'maybe we should have let him go off with his friends after all.'

'Camping with a bunch of yobs? Not on!'

'You're too hard on him.'

'He'll appreciate it later.'

'At his age you need some freedom, Don. A life of your own.'

'Ho!' Mr Phelps snorted. 'Freedom to act like an idiot, you mean. Freedom to roam the streets and vandalize bus shelters. Freedom to terrorize old people and mess yourself up with drugs. Some freedom that is!'

'What makes you think Martin would behave like that?'

'Oh, come on, Mary. You've seen the rubbish who hang around our place. I passed a gang of them the other night. Half of them smoking their heads off while they watched the other half make a meal of the local females. About which enough said!'

Mrs Phelps sighed. 'That's a kind of learning too, I suppose.'

Her husband flicked a hand at a bombarding fly. 'Well, as far as I'm concerned, it's a lesson Martin can do without, thanks.'

For a few moments neither spoke.

Mr Phelps whisked at more attacking flies, but with less ferocity now.

'Why not go for your walk?' Mrs Phelps said when she was sure the storm had blown over.

Her husband stood up in one smooth movement without using his hands. 'Perhaps I will.' He tucked his shirt in and hitched his trousers. 'There's a long barrow just north of us. No record of it being excavated. I'll poke about there for a while. Might be interesting.'

He collected his stick from the back of the car, said, 'See you in a couple of hours,' and stalked away.

From his seat in the caravan Martin watched his father stride across the field, climb the gate in the hedge and disappear up the lane. Then he returned his gaze to the map lying on the table at his elbows. A week ago he had been looking at it with excited anticipation. Now he regarded it with distaste. Nothing ever turned out as well as you hoped.

He slipped out from behind the table, took an apple from the basket in the food cupboard, bit into its juicy crispness, went to the door and sat on the step, his feet square on the ground.

The noise of his munching was loud in the country silence.

'Enjoying it?' his mother said.

Martin nodded, knowing she was watching from behind her dark glasses.

'He'll feel better after his walk,' Mrs Phelps said.

Martin nodded again.

He gnawed his apple to the core, then lobbed it high over his mother's body to fall in the long grass beyond. From where it landed a small dark bird he couldn't recognize flew up, startled. If his father had still been here, he would have insisted on him looking it up in his recognition book.

'Could I help?' Mrs Phelps asked.

'Doubt it,' Martin said, squinting as he tried to follow the bird's flight into the sun.

Mrs Phelps sat up and swivelled to face him. 'Won't you tell me what the trouble is?'

'Doesn't matter.'

'You were having quite a set-to for something that doesn't matter.'

Martin shrugged. 'It's just that I say the map is wrong, and Dad says I don't know how to read it properly.'

Mrs Phelps took her sunglasses off. 'What do you say is wrong?'

Martin sighed. 'You know how he set me a route to walk this morning to prove I could use the map on my own?'

'Yes.'

'Well, I managed all right really. Just missed a couple of details. Only little things. But on the last leg down Tinkley Lane . . .'

'The one that runs along the far side of this field?'

'Yes. There's a quarry along there, about a mile away, and a bench mark, and a couple of disused farm buildings, and I got them all OK . . .'

'But?'

'In a field with a pond in it about three quarters of a mile away—eight tenths, actually, to be exact—I saw a tower.'

'And?'

'It isn't marked on the map so I put it in.'

'But Dad says it isn't there?'

Martin nodded.

Mrs Phelps put her sunglasses on again. 'But, sweetheart, I don't see the problem. Either the tower is there or it isn't.'

'That's what we were rowing about.'

Mrs Phelps laughed. 'Men! Why row? Why not just go and find out together?'

'I wanted to. But Dad wouldn't.' Martin stood up. 'He said he knew it wasn't there. He said he'd been along that way twice already since we got here and he'd never seen a tower. But I know it is there, Mum, I saw it this morning, certain sure.'

'All right, all right!' Agitation in her son's voice warned that care was needed. 'Come here. Sit down. Let's have that shirt off. Get some sunlight on you. You're as bad as your dad. You both think you'll evaporate if you get sun on your body.'

Reluctantly, Martin tugged his shirt off and sat so that his mother could rub sun oil on to his back.

'This tower,' she said as she anointed him, 'what did it look like?'

'A bit weird really. Built of stone and quite high. Fifteen metres. Twenty maybe. And it was round. With little slit windows, with pointed tops like in a church. But there wasn't a spire or anything, it was just flat, with battlements round the top like a castle. There was a biggish door-way at the bottom, with an arch like the windows. But there was no door. And the wall was partly covered in ivy, and weeds and even clumps of flowers were growing out of the cracks between some of the stones.'

'How exciting. Lie down and I'll do your front.'

'No, I'll do myself.'

Martin took the tube and began oiling his chest.

'Did you go inside?'

'I started pacing towards it because I wanted to try and fix its position on the map exactly. But after thirty paces, well before I even reached the pond . . . I don't know . . . the air went chilly. Just all of a sudden. Like I'd come up against a wall of cold.'

He stopped rubbing the oil and looked at his mother's masked eyes.

'Made me feel a bit scared. Don't know why. There weren't any cattle in the field, nothing to be scared of, you know. But I stopped pacing and just stood. And then I noticed how quiet the place was. I mean quiet in an odd sort of way.'

Martin paused, his eyes now not focused, though he was looking straight at his mother.

'And what was so odd?' Mrs Phelps said as calmly as she could.

Martin's eyes focused again.

'No birds,' he said. 'None flying anywhere near and not a sound of any birdsong either. Not even insects. Nothing. Just dead silence.'

Mother and son stared at each other.

'Perhaps a kestrel lives in the tower? Or some other bird of prey?'

Martin shook his head.

'You can't be sure.'

'Can.'

'How?'

'Went in.'

'Even though you were scared?'

'I'm trying to tell you!'

'All right, OK, I'm listening.'

'It was pretty hot this morning, right?'

His mother nodded.

'A heat haze, just like now?'

'Was there?'

'I didn't notice either till I was in the field looking at the tower. I'd noticed about the birds and was looking at the tower. It seemed normal, just an old stone building, you know. The field all around is long grass, like this one, with a tall hedge, and a wood opposite from the lane side. And it was while I was looking at the wood that it hit me.'

He stopped, uncertain of himself.

'Go on, sweetheart,' Mrs Phelps said.

'Well, everything, the wood and the hedge and the grass in the field, even the pond—everything was shimmering in the haze. But the tower . . . It wasn't. It was quite still. The shape of it was clear cut.'

Mrs Phelps gave an involuntary shudder. She didn't really believe Martin's story. Not that he would lie. He never lied. But he did get carried away by his imagination sometimes. Even so—a tower standing cold and silent in the middle of a summer field. She shuddered again.

Curious how a few words, just by association, can make you feel cold on a lovely day in hot sunshine.

She came back to herself. Martin was still telling his story and she had missed something. She said, 'Sorry, lovey, I was distracted. What did you say?'

'The tower,' Martin said. 'It was cool inside, wonderfully cool, and restful.'

'Wasn't it locked up?'

'No, I told you, I went straight in. There was a doorway but no door. And inside the place was smelly, really stank, like empty places often do, don't they, as if people have used them for lavatories. But it was quite clean, no rubbish or anything. A round-shaped room with a bare earth floor. And one of the little pointed windows with no glass in it. And a stone stairway, that started just inside the door and curled up round the wall to a floor above. No banister, just the stone stairs in the wall.'

'No sign of life?'

'Nothing. Deserted. And very cool. Really nice after the heat. Well, anyway, I thought it must have a smashing view from the top, so I climbed the stairs. Thirty-two. Counted them. Eighteen to the first floor, and fourteen to the top. The first floor was just old wooden boards. A few bird droppings but nothing else.'

'And safe. Not rotten or anything?'

'No. I wouldn't have gone on if it hadn't been safe, would I? I'm not that stupid, whatever Dad thinks!'

'It's just his manner. So was there a good view?'

'Not really. After the field there's trees in the way in most directions. But it was nice. There's a parapet so you can't fall off. And it was just as cool up there as inside. I'd have stayed longer, but I knew if I didn't get home in reasonable time, Dad would start getting at me for taking so long to do a simple route. So I came down, paced the distance back to the lane, marked the position on the map, and came back.'

Mrs Phelps took a deep breath. 'What a story!'

Martin glared at her. 'It is *not* a story. It's what happened.'

His mother leaned to him and hugged his face to hers. 'Yes, my love, I know,' she said. 'I mean, what a strange thing to find a tower like that and it not be on the map.'

Martin pulled free. 'Don't you start!'

Mrs Phelps leaned back on her hands. 'Did you tell your father all this?'

Martin grimaced in disdain.

'No,' his mother said. 'Best not to, I suppose.'

'He wouldn't believe me about the tower being there. So you know what he'd say about the rest. Rubbish, he'd say, pure imagination.'

Mrs Phelps thought for a while then stood up and adjusted her bikini. 'Look, why don't I slip into something respectable and you can show me your tower? That'll settle matters.'

Martin shook his head.

'Why not? If I've seen it he can't go on saying it isn't there.'

'But that'll only make it worse. He'll get angry and say we ganged up against him, that I got you to take my side, that I can't stand on my own feet.'

Impasse.

After a sullen moment Mrs Phelps said, 'I'll tell you what. You go on your own, and double-check the position of the tower. After all, you just might have made a mistake. Then come back and tell me. After supper this evening, I'll suggest we take a walk, and I'll make sure we go along Tinkley Lane past the tower. That way, we'll all see it together and your father won't be able to say you're wrong. How about that?'

Martin considered.

'OK,' he said, cheering up. 'But I know it's where I said it was.'

'Course it is, my love. But make sure. And while you're gone I'll fix supper so that everything's ready when your father gets back.'

Martin pulled on his shirt, collected his map from the caravan, folded it so he could hold it easily and see the area round the tower, gave his mother a tentative hug, and set off across the field.

Mrs Phelps watched her son out of sight before going inside, pulling on a pair of jeans and an old shirt of her husband's, and slipping her feet into her sandals.

Martin sauntered down the lane, stifled by the heat cocooned between the high, dense hedgerows. Wasps and flies whirred past his head. A yellow-hammer pink-pinked behind him. Straight above, crawling across the dazzling blue, a speck of aeroplane spun its white spider thread.

His shirt clung uncomfortably to his oiled body. He glanced up the lane and down, and, seeing no one, tugged his shirt off and used it as a fly-whisk as he walked along. Usually he kept himself covered, too embarrassed by his scrawny build to show himself in public. Boys at school called him Needle.

Even without his shirt he was sweating by the time he reached the gateless opening in the hedge that led to the tower. And sure enough, there it was, looking just as it had in the morning. This time he noticed at once how coldly it stood and clearly outlined while all around grass and flowers and trees and rocks and even the pond at the foot of the tower shimmered in the haze. And while he looked, just as that morning, he felt a nerve-tingling strangeness. He tried to work out what the strangeness was and decided it was like knowing something was going to happen to you but not quite knowing what.

There must, Martin thought, be some ordinary explanation. His father would probably know what it was, and would tell him, if only he would stop insisting that the tower wasn't there, and come and see for himself while the heat haze was still rising. By this evening, when his mother tricked his father into seeing the tower, the haze would have vanished into a dew.

As he checked its position on his map, Martin remembered the coolness and how much he had wanted to stay in the tower. Now there was nothing to hurry back to the caravan for. He could stay and enjoy himself. He might even make a den, a secret place where he could come and be by himself during the rest of the week. Nor had he properly explored the building; there was bound to be something interesting if he looked carefully enough. There was also the pond; there might be fish to be caught. And if he wanted to sunbathe, the tower roof was a good place; no one could see him lying behind the parapet, but he would be able to spy anyone approaching across the field. He might even go home after the holiday with a useful tan.

He was about to enter the field when he heard a shout. A cry, in fact, rather than a yell. A girl's voice, high-pitched and desperate. Coming from the direction of the tower.

Shading his eyes with a hand, he searched the tower but could see no one.

The cry came again. And suddenly he knew what caused the strangeness he felt. It was as if he had been waiting for this cry, that it had reached him as a sensation long before he heard it as a sound in his ears.

As he stared at the tower with fixed unblinking eyes, he saw a girl's head, then her body appear above the parapet till she was revealed to her waist. She was about fifteen or sixteen and wearing a sleeveless white summer-loose dress. But from this distance it was difficult to see her features clearly, which anyway were partly hidden by long dark hair that fell around her shoulders.

She grasped the wall of the parapet with one hand. The other she raised above her head and waved urgently at Martin. At first he thought she was only excited, perhaps pretending to be frightened by the height. But then she cried out again in that high-pitched urgent voice.

She seemed to be shouting, 'Come back, come back!' and waving him towards her.

But that could not be. He had never seen her before.

Puzzled, Martin did not move, except to raise his own hand and wave back in a polite reflex action.

Still the girl waved and cried, 'Come back, come back!'

She's mistaken me for someone else, Martin thought. But even as he thought this, smoke began to drift up from the tower behind the girl, first only a thin blue smudge in the air, which quickly became a thicker feathering, and then, after a belching puff, a dense, curling ribbon that streamed straight up into the sky, grey-white against the deep blue.

As the smoke thickened, the girl's cries became more panic-stricken, her hand-waving more frantic.

Which at last brought Martin to life again. Dropping his shirt and map, he sprinted towards the tower.

Mrs Phelps gave her son a few minutes' start before setting off after him. But she got no further than the gate when she met her husband striding down the lane towards her. She knew at once that he was excited from the jaunty way he was windmilling his stick.

'You'll never guess,' he said as he approached.

'What?' Mrs Phelps grinned, expecting some story about her husband finding an almost extinct flower or spotting a rare bird.

'Just been talking to an old farmer. Asked him if he knew of a stone tower anywhere in the district . . .' He paused, enjoying the drama.

'And?'

'At first he said no. Nothing of that sort round here, sir!' Mr Phelps, who prided himself on his talent for mimicry, imitated the farmer's accent. 'Then he remembered. Ah, wait a minute, sir, he says, yes there were one. But that were years back, sir, when I were a boy, like.'

Mrs Phelps caught at her breath.

Her husband went on, unaware. 'I quizzed him—without letting on about Martin, of course. Apparently, there used to be an old teasel tower where the pond is just down the lane from here. You know the sort. You always say they look as if they're straight out of a fairy tale. Sleeping Beauty, Rapunzel and all that rubbish. And we came across a teasel growing wild just the other day, remember? Rather like a tall thistle, with a large very prickly head. Well, it was the heads they dried in those towers and then used them for raising the nap on cloth. Fascinating process . . .'

'Yes, darling, but . . . ?'

'. . . They cut the dried heads in two and attached them to a cylinder which revolved against the cloth in such a way that the prickles snagged against the fabric just sufficiently to scuff the surface.' Mr Phelps chuckled. 'Teasing it, you might say!'

'Don . . .'

'And do you know, Mary, they still haven't been able to invent a machine that can do the job better. Isn't that extraordinary!'

'Don, the tower—what did the old man tell you?'

'I'm just coming to that. According to the old chap, one day during a long hot summer like this, the tower burned to the ground.'

'Burned . . . ?' Mrs Phelps flinched.

'Hang on, that isn't all. A young girl is supposed to have died in the blaze. The old chap told a marvellous tale about how she was meeting her boyfriend there in secret and somehow the fire started, no one ever found out how, and the girl got trapped.'

'Don, listen . . .'

'The boyfriend ran off, scared he'd be caught with the girl, I expect. You know how strict they were in those days about that sort of thing, and quite right too. The wretched boy deserted her, poor thing, and she died in the flames. Young love betrayed by cowardice.'

'He's gone there,' Mrs Phelps said bleakly.

'A nice yarn but all nonsense, of course. However, it does look as if there might have been a tower somewhere near where Martin thought he saw one. Isn't that odd!'

Mrs Phelps turned away and set off at a jog down the lane.

'Hang on, Mary,' Mr Phelps called after her, 'haven't finished yet.'

'Got to find him,' his wife called back.

'But wait!' Mr Phelps waved his stick. 'I want Martin to take us to where he thought he saw the tower.'

Without turning, Mrs Phelps shouted back, her voice carrying her panic, 'He's gone there already!'

Hearing at last what his wife was saying, Mr Phelps sprinted after her, ungainly in his walking boots. 'Gone there?' he called as he ran.

'To check. We must catch him.'

'Steady! Wait!' By the time Mr Phelps reached his wife he was almost speechless from lack of breath. He seized her arm and pulled her to a stop. 'Mary, you're being hysterical. What is all this?'

'Can't you see?' Mrs Phelps panted. 'Martin wasn't wrong!'

'Having us on!'

'No! There! To him, it was there!'

'Rubbish!' Mr Phelps leaned forward, both hands on his stick, re-covering his breath. 'He'd found out. Only pretending he'd seen it. Some kind of joke.'

'No, no, no!' Mrs Phelps was near to tears with desperation.

Her husband glared at her. 'Pull yourself together, Mary, for heaven's sake!'

As if she had been slapped, his wife's tears suddenly gave way to anger. She glared fiercely back at her husband. 'Don't you speak to me like that, Don! You're not in school now! Don't you dare condescend to me! You think you know everything. To you the world is just one big museum of plain straightforward facts. Well, let me tell you, you don't know everything. There's more to this world than your boring facts! And for once I don't care what you think. I believe Martin saw that tower. He's gone back there. And I'm going after him. I'm afraid what might happen if he sees it again. Call that a mother's intuition. Call it what you like. But I *feel* it. That's all I know. Now, are you coming or aren't you?'

Mr Phelps stood open-mouthed and rigid with astonishment at his wife's outburst.

By the time Martin reached the door of the tower smoke was billowing from every window and crevice. Instinctively bending almost double, he ran inside. The force of the air being sucked in through the doorway pressed against his bare back like a firm hand pushing him on. At once he found himself engulfed in blinding, choking fumes, could hear the roar of flames from across the room, could feel their blistering heat on his skin.

But still from above came the girl's panic-stricken cries.

Without thought or care, he threw himself to the left and on to the stairs. He pounded up them, stumbling, coughing. Hardly able to see for smoke, he kept his left hand pressed against the wall for fear of veering to the edge of the stairs and falling off into the furnace on the floor below, from where flames were already leaping high enough to lick the exposed floorboards of the room above. He held his right arm against his face, trying to protect it from the scorching blaze.

On the first floor flames were already eating at the boards. The dry wood was crackling; small explosions were sending showers of sparks cascading across the room. And, mingled with the suffocating fumes, the stench of burning flesh was so strong that Martin retched as he staggered on hands and feet now up the second flight of stairs. By the time he reached the trapdoor that gave on to the roof he was choking for breath, his smoke-filled eyes were streaming with tears and all down his right side he felt as if his skin were being peeled from him like paint being stripped by a blow-lamp. The tower had become one giant, roaring chimney.

Martin hauled himself up into the air, gulping for breath. Once on the roof he clung for a moment to the parapet, unable to move till he recovered his strength. But he knew there was no time to spare. Through tear-blurred eyes and the fog of smoke swirling about him, he looked round for the girl and saw her only an arm's length away still waving and crying desperately in the direction of the road.

'Here!' he tried to shout, 'I'm here!', but the words clogged in his parched throat.

So he reached out to take her by the shoulders and turn her to him.

'Surely, we're nearly there!' Mrs Phelps panted.

Clumping along beside her, Mr Phelps, breathless too and sweating, said, 'That beech tree. Just there.'

Seconds later Mrs Phelps spotted her son's shirt and map lying abandoned in the road. 'Don!' she cried, rushed to them and picked them up. 'They're his!'

She turned and saw the gap in the hedge, and dashed towards it. But her husband, arriving at the same instant, pushed her aside and ran ahead into the field, causing Mrs Phelps to fall to her knees. 'Oh, God!' she pleaded, and, finding her feet again, stumbled after him.

'Martin . . .!' Mr Phelps was calling when both he and his wife were brought to a sudden stop.

Across the field, high above the pond, they saw their son floating upright in the air, his arms outstretched as if reaching for something.

'Dear Lord!' Mr Phelps muttered.

But neither he nor his wife could move. Spellbound, they could do no more than watch as their son took hold of that invisible something for which he was reaching and clutched it eagerly to him in a passionate embrace. For a long moment he remained like that, his body utterly still, until, suddenly, he opened his arms wide, peered down and, in a strangely slow, dream-like movement, as if from a high diving board, launched himself earthwards.

The instant Martin's body hit the water, Mrs Phelps came violently alive.

'Martin!' she screamed and hurtled across the field.

Her scream seemed to bring her husband back to his senses. He sprinted after her, yelling, 'Mary . . . Mary . . . Careful!'

But Mrs Phelps paid him no heed. By the time she reached the pond her son's body had surfaced and was floating face down in the middle. She plunged in headlong, her arms flaying, but found herself at once entangled in clinging weeds that grew around the edge and prevented her from making any progress.

Galloping up behind her, Mr Phelps made no attempt to swim, but ploughed in till he was wading waist-high towards his son, his frantic strides churning the water to froth around him and his boots so disturbing the stagnant mud on the pond's bottom that it belched up great bubbles of putrid gas in his trail.

As soon as they had lifted Martin on to the bank Mr Phelps said, 'Leave him to me!', and with a sureness and skill that surprised his wife, began reviving their son with the kiss of life.

It was only when Martin was breathing properly again that Mrs Phelps noticed the ugly blisters covering the right side of his body. She was sitting with Martin's head cradled in her lap and had been going to cover him with his shirt. Instead she looked at her husband who was kneeling at her side and saw that he too had seen the burns.

'We must get him to hospital,' she said, working hard to keep the shock from sounding in her voice.

Mr Phelps nodded.

Martin opened his eyes. 'Mum,' he said.

'Hush, sweetheart. It's all right. You're safe now.'

Martin blinked in the bright sunlight, and coughed up water. His mother eased his position, holding him so that he could breathe easily.

'Is the girl safe?' Martin asked when the spasm was over.

His parents glanced at each other.

'She'll be all right,' his mother said, smiling down at him.

Martin tried to raise himself. 'Where is she?' he asked.

His mother gently restrained him. 'She's been taken care of. Don't worry.'

'You see, Martin . . .' his father began.

'Not yet,' Mrs Phelps said as lightly as she could. 'Later.'

Her husband turned away. 'I'd better get the car and take you to hospital, old son,' he said.

Martin said, 'I told you it was there, Dad, didn't I?'

Mr Phelps peered across the empty field hidden from his son by his wife's cradling body.

'You did,' he said.

'And I got the position exactly on the map.'

'You certainly did. Well done!'

Mr Phelps looked down at his son and for a moment stared into his eyes for the first time in months. And the boy's gaze, looking frankly back at him, as though somehow he now knew all there was to know about his father, caused Mr Phelps to shudder.

Mrs Phelps observed her husband's discomfort and felt his pain. But there was nothing she could do to help him. The time for that had passed. And their holiday too was over.

'We ought to get him away from here as soon as we can,' she said gently.

Mr Phelps took a deep breath and braced himself. 'I'll only be a jiffy,' he said and set off towards the lane at a steady jog.

Mrs Phelps watched him go and suddenly felt utterly exhausted. The sun was scorching her back, but she knew she mustn't move. The warmth reminded her that Martin had said how cool it had been near the tower. It certainly wasn't now. And all around grasshoppers rasped. She listened. There was also plenty of bird noise and the loud skirl of passing flies and bees. None of the strange silence he'd mentioned.

Martin broke in on her thoughts. 'Am I badly hurt?'

'Not badly,' his mother said, brushing scorched hair from his forehead.

'Was I out for long?'

'Long enough.'

'Has the tower burned down completely?'

'Afraid so.'

'That's a pity. It was such a nice place. But the girl's OK?'

'I'm sure she is,' Mrs Phelps said with utter conviction. 'Thanks to you.'

'And I will see her again, won't I?'

'Would you like to?'

'Wouldn't mind.' Martin grinned sheepishly at his mother. 'She was quite pretty really.'

'Yes,' Mrs Phelps said, struggling against tears. 'I expect she was.'

GRACE HALLWORTH

The Guitarist

JOE was an excellent guitarist and when he wasn't performing on his own, he accompanied the singers and dancers who also attended the Singing.

After a Singing someone was sure to offer Joe a lift back to his village but on one occasion he found himself stranded miles away from his home with no choice but to set out on foot. It was a dark night and there wasn't a soul to be seen on the road, not even a cat or a dog, so Joe began to strum his guitar to hearten himself for the lonely journey ahead.

Joe had heard many stories about strange things seen at night on that road but he told himself that most of the people who related these stories had been drinking heavily. All the same, as he came to a cross-road known to be the haunt of Lajables and other restless spirits, he strummed his guitar loudly to drown the rising clamour of fearful thoughts in his head. In the quiet of early morning the tune was sharp and strong, and Joe began to move to the rhythm; but all the while his eyes were fixed on a point ahead of him where four roads met. The nearer he got, the more convinced he was that someone was standing in the middle of the road. He hoped with all his heart that he was wrong and that the shape was only a shadow cast by an overhanging tree.

The man stood so still he might have been a statue, and it was only when Joe was within arm's length of the figure that he saw any sign of life. The man was quite tall, and so thin that his clothes hung on him as though they were thrown over a wire frame. There was a musty smell about them. It was too dark to see who the man was or what he looked like, and when he spoke his voice had a rasp to it which set Joe's teeth on edge.

'You play a real fine guitar for a youngster,' said the man, falling into step beside Joe.

Just a little while before, Joe would have given anything to meet another human being but somehow he was not keen to have this man as a companion. Nevertheless his motto was 'Better to be safe than sorry', so he was as polite as his unease would allow.

'It's nothing special but I like to keep my hand in. What about you, man? Can you play guitar too?' asked Joe.

'Let me try your guitar and we'll see if I can match you,' replied the man.

Joe handed over his guitar and the man began to play so gently and softly that Joe had to listen closely to hear the tune. He had never heard such a mournful air. But soon the music changed, the tune became wild and the rhythm fast and there was a harshness about it which drew a response from every nerve in Joe's body. Suddenly there was a new tone and mood and the music became light and enchanting. Joe felt as if he were borne in the air like a blown-up balloon. He was floating on a current of music and would follow it to the ends of the earth and beyond.

And then the music stopped. Joe came down to earth with a shock as he realised that he was standing in front of his house. The night clouds were slowly dispersing. The man handed the guitar back to Joe who was still dazed.

'Man, that was guitar music like I never heard in this world before,' said Joe.

'True?' said the man. 'You should have heard me when I was alive!'

LEON GARFIELD

A Grave Misunderstanding

I AM a dog. I think you ought to know right away. I don't want to save it up for later, because you might begin to wonder what sort of a person it was who went about on all fours, sniffing at bottoms and peeing up against lampposts in the public street. You wouldn't like it; and I don't suppose you'd care to have anything more to do with me.

The truth of the matter is, we have different standards, me and my colleagues, that is; not in everything, I hasten to bark, but in enough for it to be noticeable. For instance, although we are as fond of a good walk as the next person, love puppies and smoked salmon, we don't go much on reading. We find it hard to turn the pages. But, on the other paw, a good deep snoutful of mingled air as it comes humming off a rubbish dump can be as teasing to us as a sonnet. Indeed, there are rhymes in rancid odours such as you'd never dream of; and every puddle tells a story.

We see things, too. Only the other day, when me and my Person were out walking, and going as brisk as biscuits, through that green and quiet place of marble trees and stony, lightless lampposts, where people bury their bones and never dig them up, I saw a ghost. I stopped. I glared, I growled, my hair stood up on end—

'What the devil's the matter with you now?' demanded my Person.

'What a beautiful dog!' said the ghost, who knew that I knew what she was, and that we both knew that my Person did not.

She was the lifeless, meaningless shell of a young female person whose bones lay not very far away. No heart beat within her, there was wind in her veins, and she smelled of worm-crumble and pine.

'Thank you,' said my Person, with a foolishly desiring smile: for the ghost's eyes were very come-hitherish, even though her hither was thither, under the grass. 'He *is* rather a handsome animal. Best of breed at Cruft's you know.' The way to his heart was always open through praise of me.

'Does he bite?' asked the ghost, watching me with all the empty care of nothingness trying to be something.

'SHE'S DEAD—SHE'S DEAD!'

'Stop barking!' said my Person. 'Don't be frightened. He wouldn't hurt a fly. Do you come here often?'

'Every day,' murmured the ghost, with a sly look towards her bones. She moved a little nearer to my Person. A breeze sprang up, and I could smell it blowing right through her, like frozen flowers. 'He looks very fierce,' said the ghost. 'Are you sure that he's kind?'

'COME AWAY—COME AWAY!'

'Stop barking!' commanded my Person, and looked at the ghost with springtime in his eyes. If only he could have smelled the dust inside her head, and heard the silence inside her breast! But it was no good. All he could see was a silken smile. He was only a person, and blindly trusted his eyes . . .

'Dogs', said the ghost, 'should be kept on a lead in the churchyard. There's a notice on the gate.' She knew that I knew where she was buried, and that I'd just been going to dig up her bones.

My Person obeyed; and the ghost looked at me as if to say, 'Now you'll never be able to show him that I'm dead!'

'SHE'S COLD! SHE'S EMPTY! SHE'S GRANDDAUGHTER DEATH!'

'Stop barking!' shouted my Person, and, dragging me after, walked on, already half in love with the loveless ghost.

We passed very close to her bones. I could smell them, and I could hear the little nibblers dryly rustling. I pulled, I strained, I jerked to dig up her secret . . .

'He looks so wild!' said the ghost. 'His eyes are rolling and his jaws are dripping. Are you sure he doesn't have a fever? Don't you think he ought to go to the vet?'

'He only wants to run off and play,' said my Person. 'Do you live near here?'

'YES! YES! RIGHT BY THAT MARBLE LAMPPOST! SIX PAWS DEEP IN THE EARTH!'

'Stop barking!' said my Person. 'Do you want to wake up the dead?'

The ghost started. Then she laughed, like the wind among rotting leaves. 'I have a room nearby,' she murmured. 'A little room all to myself. It is very convenient, you know.'

'A little room all to yourself?' repeated my Person, his heart beating with eager concern. 'How lonely that must be!'

'Yes,' she said. 'Sometimes it is very lonely in my little room, even though I hear people walking and talking upstairs, over my head.'

'Then let me walk back with you,' said my Person; 'and keep you company!'

'No dogs allowed,' said the ghost. 'They would turn me out, you know.'

'Then come my way!' said my Person; and the ghost raised her imitation eyebrows in imitation surprise. 'Madam will you walk,' sang my Person laughingly. 'Madam will you talk, Madam will you walk and talk with me?'

'I don't see why not,' smiled the ghost.

'BECAUSE SHE'S DEAD—DEAD—DEAD!'

'Stop barking!' said my Person. ' "I will give you the keys of Heaven, I will give you the keys of my heart . . ." '

'The keys of Heaven?' sighed the ghost. 'Would you really?'

'And the keys of my heart! Will you have dinner with me?'

'Are you inviting me into your home?'

'NO GHOSTS ALLOWED! SHE'LL TURN ME OUT!'

'Stop barking! Yes . . . if you'd like to!'

'Oh I would indeed—I would indeed!'

'DON'T DO IT! YOU'LL BE BRINGING DEATH INTO OUR HOME!'

'For God's sake, stop that barking! This way . . . this way . . .'

It was hopeless, hopeless! There was only one thing left for a dog to do. *She* knew what it was, of course: she could see it in my eyes. She walked on the other side of my Person, and always kept him between herself and me. I bided my time . . .

'Do you like Italian food?' asked my Person.

'Not spaghetti,' murmured the ghost. 'It reminds me of worms.'

It was then that I broke free. I jerked forward with all my strength and wrenched the lead from out of my Person's grasp. He shouted! The ghost glared and shrank away. For a moment I stared into her eyes, and she stared into mine.

'Dogs must be kept on a lead!' whispered the ghost as I jumped. 'There's a notice on . . . on . . . on . . .'

It was like jumping through cobwebs and feathers; and when I turned, she'd vanished like a puff of air. I saw the grass shiver, and I knew she'd gone back to her bones.

'SHE WAS DEAD! SHE WAS DEAD! I TOLD YOU SO!'

My Person didn't answer. He was shaking, he was trembling; for the very first time, he couldn't believe his eyes.

'What happened? Where—where is she? Where has she gone?'

I showed him. Trailing my lead, I went to where she lay, six paws under, and began to dig.

'No! No!' he shrieked. 'For God's sake, let her lie there in peace!'

Thankfully I stopped. The earth under the grass was thick and heavy, and the going was hard. I went back to my Person. He had collapsed on a bench and was holding his head in his hands. I tried to comfort him by licking his ear.

A female person walked neatly by. She was young and smooth and shining, and smelled of coffee and cats. She was dressed in the softest of white.

'Oh, what a beautiful dog,' she said, pausing to admire me.

He stared up at her. His eyes widened; his teeth began to chatter. He could not speak.

'GO ON! GO ON! "BEST OF BREED AT CRUFTS'S!"'

'Hush!' said the female person, reproaching me with a gentle smile. 'You'll wake up the dead!'

'Is she real?' whispered my Person, his eyes as wide and round as tins. 'Or is she a ghost? Show me, show me! Try to jump through her like you did before! Jump, jump!'

'BUT SHE'S REAL! SHE'S ALIVE!'

'Stop barking and jump!'

So I jumped. She screamed—but not in fright. She screamed with rage. My paws were still thick and filthy with churchyard mud, and, in a moment, so was her dress.

'You—you madman!' she shouted at my shamefaced Person. 'You told him to do it! You told him to jump! You're not fit to have a dog!'

'But—but—' he cried out as she stormed away, to report him, she promised, to the churchyard authorities and the RSPCA.

'I TOLD YOU SHE WAS ALIVE! I TOLD YOU SO!'

'Stop barking!' wept my Person. 'Please!'

RUSKIN BOND

Ghost Trouble

I

IT was Grandfather who finally decided that we would have to move to another house.

And it was all because of a Pret, a mischievous north-Indian ghost, who had been making life difficult for everyone.

Prets usually live in peepal trees, and that's where our little ghost first had his home—in the branches of a massive old peepal tree which had grown through the compound wall and spread into our garden. Part of the tree was on our side of the wall, part on the other side, shading the main road. It gave the ghost a good view of the whole area.

For many years the Pret had lived there quite happily, without bothering anyone in our house. It did not bother me, either, and I spent a lot of time in the peepal tree. Sometimes I went there to escape the adults at home, sometimes to watch the road and the people who passed by. The peepal tree was cool on a hot day, and the heart-shaped leaves were always revolving in the breeze. This constant movement of the leaves also helped to disguise the movements of the Pret, so that I never really knew exactly where he was sitting. But he paid no attention to me. The traffic on the road kept him fully occupied.

Sometimes, when a tonga was passing, he would jump down and frighten the pony, and as a result the little pony-cart would go rushing off in the wrong direction.

Sometimes he would get into the engine of a car or a bus, which would have a breakdown soon afterwards.

And he liked to knock the sun-helmets off the heads of sahibs or officials, who would wonder how a strong breeze had sprung up so suddenly, only to die down just as quickly. Although this special kind of ghost could make himself felt, and sometimes heard, he was invisible to the human eye.

I was not invisible to the human eye, and often got the blame for some of the Pret's pranks. If bicycle-riders were struck by mango seeds or apricot stones, they would look up, see a small boy in the branches of the tree, and threaten me with terrible consequences. Drivers who went off after parking their cars in the shade would sometimes come back to find their tyres flat. My protests of innocence did not carry much weight. But when I mentioned the Pret in the tree, they would look uneasy, either because they thought I must be mad, or because they were afraid of ghosts, especially Prets. They would find other things to do and hurry away.

At night no one walked beneath the peepal tree.

It was said that if you yawned beneath the tree, the Pret would jump down your throat and give you a pain. Our gardener, Chandu, who was always taking sick-leave, blamed the Pret for his tummy troubles. Once, when yawning, Chandu had forgotten to put his hand in front of his mouth, and the ghost had got in without any trouble.

Now Chandu spent most of his time lying on a string-bed in the courtyard of his small house. When Grandmother went to visit him, he would start groaning and holding his sides, the pain was so bad; but when she went away, he did not fuss so much. He claimed that the pain did not affect his appetite, and he ate a normal diet, in fact a little more than normal—the extra amount was meant to keep the ghost happy!

2

'Well, it isn't our fault,' said Grandfather, who had given permission to the Public Works Department to cut the tree, which had been on our land. They wanted to widen the road, and the tree and a bit of our wall were in the way. So both had to go.

Several people protested, including the Raja of Jinn, who lived across the road and who sometimes asked Grandfather over for a game of tennis.

'That peepal tree has been there for hundreds of years,' he said. 'Who are we to cut it down?'

'*We*,' said the Chief Engineer, 'are the P.W.D.'

And not even a ghost can prevail against the wishes of the Public Works Department.

They brought men with saws and axes, and first they lopped all the branches until the poor tree was quite naked. It must have been at this moment that the Pret moved out. Then they sawed away at the trunk until, finally, the great old peepal came crashing down on the road, bringing down the telephone wires and an electric pole in the process, and knocking a large gap in the Raja's garden wall.

It took them three days to clear the road, and during that time the Chief Engineer swallowed a lot of dust and tree-pollen. For months afterwards he complained of a choking feeling, although no doctor could ever find anything in his throat.

'It's the Pret's doing,' said the Raja knowingly. 'They should never have cut that tree.'

Deprived of his tree, the Pret decided that he would live in our house.

I first became aware of his presence when I was sitting on the verandah steps, reading a book. A tiny chuckling sound came from behind me. I looked round, but no one was to be seen. When I returned to my book, the chuckling started again. I paid no attention. Then a shower of rose petals fell softly on to the pages of my open book. The Pret wanted me to know he was there!

'All right,' I said. 'So you've come to stay with us. Now let me read.'

He went away then; but as a good Pret has to be bad in order to justify his existence, it was not long before he was up to all sorts of mischief.

He began by hiding Grandmother's spectacles.

'I'm sure I put them down on the dining-table,' she grumbled.

A little later they were found balanced on the snout of a wild boar, whose stuffed and mounted head adorned the verandah wall, a memento of Grandfather's hunting trips when he was young.

Naturally, I was at first blamed for this prank. But a day or two later, when the spectacles disappeared again, only to be found dangling from the bars of the parrot's cage, it was agreed that I was not to blame; for the parrot had once bitten off a piece of my finger, and I did not go near it any more.

The parrot was hanging upside down, trying to peer through one of the lenses. I don't know if they improved his vision, but what he saw certainly made him angry, because the pupils of his eyes went very small and he dug his beak into the spectacle frames, leaving them with a permanent dent. I caught them just before they fell to the floor.

But even without the help of the spectacles, it seemed that our parrot could see the Pret. He would keep turning this way and that, lunging out at unseen fingers, and protecting his tail from the tweaks of invisible hands. He had always refused to learn to talk, but now he became quite voluble and began to chatter in some unknown tongue, often screaming with rage and rolling his eyes in a frenzy.

'We'll have to give that parrot away,' said Grandmother. 'He gets more bad-tempered by the day.'

Grandfather was the next to be troubled.

He went into the garden one morning to find all his prize sweet-peas broken off and lying on the grass. Chandu thought the sparrows had destroyed the flowers, but we didn't think the birds could have finished off every single bloom just before sunrise.

'It must be the Pret,' said Grandfather, and I agreed.

The Pret did not trouble me much, because he remembered me from his peepal-tree days and knew I resented the tree being cut as much as he did. But he liked to catch my attention, and he did this by chuckling and squeaking near me when I was alone, or whispering in my ear when I was with someone else. Gradually I began to make out the occasional word. He had started learning English!

3

Uncle Benji, who came to stay with us for long periods when he had little else to do (which was most of the time), was soon to suffer.

He was a heavy sleeper, and once he'd gone to bed he hated being woken up. So when he came to breakfast looking bleary-eyed and miserable, we asked him if he was feeling all right.

'I couldn't sleep a wink last night,' he complained. 'Whenever I was about to fall asleep, the bedclothes would be pulled off the bed. I had to get up at least a dozen times to pick them off the floor.' He stared suspiciously at me. 'Where were *you* sleeping last night, young man?'

'In Grandfather's room,' I said. 'I've lent you *my* room.'

'It's that ghost from the peepal tree,' said Grandmother with a sigh.

'Ghost!' exclaimed Uncle Benji. 'I didn't know the house was haunted.'

'It is now,' said Grandmother. 'First my spectacles, then the sweet-peas, and now Benji's bedclothes! What will it be up to next, I wonder?'

We did not have to wonder for long.

There followed a series of minor disasters. Vases fell off tables, pictures fell from walls. Parrot feathers turned up in the teapot, while the parrot himself let out indignant squawks and swear-words in the middle of the night. Windows which had been closed would be found open, and open windows closed.

Finally, Uncle Benji found a crow's nest in his bed, and on tossing it out of the window was attacked by two crows.

Then Aunt Ruby came to stay, and things quietened down for a time.

Did Aunt Ruby's powerful personality have an effect on the Pret, or was he just sizing her up?

'I think the Pret has taken a fancy to your aunt,' said Grandfather mischievously. 'He's behaving himself for a change.'

This may have been true, because the parrot, who had picked up some of the English words being tried out by the Pret, now called out, 'Kiss, kiss,' whenever Aunt Ruby was in the room.

'What a charming bird,' said Aunt Ruby.

'You can keep him if you like,' said Grandmother.

One day Aunt Ruby came in to the house covered in rose petals.

'I don't know where they came from,' she exclaimed. 'I was sitting in the garden, drying my hair, when handfuls of petals came showering down on me!'

'It likes you,' said Grandfather.

'What likes me?'

'The ghost.'

'What ghost?'

'The Pret. It came to live in the house when the peepal tree was cut down.'

'What nonsense!' said Aunt Ruby.

'Kiss, kiss!' screamed the parrot.

'There aren't any ghosts, Prets or other kinds,' said Aunt Ruby firmly.

'Kiss, kiss!' screeched the parrot again. Or was it the parrot? The sound seemed to be coming from the ceiling.

'I wish that parrot would shut up.'

'It isn't the parrot,' I said. 'It's the Pret.'

Aunt Ruby gave me a cuff over the ear and stormed out of the room.

But she had offended the Pret. From being her admirer, he turned into her enemy. Somehow her toothpaste got switched with a tube of Grandfather's shaving-cream. When she appeared in the dining-room, foaming at the mouth, we ran for our lives, Uncle Benji shouting that she'd got rabies.

4

Two days later Aunt Ruby complained that she had been struck on the nose by a grapefruit, which had leapt mysteriously from the pantry shelf and hurled itself at her.

'If Ruby and Benji stay here much longer, they'll both have nervous breakdowns,' said Grandfather thoughtfully.

'I thought they broke down long ago,' I said.

'None of your cheek,' snapped Aunt Ruby.

'He's in league with that Pret to try and get us out of here,' said Uncle Benji.

'Don't listen to him—you can stay as long as you like,' said Grandmother, who never turned away any of her numerous nephews, nieces, cousins or distant relatives.

The Pret, however, did not feel so hospitable, and the persecution of Aunt Ruby continued.

'When I looked in the mirror this morning,' she complained bitterly, 'I saw a little monster, with huge ears, bulging eyes, flaring nostrils and a toothless grin!'

'You don't look *that* bad, Aunt Ruby,' I said, trying to be nice.

'It was either you or that imp you call a Pret,' said Aunt Ruby. 'And if it's a ghost, then it's time we all moved to another house.'

Uncle Benji had another idea.

'Let's drive the ghost out,' he said. 'I know a Sadhu who rids houses of evil spirits.'

'But the Pret's not evil,' I said. 'Just mischievous.'

Uncle Benji went off to the bazaar and came back a few hours later with a mysterious long-haired man who claimed to be a Sadhu—one who has given up all worldly goods, including most of his clothes.

He prowled about the house, and lighted incense in all the rooms, despite squawks of protest from the parrot. All the time he chanted various magic spells. He then collected a fee of thirty rupees, and promised that we would not be bothered again by the Pret.

As he was leaving, he was suddenly blessed with a shower—no, it was really a downpour—of dead flowers, decaying leaves, orange peel and banana skins. All spells forgotten, he ran to the gate and made for the safety of the bazaar.

Aunt Ruby declared that it had become impossible to sleep at night because of the devilish chuckling that came from beneath her pillow. She packed her bags and left.

Uncle Benji stayed on. He was still having trouble with his bedclothes, and he was beginning to talk to himself, which was a bad sign.

'Talking to the Pret, Uncle?' I asked innocently, when I caught him at it one day.

He gave me a threatening look. 'What did you say?' he demanded. 'Would you mind repeating that?'

I thought it safer to please him. 'Oh, didn't you hear me?' I said, '*Teaching the parrot, Uncle?*'

He glared at me, then walked off in a huff. If he did not leave it was because he was hoping Grandmother would lend him enough money to buy a motorcycle; but Grandmother said he ought to try earning a living first.

One day I found him on the drawing-room sofa, laughing like a madman. Even the parrot was so alarmed that it was silent, head lowered and curious. Uncle Benji was red in the face—literally red all over!

'What happened to your face, Uncle?' I asked.

He stopped laughing and gave me a long hard look. I realized that there had been no joy in his laughter.

'Who painted the wash-basin red without telling me?' he asked in a quavering voice.

As Uncle Benji looked really dangerous, I ran from the room.

'We'll have to move, I suppose,' said Grandfather later. 'Even if it's only for a couple of months. I'm worried about Benji. I've told him that I painted the wash-basin myself but forgot to tell him. He doesn't believe me. He thinks it's the Pret or the boy, or both of them! Benji needs a change. So do we. There's my brother's house at the other end of the town. He won't be using it for a few months. We'll move in next week.'

And so, a few days and several disasters later, we began moving house.

5

Two bullock-carts laden with furniture and heavy luggage were sent ahead. Uncle Benji went with them. The roof of our old car was piled high with bags and kitchen utensils. Grandfather took the wheel, I sat beside him, and Granny sat in state at the back.

We set off and had gone some way down the main road when Grandfather started having trouble with the steering-wheel. It appeared to have got loose, and the car began veering about on the road, scattering cyclists, pedestrians, and stray dogs, pigs and hens. A cow refused to move, but we missed it somehow, and then suddenly we were off the road and making for a low wall. Grandfather pressed his foot down on the brake, but we only went faster. 'Watch out!' he shouted.

It was the Raja of Jinn's garden wall, made of single bricks, and the car knocked it down quite easily and went on through it, coming to a stop on the Raja's lawn.

'Now look what you've done,' said Grandmother.

'Well, we missed the flower-beds,' said Grandfather.

'Someone's been tinkering with the car. Our Pret, no doubt.'

The Raja and two attendants came running towards us.

The Raja was a perfect gentleman, and when he saw that the driver was Grandfather, he beamed with pleasure.

'Delighted to see you, old chap!' he exclaimed. 'Jolly decent of you to drop in. How about a game of tennis?'

'Sorry to have come in through the wall,' apologized Grandfather.

'Don't mention it, old chap. The gate was closed, so what else could you do?'

Grandfather was as much of a gentleman as the Raja, so he thought it only fair to join him in a game of tennis. Grandmother and I watched and drank lemonade. After the game, the Raja waved us goodbye and we drove back through the hole in the wall and out on to the road. There was nothing much wrong with the car.

We hadn't gone far when we heard a peculiar sound, as of someone chuckling and talking to himself. It came from the roof of the car.

'Is the parrot out there on the luggage-rack?' asked Grandfather.

'No,' said Grandmother. 'He went ahead with Uncle Benji.'

Grandfather stopped the car, got out, and examined the roof.

'Nothing up there,' he said, getting in again and starting the engine. 'I thought I heard the parrot.'

When we had gone a little further, the chuckling started again. A squeaky little voice began talking in English in the tones of the parrot.

'It's the Pret,' whispered Grandmother. 'What is he saying?'

The Pret's squeak grew louder. 'Come on, come on!' he cried gleefully. 'A new house! The same old friends! What fun we're going to have!'

Grandfather stopped the car. He backed into a driveway, turned round, and began driving back to our old house.

'What are you doing?' asked Grandmother.

'Going home,' said Grandfather.

'And what about the Pret?'

'What about him? He's decided to live with us, so we'll have to make the best of it. You can't solve a problem by running away from it.'

'All right,' said Grandmother. 'But what will we do about Benji?'

'It's up to him, isn't it? He'll be all right if he finds something to do.'

Grandfather stopped the car in front of the verandah steps.

'I'm hungry,' I said.

'It will have to be a picnic lunch,' said Grandmother. 'Almost every-thing was sent off on the bullock-carts.'

As we got out of the car and climbed the verandah steps, we were greeted by showers of rose petals and sweet-scented jasmine.

'How lovely!' exclaimed Grandmother, smiling. 'I think he likes us, after all.'

PAUL YEE

Spirits of the Railway

ONE summer many, many years ago, heavy floodwaters suddenly swept through south China again. Farmer Chu and his family fled to high ground and wept as the rising river drowned their rice crops, their chickens and their water buffalo.

With their food and farm gone, Farmer Chu went to town to look for work. But a thousand other starving peasants were already there. So when he heard there was work across the ocean in the New World, he borrowed some money, bought a ticket, and off he sailed.

Long months passed as his family waited to hear from him. Farmer Chu's wife fell ill from worry and weariness. From her hard board bed she called out her husband's name over and over, until at last her eldest son borrowed money to cross the Pacific in search of his father.

For two months, young Chu listened to waves batter the groaning planks of the ship as it crossed the ocean. For two months he dreaded that he might drown at any minute. For two months he thought of nothing but his father and his family.

Finally he arrived in a busy port city. He asked everywhere for his father, but no one in Chinatown had heard the name. There were thousands of Chinese flung throughout the New World, he was told. Gold miners scrabbled along icy rivers, farmers ploughed the long low valleys, and laborers traveled through towns and forests, from job to job. Who could find one single man in this enormous wilderness?

Young Chu was soon penniless. But he was young and strong, and he feared neither danger nor hard labor. He joined a work gang of thirty Chinese, and a steamer ferried them up a river canyon to build the railway.

When the morning mist lifted, Chu's mouth fell open. On both sides of the rushing river, gray mountains rose like walls to block the sky. The rock face dropped into ragged cliffs that only eagles could ascend and jutted out from cracks where scrawny trees clung. Never before had he seen such towering ranges of dark raw rock.

The crew pitched their tents and began to work. They hacked at hills with hand-scoops and shovels to level a pathway for the train. Their hammers and chisels chipped boulders into gravel and fill. Their dynamite and drills thrust tunnels deep into the mountain. At night, the crew would sit around the campfire chewing tobacco, playing cards and talking.

From one camp to another, the men trekked up the rail line, their food and tools dangling from sturdy shoulder poles. When they met other workers, Chu would run ahead and shout his father's name and ask for news. But the workers just shook their heads grimly.

'Search no more, young man!' one grizzled old worker said. 'Don't you know that too many have died here? My own brother was buried alive in a mudslide.'

'My uncle was killed in a dynamite blast,' muttered another. 'No one warned him about the fuse.'

The angry memories rose and swirled like smoke among the workers.

'The white boss treats us like mules and dogs!'

'They need a railway to tie this nation together, but they can't afford to pay decent wages.'

'What kind of country is this?'

Chu listened, but still he felt certain that his father was alive.

Then winter came and halted all work. Snows buried everything under a heavy blanket of white. The white boss went to town to live in a warm hotel, but Chu and the workers stayed in camp. The men tied potato sacks around their feet and huddled by the fire, while ice storms howled like wolves through the mountains. Chu thought the winter would never end.

When spring finally arrived, the survivors struggled outside and shook the chill from their bones. They dug graves for two workers who had succumbed to sickness. They watched the river surge alive from the melting snow. Work resumed, and Chu began to search again for his father.

Late one afternoon, the gang reached a mountain with a half-finished tunnel. As usual, Chu ran up to shout his father's name, but before he could say a word, other workers came running out of the tunnel.

'It's haunted!' they cried. 'Watch out! There are ghosts inside!'

'Dark figures slide soundlessly through the rocks!' one man whispered. 'We hear heavy footsteps approaching but never arriving. We hear sighs and groans coming from corners where no man stands.'

Chu's friends dropped their packs and refused to set up camp. But the white boss rode up on his horse and shook his fist at the men. 'No work, no pay!' he shouted. 'Now get to work!'

Then he galloped off. The workers squatted on the rocks and looked helplessly at one another. They needed the money badly for food and supplies.

Chu stood up. 'What is there to fear?' he cried. 'The ghosts have no reason to harm us. There is no reason to be afraid. We have hurt no one.'

'Do you want to die?' a man called out.

'I will spend the night inside the tunnel,' Chu declared as the men muttered unbelievingly. 'Tomorrow we can work.'

Chu took his bedroll, a lamp, and food and marched into the mountain. He heard the crunch of his boots and water dripping. He knelt to light his lamp. Rocks lay in loose piles everywhere, and the shadowy walls closed in on him.

At the end of the tunnel he sat down and ate his food. He closed his eyes and wondered where his father was. He pictured his mother weeping in her bed and heard her voice calling his father's name. He lay down, pulled his blankets close, and eventually he fell asleep.

Chu awoke gasping for breath. Something heavy was pressing down on his chest. He tried to raise his arms but could not. He clenched his fists and summoned all his strength, but still he was paralyzed. His eyes strained into the darkness, but saw nothing.

Suddenly the pressure eased and Chu groped for the lamp. As the chamber sprang into light, he cried, 'What do you want? Who are you?'

Silence greeted him, and then a murmur sounded from behind. Chu spun around and saw a figure in the shadows. He slowly raised the lamp. The flickering light traveled up blood-stained trousers and a mud-encrusted jacket. Then Chu saw his father's face.

'Papa!' he whispered, lunging forward.

'No! Do not come closer!' The figure stopped him. 'I am not of your world. Do not embrace me.'

Tears rose in Chu's eyes. 'So, it's true,' he choked. 'You . . . you have left us . . .'

His father's voice quivered with rage. 'I am gone, but I am not done yet. My son, an accident here killed many men. A fuse exploded before the workers could run. A ton of rock dropped on us and crushed us flat. They buried the whites in a churchyard, but our bodies were thrown into the river, where the current swept us away. We have no final resting place.'

Chu fell upon his knees. 'What shall I do?'

His father's words filled the tunnel. 'Take chopsticks; they shall be our bones. Take straw matting; that can be our flesh. Wrap them together and tie them tightly. Take the bundles to the mountain top high above the nests of eagles, and cover us with soil. Pour tea over our beds. Then we shall sleep in peace.'

When Chu looked up, his father had vanished. He stumbled out of the tunnel and blurted the story to his friends. Immediately they prepared the bundles and sent him off with ropes and a shovel to the foot of the cliff, and Chu began to climb.

When he swung himself over the top of the cliff, he was so high up that he thought he could see the distant ocean. He dug the graves deeper than any wild animal could dig, and laid the bundles gently in the earth.

Then Chu brought his fists together above his head and bowed three times. He knelt and touched his forehead to the soil three times. In a loud clear voice he declared, 'Three times I bow, three things I vow. Your pain shall stop now, your sleep shall soothe you now, and I will never forget you. Farewell.'

Then, hanging onto the rope looped around a tree, Chu slid slowly back down the cliff. When he reached the bottom, he looked back and saw that the rope had turned into a giant snake that was sliding smoothly up the rock face.

'Good,' he smiled to himself. 'It will guard the graves well.' Then he returned to the camp, where he and his fellow workers lit their lamps and headed into the tunnel. And spirits never again disturbed them, nor the long trains that came later.

BARBARA GRIFFITHS

Many Happy Returns!

THE man had a nail through his head—it was a long one which went in one side, and came out the other. Apart from this, he was quite ordinary, in a baggy grey suit lightly sprinkled with dandruff and cigarette ash.

'Do come in, my dear. You're letting in the flies,' he said.

The boy held up a bright parcel. 'I've brought this for Mark.' He was on his best behaviour, and that did not include screaming and running down the garden path.

'You'd better go and find him, then, hadn't you? And is your lovely mummy coming in?' He smirked over the boy's head.

'I'll pop in for a minute, just to say hello,' said Sally.

With a courtly bow and a flourish of the hand, the entertainer ushered them into the hall.

'Hi there, Jan,' called Sally, squeezing past him.

'I'm in the kitchen,' came the reply.

The doorbell rang and the boy watched the magician go to answer it. He could see now that the nail was actually in two pieces, joined by a piece of plastic which curved around the head. He decided that the purpose of the nail was to secure a wide mat of hair which stretched from one ear to the other, and to divert attention from it. He wondered why anyone would weave such a structure.

'Don't stare. It's rude,' whispered Sally, and carried on with her conversation.

'Mr Smarty-pants? I don't think I've heard of him. Who was he recommended by?'

'Well, no one, I'm afraid,' Jan said. 'The agency says it's always murder in June; we were lucky to get anyone at all. I do hope he'll be O.K.'

'Of course he will. Of *course* he will. Cheer up, it's only once a year. Right then, I'll be off.'

'Oh,' said Jan. 'Wouldn't you like to stay for a bit?'

'What's the matter?'

'Well . . . Mark wanted the whole class, that's thirty kids. I don't even know half of them! And that old fellow doesn't really look up to it.'

'And you could do with some moral support? Say no more. I'll help you take those jellies through.'

By the time they had laid the table, the house was popping with children.

'There can't possibly be any more, can there?' said Sally.

'I do hope not. Lord, there's the bell again. I'll get it.'

On the step, all alone, stood a little boy. He was thoughtfully picking his nose.

'Where's your mum?' asked Jan.

'I always come on my own. I'm Neville.'

'You'd better come in, then,' said Jan, noticing that he hadn't brought a present, and that his nails were the dirtiest she'd ever seen. 'The others are all in the dining room waiting for the magic to begin. This way.'

The children were sitting on the floor by the open French windows. Against one wall, the entertainer was laying out entrancing cloths and boxes, the tricks of his trade, and against the other wall was a table of crisps and jellies, and sweets and cake . . .

'Mum!' called Mark. 'That strange boy, he's . . .'

'Candles!' she cried. 'Hang on a minute.' When she'd fetched them she couldn't resist lingering in the doorway to enjoy the scene. She felt utter satisfaction. It was the sort of moment, she thought, one remembers when they are grown; the children all so prettily dressed, their little faces bright with excitement and expectation, their chatter mingling with the summer sounds of bees and a distant lawn-mower . . . and was that the tinkle of a fountain? She looked over their heads and down the garden.

'Neville!' she screeched. 'Stop that at once! NOT in the sand-pit, if you please!'

The entertainer cleared his throat.

'Are we sitting comfortably?' he said, wearily raising his hands to quiet them. 'Then I shall begin. Who'd like to choose a card?' His voice swelled to drown the yelps of those with fingers crushed by Neville on his ruthless way to the front.

'It's a three of hearts,' said Neville.

'You peeped!' said another child.

'No I didn't. Bet you anything the whole pack is threes of hearts.'

'Shhh!' said Jan. The entertainer grimly carried on with the trick.

'Boys and girls, you will never guess what this card is?'

'The three of hearts,' they shouted in unison, and giggled.

'Quiet, please, do let's have a bit of hush,' implored Jan. The entertainer started taking coloured scarves from a box.

'I am about to perform a most peculiated and compuliar trick,' he said, wafting them through the air. 'Can you guess what I shall do with these pretty things?'

The children all looked at Neville.

'Wot, no bog paper?' enquired Neville, politely.

'I shall eat them,' said Mr Smarty-pants, addressing a little girl at the furthest point from Neville. He scrumpled them up and put them into his mouth. When he pulled them out again, lo and behold, they were all tied end to end in a rope. There was an impressed gasp; then they turned to look at Neville.

''E's got them up 'is sleeve. Look, up 'is left arm.'

Next came the disappearing rabbit trick. The children, who had been getting raucous, calmed down a little. They liked the rabbit.

'It doesn't really disappear, you know,' chipped in Neville. 'It's in a compartment at the back of the box.'

'Did you ever wonder,' said the entertainer, slowly and clearly, 'why you were given a name with the word "vile" in it?'

'What *we* was wondering,' replied Neville, 'is how you got the name "Smarty-pants" when you're not in the least bit smart.'

He began to chant, 'Smarty-pants, Smarty-pants, Smarty-pants . . .' only instead of the word 'Smarty', he used a word that rhymed with it. The children howled with laughter and joined in.

'That is enough!' cried Jan. 'Neville, please go and wait in the kitchen until teatime. I don't like to get cross at parties, but when poor Mr Far . . . I mean, Smarty-pants has been so kind as to come and entertain us . . .'

'Dear lady, do not concern yourself. My fee is your freedom, just sit back and enjoy the show.'

He stretched out his arms dramatically.

'Do you all know what an illusion is? Now you see it, now you don't? Good. Girls and boys, ladies, I shall now perform the greatest illusion the world has ever seen. Would the troublesome young gentleman care to assist?'

Neville stood up and sauntered towards the magician. A hush fell. The boy grinned over his shoulder, then said challengingly, 'Yeah? Go on, then.'

'First I shall need three chairs,' said Mr Smarty-pants.

Jan and Sally passed them to him. He arranged them so that two were facing each other, and one was sideways in the middle.

'Lie down, young fellow-me-lad.'

Neville lay along the chairs, his feet sticking through the bars. He turned his face to the audience, crossed his eyes and stuck out his tongue.

'I think we could well do without the sight of your charming features,' said the magician. He placed a pole across the tops of the chairs on the audience side, and flung a cloth over it so that it hung down to form a curtain. A fine cloth, it was, made of purple velvet with gold tassels all around—an odd contrast to the dirty boots sticking out.

'Now!' he said, reaching into his bag. 'What have we here?'

The children sat up eagerly.

'We have a rare and precious sword, a golden sword, which was used over many centuries by the Kings of Persia for executions. Can you all see?'

He held it at arm's length, moving it slowly from side to side. It glittered fiercely in the sunlight.

'And it's very sharp. You see this sausage?' He leaned over and took one from the table. 'Hold this, little girl. No, stick your arm out. That's the ticket.'

He swung the sword in a great arc that ripped the air with a hiss; half a sausage toppled, like a severed finger, on to the child's satin party frock. She began to sob, and Jan pulled her up on her knee for a cuddle.

'Oh dear,' she whispered to Sally, 'do you think this is safe?'

'Of course it is. He's a professional, isn't he? They have to belong to a magic circle, or something.'

'Hush, ladies,' he reproached them. 'To continue; when I give the signal, I want you all to say the magic words:

> *The sky is blue, but blood is red.*
> *Magic sword chop off his head!*

'Have you all got that?'

'Yes!' they shouted exultantly. 'Easy cheesy.'

'Right then. All together now.'

The windows rattled as thirty children bellowed the rhyme. Slowly, majestically, the entertainer lifted the sword higher and higher. He seemed to swell, to grow in stature, filling the room with his presence, like a priest in some demonic rite. The sword was nearly touching the ceiling . . . then it flashed down. There was a slight 'snick'. The muddy boots twitched violently, and fell slack. From under the cloth, a slim white forearm slipped towards the floor until the hand rested on the carpet, the fingers curving gracefully upwards. A dark liquid trickled down the chair-leg, the stain spreading evenly across the carpet.

The audience gasped. The mothers, after a moment, turned to each other. Jan pushed her fist against her mouth. She was shaking.

'Calm down, don't panic,' whispered Sally. 'We must get the children into the garden. You get them out, and I'll pull the curtains.'

'Oh, Christ!'

'Pull yourself together. Come on, quickly; they might not realize.'

A child screamed. 'Look, look, it's blood!' Another screamed, and another.

Sally was shouting, 'Just a little scratch, nothing to worry about. Come along now, we'll have some nice games on the lawn.'

She was pushing them frantically through the doors. At first they stuck, stupid as sheep, then they stampeded. She turned back to pull the curtains. The magician was slumped in an armchair. He was patting his pockets and frowning. He stuck his hand in a jacket pocket and pulled out a mouse, which he looked at vaguely, then put on the carpet. Poking around in the pocket again he produced a cigarette which he lit, lying back in the chair. The mouse scuttled across the room and climbed up on to the table; it picked up a crisp, and began to nibble delicately. It had left red footprints on the white tablecloth.

Sally swallowed hard. She dragged the curtains across and stepped out, closing the doors. The children were all waiting, pressed up against the fence at the bottom of the garden. Jan gripped her arm.

'What shall I tell his mother?' she kept saying.

'You're hurting me,' said Sally. 'For God's sake, stop being so hysterical. The mothers will be here in a minute. You've got to look after the children while I phone for an ambulance. Not that there's much point. Oh, and I'd better call the police, too, I suppose.'

'But, how shall I tell the poor little boy's mother? It's too dreadful, I just can't do it.'

'Don't worry, the police'll see to that. Now, get a hold on yourself. I'm going back in there.'

It took all her courage to force herself to go through the doors. She pulled the curtains apart and stepped inside.

As her eyes grew used to the darkened room, Sally saw that the entertainer was packing away his things. The chairs on which the boy had lain were lined up against the wall.

'What have you done with him?' she demanded. 'Where's the boy? I warn you, I'm going to phone the police.'

'He always comes,' said the magician. 'Nasty little so-and-so. Makes my life a misery.'

'But you *killed* him. He was just a child!'

'Oh, that was years ago. About twenty, I'd say. And it really was an accident, I promise you. But the little blighter won't let me alone. Perhaps he's waiting for me to improve, so he can't guess the tricks. Ha!' He stubbed out the cigarette in some jelly, which fizzed.

'Are you telling me . . . are you saying that he's a ghost?' she asked, hesitantly.

'That's right. Well, sweetie, you couldn't get stains like that off a carpet, could you?'

She looked at the carpet, at the tablecloth; they were spotless.

'There is one thing I'll say, though,' he said, smiling roguishly and adjusting the nail. 'You must admit it was a corking good illusion!'

ROBERT WESTALL

The Beach

ALAN remembered reading an old story once—perhaps by Erskine Childers—about the Germans invading England on an August Bank Holiday Monday. Because everything was shut down, and everyone flopped-out in a heatwave, the Germans had a walkover.

Their ideal landing-beach, thought Alan bitterly, would have been Southwold, Suffolk. Where his family came every year for a holiday.

There was something terribly wrong with Southwold. Instead of arriving all weary, and leaving set up for the winter, you arrived all bouncy, full of ideas, and left feeling like death warmed up.

Every year they loaded up the Volvo for the Great Adventure, with tennis-rackets, binoculars, Dad's latest model sailing-boat, guide-books to churches and pamphlets about what's-on-in-Suffolk.

And every year, by the end of a fortnight, Suffolk had defeated them.

Tennis was fun at first. Dad's great booming erratic service that hit the net with an impressive thwack more often than it went in. Mum luring Dad to the net, then lobbing him into screaming frustration. Even the fact that Anita gave a hideous shriek every time she missed, and fell on her bum every second time she hit the ball. Hilarious!

But nobody else ever came to that tennis-club. Every time you paid the lady at number seven and got the keys, you found the same footprints on the gravel court that you'd left yesterday.

And no matter how fast Dad's new yacht sailed, there was nothing you could do with it but sail it from side to side of the yacht-pond, and after an hour it was totally boring.

And after the second one, all the great Suffolk wool-churches looked the same. They all had wonderful roofs, brasses to rub, alabaster monuments gathering dead flies.

And you could have enough of morris men, brass bands and village shows.

You always ended up doing the gift-and-card shops. When Mum started doing her cards and gathering her gifts, you might as well be back home already. Because you knew the Great Adventure wasn't going to happen again this year. And every heatwave morning, as the sun climbed, you felt wearier. And in the end you just dragged yourselves down to the beach-hut, for the day.

That was the point when the sea-mist always seemed to start. The sea had been quite exciting before that, because there was an oil-rig on the horizon, and boats passing. Coasters going up to Yarmouth, and fishing-smacks with strange registration-letters, that might have belonged to Lowestoft, and mysterious grey ships that just might have been Russian spy-trawlers. And a yellow power-boat, vaulting across the waves. And Dad's binoculars were snatched from hand to hand, and violent arguments broke out, if only on the topic of was that or wasn't it a lesser black-backed gull.

But once the mist came down, there was nothing to see at all. Except mist. It seemed to hang about thirty yards off-shore, like a grey theatre-curtain that was never going to go up again. No matter how hot the day, the grey curtain hung there and, by three o'clock, your skin started getting damp with it. Alan grew furious that the sun didn't drive it away. But Mr Burleigh, the man who hired out deckchairs and was the sage everyone turned to when baffled, said that the sun *made* the mist. On cold days, the horizon was quite clear . . .

So there you sat, with the sea-wall behind you, and the mist in front. What made it worse was the breakwaters that ran down the beach every thirty yards. They reduced the long sweep of beach to little separate rooms, with floors of sloping shingle. And the same people seemed to gather in the same room every day. Just sitting there, in long rows of deckchairs against the breakwaters. Gossiping, quarrelling, falling asleep, waking up to ask what about an ice-cream or a cup of tea, or were there any sandwiches left? But mainly asleep; under newspapers, or with heads tilted on one side and their mouths open. For God's sake, why did they come here to *sleep*—when they could sleep at home for nothing? Didn't they know time was passing? That there was only a short run to Christmas and then it would be 1990 and they would be another year older, another year nearer to that old man in the end deckchair whose hands shook non-stop so that anything he did took ten minutes, even eating a sandwich?

Alan felt sometimes, especially towards the end of an afternoon, like suddenly leaping to his feet and shouting at them all, like an Old Testament prophet forecasting the end of the world.

But he didn't, of course. He would pad off in his striped orange-and-blue bathing trunks in search of the *real* instead.

Real inside the amusement-arcade. Spotty youths shoving in money like there was no tomorrow, pulling the chrome handles without a clue, just to impress the stupid girls who hung on their elbows. If you watched any particular fruit-machine long enough, you could guess when it was coming up to dropping a jackpot. Then you could drift up to the couple working it and stare rudely, 'til they got uncomfortable and moved on. Then, after three or four goes, you got the jackpot yourself; a shower of coins spilling over onto the dirty floor, among the flattened fag-ends.

But it was a dark, miserable kind of reality, that made Alan feel dirty himself afterwards.

Better to stroll along the prom and watch the bodies of the girls, walking along in their bikinis. Brown and rounded, exciting. Like the bunches of grapes hanging among the boring dusty leaves of the vine-yards in France. Single girls with fellers; bunches of girls laughing on their own.

He never tried to chat them up. He wasn't interested in their minds, which were just full of giggles, or what Bet Lynch had said in the last episode of the Street. Their minds were just an extension of the Great Dreary Desert. But their bodies were a promise of something better, that never seemed to happen. Yet the promise was nearly as good as a feast.

Sometimes, up on the prom, he'd come across newspaper placards, proof that there was life outside Southwold. But even they seemed to shrink in scope as the heatwave rolled on. From 'Gorbachov sacks party bosses' and 'New threat by Ayatollah' to 'Outbreak of foot and mouth' and 'Bather drowned'.

His other great source of the real was the sea. Just watching the waves break soothed him; letting his mind fill with their roar and rattling ebb. Like the beating of some gigantic heart. But the best was to wade out into them 'til you were up to your neck, giving little upward hops to keep your mouth clear of the wave-tops as they passed. Then to lie back and let the waves lift you; feel each one as it coursed through your body from your heels to your head. Letting your flesh become part of the wave, letting the sea have its way with you. Helpless. Very relaxing. Sometimes he fell asleep, floating, and only wakened when the waves had spun him round to face the sun, and the sunbeams forced their way in through foam-speckled eyelids.

He came back from one such trip to find his whole family asleep. Mum looked pretty cool, with her mouth shut and her big mirror-sunglasses on, and her neat plump body very brown with just a hint of red in it, and the latest Iris Murdoch paperback 'The Book and the Brotherhood' lying open face-down across her chest. Alan thought she looked so cool some passing bloke might have picked her up, if Dad hadn't been there.

But Dad was there, sprawled like a disaster-area. Anita had piled sand all over him, and he hadn't even stirred. A hairy man was Dad; beard and hairy chest, all full of drying sand. Mouth open, snoring, and all his fillings showing. Make a good book-jacket for a Stephen King chiller. The Southwold Horror.

Anita was asleep, face down in a sandy copy of 'Jackie'. Open at the problem page, but the creeping sand was erasing the problems, as it had once erased the Pharaohs.

Them all being asleep made him feel desperately cut-off; as if they'd gone off into the land of dreams and left him abandoned forever. He had a selfish panicky desire to shout or bump into their deckchairs, or trample on them by accident, just to wake them up, make sure they were really still there. But people got so mad with you, when you did that. So he just bent and looked at Mum's watch on her wrist. Only half past three. God, two hours before there was any chance of going back to the digs to get ready for supper. He lay down on the sand feeling quite hopeless. The people next door seemed to be asleep as well, but they'd left their tranny on. Broadcasting the Final Test; running down to a hopeless draw on a dying battery. The commentator was talking so slowly he sounded like he was falling asleep as well. Alan had a sudden feeling that the whole world was just running-down, like a clockwork toy that God had forgotten to wind up. The world needed *energy* to drive it, and the heatwave had sucked all the energy away.

He squinted down the beach, with his right eye as it lay against the sand; making the nearby pebbles look as big as boulders on the moon.

That was when he noticed the girl walking towards him, the only thing moving on the whole beach. He noticed her first because she had a gap of nearly two inches between her thighs. Some girls, he'd noticed, had no gap at all between their thighs, so that their thighs rubbed together as they walked in their bikinis. Others had quite a large gap; full of bikini, of course. It wasn't that a gap turned him on or anything. It was just something you noticed, if you watched a lot of girls walking about in bikinis. A gap wasn't necessarily attractive or anything . . .

But this girl was attractive. She walked proudly, head held high like a queen. Her skin was very pale, hadn't been in the sun much yet. And her bikini was black. He watched her appreciatively as she approached. Then thought sadly that, in a minute, with a squeak and swish of dry sand, she'd be past, and he'd never see her again.

But she didn't swish sand over him. He had lowered his head out of politeness as she got very near, and now he saw her long slim white toes stop dead in front of him. In the end he looked up timidly, and she was looking down at him between the beautiful black cones of her bikini. She said,

'Hello. You look a bit lost.'

'I am.' He tried to give her a bold friendly grin, but it didn't come out right, because he was staring up at her at such an angle, and getting a crick in the back of his neck.

As if she'd read his thoughts, she sat down abruptly and arranged herself cross-legged, like a buddha. The position created all kinds of exciting folds of flesh. He didn't know where to look, so he sat up quickly himself. He glanced at his parents, to see if they were watching, fearing knowing grins on their faces, and a giggle and sarky remark from Anita. But they were all lying exactly as before. He felt ashamed of his father's gaping mouth. What would the girl think?

She followed the direction of his eyes. 'S'alright', she said. 'They won't wake up for a bit.' She sounded so sure of herself, he felt slightly annoyed. Then she said,

'You're Alan Dean, aren't you? I've got a message for you.'

'How'd you know my name?' He pretended outrage; but it is not unpleasing when a pretty stranger knows your name.

'That'd be telling,' she said. Oh, God, she was one of those. He hated girls who made mysteries. On the other hand, he liked girls with long black hair, wet from the sea, that sent runnels of moisture trickling down their cleavage and under their costumes.

She smiled at him and said,

'It's no good looking at me like that. I'm dead, you see.'

He gaped at her far too long. He was far too slow in saying,

'Oh, har har!' He wasn't at all sure he liked cocksure jokey girls like this one, who enjoyed saying crazy startling things. What she meant probably was that she didn't feel sexy; that being in the sea had made her cold and shrivelled up where it mattered. The sea did that to him, too; after a bathe, he became no bigger than a winkle.

'No, I don't *mean* that,' she said sharply. 'I mean I am really dead! I'm a ghost.'

'And I'm Batman. And Robin too, in my spare time.'

She laughed out loud at that. That pleased him. He liked making girls laugh; it gave him a sense of power. He did it a lot. It was safer than making a heavy pass at them.

Then she stopped laughing and said, 'I'm serious. I am a ghost. I got drowned swimming off Walberswick yesterday. I went out too far and the current carried me away and I couldn't get back. They found my body on Dunwich beach this morning. The tide carried it south. It always does.' She gestured vaguely southward.

That was her mistake. He made a sudden snatch, and grabbed her wrist.

It was, of course, absolutely solid; bone and sinew under soft attractive flesh.

Just cold, that was all. From being in the sea.

'Gotcha!' he said. 'You're as real and solid as I am.'

'Yes' she said sadly. It really seemed to take her down a peg. She lowered her eyes, and looked at his hand holding her wrist. He was holding her tightly, though not tight enough to really hurt. But his fingers dented her sleek skin. He liked that; again he felt a sense of power.

She just didn't seem to know what to do next. Then she said, conspiratorially, in a lowered voice, 'I really am a ghost, you know. Let go of me and I'll *show* you.'

The way she said 'show' excited him more. Maybe it was a memory of other girls who had shown him things when he was younger; long ago.

He glanced furtively at his family.

'I *told* you,' she said impatiently. 'Don't worry about them. They won't wake up for a bit yet. *Look!*'

She pulled her hand away, and gestured up towards her own face.

He looked at her face intently. She seemed to be making an inner effort of some sort; though it could simply have been an effort not to laugh. The distant Southwold pier, with its few and dreaming fishermen, seemed to run in one of her ears and out the other; it would have made a very comical photograph . . .

She went on making her effort; he went on staring at her intently; he wasn't going to grumble about that. She had a face well worth staring at. Her high rounded forehead looked even higher, with her long hair pulled back by its own wetness. Wide apart eyes. When she grew up, she would look a bit like Anna Ford. The only thing that spoilt her face were the little bits of thin green seaweed. One piece came down out of her hair, and hung a little way down her rounded forehead. The other piece seemed to have stuck to the corner of her mouth. She didn't seem to know it was there. He wanted to reach out and take it off gently, but he couldn't quite pluck up the courage.

'Well?' she asked expectantly.

'Well what?'

'Can you still see my face?'

'Course I can see your bloody face.' Then he was sorry, that he'd said 'bloody'. She had a very beautiful face.

'Ooooooh,' she said, in girlish exasperation, and took a deep breath, which suddenly made her bikini exciting. 'I'll try one last time.'

And this time her face went . . . slightly blurred. Enough to make him raise his hand and rub his own eyes. He'd been staring at her too intently, too long, that was all.

But when he opened his eyes again, she had grown more blurred, even misty.

'Damn,' he said. Rubbing your eyes sometimes made them worse, particularly on the beach, when salt and sand got on your lashes. He rubbed harder, and looked again.

There was a fisherman walking along Southworld pier now. And at the point where that fisherman should have vanished behind her head . . .

He stayed in sight. He walked right across her face and out the other side, and stood on the end of the pier, looking at the sea and lighting the tiny dot of his pipe.

'Yewhat?' He went on staring stupidly at the distant fisherman. As if the fault lay in *him*. Then he came back to his senses, and switched his eyes back to her face.

Which was as solid and beautiful as it had ever been.

'That was a *trick*,' he said.

'I'll have to practise,' she said. 'It's harder with you, because you're . . .'

'I'm *what*?'

'I mustn't tell you yet . . .'

Oh, God, she was back to her stupid teasing ways again. Girls in this mood were bloody exasperating.

And yet some little doubt remained. It had been a strange trick she had pulled; making her own face as transparent as glass. It had left him feeling quite odd and lost. He reached out and grabbed her hand again. Partly to reassure himself; partly because he liked doing it.

And of course, her hand was as solid as before. He could feel the slim elegant shape of her finger-bones through her soft flesh.

But she was so *cold*. Her cold seemed to run right up his own arm. It wasn't just the cold of somebody who's been swimming; he'd been swimming himself.

It was the cold of a vase full of water, on an icy winter's day.

The sea couldn't be that cold. This was August, in the middle of a heatwave. But as he went on holding her hand, the cold worked further and further through him.

In the end he had to let go of her. He was panting; panting with *cold*.

'I *told* you,' she said. 'I'm cold because I'm dead.'

'Bollocks. You're not dead.' He used it as an excuse to examine her in every detail. The soft shine of the skin on her young shoulders; her breasts in the bikini, like little apples; the soft small roundness of her belly, with its perfect little navel . . .

'Why don't you look at my feet,' she asked. She lifted a slim white foot and waved it at him.

'What's wrong with your feet?'

'No sand on them. I've been walking with wet feet on dry sand, but there's no sand on them. Everybody else has sand on theirs. Even if they haven't been swimming.'

He looked back to the safety of his family. Sleeping Dad had caked sand on the soles of his big sprawling feet. So had sleeping Anita. Even sleeping Mum had a bit. Then he looked at his own.

'I haven't got any sand on my feet.'

'No,' she said, so sadly it terrified him, he didn't know why. He didn't dare to ask why.

'Look,' he shouted. 'You feel solid to me, so you can't be a ghost. I *felt* you. And you're walking and talking, so you can't be dead.'

Then he realised he was screaming at the top of his voice. He looked round, embarrassed, to see who he'd wakened up; who was staring at him with sleepy accusing eyes.

Nobody. The sleepers slept on as before. He might as well have never shouted. For all the effect he had had, he might as well not *exist*.

But he did exist; like the girl existed.

'Look,' he said. 'Have a biscuit, have a Kit-kat. My Mum's got some in her bag. That'll prove you're alive.'

He still thought up till that point that he was talking to a girl who was potty. Beautiful and friendly but quite potty. The only real worry he had, as he reached for Mum's big fashionable straw basket, made in Italy, was that the Kit-kats would be sticky—melting with the heat.

His hand seemed to miss the bag. He wasn't looking what he was doing; he was still looking at the girl. He turned his head with a grunt of exasperation, and grabbed the handle of Mum's bag properly.

The handle seemed to run through his fingers like the dry sand of the beach. Like it was thinner than the dry sand of the beach. Like it was the air itself.

He couldn't believe his eyes; he couldn't believe his hand. He grabbed and grabbed and the bag never moved. It might as well have been a hologram of a bag

In total panic, he turned and grabbed the girl's hands again.

'But *you're* solid!'

'Because I'm dead and you're dead. How could I eat your silly Kit-kat when I'm dead?' And she opened her pretty lips wide.

And her mouth was full of weed and sand.

'But *I'm* not dead!' he cried out.

'You were doing your floating act,' she said, 'and you drifted too far out. That yellow powerboat ran you down. They were going so fast, they didn't even notice. Nobody knows you're dead yet. That's why. I was sent to tell you . . .'

'Rubbish,' he shouted. '*Rubbish!* I'm alive, I tell you. *Alive!*'

'All right,' she said, gesturing at his family. 'Tell them you're alive. Tell everybody. See where it gets you. I tried to break it to you the easy way. But I don't suppose there is any easy way. You have to find out for yourself.'

He ran and ran. He ran everywhere about the little town of Southwold. Up the little sleepy Georgian main street, through the lazy shoppers; into the church, to try to make the vicar understand; but the vicar was too busy to notice, talking to the ladies who were polishing the brass and arranging flowers. Up to the lighthouse and the green where the old cannons still stood. Then back to the beach.

In time to see them bringing a body ashore; a body silent and floppy and naked, save for blue and orange swimming-trunks.

His swimming-trunks.

'C'mon,' said a voice at his elbow. 'It's not so bad once you get used to it. But it's funny how you ran about everywhere, just like me. I suppose everybody runs about everywhere, trying to prove they're not dead. And you suddenly find when it's too late that you love everything you thought you hated, don't you?'

She took his hand, and it was so *cold*. The cold in her started to seethe and bubble all over his body.

He suddenly shouted at her, in a rage,

'If I'm dead, why'm I not as cold as you?'

He squeezed her hand harder and harder, as if to show his rage with all the world. And her hand crushed and oozed into a freezing pulp.

He heard his mother's voice say sharply,

'Oh, Anita, what a *stupid* thing to do! Look at the mess you've made!'

And Anita say, whingeing, 'It was Alan made the mess, not me. It was only a *joke*.'

'Waste of a good ice-cream,' said Dad crossly. 'Fancy dropping it in his hand like that. Couldn't you see he was asleep?'

'I just thought it would wake him up. I didn't know he was going to *squash* it.'

Alan felt his left hand not just freezing, but sticky. He opened his eyes and the setting sun shone straight into them. He raised the hand to block out the sun's rays, and freezing drops fell on his chest. Blearily, he saw he was clutching a mis-shapen red and silver paper, from which white and brown liquid dripped. A drop fell in his mouth and tasted sweet.

'Give me that hand,' said Mum, grabbing it and extracting the silver paper, and wiping his fingers with the wet face-cloth she always carried to the beach. 'Anita, you are the *end*.'

It had all been a dream. He had fallen asleep, sprawling, mouth wide open. Just like Dad.

The girl had just been a dream, he thought again, as the yellow power-boat roared past again, was, for a moment, faintly visible through the mist, then again vanished into obscurity.

Only a horrible dream.

At least he thought so, till they climbed the long steps back into the town, and he saw her photograph under the screaming headlines of the local paper.

SUSAN PRICE

Across the Fields

A BRAZIER held the fire in the centre of the hut. Its iron bars were crumbling with rust but the coals were red-hot inside, sending out waves of heat to meet the long thin draughts of cold wind that came in through the gaps in the planking walls. The men, their bodies blackened with a coating of sweat, water and coal-dust, crowded close to the fire, shivering and trying to wipe themselves dry with old rags, shirts or sheets of newspaper.

'Never mind—Christmas tomorrow!' one of them shouted, and the others laughed. Christmas Day was the only day in the whole year the mine didn't work.

When they were more or less dry, though still filthy with coal-dust, the men pulled on trousers, shirts and jackets. In 1924, there were no pit-head baths. They crowded around the fire, shoulders jostling, trying to get warm before the long, dark walk home. From hand to hand passed the jug of beer the mine-owner left in the hut for every shift of men coming up the shaft. As they drank, or waited for their turn to drink, they listened to the wind blowing around the hut and shrieking in the gaps.

'Our Grace'll be walking tonight,' one of the men said, and there was more laughter.

There was a soft rap on the door of the hut, which only the nearest man heard. He opened it a crack, and then pulled it wide to allow someone to come in.

'Jon!' he called. 'Tha little sister here, come to walk home with thee, so thee don't get scared!'

That made all the men laugh again, and several of them began coughing badly. The girl recognised her brother's cough among them, sharp and loud. Jon almost always coughed when other people laughed.

The men crowded together to let the girl come to the fire and stand beside her brother. She was about thirteen, tall for her age and thin, wearing a long, limp skirt that almost hid her boots. On her head was a man's old cap, with a thick tartan shawl folded over it and wrapped tightly about her body. Between the cap's peak and the shawl her eyes glistened brightly, and her nose glowed a bright red from the cold outside.

She looked quickly and shyly at all the men's faces. Even though she was standing beside him, she wasn't quite sure that she recognised her brother. All the faces were black and shiny, as if they'd been polished with the black lead that her mother used on the cooking-range at home; and in the tawny, golden-red light from the fire, their faces shone gilded, as the range shone by the light of the fire. But their eyes glittered white, and every glance and swivel of their eyeballs seemed exaggerated and comic and horrible all at once. And their lips, washed by the beer, were bright red.

With a final cough, the man beside her said, 'What's up, Emily?' Then she knew for sure it was Jon.

'Have tha been paid?' she asked, and jumped as all the men around her laughed aloud.

'After thy money! Her's learning early!' one said.

'I shall be paid tonight,' Jon replied.

'Mother wants thee to fetch the meat for our Christmas dinner.'

Jon nodded, and took the jug from the man beside him. As he drank, the other miner asked the girl, 'Thee walk here on thy own, me flower? In the dark?'

She nodded.

'And tha weren't scared?' he asked. He grinned at her.

From the other side of the brazier, another man said, 'Did tha meet Our Grace?'

'Ar, with her dead white face and her long wet hair hanging down her back,' said another, 'and her eyes staring, and her hands reaching out for whoever her can find—'

The miners laughed as the girl turned aside from them, pretending she wasn't interested. She knew who they were talking about: everyone in the neighbourhood knew the story of Grace, the gypsy girl who had drowned herself in the flooded clay-pit and now, so people said, walked over the fields at night, trying to find and drown others.

'Jon, hurry up,' Emily said. 'We've got to get that meat.'

'Plenty of time,' Jon said. It was true. The market would stay open until at least nine, and it could only be about seven now.

'Her don't want to be out late,' said a miner, and nudged Jon. 'If tha'm out late, tha might meet Padfoot.' He stooped towards Emily. 'Tha sure tha didn't hear Padfoot padding along after thee as tha come along that path?'

'I don't believe in ghosts,' Emily said, and the hut was filled again with the row of the miners' laughter.

'Hey, be serious, though,' said another miner.

'Have thee ever heard that screaming as tha was walking home?' asked a third man. 'I remember the time—'

Emily moved close to Jon and looked pleadingly up at him. She didn't want to hear any more of these frightening stories. Jon smiled his red-lipped smile and shouted, 'Happy Christmas, lads! We'm going.'

He reached out and opened the door of the hut, letting in a broad, cold blast of air as he and Emily moved out into the darkness, followed by a cheery, beery chorus of, 'Happy Christmas! Happy Christmas, little un! Happy Christmas!'

Outside in the dark, another fire burned near the mine-shaft, an open, brick-lined hole in the ground. It was the only light to be seen nearby; beyond its flickering was deep darkness. Jon passed by the fire with his quick, long stride, and Emily hurried after him, her boots clop-clopping on the stony, hard-frozen ground. Above them glittered a wide expanse of silver stars.

A black shape loomed up ahead—it was the mine office. They rounded the building, and Emily was glad to see yellow lamplight spilling from its windows. She waited outside, leaning against the wooden wall and hugging herself inside her shawl, while Jon went in to hand over his candle-can and collect his money. Emily was cold and wished he would hurry up. Even there, in the mine yard, she didn't like the dark. She couldn't help thinking that Our Grace might suddenly whip into sight, with her long wet hair, her white drowned face and her reaching hands. Even the knowledge that Jon and the light of the mine office were only a step behind her didn't make her feel any better. She would still have *seen* Grace—her swollen drowned face and her mouth moving as she called your name.

Quickly Emily pushed the door and went into the office, to stand close behind Jon, so close that she touched him. Being near her brother always made her feel better. He never seemed to be afraid of anything: not of going underground, nor of the dark, or big dogs, or strangers, or mice or spiders or anything. Yet still she looked fearfully towards the door, wondering if the yellow light of the oil lamp would really keep Grace out of the office if she were in the yard.

Jon felt her touch against him, looked down and smiled. 'Come on, Chuck,' he said, moving towards the door. She followed him. It meant going out into the dark again, but at least now she would be with Jon, and she didn't fear ghosts as much while he was with her. He walked to work in the dark most days, he worked all day in the dark and walked home again in the dark, and he thought nothing of it. Ghosts didn't come near people who didn't believe in them, did they? So Emily hoped.

Jon had worked hard all day, but he still walked fast as he led the way, by dark, unlit field-paths, towards the town of Oldbury and its market. Emily had to put many a hop and skip in her walk to stop herself from falling behind. Slipping one hand out of her shawl, she gripped him by the belt to help herself.

'Here,' he said. 'Keep thy hand warm.' And he slipped her arm through his, and held her hand in his dirty warm one. His hands were always hot, as if he had a fire burning in him. But she was still out of breath by the time they reached Oldbury.

The market place was lit by flaring white gas lamps with pitch black shadows between pools of light. There were still many people about: all those who had delayed shopping for their Christmas dinner as long as possible in order to buy cheap. Jon and Emily kept their arms linked as they pushed through the crowds and made their way to the butchers' stalls, where blood had collected in pools between the cobbles, and where chickens' heads and legs lay scattered everywhere. Even in the cold, there was a bad smell of blood and flesh and chickens' guts.

Jon was tired and wanted to get home, bath and sleep, so he didn't take long about marketing. On one stall he spotted a large goose hanging by its legs.

'I bet,' he said to Emily, 'that he can't sell that. Too big. Nobody wants it. How much for the big 'un, mate?' he called to the stallholder, pointing to the goose.

The stallholder looked up at the bird and pulled a face. He knew that he wasn't going to sell the bird, and he had no way of keeping it fresh to sell another day. 'Seven and six,' he said.

'I'll give thee five shilling,' Jon said, and the stallholder took the bird down without another word, and began wrapping it in newspaper.

Emily wasn't happy. 'Too much!' she whispered.

'It's Christmas,' Jon said, and went on to buy sweets for her and for the two other sisters and three brothers at home.

'We'll have no money *left*,' Emily said, wanting the sweets, but afraid of what their mother would say.

'It's my money,' said Jon.

*

They started walking home, Jon's pockets stuffed with bags of sweets, and his arms wrapped round the goose. Emily held on to his belt to help her keep up, her hand warmed by the shelter of his jacket and the heat of his body through his shirt. She was tired, having been up early to scrub the kitchen floor before going to school, then running errands after school and finally coming on this long walk with her brother. She leaned her head on his arm as they walked.

Once they were out of town, they were faced with a long, long road home. Jon suddenly stopped walking, hugging the goose to himself and lowering his head. Emily knew that he was overcome with the thought of how far they had yet to walk before they were home. And then he still had to bath before he could go to bed. 'It'd be shorter,' he said, 'if we cut across the fields.'

Emily straightened up, lifting her head from his arm. She didn't like the idea at all. The fields were wide, cold, empty and dark. But she had to give a more sensible reason than that. 'It's dangerous,' she said. 'What about all the old pit-workings and quarries? We might fall in one.'

'I'm not walking all the way round,' Jon said, turning off the road and striking out across the rough ground of the field.

Emily let go of his belt and stood for a moment. She thought about walking home by herself. She looked about, up and down the road, but there was no one in sight, and the roadway, lit only by widely spaced gas lamps, seemed darker without Jon. And Jon, with his quick, long stride, and without her hanging on his belt, was already growing smaller, fading into the darkness. Even walking across the fields, she quickly decided, was better than walking all that way by herself, thinking about drowned Grace, and the ghost dog, Padfoot, whom you saw when you were going to die.

'Wait for me, Jon!' Hugging her shawl about her, Emily ran from the road over the field. The frozen ground was just as hard underfoot as the pavement, and frozen leaves rustled under her boots. Jon stopped and turned, waiting for her. Breathless, she caught up with him and wrapped her fingers about his belt again, under his jacket.

'We'll soon be home,' he said. 'Have a mincepie afore we go to bed.'

They didn't waste breath on talking after that. Emily was surprised, as always, that Jon could walk so quickly after spending all day crouching underground, hacking at rock and coal. He swung on, stride after quick stride, hugging the dead goose to his chest, his head lowered to watch where he put his feet, his breath drifting before him in puff after puff of white mist. Emily's own breath wreathed her face as she panted beside him, forced to work her legs just a little too fast, so that her hips ached. Her heels jolted hard on the ground and shook her with every step. Her throat was raw from gasping at the freezing air, but she didn't ask Jon to slow down. After all, she thought, peering around them into the dark, the quicker they walked, the sooner they would be home and safe from the night.

The fields around them could only be felt as a cold open space, over which the wind blew to scrape at them. Nothing could be seen but blackness; even the path beneath their feet was only a dimmer grey in the darkness. Emily hoped they were on the right path: in the dark, it could be any path. And anything could be out there, in the darkness, hidden from them.

As they walked, Emily kept looking all round, glancing back over her shoulder every few seconds, and squinting her eyes to peer into the darkness ahead. If there was any danger, she wanted to see it before it reached them. But despite this care, she didn't see the man coming. She only heard his voice, suddenly barking out in the darkness on Jon's other side. 'Evenin'.'

Emily leaned around Jon and saw a stranger walking beside her brother. In the dark, she could just make out the darker area of his working clothes and the pale white stripe of his muffler. Between the muffler and the dark cap was the not-so-pale blur of his face.

'Evenin'',' Jon said, friendly and unafraid, while Emily clung more tightly to his belt and pressed closer to him. The man was not the ghost she had feared, but now she was afraid that he was a robber or a murderer, who'd been waiting for them on this dark field path. 'Happy Christmas,' her brother added.

'Oh,' said the man, his deep voice grumbling through the dark, cold air. 'It ain't Christmas yet. Not 'til the last stroke of midnight.'

Their feet crunched on the frost-hardened path—Jon's light, quick, steady tread and Emily's skip, hop and jump. She listened, but the stranger's feet made no sound.

The stranger spoke again: 'Where thee going?'

'Home,' Jon said. 'As quick as we can.'

'What's thy hurry?' asked the stranger. 'Why don't tha come to the match? Tha could win a prize; strong lad like thee.'

'Match?' Jon asked, and Emily tugged at his belt and whispered, 'Jon!' But he either didn't hear her or took no notice.

'Wrestling match,' said the stranger. 'I know thee for a good wrestler, lad.'

'Jon, we've got to get home,' Emily said.

'There's prizes?' Jon asked. Their family always needed money or extra food, especially at Christmas. Whether the prize was money or a cake or another goose, it tempted Jon.

'There's prizes,' said the stranger, and Emily didn't like the way he said it—as if there were other things he wasn't saying.

'A bout or two then,' Jon said, not seeming to notice anything odd about the way the man had spoken. Emily tugged at his belt but he ignored her, and she could have wept with anger and disappointment. She so much wanted to get home and safely into the warmth and light.

'Oh Jon, let's go home,' she wailed. 'Tha'm tired. Come home, go to bed.'

Jon looked round. 'Thee run on home,' he said, sounding bad-tempered.

Emily looked ahead at the thin path of hard dirt that ran through long, grey tussocks of wilted, frozen grass and leafless bushes, and quickly faded into black winter darkness. She almost did as he said: she could see herself, in her imagination, running hard along the path until she reached the safety of streets and houses. In imagination, she could feel her running feet hitting the ground.

But she was afraid of what she might meet on her own, without Jon's warmth and confidence to keep the ghosts away. And she was afraid to leave her brother alone too, without her fears to warn him, trusting and friendly as he was. As he protected her, so, she felt, she protected him: they should stay together. Who knew who this stranger was, or what he really wanted? He might kill Jon to get the goose.

'I'll come with thee,' she said, in a small, frightened voice.

She imagined the man taking something heavy from his pocket, like a brick or an iron bar, and hitting Jon on the head with it, and she knew she couldn't stop him, but she also felt, fiercely, that she could try. She could kick the man hard; she could bite him till he bled. She could shout and shout, louder than she'd ever shouted; she could run and fetch help. Even if she couldn't stop the man hurting Jon, she could make sure he didn't get away with it.

The stranger left the path and struck off through the long, crunching, frozen grass of the field. Jon followed him and Emily, clutching at Jon's belt, followed Jon. Whenever she could, Emily peered around Jon at the stranger, trying to see what he looked like so that she could describe him to the police if she had to. But she could never see his face clearly. It was always hidden by his cap, or by his turned-up collar and muffler. She thought he had a dark moustache; she thought his cheeks and chin were darkened by beard-stubble; but that was as much as she could tell.

Just you try anything, she thought at him. Just you try. I'll kick your feet from under you. I'll bite your fingers off. I'll—she wished very much that she was bigger and stronger.

They were very far from the path now, and when Emily looked around and behind them, she saw nothing but deep, blue-grey darkness, with black shapes of low bushes emerging from it. But from ahead came a noise. It was a murmur, buzzing and rising and falling: the sound of voices clamouring together as they had clamoured in the market-place—but here the sound had a colder, more frozen note as it faded and was lost in the open fields. She wanted to ask Jon, one more time, not to go to this meeting, but to come home with her—but she knew that he wouldn't change his mind now.

There was light ahead: red and golden light, shining out of the darkness like a jewel. Black shapes moved across it, blocking out its light and then letting it shine again—a fire with people moving around it. Jon picked up his heels and walked even more quickly, to reach the fire and the people, and Emily had to run to stay with him. She felt tears in her eyes as she ran towards what frightened her.

They came nearer to the fire, and felt its heat blow towards them on the wind, bringing a shower of sparks and cinders together with an ashy smell of burning. The stranger began to clap his hands and shout, 'Here we be, here we be! Here's a lad to give we a bout! Here's a lad who'll bet his wages, his goose, and his heart and soul!'

Emily didn't like the sound of that; and she didn't like it when the people left the fire and came to meet them, crowding around them so that they were hemmed in. She didn't like it when men pressed close and began to slap Jon on the shoulders, because she was so small among them that she felt she was being smothered in the crowd, and because she was afraid she would lose her grip on Jon's belt and be pushed away from him. She took hold of his belt with both hands, and let herself be dragged almost off her feet as he was carried forward in the noise of the crowd, closer to the light and heat of the fire.

A dark young man, as tall as Jon but broader, stood squarely between them and the fire. His face was in deep shadow and couldn't be seen. He started to take off his jacket, and as he did so, he said, 'For the goose.'

Jon grinned and passed the goose to Emily. She took it, soft, limp and heavy, in her arms. Jon took off his cap and put it on Emily's head, on top of the shawl and cap she already wore. He unwound his muffler and hung it around her neck; and he took off his jacket and draped it around her shoulders. Then, in his shirt-sleeves, in the bitter cold, he bent at the knees and held his arms out to the other young man. The crowd around them backed away to give them room.

Emily hated being there and having to watch. She felt desperately that Jon must win—felt it so much that it hurt—not only because he was her brother but because if he lost the goose, the whole family would have to go without Christmas dinner, and the five shillings spent on it would be wasted. She didn't think they would dare go home and face her mother after spending five shillings on a goose and then losing it.

And wrestling was a rough game. The other man looked heavier than Jon. If he was a better wrestler as well, then Jon could be badly hurt, and if Jon was hurt, then he wouldn't be able to work, and they were always short of money even when Jon was in work. Jon had to win, he *had* to, he *had* to! She hugged the goose tightly, and swallowed over a painful, hot lump in her throat.

The two men had wrapped their arms around each other, and were now trying to crush the breath from each other's ribs while struggling to trip each other with their feet. Emily watched, her unblinking eyes watering in the cold, wishing hard for Jon to win. But the fear that he would lose was equal to all her hope. It was unbearable—unbearable to hope and fear so much, and she had to turn away from the wrestlers.

She found herself looking instead at the faces in the crowd, lit warmly red and gold by the light of the fire. And her eyes picked out one woman's face. She had seen that woman somewhere before—

She jumped as a shout went up all around her, shaking the cold air. Jon was on the ground. The other had thrown him down. As she watched her brother got up and again they wrapped their arms around each other.

Emily looked again for the woman in the crowd. She couldn't see her any more, but she noticed a man. She knew his face too, but couldn't think of his name . . .

There was another shout, and Jon was on the ground again. Jon was losing! Oh, Jon! she thought, hugging their goose, their Christmas dinner, which they were going to lose: how could thee win when thee were so tired? Why didn't thee come home with me?

She had to look away again. She couldn't bear to watch. And there was another face she knew: the face of a boy this time. Now she knew that boy's face very well. Who was he . . . ?

The crowd shouted a third time, but Emily didn't look to see which of the wrestlers had been thrown. She remembered where she had seen the boy before. He had been in her class at school—had it been last year or the year before? But he was no longer at school because—she turned even colder as she remembered—because he had died. He had died of consumption. She had seen his funeral go past in the street. They had prayed for him at school, and had been asked to remember him. Dead and buried, that boy, yet here he was at this Christmas Eve wrestling match, out in the wild, dark fields.

She felt a tugging at the goose in her arms, and looked up into the face of the dark young man, Jon's opponent. He was taking the goose from her. 'I won,' he said. And he wasn't even out of breath.

Emily let him take the goose, because he had won it and because she was afraid. She remembered where she had seen the woman she had noticed earlier . . . That woman had lived three doors away from them when Emily had been a little girl, until she had gone away. It had been a long time before Emily discovered that the woman had died. And the man she had noticed . . . She had seen the man with Jon. Long ago, when Jon had first started working down the pit, he had worked with that man. Emily had seen him outside the pub, laughing and joking with Jon. And Jon had gone to his funeral after he had been killed by a roof-fall in the mine.

Shrinking in on herself, hugging herself small, she glanced quickly at the crowd about her, and thought: dead, all dead. We're in company with the dead.

Jon had got to his feet, and had come over to her and the young man who now held the goose.

'I wasn't ready,' he said, breathing hard and short, out of breath. He coughed before adding. 'Again. I'll win the goose back.'

'Jon,' Emily said, reaching out for him. 'No.' She wanted to tell him about the people around them. She wanted to point out the dead neighbour-woman and his dead workmate and her dead schoolfriend. But her voice squeaked like a mouse, and Jon took no notice of his nervous little sister.

'The goose if thou win,' said the dark, dead young man. 'What if I win?'

Jon reached into his trouser-pocket, and they heard the jingle of coins.

'I've no use for money,' said the dark young man.

Jon dropped the coins back into his pocket and looked up in surprise. 'What, then?'

Emily felt all the people around—all the dead people—move closer; and she darted to Jon and put her arms around his waist. He absentmind-edly dropped his arm around her shoulders as he waited for an answer.

'Thy heart and soul,' said the dark young man.

Emily hugged Jon tighter in warning, but Jon laughed and coughed, and said, 'Me heart and soul? What use be them to thee?'

The fire flared and its red light glowed over the dark young man's face, showing the damp twist of his hair and the deep hollows above and below his eyes, the skin stretched tight over his cheekbones, and the shape of his teeth showing through his lips.

As Emily held on to Jon, she felt him start with shock. 'Tom Rugeley!' he cried, drawing a long breath of cold air, which made him cough. Emily, hugging him, felt the coughs shake him. 'Tha'm dead, Tom,' Jon said. And then he said, to himself, 'I'm dreaming.'

'Bet me thy heart and soul,' said Tom Rugeley. 'I'll dance to the beat of thy heart—mine don't dance no more. I'll feel with thy soul—mine don't feel no more. If I win, I'll live in thee—and thou won't live no more.'

Emily felt Jon's arm tighten around her, and his other arm come round her too. He lifted her right off her feet, up to his chest, and she felt him move a step or two. He was going to run and take her with him. But then he stopped, and looking about, Emily saw the people all around them coming closer, their arms held out to block their way. Jon's grip on her loosened, and she slipped back to the ground. There were too many of the dead, all around them and all too strong. They could not run away.

'Then we'll wrestle,' Jon said, 'but here's the wager. If I lose, me heart and soul. But if I win, the little wench goes home with the goose.'

When she heard that, Emily's heart swelled and grew full and sore with love and gratitude. Tears pressed against the backs of her eyes, and she took Jon's warm hand in both of hers and held it tight.

All around them the dead murmured and whispered, and to the front of the crowd came pushing the dead women, the young girls, and the little girls who had died as children. They all stared at Emily with their sunken eyes and there was one—Emily shivered and hid her face against Jon's shirt-sleeve—there was one with long black hair hanging over her shoulders that dripped water on to the ground even in this freezing weather. A man's voice from the back of the crowd called, 'Grace!' and she turned her head, that one, water flying from her hair. And the whispering, the murmuring from all the dead women and girls said, 'But we want her. We want her . . .'

'Then it's a good wager!' Jon said. 'More to win, more to lose! My heart and my soul against the little wench and the goose. What tha say, Tom?'

Tom Rugeley looked around at the dead, and then he looked back at Jon and slowly, despite the cold whispering in the air, he nodded.

Jon pushed Emily gently away from him and the second wrestling match began.

Emily watched this time, gritting her teeth until her jaws ached as Jon strained to throw the dead man and not be thrown himself. By sheer skill, he got his foot around the foot of the dead man, and threw him over his hip to the ground. But the dead man got up again at once—no struggle can tire nor fall hurt a dead man—and closed with Jon again. And Emily watched, her heart aching more each time, as her brother was thrown once, twice, three times, and lost the match.

How else could it have ended? Jon had worked all day, and walked to market and back, and fought one bout already, while his opponent would fight always with the same untiring strength. He had lost, and now he lay on the hard, frozen ground where he had been thrown, while all the dead turned to Emily.

'New lives for old,' said Tom Rugeley. 'Who shall I give the little wench to?'

'Thou hasn't won me!' Emily said. Her voice shrilled out through the dark, sharp with fright. 'Jon lost, so tha've won him, heart and soul. But tha've not won me.'

'Art going to wrestle?' asked Tom Rugeley, and around them came the dry laughter of the dead.

Emily ran across the little open space at the centre of the gathering, to where Jon half-sat, half-lay on the ground. She took his jacket from around her own shoulders and put it around his. 'I can't wrestle,' she said, 'but I can riddle. I'll ask thee a riddle. If tha can answer it, thou shall ask me one. First one who can't answer is the loser.'

'But what's the wager?' asked the dead man.

'If I lose, tha win us both,' said Emily. 'If I win, tha lose us both. Win all, lose all.'

The dead crowded close; the dead whispered and shook their heads. But Emily said, 'Fancy a dead man being scared to take a bet!'

'You're on!' said Tom Rugeley.

'And I'll ask the first riddle,' she said. And she asked the hardest one she knew—one she had learned at school:

'In a hall as white as milk,
Lined with skin as soft as silk,
In a fountain crystal clear,
A golden apple does appear.

No doors there are to this stronghold,
But thieves break in and steal the gold.
What is it?'

'That's an old one,' said Tom Rugeley, 'and the answer's known to all
of us here. It's an egg. And now I ask one. How many wild strawberries
grow in the salt sea?'

Emily was kneeling on the ground beside Jon, and she looked into his
face, hoping he might know the answer. She could hardly see his face in
the dark, but even so it was plain that he had no more idea than she had.
'How many wild strawberries . . . ?' she said, and knew that the answer
must be a tricky one.

And then it seemed to her that she had heard the riddle before, and
knew the answer. She snatched at it without wondering what it
meant—'As many as fish swim in the forest!' She saw by the way the
dead people's shoulders sagged in disappointment that she had given the
right answer.

'Here's my next riddle.' It was another hard one she'd been taught at
school:

'White bird featherless
Flew from Paradise,
Landed on the castle wall.
Along came Sir Landless
Took it up handless
Rode away horseless
To the King's white hall.
What is it?'

'Another old riddle,' said Tom Rugeley. 'What's old we know. The
answer is: a snowflake in the wind. Here's my riddle: How quickly can
you travel round the world?'

This is hard, thought Emily. The dead man knew far better riddles
than she did. She had no idea of how long it would take to travel even
to Wales. But then the answer suddenly jumped into her head.

'If you get up with the sun, and keep up with the sun, you can travel all
round in the world in one day—like the Sun does. And here's my riddle.'

And, she thought, I had better make it a good one, a new one, because
I might not be able to answer another one of his. She thought: make it
a new one. The dead know all the old riddles. And she began to think
frantically, while the ghosts waited. Hurry, hurry! she kept telling herself. Think of the answer first, then make a riddle to fit it. She thought

so quickly that when she spoke the beginning of the riddle, she had no idea how it would end.

'*I nothing fear but morning bird-song.*
My heart is still, but still it longs.
By day I am gone, by night I show clear
Now riddle-me-ree-a.
What be I?'

To her relief, Tom Rugeley didn't answer. He stared at her, and then looked around at the other dead. 'A new riddle,' he said.

'Can't thee answer it?' Emily asked. 'Tha've lost if tha can't.'

'I can answer it, I can answer it. "By day I am gone, by night I show clear . . . ?" '

Emily and Jon sat together on the cold, hard ground, and they looked at each other, and they waited. All around them, the dead whispered together.

'Dost thee give up?' Emily asked. 'Is it too hard?'

'Gone by day but clear by night,' said Tom Rugeley, 'It's the moon.'

'No,' Emily said.

'Then it's the stars,' said another of the dead.

'No,' Emily said.

The dead looked at each other. 'Can't be the sun,' one of them muttered.

'Dost give up?' Emily asked.

The night drew on, and it grew colder and colder. Emily and Jon sat wrapped in her thick, heavy shawl, huddling close together to keep warm amidst the cold company of the dead.

' "I nothing fear but morning bird-song," ' said Grace, the drowned girl whose hair never stopped dripping water. 'Is it a worm?'

'No,' said Emily, her head leaning on Jon's shoulder because she was so tired she couldn't hold up its weight.

' "My heart is still, but still it longs," ' said the dead man who had led them there. 'I can't make owt of that.'

'It's a stupid riddle!' said Tom Rugeley.

'Does that mean thee give up?' Emily asked.

'No!' And on and on went the guessing game, until midnight was passed, and then more hours, and there came the coldest, darkest time of the night, when Emily and Jon shivered together despite the shawl, and the deep cold set Jon coughing again.

The dead couldn't guess the answer to the riddle, but they wouldn't give up their chance of winning living hearts and souls either.

'It must be the moon! It can only be the moon!'

'No,' Emily said, her eyes closed.

'Then it's the stars—has to be!'

'No.'

' "My heart is still . . ." It must be something dead,' said one of the ghosts thoughtfully, and Emily opened her eyes and held her breath. But the right answer didn't come.

But though they went on trying, the ghosts could not guess the answer. They went on trying until the sky was grey, and the air still colder than it had been all night. They went on trying until, from far over the field, came the first morning cock-call, the first cock-crow of Christmas Day. And on Christmas Day, and the twelve days of Christmas, ghosts and the dead and witches have no power.

As the cock crowed a second time, a rustle of movement ran through the crowd of dead. They drew back from Jon and Emily and looked at each other. And as the cock crowed a third time, they turned and ran away across the dark field. Without a sound they went: no shouting, and no sound of feet on the ground. They vanished into the deep grey of the morning twilight, running for their graves in all the little churchyards round about.

Jon and Emily knelt up on the hard, cold ground, and watched them go. Jon put his arms round Emily and hugged her tight.

They got to their feet, moving very stiffly and slowly because they were so cold. Jon picked up the goose and checked that his pockets were still full of sweets, and then they went on slowly across the fields to home.

They lived in a little house that was one in a long row. Jon lifted the latch and they went in. Their whole family was gathered in the little room. Mincepies were being made at the table: one sister was rolling out the pastry; a little brother was cutting the pastry out with a cup; another was greasing tins. Their mother was putting mincemeat into the cases. Everyone stopped what they were doing and looked up as they went in.

'Where have thee been?' their mother shouted.

Jon and Emily looked at each other.

'We come across the fields and we got lost,' Jon said.

'I thought the bogey-man'd had thee,' said their mother.

Jon and Emily looked at each other again. Jon handed the goose over to his mother.

'All of thee—upstairs!' said their mother to the children. 'Jon's got to have a bath. There's hot water in the copper, Jon.'

All the children left the mincepies and went through to the stairs. Emily followed them, and after her came Jon, on his way to get the tin bath from the yard. At the foot of the stairs he stopped her and whispered, 'I think I know the answer . . . Is it "A ghost"?'

Emily grinned, nodded, and went on up the stairs.

'If you want to hide something,' Jon said, 'put it in full view.' And he went to fetch the bath.

Afterwards they had roast goose for Christmas dinner, and mincepies; and when Jon walked to work in the dark early the next morning, he didn't go across the fields, even though the twelve days of Christmas still had eleven days to run.

TIM WYNNE-JONES

The Clearing

THE boy stopped at the top of You-and-Me-Pal Hill and kicked off his skis. He leaned against a rock. The sun was high and the glare on the snow hurt his eyes. He hurt everywhere. But at least he was outside again, moving through the windless day, his skis breaking a new trail.

He got his breath back. He couldn't shake the dizziness but he settled into the middle of it, found somewhere there that wasn't moving. Down the high meadow was Far-Enough Swamp, though he couldn't see it through the cedar and balsam that hugged the reedy shore.

'This is rich land,' his dad had said once. 'Where else you gonna find a swamp with a fir collar?'

The boy trained his eyes at a break in the trees. If this was a time-travel story, someone would come now. Maybe a Mohawk brave silently tracking a white-tail deer. He was ready. He would jump out at the deer and scare it—herd it—back into the path of the brave's arrow. It was a cold winter. The brave would be thankful. He might take the boy back home to meet his dad and mom.

The boy watched and waited. Nothing.

Rich land—what a joke. Solid granite with a rind of dirt only Pollyanna could call soil. Farmers had once tried to cultivate this area. Snow-rounded pyramids of rocks along the cedar fence lines testified to their efforts; those and straggly apple orchards gone wild. But these meadows had been turned over to the hardier grasses—to juniper and thorn and prickly ash; to the fir trees that ringed Far-Enough Swamp.

The boy took a deep breath of bright, cold air. It was minus ten degrees Celsius, but he took off his gloves. They were wet inside with sweat, like the sheets of the bed he had left behind, clammy and constricting.

Where was his time-travel connection? In those stories the hero was always lonely, and he was lonely. The kid in a time-travel story was usually sick, too, and he was sick. For how long now, he didn't care to recall.

He started to shiver. Then he slipped back into his skis and shooshed down the meadow towards the gap in the trees that led to the swamp.

On the swamp there were many tracks: brush wolf and fox and rabbit. No humans. He followed the path of two wolves who seemed to be going more or less his way.

There was a wire fence property line right through the middle of the swamp. He climbed over it without taking off his skis. He imagined himself making an escape. He pushed himself hard, ducking invisible enemy fire, until the fence and his imaginary enemy were lost to view around a bend in the meandering waterway. Deeper and deeper he escaped into the silent forest, a graveyard of grey stumps and the spiny skeletons of trees.

He was trespassing now. This was Ken Axelrod's land and, after crossing the dyke, the Starkweathers, the Beresfords, the Strongs, the Frosts. But after that, he couldn't say anymore where he was. There were no signs of civilization out here and, in his dizziness, the sun was no help—it seemed lost itself. The only thing he knew for sure was that he was heading away, his sick bed slipping farther and farther behind.

At last he saw something in the distance that was not dead, not stumps. A hockey rink in a clearing. Rag-tag nets; sticks, broken or intact, stuck in the snow bank like a rickety fence; a bench carved out of ice with an old pine plank on top. A frozen toque.

Coming to the rink, the boy slipped out of his skis. He sat on the bench. He noticed the snow shovels. Suddenly, sick and tired as he was, an idea started ticking over in him.

There was three or four centimetres of fresh snow on the rink. The boy pushed at the snow with his foot; it flew up like so many feathers. He started to shovel. The joke of it flowed like fresh blood to his aching muscles. He shovelled like a boy possessed. He laughed a little to himself. He whistled.

Then, just as suddenly, he stopped. Looking up, he saw someone in the trees at the swamp's edge staring at him. He felt cold all over.

'Hey,' the boy on the ridge called to him. 'Hi.'

Shaking, he dropped the shovel and ran for his skis. He fumbled with his binding. There was no such thing as time travel. There was only wishful thinking. This should not have happened.

The boy was coming. 'It's all right,' he cried.

But it wasn't all right. The intruder was stomping, sliding down the slope of the woods to the shoreline.

The skier turned himself towards home. His tips crossed and he fell over hard, then clambered to his feet again.

'Wait,' the intruder cried. 'Don't go.'

But the skier pushed himself off, digging his ski pole tips through the downy snow into the ice itself. Heaving himself homeward, following his tracks.

'Hey, I can help,' yelled the intruder, coming nearer, crossing the ice, slipping, recovering.

But the skier was off. The other boy would never catch him now.

'Come again,' the intruder called after him.

Ben watched until the skier was out of sight. He took over shovelling where the other boy had left off, stopping often and staring out across the swamp. The sun was sitting low behind the hills, casting long blue shadows. Sometimes he fancied he saw the boy far off, a lean shadow disentangling itself from those of dead trees.

The wind picked up. Already the ski tracks were sifting over. Ben pushed the snow around in a desultory way. After a while he heard his father coming. He put his shoulder down and heaved snow manfully.

'Yowzers!' said his father, with enough surprise in his voice that Ben laughed inside. 'Good work, Ben.'

'Ah, it was nothing,' said Ben, huffing it up a bit.

'Pretty industrious,' said his father. Ben thanked him. Out of the corner of his eye he caught his father scratching his head. 'I came to give you a hand.'

Ben stopped, sucked in a bucketful of frosty air. 'I can handle it, Dad,' he said, leaning on his shovel.

His father waited a minute more while Ben went on shovelling.

'I'm sorry about the fight,' said his father. Ben scraped his shovel over the ice.

'That's okay,' he mumbled, without turning around.

'It's just that . . .' his father began, '. . . sometimes it's as if you didn't really move out here with us at all.'

'That's dumb!' Ben wanted to shout. 'Where am I? Back home in the city? What choice does a twelve-year-old have but to be wherever his parents take him!' But he didn't say a thing, because it would come out wrong and ungrateful and the argument would start all over again. And that would ruin the wonderful joke of this magically cleared rink.

After some more minutes his father said, 'It'll be dark soon,' and he headed back towards the woods, the path, the house. When he was out of sight, Ben surveyed what was left of the smooth blanket of snow on the ice and went to work with a vengeance. It was some creative shovelling he did. Then he went home hungry for supper and ready to make up properly.

In the snow still left on the rink, he had written

COME AGAIN

Before the school bus the next morning he ran down from the house to check. His message was mostly gone. The rink was clear, but it appeared to be the work of the wind.

Over the next few days it warmed up. Then it froze. Then it snowed a whole night. Then the sun shone hot. It was a winter spell set on killing a swamp skating rink. But Ben's father wasn't the kind of man who gave up on a pet project easily. He and Ben tried to keep the surface smooth, mostly for Ben's sisters. Ben liked hockey, but he hadn't really gotten to know anyone much since they'd moved to the valley and playing hockey by yourself was—well, you could only score the winning goal in the final game of the Stanley Cup so many times before the thrill wore off. But whether he used the rink or not, he and his father would come down, often in the chill of the night, and fill buckets with water from a hole to spread as best they could—'Smoother, Ben, smoother'—under the icy moon.

Ben would always have his eye open for the stranger. He would look up suddenly across the swamp.

'Did you hear that?' he would say.

'You're a jumpy customer,' his father would answer, not listening long enough or hard enough, shaking his head and chuckling to himself.

Ben asked on the school bus who the kid might be. It gave him something to talk about.

The weather heated up unseasonably. The top of the rink in the clearing thawed, then froze again from the top down, leaving a sandwich of water between the new ice and the thick grey ice below.

That was the first time Ben saw the mayfly wrigglers. The water nymphs swam up through cracks in the thick ice and got themselves stuck in the watery sandwich. Having escaped from the winter dark at the bottom of the pond, they swam like crazy black writing in the sunlight. They were stuck there. They were not alone. Ben saw a black splotch under the new ice. He was just wondering how a puck had got there when the splotch moved.

'Look at this!' he cried.

'Bullfrog tadpole,' said his dad. 'It'll die there, unless it finds its way back down. Shouldn't have been so nosy.'

Ben wanted to watch it, but the new ice wasn't very thick, and his father didn't want him to go through and wreck the surface. They went up for dinner with the tadpole, big as a puck, in Ben's head. It swam around just under his skull, wanting out.

That night the moon was full again. And whether it was the moon or the trapped tadpole or just life, Ben and his folks got into another fight.

Ben wasn't ever sure how these things happened. He was usually reading an Archie comic at the time or rearranging his baseball card collection. The argument was always over something he had said or hadn't done or had implied or had complained about.

In his room, with a slammed door separating him from the family, Ben opened his journal to the last page where he kept his fight record.

Mom	Dad
x x x x x x	x x x x x x x x

He added a new x to Mom's column. She was catching up to Dad. He could still hear her pounding about downstairs, her voice raised for him to hear, door or no door.

He never got hit, but the words were big and noisy, like God yelling at Moses: words that blew your ears off.

Reaching for his baseball dictionary, Ben flipped to 'earned run average.'

earned run average *n.* (ERA) A pitcher's statistics representing the average number of runs legitimately scored from his deliveries per full nine-inning game (27 outs).

He tried to figure out his earned fight average *n.* (EFA). Earned—how did you determine that? What was average? What made a fight legitimate? Did he ever win any?

Ben messed with his pen on some scrap paper while his heart turned around in his chest like a dog looking for some place to settle down. Then he started to draw: a guy sliding into second just under the ball; just under the sweeping hand of the second baseman. Safe. When spring started again, there would be baseball. If he could just make it through this endless winter to baseball . . .

He turned the pages in the journal to the entry he had written about the Phantom Shoveller. He had painted a little comic strip in watercolours. In the picture Ben cried after the shoveller, 'Come back, come back, I've still got the driveway to do!' Now he noticed the date on the page. It had been the day of the last full moon.

His dad suddenly opened the door, and Ben slammed the journal shut. Later he wasn't quite sure why the apology he tried to make resulted in another yelling match and another slammed door. He sat on his bed for a long time, trying to figure out whether this was actually a new fight for which he should reward his father with an x, raising his EFA, or whether this was just the same fight he had been having with his mom and into which his dad had entered, kind of like a reliever in the late innings of a game.

Nobody came to kiss him goodnight. He didn't change into his pyjamas. He didn't turn out his light. He stomped, boiling mad, downstairs and made himself some toast just after his parents had put the girls to bed. He made several trips to the bathroom. In short, he gave them every opportunity to crab at him some more, so that he could stumble through a real apology. Then everyone could make up and get the whole thing out of the way, and he could get to sleep. Instead, they left him to stew in his own juices.

Finally he heard them in the bathroom preparing for bed. Surely now they would notice his light. The door was wide open.

They didn't. He heard them turn out their own lights without so much as looking in on him.

They were treating him as if he were gone. As if maybe they had left him back in the city.

Ben flicked out his own bedside light and sat, arms crossed tight on his chest, breathing heavily in the dark. But it was not really dark; there was a full moon. It was almost bright enough to read by. Bright enough to leave by.

He was as quiet as a mouse until he was out of the house and then he slammed the door good and loud. Just one more slammed door in a night of slammed doors.

He was halfway to the clearing before he realized where he was heading. He had never been out in the woods so late—not alone, at least. Once the family had skated under the full moon with a bunch of neighbours, and even his sisters had stayed up until almost midnight. But on that occasion the bright night had been filled with chatter and hot chocolate, and he had not heard the noise the night makes all on its own. In the dead of winter, that noise is Silence.

Silence was something he had never heard in the city. It was a Silence to fill the wildness of the eastern forest; a silence as tall as the pines, as wide and as deep as the swampland. It filled him with an urgent longing.

He stood among the trees on the shore looking out at the shining rink. He waited for his father to come tromping through the brush after him. 'Ben, Ben, this is ridiculous!' Then he could hurl himself at his father's chest and into his arms. But his father didn't come, and the Silence grew around him.

Then, because he had to do something to occupy his runaway mind, he slithered down the snowy bank to the swamp and walked quickly out across the clearing to the rink. There was a wind out there he had not felt in the shelter of the trees. It was a sound, anyway, almost soothing.

It took some time to locate the huge tadpole. On his knees to better spread out his weight, Ben watched it for several moments fearing that it was already dead, perhaps frozen into place, for the night had turned cold. Then it moved, squirming slowly but too stupid cold to look for the hole through which it had slipped into this place between places.

'Yes!' said Ben, and in a flash he was on his feet again and searching for his father's axe. He brought the axe down hard on the new ice— once, twice, three times—before finally cracking it. That woke the tadpole up!

'It's for your own good,' said Ben.

The tadpole didn't swim far. It was trapped every which way, in the last pool of unfrozen water, a pool no more than a metre in diameter.

Ben whacked some more. Each whack sounded like a gunshot. Finally, with one last, mighty swing—Splat!—water sprayed up at him. He had broken through. He chipped away the chunks of surface ice, brought over the coffee can that his father used as a small bucket, and attempted to catch the frantic prisoner. He had made several dives at it, and his cuffs were getting pretty wet, when someone spoke.

'You gonna destroy the whole rink?'

For one wild, midnight second, Ben thought it was the tadpole. Then he swung around so fast that the bottom half of him slid into the pond.

There, just behind him, stood the phantom skier.

'The rink,' said the boy. 'You destroying it?'

'No,' said Ben. 'There's this tadpole.' He clambered up, shaking his cold, damp leg to get some of the water off it. The boy approached him cautiously. Ben backed off a little. The boy bent down and looked into the hole. Ben saw the sweat stand out on his cheek and forehead, saw that he was shivering badly.

The stranger bent down. 'Can you catch him?' he said.

Ben dropped to his wet knees beside the boy and picked up the coffee can. The stranger leaned back on his haunches, watching as Ben lowered the can into the shallow icy pond, quite suddenly an expert at the moonlight capturing of trapped tadpoles. In one deft swoop he swooshed the can out of the pond, triumphant. The two boys peered into it together and then ventured to look at each other.

'Come on,' said Ben. He led the other boy to the hole his father kept open at the edge of the rink in order to draw water from the swamp

below. It was covered with a bucket. 'Here you go,' said Ben, emptying
the can into the hole. With a flip of its tail the creature was gone. The
two boys watched the darkness for a moment.

'In a cartoon,' said Ben, 'the tadpole would come to the surface and
wink or something.'

'Or there would be a bubble,' said the boy, 'and when you popped it
the word "thanks" would come floating out.'

They smiled at each other. It was only a fleeting smile. Each of them
had things on his mind. The stranger looked back to the axe hole in the
rink.

'I'll have some explaining to do,' said Ben. 'But I think my dad will
understand.'

'You took some initiative,' said the boy, the tail of a smile reappearing
on his pale face.

'Right,' said Ben. 'I was industrious.' They both laughed. Then, because he couldn't hold it any longer, Ben said, 'Who are you?'

It was exactly the wrong thing to say. The boy's face seemed troubled
again. He looked back at the hole in the rink and then at the open hole
in front of them and then all around, as if he was looking for something,
some way to explain.

'I didn't mean to be rude,' said Ben. But it was already too late. The
boy stood up, tall and thin—too thin. Head down, he went for his skis.
'Wait,' said Ben, desperate now, for he was losing people all over the
place' tonight.

'I can't stay,' said the boy.

'Then I'll come with you,' said Ben, following him, staying close
enough to touch the boy's elbow.

'You can't,' said the boy, pulling his arm out of reach. He clipped on
his skis.

'Why not?' said Ben.

The boy was breathing hard. He started moving, finding his tracks in
the snow. 'You won't be able to keep up,' he called over his shoulder.

Ben started after the boy on foot. 'Just watch me,' he shouted, breaking into a tight and cautious run. 'I can't go home. Wait up.'

Across the moonlit swamp he pursued the skier, falling farther and
farther behind. 'I'll get lost,' he yelled. 'And it'll be your fault!'

'Go home,' the boy called back at him.

It started to snow, one more curtain between Ben and home and
between Ben and the boy, now almost out of sight. But Ben wasn't
going to let go of him. He followed the tracks. How hard it was to move
on this land without skis! His legs were city legs: pavement hard and

strong, but he could not keep his footing on the snow-covered swamp. He would break through the crust here, slip out on the ice there. But he kept going.

At one point the ski trail joined up with the tracks of a pair of coyotes—brush wolves they called them around here. Ben faltered in his stride.

'Please!' he called out across the swamp. 'I don't want to be somebody's dinner.'

'Go home.'

Then, finally, the tracks came to a fence, and not far beyond that headed towards the shoreline, the woods. In the fringe of trees there was no wind and Ben paused for a moment to catch his breath. He looked back across the swamp. The snow fell quietly. Already it had laid fine tissue in his footsteps. How much longer would there be a path to follow home?

Then, behind him, back in the direction he had come from, the coyotes howled. It was a mad yip, yip, yipping. The sound zinged through him. He was not the only crazy one on the prowl tonight. It was the moon they wanted, not him, he told himself, but the sound was enough to send him quickly on his way, after the boy.

At the top of the meadow he stopped at a rocky outcropping. Looking down the other side, he thought he saw a striding shadow slip into the woods. 'Yes!' He tore off in pursuit. Sinking into the deep drifts of the meadow, scratching himself in the prickly ash, pressed on by the baying coyotes, following tracks that grew fainter and fainter under the snow-beclouded moon.

He emerged at last from an old logging road at a small, neat cottage with the lights still on. It was like something from a fairy tale, with him as the miserable, poor straggler. Unable to move another step, breathing heavily, soaked with sweat and numb where the icy water of his tadpole rescue mission had soaked through his jeans, he leaned against a tree. He caught his breath and watched the uncurtained windows of the cottage. He could make out a woman reading by a fire. No one else.

Ben gathered up what was left of his shredded courage and marched up to the door. When he was close enough, he checked the walls to make sure they were not gingerbread.

He had no idea what he was going to say. His mind was muzzy with the cold and a buzzing tiredness of limb and spirit he had never experienced before. He would have to say something, he told himself, and though words would not form in his head, he knocked again and again. Then the woman was at the door, opening it in a hurry, keeping back a barking, slathering golden retriever with her foot, and all Ben could think to say was 'I'd like to phone my mom, please.'

She took him in. The dog bounced on him. A man appeared in his undershirt and cleared a place by the fire. Tea came, and blankets. The man made a joke about what Ben's chattering teeth were saying in Morse code, and by then Ben could actually laugh a little, though he had no right to laugh or even to be alive, he reckoned, all things considered. He told them about the coyotes. They had heard them, too.

The woman got his phone number and talked to his mom. She turned to him. 'She's on her way.'

Then Ben asked if a boy lived there.

'No,' said the woman, shaking her head. 'A daughter off at college. No boy.' So he didn't tell them about the skier.

It was Ben's dad who came because the coyotes had woken up both the girls with full-moon nightmares, and Mom was feeding them full-moon carrot cake and hot milk.

'So you'll be coming home to a party,' his father said, squeezing him tightly. No one asked any questions. Ben didn't try to explain. Dad had met the couple, the Robbs, at some valley shindig. He couldn't thank them enough.

'Ah, heck,' said Mr. Robb. 'It kind of livens up a dull evening.' And then it was time for Ben to change into the warm clothes his father had brought along and head home.

At the front door, Ben noticed a pair of skis. They were leaning in the corner of the mud room. They were just like the ones the boy had worn. But they weren't wet at all. The woman noticed him looking at them, and she got a frown on her face, which made Ben feel bad. He concentrated on putting on his boots. His hands were shaking badly.

They were climbing into the car and Dad was tucking him into the passenger seat like a little kid when the door of the cottage reopened and Mrs Robb called out to Ben's father. He closed Ben's door and went back to the house. Ben watched them talking through the oval window of the front door. Then, amazed, he saw the woman handing the red skis to his father. Meanwhile, Mr Robb opened a closet and emerged with ski boots and poles. Then it was goodbye all over again and Dad was making his way to the car laden down with this mysterious treasure. The skis wouldn't fit in the trunk so they had to be shoved into the back seat with the tips hanging over Ben's shoulder.

'They're for you,' said his father with a catch in his voice. 'Make getting around out here a whole lot easier.' He didn't say anything about running away.

And he didn't say any more just then. Ben looked at him in the dashboard light and saw that he was choked up about something.

'It was the last thing they had left of their own son,' his father said at last. There was a long pause. Snow fell. Ben kept his eyes on the road.

'It's been five years.'

They turned onto a now familiar road.

'He was your age.'

Neighbours' mailboxes glided by: the Beresfords, Strongs, Frosts.

'They wanted me to thank you.'

Thank him? Ben was puzzled. They pulled into the driveway and stopped the car and had a big shaky hug together. Over his father's shoulder, Ben could see his mom in the kitchen, the girls sitting in their nighties. He wanted to get in and be a part of it.

Ben and his dad climbed out of the car wrestling the skis out with them.

'They just couldn't seem to let him go,' said his father.

And far away the coyotes started yip, yip, yipping at the moon.

JOHN GORDON

The Burning Baby

THE morning after Barbara Pargeter disappeared, Bernard Friend rang the police.

'My God,' he said, 'I've just seen her parents and they're in a terrible state.'

'Do you know the girl, sir?'

'Yes, I most certainly did. She was a nice kid.'

'Still is, sir, we hope.'

'Good grief!' He sucked in his breath. 'What a terrible mistake.'

'Quite understandable, sir.'

'Excuse me.' Bernard Friend wiped grease from his hands on to his overalls. He was sweating.

'Are you still there, sir?'

'I'm sorry, officer, but I was just thinking how I could have said the same thing to her parents . . . the same slip of the tongue. I can't imagine what it might have done to her poor mum and dad.' There was silence at the other end of the line, and he wiped his hands again. 'They are very emotional about it,' he said. 'Very emotional.'

'Yes, sir.'

'Because Barbara Pargeter *is* a lovely little kid.'

'She's nearly sixteen, sir.'

'I know, I know—but time passes so quickly. It seems as if it was only yesterday when . . . but I mustn't say everything that's in my heart at this moment in time. And I know—I mean I've been told—that girls of her age are a problem, aren't they? Not that I've had any experience of it. Not like you—someone in that line of business, girl business, as you might say.'

Bernard Friend chuckled, but when there was still no response he added, 'I suppose you have to deal with flighty little bits all the time, isn't that so? That way you must get to know what they are like, girls of that age. Always in trouble, I shouldn't wonder.'

'Often enough, sir.'

'And was she?'

'A flighty bit? Not that I'm aware of, Mr Friend.'

'I mean was she in any trouble you know of?'

Papers were turned over. 'May I ask exactly where you live, Mr Friend?'

'I'm just down the lane from the Pargeters. I have the garage. Friend's Motors.'

'Ah,' said the policeman, 'now I've got you. The old car dump.'

'Garage.' His tone was pained. 'I spend time and energy working for our little community and then a couple of them object to my business and it's instantly branded. Old motors are only part of my enterprise.'

'Just trying to get you in my sights, Mr Friend.'

'I'm having it landscaped because I am a caring sort of person. Which is why I am ringing you at this present moment in time when everybody is distressed about Miss Pargeter.'

'Did I understand you to say that she had some sort of problem, Mr Friend?'

'No. Not as far as I know.'

'I'm led to believe Barbara was an attractive young lady.'

The sudden use of her first name made Bernard Friend clench his jaw. She had been missing for only one night but already the police were referring to her as *Barbara* as if her photograph had been on television, and journalists had been writing headlines.

'Attractive?' he said. 'I don't know. Well . . . yes, maybe to a certain sort of individual.'

'I see.' The voice was flat, as if the policeman was taking notes. 'Can you tell me when you last saw Barbara, Mr Friend?'

Bernard grunted to indicate that he had to think. 'Hold on a sec.' He gazed at the calendar on his office wall, working it out, and he used the pause to brush a fingertip under each eye to clear the beadlets of sweat. 'It was the day before yesterday, I believe. Yes, that was it—I was on the pumps when she went by. On her way home, I presume.'

'And how did she seem? Did she say anything?'

'Nothing, really. Just "Hello, Mr Friend"—something like that. That was about teatime. I didn't see her after that. She was normal, absolutely normal, poor kid.'

The officer, writing, repeated Bernard's words—'. . . and she said, "Hello, Mr Friend".'

'If you are taking a statement, I'm very willing to help in any way possible—join a search party,' said Bernard. 'Anything.'

'We hope that won't be necessary, Mr Friend. She's only been missing for one night, and our other enquiries may turn something up.'

With the phone back on the hook, Bernard Friend gazed for a long time at the calendar before he realized he was looking at the picture of a girl; a naked girl with very long legs.

He was reaching to take it down when he paused. What garage didn't have such a calendar? People must have noticed it there, and to remove it would only make them think. Barbara herself had seen it.

He felt sweat on his back, but only for a moment—a cold dampness, soon gone. Barbara didn't matter any more. The damned calendar could stay where it was. It wasn't the calendar that was the problem; it was the breakdown truck. Once again the quick sweat came, but was soon mastered. The truck was far away; out of reach of any search parties around the village. Bernard Friend went back to work.

He was in the inspection pit, draining the sump of a Passat, when he saw a girl's feet as she walked across the floor towards him.

'Hello,' he called.

There was no answer.

'Who's there?' He saw her shoes and ankles. They seemed familiar. 'Who is it?'

There was a snuffle as if the girl was holding back her tears.

'Oh, hell!' He had tilted the can he was holding and black oil spilled down the front of his overalls. He cursed again and climbed out.

'So it's you,' he said to the girl. 'Look what you made me do.' He picked a handful of waste from the bench and rubbed at the oil. 'These overalls are clean on today,' he said. Then he realized, sickeningly, that he must not admit to having changed his clothes since yesterday. 'Well, nearly clean. I've only had them on a week.' He looked down. The knees and arms were already dirty, thank God. 'Only a week,' he said, 'and look at them.'

The girl obediently regarded his oily front, and nodded. The edges of her nose were red and her eyes were moist. 'You're a mess,' she said, and then put her knuckles to her mouth and added, 'but where can Barbara have got to?' She wore a dark blue anorak and a grey school skirt. Her fair hair straggled down her cheeks and its untidiness made her appear younger than she was. 'I'm scared, Bernie,' she said.

'There's nothing to be scared of.' He had a broad, handsome face and a dark moustache. It was a face taken from a movie poster, but the wide-shouldered, muscular body beneath it was not tall. He was barely the height of the girl who stood in front of him.

'Why are you scared, Julie?' he said. 'She's only gone to a party, I expect, and spent the night with some feller.' His deep laugh rumbled in his chest. 'Some young chap's to blame.'

Julie pulled her hands inside her sleeves. 'Don't you mind?' she said.

'Me?' He raised one dark eyebrow. 'Why should I mind? I'm old enough to be her father.'

'I know, but . . .'

'But what, Julie?'

Faced with the intensity of his gaze, her eyes fell. 'She used to talk to you, Bernie.'

'Only out there by the pumps, Julie. You know that. Only by the pumps where everybody saw us.'

'She was in trouble, Bernie.' The words came out in a wail, and Julie's brimming eyes gazed tragically into his. 'Trouble . . . you know what I mean.'

'I'm afraid I don't, Julie.' His mouth had gone dry and his lips wanted to stick together.

'She said you knew all about it, Bernie.'

'Me? Why me?' The pitch of his voice rose suddenly and alarmed him. 'Excuse me, Julie, I've got a frog.' He cleared his throat. 'That's better.' He frowned, thinking earnestly. 'All she ever told me, Julie, was that she wasn't doing too well at school.'

'That wasn't it, Bernie. She wasn't bothered about that.'

He looked at her. This skinny girl was so bedraggled he thought it must be raining, and he could not prevent his eyes turning to the open door. Outside there was cold November sunlight but no rain. It was her misery that made her look like this, and girls in her state were dangerous. 'Just what did she tell you, Julie?' he asked softly.

'She was in *trouble*.' It was a whine of annoyance at his lack of understanding. 'She was going to have a baby!'

'I don't believe it!' There were flecks of white at the corners of Bernard Friend's mouth. 'I just don't believe it.'

'It's true. She was pleased about it.'

'Pleased?' But he knew very well what Barbara Pargeter had thought about having a baby, and a spurt of anger kept his voice strong and level. 'Did she tell you who the father was?'

Julie shook her head.

'Nothing about him? Nothing at all?'

Julie shook her head again. 'She just said she was pleased.'

'Then what are you bothered about, Julie?' His voice rumbled with a relief he had to disguise. 'I mean you *should* be bothered—I'm bothered about what you've just this minute told me—but if she was *happy*, it doesn't seem so bad.'

'If she was happy why has she run away? It doesn't make sense, Bernie.'

Two days ago he had enjoyed being called Bernie by kids, had encouraged it even, but now, on this girl's lips, it was too familiar, incriminating. 'I don't know why you're telling me all this, Julie,' he said. 'I don't know you well enough, do I? All I ever did was chat to you two girls as you went by—when I wasn't busy.' He picked up a wrench, hinting he wanted to get on with his work. Then he put it down. 'Does anybody else know she was pregnant, Julie? Have you told anyone?'

'No, Bernie, I couldn't—not until I'd told you. She said I could tell you.'

'Why me?' He smiled, but his jaw tightened. The poisonous little bitch had been spreading hints. 'That Barbara,' he shook his head, 'she had . . . she *has* some funny ideas. Always romancing about something, isn't she?' He tried to get Julie to agree. 'That's what she is, isn't she—a romancer?'

Julie nodded.

'I doubt if she really is pregnant, Julie, don't you? Not pregnant at all—just romancing. So I wouldn't say anything about it until she turns up—not a word to anybody. It would only get her into more trouble, now wouldn't it?'

'I suppose so, Bernie.'

'And not so much of the Bernie, young lady.' Playfully he waved the wrench at her. 'I'm Mr Friend to you—as I always was to your friend.'

'But Bernie . . .'

'And not a word to anyone until she turns up.' He walked with her to the door. 'Not a word, young lady, or you'll have Mr Friend to answer to.'

He went back, still clutching the wrench. It was very clean in his oily hands. Too clean. He had burnished it too thoroughly, using a blowtorch on it, burning off every trace that may have stuck to it. Washing would have been useless. Particles always lodged in waste pipes and drains, and could be found. Burning was the only way. But he had made it too clean; no garage man had a wrench as spotless as this. Bernard Friend dropped it on the floor and trod on it.

In The Doves that night he criticized the police. 'One of our young girls goes missing,' he said, 'and they're not doing a blind thing.'

'Pound to a penny she's in London,' said the landlord.

'With some young feller,' said Bernie.

'I reckon Bernie wishes it was him,' said someone else, and there was a laugh.

Bernard Friend's pint was half-way to his mouth, but he put it back on the bar and stood for a moment gazing at the floor. 'In the circumstances,' he said, raising his head as if from prayer, 'that isn't a very funny remark. I always found her a very pleasant young lady.'

'But she was just ready for it, wasn't she, that one? You must've known it, Bernie. Waltzing past your place, flaunting it.'

Bernie made no response and shamed the bar into silence. He took a drink, and said, 'There ought to be a search—a really big search.'

His earnestness was genuine, and it showed. He wanted a search—he needed a search around the village, every nook and cranny. It could only be then, after the search was over, that he would be able to bring the breakdown truck back to his yard. He couldn't have it standing there while police dogs sniffed around it. And time was running out. That truck had to be in his yard by tomorrow.

'If the police aren't going to do anything,' he said, 'we ought to organize our own search parties.'

'That's right, Bernie,' they agreed, but as it happened the police were ahead of him. The first parties were out early the next morning, and it was Bernard Friend himself who suggested that the search should begin in his scrapyard.

'You never know what kids might get up to,' he said, and he watched the dogs nosing among the piles of old cars as he stood by with a crowbar to jemmy open locked boots.

Nothing was found, but then he turned to a tumbledown lean-to built against the back wall of his garage. 'As I told your officer, I'm tidying this place up a bit,' he said to the inspector. 'So that old shed has got to come down. OK if I go ahead?'

'I don't see why not, Mr Friend.'

'Everyone calls me Bernie, inspector—even the kids sometimes.' It was a bit of insurance, just in case Julie said something. 'Cheeky young devils.'

'It's the way they've been brought up,' said the inspector. 'They're not like we were.'

'They're not all bad.' Bernie took a breath. 'As a matter of fact I'm going to use that old shed to give them a bit of a treat.'

'How's that, Bernie?'

His name, coming from beneath a peaked cap, was an intimacy that he did not, after all, care for, but he managed to smile. 'Guy Fawkes night tomorrow,' he said, 'so I thought I'd use the timber to give 'em a good old bonfire on my paddock.' He pointed to rough ground alongside the heaped cars. 'Maybe it'll help to take their minds off this ghastly business.'

'It's not ghastly yet, Bernie. She could still turn up.'

'Of course, of course.' He looked up at the eyes half hidden in the shadow of the cap. 'I just keep thinking you're going to find her some-where . . . find her, you know . . .'

'Dead?' said the inspector. 'That remains to be seen.' He turned away. 'Watch how you go, Bernie.'

Bernie knew that the bonfire was a stroke of genius. When Barbara's body had first sagged against him and he had lowered her to the floor of his office, his first impulse had been to take her miles away and bury her.

He had even rolled her in the strip of old carpet pulled from under his desk, but then, as he lifted her to carry her out to the boot of his car, he had suddenly realized what he was doing. He was acting as if he was in a movie. The roll of carpet, the car boot, the scraped grave. He had seen it many times. And every real-life murderer did the same. They copied the movies. And if there was a pattern for murderers, there was also a pattern for the police. They knew where to look.

So he had left her on his office floor while he backed his breakdown truck into the garage. Then he emptied the tool chest behind the cab. It was cramped, but Barbara was not a large girl and he got her in. Then he padlocked the chest and, for extra safety, put spot welds at the corners of the lid, disguising their newness with dirt.

By the time he had loaded a scooter into the back it was dark, and it was unlikely that anyone had seen him drive out of the village. Eight miles away, in town, he parked in the yard behind a garage he often did business with. They would think nothing of it. Then he rode the scooter home.

The truck was still miles away when Bernard Friend took the morn-ing off to help in the fruitless search. In the afternoon he began to pull down the shed and build the bonfire in the middle of his paddock. Several kids came to help him, Julie among them, but her mind wasn't on it. Every now and again she would stand still and look around.

'Come on, Julie,' he called. 'We'll never get done at this rate.'

'I just wish I knew something,' she said. 'I just wish I knew where she was.'

One of the mothers came into the paddock and Bernie went up to her. 'I thought this would take their minds off things,' he said. 'Keep them active and stop them moping.'

She looked apprehensively at the pile of wood. 'It's going to be very big, isn't it, Mr Friend?'

'Might as well give them a good time,' he said, and smiled sadly. Then a group tilting a roof beam against the heap caught his eye and he broke off to tell them to be careful. 'Young tearaways,' he said, 'but don't worry, they're safe with me.'

'You're very good to think of all this, Mr Friend.'

'I'm doing myself a service at the same time.' He grinned broadly, feeling suddenly on top of his problem. 'There's too much old rubbish lying around, I must admit, so everybody's going to be pleased with good old Bernie when it's done.'

He was still smiling to himself when he helped Julie roll an old tyre up the slope of the paddock. He had constructed a tunnel of tyres in the centre of the bonfire and was still adding to it. Julie stooped to gaze inside.

'It's dark in there, Bernie,' she said.

'Mr Friend,' he corrected her.

'Yeh, Mr Friend.' She looked sideways at him.

'That's better, Julie. Show a little respect to your elders.'

Suddenly her eyes filled with tears. 'I hope some little kid doesn't get in there to hide. That would be terrible.'

'Julie, Julie,' he said. 'Cheer up. Can you see a caring person like myself letting that happen?'

'I was just thinking that Barbara might want a place like that to shelter, Bern . . . I mean Mr Friend. Suppose she's hurt herself and is lying out there in the woods somewhere.'

He carefully did not put his hand on her shoulder, and he raised his voice so that all the helpers could hear. 'I'm quite sure Barbara is safe, Julie. Wherever she is. Somebody is taking good care of her—very good care.' He covered the mouth of the tunnel and put more timber over it. 'Nothing can get in there now, Julie. Not a living soul.'

Julie gave him a watery smile. 'You make me feel a lot better, Mr Friend,' she said.

'Good girl.'

It was late before the bonfire was finished, and later still before Bernard Friend rode his scooter over to town. The breakdown truck stood behind the garage in the darkness. He had a story ready, a towing job he had to do next day, but the garage was closed and nobody spoke to him or, he was certain, even saw him.

A light drizzle was falling as he put a strap around his scooter and used the breakdown crane to crank it into the back of the truck. It clanked suddenly against the tool chest. 'Sorry,' he said, and for the first time realized that a dead girl lay curled up within inches of him. He had been so busy he had not even checked the lid of the chest. He looked carefully around the yard. There were parked vehicles everywhere and many shadows, but nothing moved. Even then he gave the lid only a quick glance and tugged at it once. Nobody had interfered. It was shut tight.

Bernard Friend was whistling as he drove out of the yard. Even the drizzle lifted.

It was very late that night when a bright light flickered briefly in his garage and the welds that held the tool chest lid were cut through. Tarpaulins shrouded the truck as he lifted the lid, and soon afterwards the last glimmer of light went out in the garage and the whole village was dark and still under the stars.

Minutes went silently by before, very slowly, a shadow detached itself from the darkened garage and moved towards the open ground of the paddock. The shadow was broad, made broader by the bulk of something it cradled in its arms, but Bernard Friend had powerful muscles and moved lightly despite the weight. The only sound was the breath in his nostrils, like some night-wandering animal snuffling for food.

He lowered his burden and looked around. The dark trees collected extra shadows to shroud the hillside above him, and the stars pricked the empty sky like the frost that was beginning to whiten the grass. The pyramid of the bonfire was a tent where, cautiously, he drew back the doorflap of old timbers and revealed the deeper blackness of the tunnel inside. Stiffened by its roll of carpet, the body slid into its tomb.

Bernard Friend piled extra wood over the entrance and made one more journey to pour sump oil into the centre of the pyre before he drew back and left the frost to crystallize over his footprints.

Nothing now to do but wait and watch. The thought had occurred to him that he might make the bonfire blaze tonight and blame it on spoilsport youths, but surely someone, some busybody aroused by the flames, would then make an attempt to put it out. No, he would keep watch. Then there would be no risk.

Nevertheless it was going to be a cold night. His bungalow was behind the garage, out of sight of the paddock, so he had to keep watch from the workshop.

He put on extra clothes, but still he shivered. And all because of that stupid Barbara kid. She had said she wasn't going to get pregnant . . . she had promised him over and over . . . and then she had let it happen. And she'd been proud of it.

His fists clenched as if they once again held the wrench. She should never have told him—not just at that moment, not smiling, not pretending she'd done something clever. Anger licked through him again. She'd asked for it. His fist hit the bench . . . with the same short, powerful jab that had brought the wrench down across her stupid smile.

He grunted and leant forward to rub the dirty window pane. Nothing stirred outside. The bonfire was neat and high. He was a good mechanic, everyone said so, and this was a job well done. He thought it through again. Nothing would go wrong. He was so certain of it that he was dozing when the first light dimmed the stars, but nothing had disturbed the dark pyramid.

Once during the day he came outside after answering the telephone to find kids piling new rubbish on the bonfire. He had yelled at them before he'd had time to think, but at least it had made them leave him alone until late afternoon. Then Julie came up to him.

'Bernie,' she said, 'I mean Mr Friend. Sorry.'

'That's all right, Julie.' He smiled at her. She stood in front of him in the forlorn way she'd always had. Barbara had been the dominant one, had bullied her and sent her away whenever she'd wanted to be alone with Bernie in his office. Which was often enough. He'd miss it. 'What is it, Julie?' he asked.

'Everybody wants to know what time we're going to start.' She smiled at him. 'They're ever so keen.'

He glanced out through the garage door. The sun was already behind the hill, and he could not delay much longer. But suddenly he feared what the flames might show. He had to have time to pile on more wood. 'How about seven?'

'That's too late,' she whined.

Shut up. The words were in his mind but they stayed inside him. Ridges showed in his cheeks. Shut up, or you'll join your stupid friend. When he did speak he kept his voice calm. 'I keep putting it off in case Barbara turns up,' he said.

Again the moisture in her eyes. 'I wish I knew where she was. Haven't you any idea at all, Mr Friend?'

'Julie.' His voice rumbled towards her. 'How old are you, Julie?'

'Sixteen,' she said.

Then stop behaving like a kid of twelve, he yelled in silence behind his teeth. Aloud, he said, 'Well, I'll put you in charge, Julie. Tell them I won't have anybody here before half past six.' He realized he had to make more torches so that every point should be touched with flame and no dead patches could show what lay there.

'Thanks ever so much, Mr Friend,' and she turned away. His hatred burned at her back as his eyes watched her leave the yard.

They were early, as he knew they would be, but he was ready for them. The torches touched, and the smoke went up into a clear sky. But all was not well. The flames burned sullenly as if reluctant to advance into the dark heart of the pyramid. And faces, flickering in the uncertain firelight, ringed the paddock, observing every detail.

A boy advanced and poked at one of the dwindling firespots with a stick.

'Stop jabbing at it!' Bernie snatched the stick, and the boy backed away, startled. 'I'm the only one who can make it go. Stand clear—all of you!' He ran into the garage and came back carrying a can.

It was a dangerous mixture that Bernard Friend flung at the smouldering wood. In an instant flames whirled in a spiral and bit deep with a roar that flung forked leaves of fire at the timbers and tossed the white petals of an enormous flower high into the sky. And the heat, pressing on uncovered skin, pushed everyone back.

'She's away!' shouted the boys, and soon rockets flew to burst among the stars, and girls screamed as crackers exploded in the grass.

Many eyes watched the flames, but none so closely as Bernie's. The heart of the bonfire had become a blazing city where red towers of glowing wood were eaten away in the heat and collapsed into the scorching alleyways. Blue flames, so hot they were all but invisible, danced like devils in the streets, and white fragments, lighter than snowflakes, broke free and rode the hurricane that, feeding on itself, peeled layer after layer from the silent, waiting depth of the heap.

The tyres showed. Bernie risked the heat to throw fallen wood towards them. Their black rubber bubbled and sent out smoke so dense it made shadows even inside the glare of the blaze until, unable to resist it for a moment longer, the smoke lost its blackness and was transformed into greasy flame.

Julie saw Mr Friend's face, always so broad and brown and now reddened by fire, take on a new shade. A paleness, in spite of the heat, seemed to shine there, and she was watching him and not the blaze when the first tyre split open.

His lips had parted, and his strong white teeth shone whiter, but his eyes had narrowed and pierced the flames. She turned away from him to see what held him so fast.

What she saw was a roar of blue emptiness under the arch of the gaping tunnel, and on its floor a shapeless shape lying there, a flaking, shrinking, dwindling darkness in the heart of it all. But at that moment the bonfire collapsed inwards in a firestorm of such intensity that it sucked the oxygen out of the November night and made the watchers reel back, gasping for breath.

She turned to Mr Friend, wanting to ask what it was that she had seen, but now he was circling the blaze, stooping to throw every scrap of wood towards the centre. He never stopped. He was still doing it when the last firework had punctured the sky, and the last straggler had left for home.

Julie was the last of all. She had left the paddock and was turning the corner of the garage when the thought of Barbara tugged suddenly at her heart and she knew she had to ask if, somewhere among the hills, Barbara could have seen the bonfire at this moment and might have been dragging herself towards it. She turned back.

Bernard Friend was silhouetted against the mound of red embers. He was raking into it, stirring up chrysanthemums of sparks. He did not hear her as she approached over the trodden grass.

'Bernie,' she said softly.

He stopped his raking, listening, not sure where the voice came from.

'Bernie,' she said again, and he looked over his shoulder.

Julie could not see his face. All she was aware of was that he dropped his rake and backed away from her, skirting the edges of the fire, putting it between her and himself. Now, with the glowing heap between them, his face became visible. She could not account for the fear that pulled down the corners of his mouth.

'It's only me, Bernie,' she said, and took a step forward. It was then that she saw what it was that terrified him. It was the bonfire, the mound of redness.

Bernie knew it had consumed everything. Every atom. He knew no trace of Barbara remained. And no trace was ever found, but that night, under the stars, the dying bonfire rustled and stirred.

Julie saw the embers heave in just one place, as though the red heap had become brown, cool earth and some small animal burrowed there. The glowing ashes turned again and then, from the centre, there arose a small entity, a little shape of fire. It had a small torso, small limbs, and a head of flame. And it walked.

Bernard Friend was caught against the fence. He tried to shuffle sideways, but his clothes snagged on the wire and he was held in a crouch. He struggled, but the wire bit deeper and he was still crouching when the little figure, clothed in heat, trod unsteadily towards him.

Julie saw Bernard Friend slip and fall. He sat with his back against the fence, and she saw the burning baby come up to him, hold out its arms and wriggle into his lap.

Bernard Friend had made sure that his working overalls showed the mark of his trade; oil had soaked into them. And now, at the baby's touch, flames ran along his legs and arms and sat on his shoulders like wings. He was drenched in fire.

He cried out, but the fire had reached his lungs and the scream that came forth was made visible. It was a torch, a gush of flame from his blistering lips. The whole village heard it, but only one saw it.

Julie watched, and Bernie burned.

BIOGRAPHICAL NOTES

'A School Story' by M. R. James. First published in *More Ghost Stories of an Antiquary* (Arnold, 1911).

M[ontague] R[hodes] James (1862–1936) spent his childhood in Suffolk, where his father was Rector of Livermere. He was educated at Eton and King's College Cambridge. Very early he distinguished himself in antiquarian, biblical, and other studies; and he became Provost first of King's and then of Eton. His classic ghost stories are mainly collected in *Ghost Stories of an Antiquary* (1904) and *More Ghost Stories of an Antiquary*.

'A School Story' was for the boys of King's Choir School at Christmas (see Introduction), and James's closest connection with the school would have been while he was Dean of the College. That ended in the summer of 1905, when he became Provost. So it is arguable that the story should be dated at least as early as Christmas 1904.

The setting of the story—a school 'near London', described in detail—was identified by James as his own prep. school: Temple Grove, East Sheen.

The text of the story presents a puzzle: can M. R. James really have begun a ghost story for young boys with a smoking-room discussion of 'The Folklore of Private Schools'? And how unlike James to call the first of his reminiscing characters by a mere letter of the alphabet: A. Stranger still, perhaps, A.'s interlocutor has no name at all, although he tells the tale.

The MS of 'A School Story', as it went to the printer, can be inspected in the Modern Archive of King's College. The first two pages of the MS and the last page are of quite a different size from the rest, much smaller; and, although the handwriting on these smaller pages is the same as on the larger, the effect is different: perhaps a different pen, a different ink, or written in different circumstances—in haste, for instance.

At the beginning of the story, the change from the small pages to the large shows no problem, except that two lines at the top of the first large page roughly duplicate what is at the bottom of the preceding small page: these two top lines have been crossed out, to make the flow perfect. This suggests the possibility that the two small pages are some kind of rewrite which was spliced on to the main story in the large pages.

This supposition is strengthened when one reaches the change back from the last large page to the single small page at the very end of the story. Here there is a good deal of crossing out and writing in. A name, 'Mr Selby', is crossed out, and 'the narrator' is substituted. A little further on, another crossed-out passage gives another name which was not allowed to appear in the published text: 'In the course of that summer, Mr Jones paid a visit to a country house in Ireland.'

So, originally, there were a Mr Selby and a Mr Jones in what one may call the framing of the story. Why did they disappear? And why does what seems to be a tête-à-tête conversation between A. and his anonymous friend at the beginning of 'A School Story' become, at the end, something rather different: 'There had been more than one listener to the story and . . . one such listener was staying at a country house in Ireland. . . .'

Such confusion, inconsistency, and clumsiness may have more than one explanation. It strongly suggests, however, some kind of rewriting, in haste, at the beginning and—therefore—also at the end of 'A School Story'. Perhaps M. R. James realized (or had pointed out to him), rather belatedly, that the 'framing' he had designed for an audience of young boys was not suitable for an adult readership. Hence the hurried rewriting, without matching paper.

If I am right in my supposition, the change from the new 'framing' to the original main narrative probably comes at about the sentence beginning: 'It happened at my private school . . .' (p. 2, l. 5).

'Out of the Sea' by A. C. Benson. First published in *The Isles of Sunset* (Isbister, 1904).

A[rthur] C[hristopher] Benson (1862–1925) was one of the three sons of Archbishop Benson (1829–96) who distinguished themselves as writers. He was educated at Eton and Cambridge, and returned to Eton as a master. In 1915 he became Master of Magdalene College Cambridge.

At Eton he told Sunday evening stories to the boys of his house (see Introduction). These, in expanded form, were published in *The Hill of Trouble* (1903) and *The Isles of Sunset*; and the two collections were successful enough to be republished together in 1911 as *Paul the Minstrel*.

Ghost stories were only a small part of Benson's enormous literary output, which also included essays of all kinds and verse ('Land of Hope and Glory' is his). His literary hyperactivity was offset by depressions, leading sometimes to breakdown. His ghost stories often have nightmarish depths which seem reflections of dark inner trouble—in his own words, 'the satyr lurking in the bushes'.

'Out of the Sea' is one of the simpler stories. Like other Benson tales, its language is pseudo-archaic.

'Manfred's Three Wishes' by H. F. W. Tatham. First published in *The Footprints in the Snow* (Macmillan, 1910).

H[erbert] F[rancis] W[illiam] Tatham (1861–1909) came of a wealthy family, and was educated at Eton and Cambridge. Without effort he gained a Double First in Classics. He returned to Eton as an assistant master, and remained there for twenty-three years until his accidental death on a mountain walk in Switzerland.

The Footprints in the Snow was published posthumously by Tatham's brother, who found the seventeen stories in typescript as if nearly ready for the printer. They were, like A. C. Benson's, for Sunday evening reading to the boys of

Tatham's house. Most of the stories are short, often mystical rather than ghostly, and strongly moralistic. It is difficult to imagine how effective Tatham was as a storyteller with such material. In a prefatory 'Memoir' to *The Footprints in the Snow* A. C. Benson (a contemporary and close friend) says Tatham's 'utterance was indistinct'. As a boy, he had had 'rather a quick confused utterance, and prefaced statements with certain obscure sounds'.

In his 'Memoir' A. C. Benson is clearly mystified by his friend, whose undoubted intellectual abilities were not matched by achievement. M. R. James, another friend, dismissed the matter briskly with the phrase 'incurably unambitious'. Perhaps so; yet there are hints even in the stories of an unexpected and complex personality. A. C. Benson said that Tatham 'developed into a very strong Radical' (ibid.)—although Benson's idea of what 'a very strong Radical' was has to be taken into account. Tatham's temperament was placid, stagnant; yet he could be passionately protective of animals. As a boy he had been fined in a police court for assault on a man beating his dog. He liked toads ('dry and weak'); and he had an empathy with cats: 'He told me how in the drawing room of his home in London he picked up the family cat and carried her to the window and made her look out into the street. After contemplating the busy scene for a few seconds, she looked up at him and gave a heavy sigh. He put her back on the sofa' (M. R. James, *Eton and King's*, 1926).

'The Light in the Dormitory' by William J. Wintle. First published in *Ghost Gleams: Tales of the Uncanny* (Heath and Cranton, 1921).

William J[ames] Wintle (1861–1934) was a journalist and writer of very varied non-fiction. *Ghost Gleams* seems to have been his only venture into the supernatural and his only book for children (see Introduction).

The book has never been reprinted, although individual tales have been anthologized—for instance, 'The Ghost at the "Blue Dragon" ' (in *The Mammoth Book of Ghost Stories 2*, 1991). This story suggests that Wintle knew the work of M. R. James, particularly 'Oh, whistle and I'll come to you, my lad'. Wintle's Professor Lampeter of Cambridge takes a twin-bedded room in the 'Blue Dragon' and, in the middle of the night, is nearly thrown to his death through the bedroom window by a supernatural occupant of the second bed.

There are fifteen stories in *Ghost Gleams* ranging from the mild 'The Light in the Dormitory' to the horrific 'The House on the Cliff', where someone holidaying alone on a remote headland is slaughtered by a supernatural bird-being. 'The Voice in the Night' includes ghost, werewolf, and vampire.

In his Foreword Wintle says:

These tales . . . were written in answer to the insistent demand, 'tell us a story.' from eight bright boys whose names stand on the dedicatory page; and they were told on Sunday nights to the little group crouching over a wood fire on a windswept island off the Western shore. They were so fortunate as to meet with approval from their rather critical audience. Truth to tell, the gruesome ones met with the best reception.

'Miss Jemima' by Walter de la Mare. First published in *Joy Street No. 1* (Blackwell, 1923).

Walter de la Mare (1873–1956) came of a well-off family in Kent and spent the first twenty years of his career working in an oil company. Meanwhile, he was writing poetry, mainly for children. His first book (under the pseudonym of Ramal) was *Songs of Childhood* (1902). He also wrote stories, for both adults and children, and compiled a classic anthology for children, *Come Hither* (1923). For his own *Collected Stories for Children* (which includes 'Miss Jemima') he was awarded the Carnegie Medal in 1947.

'Miss Jemima' was considered, by Forrest Reid (1875–1947), to be 'a tale of the supernatural'; and Reid excuses a certain whimsicality in the reporting of the speech of the child, Susan: ' "Miss Jemima" is so delightful a thing, so essentially fine and true, that to mention Susan's two "exacalys" and her one "quincidence" as having aroused momentary uneasiness goes very much against the grain' (Forrest Reid, *Walter de la Mare: A Critical Study*, 1929).

In the *Collected Stories* (1947), published within de la Mare's lifetime, the two 'exacalys' were corrected, but not the 'quincidence'. In the 1947 text, the status of Miss Jemima was changed by the putting of quotation marks round the word 'aunt' (p. 35, l. 24 of the 1923 text used here).

'Johnny Double' by Arthur Machen. First published in *The Treasure Cave*, edited by Lady Cynthia Asquith (Jarrold, 1928).

Arthur Machen (1863–1947) was born and brought up in Wales, but settled in London to work: he catalogued books, made translations, wrote for newspapers, and for several years acted in Sir Frank Benson's Shakespeare Repertory Company. He was deeply interested in the occult, and was well known for his tales of supernatural evil and horror.

Machen was the unintentional originator of a modern myth. He was a journalist at the time of the British retreat from Mons at the beginning of the First World War. The retreat was halted only after appalling British losses; and on 29 September 1914, in the London *Evening News*, Machen wrote a fantasy ('The Bowmen') about the archers of Agincourt coming to the aid of the British: 'the soldier . . . saw before him beyond the trench a long line of shapes, with a shining about them. They were like men who drew the bow.' Perhaps the word 'shining' started the rumours (always traceable back to the Machen fantasy) that Divine intervention by angels had saved the British. No disclaimer by Machen ever availed: and the myth still survives as 'the Angels of Mons'.

One of Machen's admirers was Lady Cynthia Asquith (1887–1960) who supplemented her family's income by the compilation of various miscellanies, particularly ghostly ones. She wrote retrospectively of Machen: 'By far my favourite writer of the literature of awe was Arthur Machen. I thought him matchless at conveying by suggestion the sense of mystery at the heart of things. How he thrilled me by his power of hinting at the existence of something that lurked behind life—something indefinable but ineffably evil! He frightened me so much more than, for all his great technical skill, did M. R. James' (Cynthia Asquith, *Remember and be Glad*, 1952).

It was bold of Lady Cynthia to include a Machen story for children—probably his only one—in her children's *Treasure Cave* (where 'Elsie Piddock Skips in her Sleep', for instance, was also a story). Whether Machen felt inhibited by the juvenile readership, or whether Lady Cynthia gave him solemn warning (or even edited his MS), 'Johnny Double' is quite unlike the strong meat Machen usually offered his readers. The murder and murder-trial that make the climax of the story are presented so remotely and even confusedly that readers must feel that Machen was deliberately ignoring the Grand Guignol possibilities of his own plot.

'Elsie Piddock Skips in her Sleep' by Eleanor Farjeon. First published in *The Treasure Cave*, edited by Lady Cynthia Asquith (Jarrold, 1928).

Eleanor Farjeon (1881–1965) came of a literary and theatrical family—her account of her childhood in *A Nursery in the Nineties* (1935) is a classic. Her early book of stories, *Martin Pippin in the Apple Orchard* (1921) was considered to be for adult reading, but thirty years later, after the War, it went on to the children's list—a striking illustration of changing reading tastes and assumptions, affecting ghost fiction as well as other kinds.

All her life Farjeon wrote plays, prose fiction, and poetry, mostly for children. In 1955 she made a choice of her own stories in *The Little Bookroom* (illustrated by Edward Ardizzone), which won the Carnegie Medal and the Hans Christian Andersen International Medal. Farjeon also wrote (for adults) of her friend, the poet Edward Thomas, who was killed in the First World War: *Edward Thomas: The Last Four Years* (1958).

'The Tiger-Skin Rug' by Lucy Boston. From an unpublished MS. The story dates from 1933, when Lucy Boston was writing a number of ghost stories. The mystifying title, 'An Asylum Story', which appears on the first page of the MS, has been replaced for this anthology by the straightforward, 'The Tiger-Skin Rug.'

Lucy M[aria] Boston (1892–1990) was born in Southport into a well-off, devoutly Methodist family. She was an undergraduate at Oxford until she left to nurse during the First World War. She led a very independent and adventurous life, settling at last in the ancient Manor House at Hemingford Grey, near Huntingdon. Much of the rest of her life was devoted to restoring the house, to beautifying its gardens, to music, to patchwork quilting—and to writing.

Her first book about Green Knowe (always to be identified with the Manor) was *The Children of Green Knowe* (1954), written when she was over 60. It would have appeared on the publisher's adult list but for Lucy Boston's insistence on illustrations (by her son, Peter Boston, who has illustrated all subsequent Green Knowe books). Lucy Boston was always impatient of publishers' categorizations: 'Is there a conscious difference in the way I write for grown-ups and children? No, there is no difference of approach, style, vocabulary, or standard. I could pick out passages from any of the books and you would not be able to tell what age it was aimed at' (talk by Lucy Boston to the Children's Book Circle, Nov. 1968).

The Green Knowe books for children—six in all—are among her best known; and *A Stranger at Green Knowe* (1961) won the Carnegie Medal. Boston had always a transcendent sense of the past in her house, and therefore of the *presence* of past inhabitants. In this way, several of the Green Knowe stories are nearly ghost stories.

The MS of *The Tiger-Skin Rug*, found in the Manor House after Lucy Boston's death, was written several years before she moved there. It is quite separate in every way from the Green Knowe stories, as are two other Boston ghost stories: 'The Curfew' (in *The House of the Nightmare and Other Eerie Tales*, 1967) and 'Many Coloured Glass' (in *The Haunted and the Haunters: Tales of Ghosts and other Apparitions*, 1975).

'Elisabeth the Cow Ghost' by William Pène du Bois. First published in New York (Nelson, 1936).

William Pène du Bois (1916–93) was born and lived in America, but had his schooling partly in France. He wrote over twenty separately published stories for children, always with his own illustrations. With *The Twenty-One Balloons* in 1948 he won the Newbery Medal for 'the most distinguished contribution to American literature for children'. In his acceptance speech du Bois said: 'As a child I hardly read at all, although I loved to look at books. I was the sort of fellow who just looks at the pictures. I try to keep such impatient children in mind in making my books' (*Newbery Medal Books 1922-55*, Horn Book Papers Vol. I, 1955).

The French education that du Bois received was, by his own account, ferociously disciplinarian, but not (for him, at least) unprofitable. But it left him with—among other things—a wistfulness which his sister, Yvonne, described: 'Billy himself was always good—he says he never had the courage to be bad. He rather envied the bad boys, the pranksters, but he was too shy' (ibid.). A subversive and very understandable wish not to be permanently pigeonholed as good (or 'gentle') lies at the heart of Elisabeth's story. Note that the scene is set in Switzerland, but in *French-speaking* Switzerland—all the names are French.

'Georgie' by Robert Bright. First published in New York (Doubleday, 1944).

Robert Bright (1902–88), born in Massachusetts, had a varied career in journalism, publishing, education, and welfare work. For a good deal of that time he was also writing, for both adults and children.

Georgie was only his second children's book, to be followed by nine more books of Georgie's adventures, all illustrated by the author. Altogether, Bright wrote some twenty picture storybooks for younger readers; he also wrote four adult novels.

The genesis of *Georgie* has been described in the Introduction to this book. Perhaps all that can usefully be added is Bright's own interesting comment on the economics of children's book publication, from one author's point of view: 'I intended to make a career as a novelist. But, by the time I had published my third novel, I realized that, while I was gaining critical success, I was not getting sufficient return to support a family. I had to be sensible, and so, sensibly, I turned to writing and illustrating picture books for children' (quoted in D. L. Kirkpatrick (ed.), *Twentieth Century Children's Writers*, 1978).

'All in the Night's Work' by David Severn. First published in *Junior 4* edited by Freda Lingstrom, Audrey Harvey, and André Deutsch (London: Children's Digest Publications Ltd., Mar. 1947).

David Severn (b. 1918) is David Unwin, son of the publisher, Sir Stanley Unwin. He has been a writer all his life. His books for children include *Dreamgold* (1949) and *Drumbeats!* (1953). Both are adventure stories triggered by magic which is only a step away from the supernatural.

'All in the Night's Work' is described by the editors' prefatory note as 'a story about two boys who try to find out if an empty manor house is really haunted'. In fact, the two 'boys' could just as easily be two young bachelors (and, for romantic element, there is a sister: one ghost-investigator 'wanted badly to win her praise, to do something she would admire').

Junior was an irregularly published miscellany for 'young people with ideas'. It addressed its readers with the idealism of the period:

> By sending us constructive suggestions and by letting us have your own contributions and letters to publish, you are helping to shape *Junior*, to make it—as it should be—your book. . . . *Junior* itself is exchanging stories, articles, illustrations, cartoons and ideas in general with the French, Italian and Swiss *Juniors*. In fact, *Junior* is not only a book to read, a book which you have helped to make, but a means of communicating ideas and of founding new—and let's hope—lasting friendships.

The English *Junior* lasted for about four years; the other *Juniors* not so long.

'Richard' by Christopher Woodforde. First published in *A Pad in the Straw* (Dent, 1952).

Christopher Woodforde (1907–62) was born and brought up in Somerset, and became an Anglican priest. Antiquarian interests took him on visits to old churches; and he made himself an expert on English stained glass, writing several books on the subject.

From 1948 to 1959 he served as Chaplain of New College Oxford and sometimes took dormitory duty in the Choir School. On Friday nights he would turn up in the senior dormitory (eight boys aged about 13), seat himself on the end of a bed, and begin to talk, his talk soon turning willingly, at the boys' request, into the telling of what seemed an impromptu ghost story. In fact, his stories were carefully prepared: his son, Giles, remembers driving with him on church expeditions (rather like the eponymous Richard) when his father would try out on him the dialogue for a story. Later, the told stories were written down, and in 1952 some of them—many remained in MS—were published in the single collection.

As his friend David Cecil pointed out, Christopher Woodforde's tales were something of a literary novelty. It puzzled *The Times'* obituarist that the Chaplain had written 'for boys—or was it for adults? There was a curious matter-of-fact maturity about them' (13 Aug. 1962).

There are twenty stories in the collection, varying greatly in the kind of supernatural featured. About half of the stories have, as titles, boys' names—probably a kind of jocular compliment to the listeners. Illustrating the stories are eleven chapter heads. The one for 'Richard' shows the old bass wind instrument, the serpent, with its snake-like bends, a visual gloss for the musically uninformed. Another Woodforde ghost story, 'Cushi' (also from *A Pad in the Straw*), can be found in *The Oxford Book of English Ghost Stories* (1986).

'The Wee Ghostie' by Alison Uttley. First published in *The Little Knife who did all the Work* (Faber, 1962).

Alison Uttley (1884–1976) was born and brought up in Derbyshire, a rural childhood reflected in one of her early books, *A Country Child* (1931). She was a science teacher until her marriage in 1911. Some years later she began writing for children, enormously and successfully. Two of her best-known series for younger children are the *Little Grey Rabbit* books (from 1929) and the *Sam Pig* books (from 1940).

'The Wee Ghostie' is one of Uttley's rare stories of the supernatural. But *A Traveller in Time* (1939), for older children, is a story carried by fantasy, dream, or time-slip, with near-ghostly effect.

'The Haunted Trailer' by Robert Arthur. First published in *Alfred Hitchcock's Ghostly Gallery* (Random House, 1962).

Robert Arthur Feder (1909–69) was born in New York and at first earned his living as an oil-worker, in his spare time writing fiction for pulp magazines. In 1937 he went to Hollywood, and for the next thirty years wrote film-scripts, also magazine stories and radio scripts.

All this writing so far had been for an adult market: now, dropping his last name, Robert Arthur Feder became Robert Arthur, children's writer. He specialized in stories of mystery, horror, and the supernatural; and he was prolific.

In his Introduction Alfred Hitchcock thanks Arthur for his 'invaluable assistance' in compiling *The Ghostly Gallery*: in fact, Arthur himself may have ghosted the compilation. Certainly he was ghost-editor of several Hitchcock anthologies for adult readers.

No less than three of the eleven stories in *The Gallery* are by Robert Arthur. To go by the evidence of the Acknowledgments, *The Haunted Trailer* was not an already published story, originally for adults (as most of the rest were): we can assume that it had been written originally and specifically for young readers. Alfred Hitchcock makes clear exactly how young in his facetious Introduction: his concern is with 'the two most misunderstood groups in our society . . . teenagers and ghosts'. Interestingly, five years later, the Puffin edition extends the readership: the stories are 'for fearless readers of ten upwards'.

'The House that Lacked a Bogle' by Sorche nic Leodhas. First published in *Gaelic Ghosts* (Holt, 1963).

Sorche nic Leodhas was the Gaelic pseudonym invented for herself by the American writer, Mrs Leclaire Alger (1898–1969); she said it meant 'Claire, daughter of Louis'. Her father, Louis Gowans, was—like her mother—of Highland descent, and her grandparents had been born in Scotland. Leclaire Alger, as a child, was thought too delicate to go to school, and her father taught her at home. Later she trained as a librarian, and worked—in libraries for many years as a story-teller to children.

Meanwhile, she was always writing. Her work for children was based mainly on Scottish folklore and song, as in *Always Room for One More*, which won the Caldecott Medal in 1966. She herself never visited Scotland, but shared in her family's strong sense of Scottishness:

> The collecting of old Scottish stories, superstitions, songs and poems is a traditional occupation in our family. It goes back for generations on both my mother's and my father's sides. None of us has ever bothered with stories that have been published, preferring to keep only those which have come down by oral tradition . . . .
>
> We have found stories in all sorts of places. Of course, there are hundreds that have come down to us through our own family. They may be found at big clan gatherings where a number of clans may have representatives, at the outings of separate clans, at Gaelic Club meetings, at ceilidhs, big and little. I've found stories along the docks of the East River, in New York; along the edge of a soccer field, with the game over and folk ready to talk; in the engine-room of an old coastwise liner; in a cabin on a Pennsylvanian hillside; in the kitchen of a Nova Scotia farmhouse over a plate of scones and a cup of tea. (*The Third Book of Junior Authors*, 1972.)

Alger always liked to work on the less well-known folktales—even on forgotten ones newly discovered by herself. Perhaps this gave scope to her inventive imagination. Certainly it is difficult to believe that *The House that Lacked a Bogle* is from genuine folklore: it seems to be cheerfully parasitic upon it. Alger herself was evasive on the subject: '*The House that Lacked a Bogle* was some of my father's nonsense (so my mother said), and where he got the story, I can't say.' (Introduction to *Gaelic Ghosts*, 1963.)

'The January Queen' by Pamela Ropner. First published in *Winter's Tales for Children 2*, edited by Caroline Hillier (Macmillan, 1966).

Pamela Ropner was born in Scotland in 1931. Her education was at an Edinburgh girls' boarding school, which was evacuated during the Second World War to a country mansion not unlike the one described in 'The January Queen'. The story interestingly combines two genres in children's fiction: the school story and the ghost story.

Since 1963 Ropner has lived in Norfolk ('which I love'). She has written several books for children, beginning with *The Golden Impala* (set in South Africa) in 1958. Her stories are mostly for older children, and her themes are often tinged with the supernatural.

Winter's Tales for Children (later renamed *Young Winter's Tales*) was a miscellany appearing annually during the period 1965–78. It specialized in previously unpublished poetry and prose, fiction and non-fiction, for children. It used work by unknown as well as known authors, thus giving a chance to new writers.

'Brownie' by R. Chetwynd-Hayes. First published in *The Third Armada Ghost Book* edited by Mary Danby (Mayfair/Collins, 1970).

R[onald] Chetwynd-Hayes was born in Middlesex in 1919, the son of a cinema-manager. His career has been varied and enterprising, including salesmanship for Harrods and the Army and Navy Stores. From 1973 he has been an editor and writer, prolific in stories of horror and terror, usually *not* for children. Two horror films, *From Beyond the Grave* (1973) and *The Monster Club* (1980) have been based on his work. He has said of his own stories that, in general, they contain humour, pathos, and 'chilling situations'.

The Armada Ghost Books were a popular series: the last to be published was *The Fifteenth Armada Ghost Book* in 1983. Each book contained up to a dozen stories for young readers, many originally written for adults and now re-presented. 'Brownie', however, was specially written for *The Third Book*. The blurb promises its readers 'creepy fun'.

'The Ghost of Top Wood' by Michael Kenyon. First published in *Allsorts 7* edited by Ann Thwaite (Methuen, 1975).

Michael Kenyon was born in 1931 in Yorkshire and was educated in England. Thereafter he divided his life between England, France (seven years), and the USA. He has settled on Long Island, New York.

Kenyon's writing for adults has included journalism, especially travel articles, and some twenty mystery novels. For children his writing has been much less: 'The Ghost of Top Wood' was a 'one-off', as Kenyon rather wistfully describes it.

Credit must go to *Allsorts* for finding a new writer for children, even if he did not continue long in that line. *Allsorts* was published annually during the years 1969–75, and included stories, poems, pictures, and all kinds of puzzles and idea-provokers. In fact, it was for 'all sorts of children with all sorts of interests'. It aimed at a readership of 7–10 years. Ann Thwaite, the editor, is a writer of children's books and the biographer of Frances Hodgson Burnett and A. A. Milne.

'The Old White Ghost and the Old Grey Granddad' by Dorothy Edwards. First published in *The Magician who Kept a Pub and Other Stories* (Kestrel, 1975).

Dorothy Edwards (1914–82) was born in Teddington, Middlesex, and began her career as a secretary. She became one of the 'voices' on the BBC radio series, *Listen with Mother*, and wrote many of the stories broadcast for very young children. Among the best known are the *My Naughty Little Sister* stories, ten of them published before her death. She also edited story-collections for the same age-group.

In 1975 Dorothy Edwards won The Other Award with *Joe and Timothy Together*, for younger readers; and in 1981 she won the same Award with *A Strong and Willing Girl* for older readers.

For older readers, too, she wrote ghost stories of some unpleasantness—for example, 'The Damp Spectre' in *Ghosts and Shadows* (1982). But 'The Old White Ghost and the Old Grey Granddad' is a clever blending of Edwards's two kinds of writing: it is indeed a ghost story, and yet it is a tale very comfortable for quite young readers.

'Looking for a Ghost' by Margaret Mahy. First published in *The Second Margaret Mahy Story Book* (Dent, 1975).

Margaret Mahy was born in 1936 in New Zealand, where she trained as a librarian, and where she still lives. Her enormous output of children's stories and her high reputation have extended across the world: she has won the Carnegie Medal twice, with *The Haunting* in 1982 and with *The Changeover* in 1984. These are novels for older children sometimes with supernatural themes illuminating family relationships. Mahy's range reaches also to the youngest, in picture books.

The Margaret Mahy Story Books—all three of them solidly Mahy—include poems as well as stories. Mahy, by her own admission, has 'an almost fanatical belief in the importance of reading aloud to children'; and 'Looking for a Ghost' has some of the recognizable patterning of oral narrative. It also, in miniature, gives a testing—and a tasting—of the supernatural for younger children.

'At the River-Gates' by Philippa Pearce. First published in *The Shadow-Cage and Other Tales of the Supernatural* (Kestrel, 1977).

Philippa Pearce was born in 1920 in Cambridgeshire and grew up there. She worked for more than ten years in radio (BBC School Broadcasting) and then in children's publishing. Meanwhile, she had begun writing for children. Her second book, *Tom's Midnight Garden* (1958) won the Carnegie Medal, and *The Battle of Bubble and Squeak* (1978) won the Whitbread Award.

Philippa Pearce has written a number of ghost stories for children, most of them collected in *The Shadow Cage* and *Who's Afraid?* (1986).

'Somebody lives in the Nobody House' by Ruth Park. First published in *Spooks and Spirits* edited by Margaret Hamilton (Hodder, 1978).

Ruth Park was born in New Zealand: 'Until I was seven, I was a forest child. My father put roads through much recently-surveyed country, the dense forest of the New Zealand bush. My mother and I went with him and camped by available streams. I had no children to play with, but I had a good imagination.'

Ruth Park became a journalist and moved to Australia (where she still lives). With her husband, she has wandered through the outback, working 'at all sorts of jobs, from shearer's cook to fruit picker, and in between I wrote'. She has published more than fifty books, about half of them for children. She has won several awards, including the Australian Children's Book of the Year Award for *Playing Beatie Bow* (1980). A collection of short stories was published in 1989 under the sinister title of *Things in Corners*.

'The Ghostly Goat of Glaramara' by J. S. Leatherbarrow. First published, under the title 'The Silvery Tinkle of a Bell' in *Berrow's Worcester Journal* (27 Dec. 1979).

J[oseph] S[tanley] Leatherbarrow (1908–89) was born and bred in Lancashire. As an Anglican parson, he worked in parishes there for many years, then in Worcestershire, where he retired. He was a Canon of Worcester Cathedral and a Fellow of the Society of Antiquaries. He wrote several books on local and church history.

He also wrote ghost fiction. This dated from his work in the 1930s with youth and Scout groups:

> Since boyhood I have been an avid reader of the work of M. R. James, particularly his *Ghost Stories of an Antiquary*, which I bought in 1931 with the object of reading them aloud to groups of young people in my first parishes. When the supply ran out, they said, 'Write us some of your own', and that is how I first began to devise these stories in respectful imitation of my mentor.

Some forty years later four Leatherbarrow stories appeared as Christmas features in the weekly newspaper, *Berrow's Worcester Journal*; and the first was the story of the ghostly goat, under the title of the last words of the story, 'The Silvery Tinkle of a Bell'.

In 1983 Leatherbarrow paid for the private printing of a dozen of his stories, including the goat story. The collection was entitled *A Natural Body and a Spiritual Body* (from 1 Corinthians 15: 44) and has the Introduction from which I have quoted above. In this booklet the title of 'The Ghostly Goat of Glaramara' must be the author's own choice, whereas, in the *Journal*, 'The Silvery Tinkle of a Bell' may have been a piece of sub-editing. (There are subtitles in the course of the story, such as *Crash!* and *Horrified* which must surely be editorial.) With the exception of the title and subtitles, the whole of the story here is from the *Journal*. Whether this was exactly what Leatherbarrow's young audience originally heard, we cannot know; but we may doubt it.

The opening of the story pays tribute not only to M. R. James but to Lord Halifax—the same Lord Halifax (1839–1934) who made 'his own original ghost story in bricks and mortar' (see Introduction). Halifax's fascination with the supernatural led to his making a manuscript collection of ghost stories, 'true' and invented. He used to read aloud from it to his children on special occasions, such as Christmas:

> Many is the time that after such an evening we children would hurry upstairs, feeling that the distance between the Library and our nurseries, dimly lit by oil lamps and full of shadows, was a danger area where we would not willingly go alone . . . I well recollect my mother protesting . . . against 'the children being frightened too much'. My father, however, used to justify the method as calculated to stimulate the imagination, and the victims themselves, fascinated and spellbound by a sense of delicious terror, never failed to ask for more.
>
> (Foreword to *Lord Halifax's Ghost Book: A Collection of Stories of Haunted Houses, Apparitions and Supernatural Occurrences*, 1936.)

Two *Halifax Ghost Books* were published posthumously in 1936 and 1937. They must have been newly read by the young Revd Leatherbarrow and, together with the stories of M. R. James, fired his imagination and his writing.

'She was Afraid of Upstairs' by Joan Aiken. First published in *The Methuen Book of Strange Tales* edited by Jean Russell (Methuen, 1980).

Joan Aiken was born in Rye, Sussex, in 1924, into a literary family. (Her father was the American poet, Conrad Aiken.) She did not go to school until she was 12, but was writing poems and stories from the age of 5. After leaving school she worked for the BBC (briefly), for the United Nations, and as a features editor on *Argosy* magazine. Eventually she became a full-time freelance writer.

Aiken has written fiction for both adults and children. For children her many short stories and novels are marked by their originality and often high spirits. In 1968 she won the *Guardian* Award for *The Whispering Mountain*.

The supernatural is the theme of many Aiken stories for children. There are several short story collections whose titles declare what they are—for instance, *A Fit of the Shivers* (1990). Her range is wide—something, for instance, especially for dog-lovers: 'Humblepuppy' in *A Harp of Fishbone* (1972); 'Crusader's Toby' in *The Faithless Lollybird* (1977); and 'Lob's Girl' in *A Goose on your Grave* (1987). In ancient times, the ghost-dog—especially the Black Dog—was usually a dreaded apparition: Aiken's ghost-dogs must seem desirable—if unpredictable—playmates to the children who read about them.

'The Extinguished Lights' by Isaac Bashevis Singer. First published in *The Power of Light: Eight stories for Hanukkah* (Farrar, Straus & Giroux, 1980).

Isaac Bashevis Singer (1904–91) was born and grew up in Warsaw, the son of a rabbi. In his early thirties he emigrated to the USA and became a naturalized citizen in 1943. He worked as a proofreader, translator, and journalist, and became an original writer of great distinction. His honours included the Nobel Prize for Literature (1978).

Singer did not begin writing for children until he was over 60. Many of his stories are based on the folklore of his childhood—often ironic–comically told, as in *The Fools of Chelm and their History* (1973). Some, such as 'Zlateh the Goat' (1967), are original, but still within the old Polish Jewish tradition. In 1970 he received the National Book Award for Children's Fiction.

Although Singer became English-speaking, his first language was still Yiddish, and he always preferred to write in it. His texts were then translated by others but with his collaboration or under his supervision. 'The Extinguished Lights' does not count as a translation in the ordinary sense, and therefore qualifies for inclusion here.

'Who's a Pretty Boy, Then?' by Jan Mark. First published in *Black Eyes and other Spine Chillers*, compiled by Lance Salway (Pepper Press, 1981).

Jan Mark (b. 1943) attended art school and became a teacher. She sprang into prominence with her first book—a novel for children, *Thunder and Lightnings* (1976), which won both the *Guardian* Award and the Carnegie Medal. She won the Carnegie Medal again in 1983 with *Handles*.

Jan Mark writes for adults as well as for children. For children her short stories have often been scary: a recent collection is *In Black and White* (1991). A story, not in itself either scary or supernatural, should be read by anyone interested in the psychology of the tale of terror: 'Nothing to be Afraid of' (published 1980 in a collection under that title). Here Mark anatomizes the addiction of a child to fear; the story is shrewdly comic, but never cruel.

The Oxford Book of Children's Stories (1993) is edited by Mark. She includes M. R. James's 'Wailing Well' with the illuminating comment: 'Although "Wailing Well" is quite as nasty as anything he wrote for adults, it is interesting to see how James lightens the atmosphere by admitting a farcical element.'

'Uninvited Ghosts' by Penelope Lively. First published in *Frank and Polly Muir's Big Dipper* (Heinemann, 1981).

Penelope Lively was born in 1933 in Egypt and passed her early childhood there. She was educated in England, where she has lived since.

Her first notable book for children (there were three earlier fantasy–historical novels) was *The Ghost of Thomas Kempe* (1973), which won the Carnegie Medal. The story hilariously brings together the twentieth and the seventeenth centuries through the mediation of an irascible ghost. Another outstanding book is *The House in Norham Gardens* (1974); the susceptible imagination of a child in a North Oxford suburb summons the ghost of a primitive tribe from the remoteness of New Guinea: 'Their world is peopled with ghosts, and they live with spirits as easily as with tree and mountain and river.' Another ghostly novel for children, *A Stitch in Time*, won the Whitbread Award in 1976.

Lively's continuous interest is in the interactions of time and place: 'Places have a past . . . They are now but also then' ('Children and Memory', *Horn Book Magazine*, Aug. 1973). Her non-fiction has included *The Presence of the Past: An Introduction to Landscape History* (1976).

Such themes need novel-length for development. Lively has also written a number of short stories for children, but—so far—only one about revenants: the light-hearted 'Uninvited Ghosts'.

Penelope Lively has written more than ten novels for adults: *Moon Tiger* won the Booker Prize in 1987.

'The Bride' by Farrukh Dhondy. First published in *Trip Trap* (Gollancz, 1982).

Farrukh Dhondy was born in 1944 in India, where he was educated. He then came to England for further study at the universities of Cambridge, Leicester, and—much later—York. He taught in a London comprehensive school and at the same time began writing for children, finally becoming a full-time freelance writer. He has written for publication, for the stage, and for television. He also has editorial responsibility for multi-cultural programmes on Channel 4.

Dhondy's first book, *East End at your Feet* (1976), caused a sensation, and won The Other Award from the Children's Rights Workshop, which seeks to encourage, among other things, 'a progressive attitude towards ethnic minorities'. He has written five more books for children, of which *Come to Mecca and Other Stories* (1978) also won The Other Award.

'The Bride' is like several other Dhondy tough–tender stories in presenting the interaction of Asian and white children—who, in the course of this story, become young adults. (That is the readership aimed at.) It is unusual in being a ghost story.

'Ivor' by George Mackay Brown. First published in *Shades of Dark* compiled by Aidan Chambers (Patrick Hardy Books, 1984).

George Mackay Brown was born in 1921, the youngest of six children, in Stromness, Orkney, where he still lives. His father was a postman cum tailor. At school he was 'a reading boy' (as he describes himself), but not of the recommended books of Scott and Dickens: he preferred *The Wizard*, *Hotspur*, and other boys' magazines. Books, anyway, had little chance in his childhood:

> For years I loved football more than anything else in life . . . I invented imaginary football teams—a score of them, maybe, in a first league and a second league, and I had them playing against each other in the wildly exciting arena of my mind. . . . Hours and months I spent in this fantasy world, and for me at the age of ten it had all the excitement and delight that later I got from writing stories and poems.
>
> (Quoted in *Contemporary Authors: Autobiography Series* vol. 6, 1987.)

He remembers writing his first poem, sitting alone on a Saturday morning in a field where (he supposes) his friends had failed to turn up 'for a kick or two at the ball'. He remembers his first story, when, as a young man, he was already writing occasional non-fiction for the *Orkney Herald*. One day, on impulse, he wrote a short story to fill his slot. The story came easily (and was published): he had been given 'the freedom of narrative' (ibid.).

In spite of indifferent health, Brown attended a Scottish college for young working men and women and, later, Edinburgh University. He was writing seriously; his first book was published in 1954. He became a poet of distinction: since the 1970s his poetry and stories have been used in song cycles, cantatas, and other works by the composer, Peter Maxwell Davies. A story from his second book of tales for children, *The Two Fiddlers* (1974), was adapted for children to play and sing as an opera in 1978.

George Mackay Brown's stories for children, like all his other work, are steeped in a sense of Orcadian landscape and people, history, and legend. He has rarely left Orkney: 'I know that if I'd moved about I would have got a sort of mental indigestion and been unable to work . . . If you stay put, you can travel in your imagination' (quoted in Maggie Parham, 'A Writer's Vocation' in the *Tablet*, 12 Mar. 1994).

'Siren Song' by Vivien Alcock. First published in *Ghostly Companions* (Methuen, 1984).

Vivien Alcock was born in Worthing, Sussex. She attended art school, and for some years worked as a commercial artist. After that, she allowed marriage and a child to keep her at home, where she painted for pleasure, until painting gave way—rather late in her career—to writing. Her first book, *The Haunting of Cassie Palmer*, a story of the supernatural, was published in 1980. Since then she has published a dozen books for children, and has established herself as a notable writer.

Alcock has written several ghost stories for anthologies, and also published her own collection, *Ghostly Companions*. *The Stonewalkers* (1981) is a novel of the supernatural.

Ghosts and ghost fiction are said to have suffered from the coming of electric lighting: fewer ambiguous shadows, less menacing darkness. 'Siren Song' shows that modern technology has its ghostly uses.

'The Tower' by Aidan Chambers. First published in *Shades of Dark* compiled by Aidan Chambers (Patrick Hardy Books, 1984).

Aidan Chambers was born in 1934 in Chester-le-Street, Co. Durham, and was a teacher until his writing began to earn him a living. He is mainly a novelist for young adults: the best known of his books so far is probably *Dance on My Grave* (1982); a more recent novel is *The Toll Bridge* (1992). Chambers also has a keen interest in ghosts and ghost stories, best described in his own words:

> In the late sixties I was asked by a publisher to compile a book of my favourite ghost stories. That led to my writing some of my own for a second volume. Before long I'd written five books full of my own stories, compiled nine

collections of stories by other writers, and produced a non-fiction book about what we think we know about real ghosts.

'The Guitarist' by Grace Hallworth. First published in *Mouth Open, Story Jump Out* (Methuen, 1984).
Grace Hallworth was born and brought up in Trinidad.

I was telling stories to my dolls at the age of four or thereabouts, mainly retelling from books I read, but also invented stories . . . I graduated to telling stories to children in the immediate neighbourhood during the holidays when we were allowed to stay up until 9 p.m. and to meet on the porch of the houses of friends. There was also a fair amount of story swapping at primary school.

As an adult, Hallworth told stories professionally in Public Libraries not only in the Caribbean but also in Toronto, New York, and in the UK. This led to the publication of collections of her stories, of which *Mouth Open, Story Jump Out* is the third.

On authenticity, Hallworth has said: 'I don't believe "The Guitarist" is pure anything, but that it comes out of a folk tradition' and such traditions have 'ramifications . . . almost impossible to sort out'. She sees herself as only one of many 'inventive raconteurs'.

The telling of stories, whether traditional or newly invented or—most often, perhaps—a blend of both, has been an essential part of Caribbean culture. In her Introduction to *Mouth Open, Story Jump Out* Grace Hallworth writes: 'I remember a time when stories about supernatural beings were a strand in the web of stories which were told orally in Trinidad and Tobago. They were part of the normal exchange of news and events and were related as true happenings.'

'A Grave Misunderstanding' by Leon Garfield. First published in *Guardian Angels: Fifteen New Stories by Winners of the Guardian Children's Fiction Award* edited by Stephanie Nettell (Viking Kestrel, 1987).
Leon Garfield was born in Brighton, Sussex, in 1921. After the Second World War, he worked as a laboratory technician in a London hospital for twenty years. During that time he was writing, and in 1964 his first book, *Jack Holborn*, was published, a story of sea-adventure set in the eighteenth century. Most of the succeeding novels and stories are similarly period pieces; but the favourite centuries—eighteenth and nineteenth—are always distinctively Garfield: authentic in detail, but idiosyncratically presented, with outrageously witty and comic effects of language.

In 1967 *Devil in a Fog* won the *Guardian* Award; in 1970 *The God Beneath the Sea* (a re-presentation of Greek myth), written in collaboration with Edward Blishen, won the Carnegie Medal; in 1980 *John Diamond* won the Whitbread Award; and in 1981 *Fair's Fair* won the Children's Book Award of the Federation of Children's Book Groups.

Ghost stories attract Garfield, with his 'passion for secrets and mysteries'. Such stories give the writer opportunity not only for suspense and shudders, but also for probing deeply into human motivation and morality. Outstanding in this way are *The Ghost Downstairs* (1972) and *Mister Corbett's Ghost* (1969). This second story was made into a film, the last in which John Huston starred.

So 'A Grave Misunderstanding' is untypical: modern in period, anecdotal in effect. But as a Garfield *jeu d'esprit* it justifies itself.

'Ghost Trouble' by Ruskin Bond. First published by Julia MacRae Books, 1989.

Ruskin Bond is an Anglo-Indian writer, born in India in 1934, and now living in the Mussoorie Hills below the Himalayas. He has always been a writer: 'My early stories, when I was in my twenties, were about my own childhood in India. . . . Although my father was British, I grew up as an Indian. There has been no division of loyalties, only a double inheritance' (quoted in D. H. Kirkpatrick (ed.), *Twentieth Century Children's Writers*, 1989).

Bond's first book, *The Room on the Roof* (1957), won the John Llewellyn Rhys Memorial Prize. *Our Trees still grow in Dehra* won the Sahitya Akademi Award for English Writing in India in 1992. Bond has written many short stories, essays, and novels and over thirty stories for children. Among the best known of these are probably *Angry River* (1972) and *Getting Granny's Glasses* (1985).

Ghost stories have interested Ruskin Bond from a very early age:

When I was ten or eleven, my stepfather took me along on one of his shikar trips into the forests near Dehra. I dreaded these excursions. The slaughter of wild animals never did appeal to me . . . But during one such week in the forest, I discovered that the forest rest-house in which we were staying had a shelf full of books concealed in a dark corner. I feigned a headache and stayed back while the adults fanned out into the forest with their weapons. One of the first books I discovered was a tome called *Ghost Stories of an Antiquary* by M. R. James. I was hooked . . . Masterpieces such as *Oh, whistle and I'll come to you, my lad*, *The Mezzotint*, and *A Warning to the Curious* influenced me in more ways than I can tell and made me an addict of this genre of writing. (Introduction to *Indian Ghost Stories*, 1993).

In an Introduction to a collection of his own fiction, *Time Stops at Shamli and Other Stories* (1989), Bond says: 'Ghosts are intangibles and can mean different things to different people'; and he acknowledges the influence of Lafcadio Hearn (1850–1904) and 'his superb stories of the supernatural'. He quotes Hearn's belief that 'the ghostly always represents some shadow of truth. The ghost story has always happened in our dreams and reminds us of forgotten experiences, imaginative and emotional.'

'Spirits of the Railway' by Paul Yee. First published in *Tales of Gold Mountain* (Groundwood Books, 1994).

Paul Yee, born in Saskatchewan in 1956, is third generation Chinese-Canadian. His books for children include *Teach me to Fly*, *Skyfighter* (1983), *The Curses of Third Uncle* (1986), *Roses sing on New Snow* (1991), and *Breakaway* (1994). He has also written *Saltwater City: An Illustrated History of the Chinese in Vancouver* (1988). All these books have been published in Canada.

'Many Happy Returns!' by Barbara Griffiths. First published in *Frankenstein's Hamster* (ABC, 1990).

Barbara Griffiths was born in Plymouth in 1948. She went to various art schools including (finally) the Slade. She has exhibited in London and illustrates her own work. Another collection of her stories, under the title of *A Gruesome Body*, appeared in 1994.

'The Beach' by Robert Westall. From an unpublished MS written 1990–1.

Robert Westall (1929–93) was born and brought up on Tyneside. He went to art school, taught art for many years and wrote art criticism for the Press. His first book for children, *The Machine Gunners* (1975), won him immediate recognition. For that book and also, later, for *The Scarecrows* (1982), he was awarded the Carnegie Medal. In 1989 he won the Smarties Prize with *Blitzcat*, and in 1991 the *Guardian* Award with *The Kingdom by the Sea*.

In collections of short stories by Robert Westall, some or most of the stories concern themselves with the supernatural: *Break of Dark* (1982), *The Haunting of Chas McGill* (1983), *Ghosts and Journeys* (1988), *A Walk on the Wild Side* (1989), *The Call and Other Stories* (1989), *Fearful Lovers* (1992). His novels for children include *The Watch House* (1977) and *The Promise* (1990): both are supernatural stories.

Westall once acknowledged, without resentment, that 'people say my writing is all cats, ghosts and World War II'. His realism is often violent, but he was also attracted to the subtler possibilities of the supernatural: 'I have been moving deeper and deeper into the world of the supernatural . . . Perhaps I use the supernatural as a viewpoint to comment on the inner world of psychology.'

'Across the Fields' by Susan Price. First published in the anthology *Haunting Christmas Tales* (Scholastic, 1991).

Susan Price was born in 1955 in Staffordshire, and grew up there. She left school to become a shop-assistant, but by then had already written her first book, *The Devil's Piper*, a fantasy, published in 1973. *Twopence a Tub*, about a pit strike in 1851, won The Other Award in 1975; and *The Ghost Drum* won the Carnegie Medal in 1987.

In her writing Susan Price combines an interest in the history of the working people of the Black Country, where she lives, with a love of folktale and legend—and ghost story.

'Across the Fields' was partly inspired by a Cornish folk-story I first came across as a teenager . . . The story was about a couple of tin-miners who are benighted on the moors and are brought to a wrestling-match between demons by the Devil. The older and more devout of the miners despatches the demons by praying aloud.

I set my version of the story in my own Black Country, so the miners became coal-miners. Then I took a lot of the background from the family stories I was told again and again as a child. The hero of the story is really my grandfather as a young man; the heroine is one of his younger sisters. The account of the girl going to meet her brother from work, and their going to the market to buy cheap food, and the description of the market, are all from these family stories. So is the ghost of Gracey Mary, who drowned herself, and now drowns others.

'The Clearing' by Tim Wynne-Jones. First published in *Some of the Kinder Planets* (Groundwood Books, 1993).

Tim Wynne-Jones was born in Cheshire, England, in 1948. At the age of 4 he was taken to Canada, where his father had found work in the north of British Columbia. Since 1980 Wynne-Jones has made his living by writing for the theatre, for television and radio, and for book-publication. He has written more than thirteen books for children, published variously in Canada, the USA, and Britain. *Some of the Kinder Planets* won the Canadian Library Association Children's Book of the Year Award and also the Governor-General's Award, Children's Literature. *The Book of Changes* (1994) is a recent collection of his stories for young readers.

With his wife and three children, Wynne-Jones now lives in a part of Canada not unlike the landscape of 'The Clearing': 'on seventy-six acres of rock, swamp and pine-forest in eastern Ontario.'

'The Burning Baby' by John Gordon. First published in *The Burning Baby and Other Ghosts* (Walker, 1992).

John Gordon was born in 1925 in Jarrow, Co. Durham, and educated at Wisbech in the Fens. Thereafter his life and the landscapes of his imagination have remained mostly East Anglian. He worked for many years on provincial newspapers; but in 1968 published his first novel for children, *The Giant under the Snow*. This story and those that have followed—some fifteen books altogether—are nearly all supernatural in their dynamic.

Gordon once said: 'Ghosts are subversive, and that's nice.' 'Nice'—what a word to associate with a John Gordon ghost-story, which can so easily and skilfully topple itself into the horrific! But Gordon explains:

> I write about the supernatural because it makes a good story and disturbs the commonplace. I like to take an ordinary town or village and make it as real as I can. This is very important, because the supernatural, the imagination, are nothing if they are not anchored in reality. Once this is done, it is possible to concentrate on some event which turns the world upside down and causes

the people in it to see things they had never dreamt of and experience feelings they had never known.

(Quoted in D. H. Kirkpatrick (ed.), *Twentieth Century Children's Writers*, 1978.)

On the suitability of the ghost story for young readers, he has said: 'Every subject can be dealt with; it is only the technique used that indicates the audience' (*The Thorny Paradise; Writers on Writing for Children*, ed. Edward Blishen, 1975).

ACKNOWLEDGEMENTS

The editor and publisher gratefully acknowledge permission to include the following copyright material:

Joan Aiken, 'She was Afraid of Upstairs' from *The Methuen Book of Strange Tales* (Methuen, 1980). Reprinted by permission of Reed Consumer Books Ltd. and A. M. Heath & Co. Ltd.

Vivien Alcock, 'Siren Song' from *Ghostly Companions* (Methuen, 1984). Reprinted by permission of John Johnson Ltd.

Robert Arthur, 'The Haunted Trailer' from *Alfred Hitchcock's Ghostly Gallery* (Random House, 1962, Puffin, 1962). Reprinted by permission of Cowan, Liebowitz & Latman, PC, on behalf of Ms Elizabeth Arthur and Mr Andrew Arthur.

William Pène du Bois, 'Elisabeth the Cow Ghost'. Reprinted by permission of the Estate of the author and the Watkins/Loomis Agency.

Ruskin Bond, 'Ghost Trouble' (Julia MacRae, 1989). Reprinted by permission of Walker Books Ltd.

Lucy Boston, 'The Tiger-Skin Rug', copyright © the Estate of Lucy Boston. Reprinted by permission of Diana Boston, The Manor, Hemingford Grey.

Robert Bright, 'Georgie', copyright 1944 by Doubleday, a division of Bantam Doubleday Dell Publishing Group, Inc. Used by permission of Bantam Doubleday Dell Books for Young Readers.

George Mackay Brown, 'Ivor' from *Shades of Dark*. Reprinted by permission of the author.

Aidan Chambers, 'The Tower' from *Shades of Dark* (Patrick Hardy Books, 1984). Reprinted by permission of the author.

Ronald Chetwynd-Hayes, 'Brownie' from *The Third Armada Ghost Book* (Mayfair Books, 1970). Reprinted by permission of the author.

Walter de la Mare, 'Miss Jemima' first published in *No. 1 Joystreet* (Blackwell, 1923). Reprinted by permission of the Literary Trustees of Walter de la Mare and The Society of Authors as their representatives.

Farrukh Dhondy, 'The Bride' from *Trip Trap* (Gollancz, 1982). Reprinted by permission of David Higham Associates Ltd.

Dorothy Edwards, 'The Old White Ghost and the Old Grey Granddad' from *The Magician Who Kept A Pub*, copyright © Dorothy Edwards, 1975. First published by Viking Kestrel. Reprinted by permission of Penguin Books Ltd.

Eleanor Farjeon, 'Elsie Piddock Skips in her Sleep' from *The Treasure Cave* (Jarrold, 1928). Reprinted by permission of David Higham Associates Ltd.

Leon Garfield, 'A Grave Misunderstanding' from *Guardian Angels* (Kestrel, 1987). Reprinted by permission of John Johnson Ltd.

John Gordon, 'The Burning Baby' from *The Burning Baby and Other Ghosts*, copyright © 1992 John Gordon. Reprinted by permission of Walker Books Ltd.

Barbara Griffiths, 'Many Happy Returns!' from *Frankenstein's Hamster* (All Books for Children, 1990), copyright © 1990 by Barbara Griffiths. Reprinted by permission of ABC, All Books for Children, a division of the All Children's Company Ltd., London.

Grace Hallworth, 'The Guitarist' from *Mouth Open, Story Jump Out* (Methuen Children's Books, 1984). Reprinted by permission of Reed Consumer Books Ltd.

Michael Kenyon, 'The Ghost of Top Wood' from *Allsorts* (Methuen, 1975). Reprinted by permission of the author.

J. S. Leatherbarrow, 'The Ghostly Goat of Glaramara' from *Berrow's Worcester Journal*, 27. Reprinted by permission of Mrs E. I. Leatherbarrow.

Sorche nic Leodhas, 'The House that Lacked a Bogle' from *Gaelic Ghosts*, copyright © 1963 by Leclaire Alger. Reprinted by permission of Henry Holt & Co., Inc.

Penelope Lively, 'Uninvited Ghosts' from *Frank and Polly Muir's Big Dipper* (Heinemann, 1981). Reprinted by permission of Reed Consumer Books Ltd.

Arthur Machen, 'Johnny Double' from *The Treasure Cave* (Jarrold, 1928). Reprinted by permission of Mrs Janet Pollock.

Margaret Mahy, 'Looking for a Ghost' from *The Second Margaret Mahy Storybook* (J. M. Dent, 1975). Reprinted by permission of the Orion Publishing Group Ltd.

Jan Mark, 'Who's a Pretty Boy, Then?' from *In Black and White*, copyright © Jan Mark, 1991. First published by Viking Kestrel. Reprinted by permission of Penguin Books Ltd. and Murray Pollinger.

Ruth Park, 'Somebody Lives in the Nobody House' from *Spooks and Spirits* (Hodder & Stoughton Ltd.), copyright © Ruth Park, 1978. Reprinted by permission of Curtis Brown Ltd., London, on behalf of the author.

Philippa Pearce, 'At the River-Gates' from *The Shadow Cage*, copyright © Philippa Pearce, 1977. First published by Viking Kestrel. Reprinted by permission of Penguin Books Ltd.

Susan Price, 'Across the Fields' from *Haunting Christmas Tales* (Scholastic Children's Books, 1991). Reprinted by permission of A. M. Heath & Co. Ltd.

Pamela Ropner, 'The January Queen' from *Winter's Tales for Children 2* (Macmillan, 1966). Reprinted by permission of the author.

David Severn, 'All in the Night's Work' from *Junior 4* (Lingstrom / Deutsch / Harvey, 1947). Reprinted by permission of the author.

Isaac Bashevis Singer, 'The Extinguished Lights' from *The Power of Light: Eight Stories for Hannukah*, copyright © 1980 by Isaac Bashevis Singer. Reprinted by permission of Farrar, Straus & Giroux, Inc.

Alison Uttley, 'The Wee Ghostie' from *The Little Knife who did all the Work* (Faber & Faber Ltd., 1962). Reprinted by permission of the publishers.

Robert Westall, 'The Beach', copyright © Robert Westall, 1991. Reprinted by permission of the author's estate.

Christopher Woodforde, 'Richard' from *A Pad in the Straw* (J. M. Dent, 1952). Reprinted by permission of Giles Woodforde.

Tim Wynne-Jones, 'The Clearing' from *Some of the Kinder Planets*, copyright © 1993 by Tim Wynne-Jones. A Groundwood Book/Douglas & McIntyre. Used with permission.

Paul Yee, 'Spirits of the Railway' from *Tales of Gold Mountain*, copyright © 1989 by Paul Yee. A Groundwood Book/Douglas & McIntyre. Used with permission.

Any errors or omissions in the above list are entirely unintentional. If notified the publisher will be pleased to make any necessary corrections at the earliest opportunity.